T0160374

SASKIA DE COSTER (Belgium) is a visual artist, playwright and regular participant in television debates, as well as an author. She is also manager of Andermansland, a company that brings words into action in public space. She has seven novels to her credit, five of which are currently translated. Her work is described as haunting, appealing, and unforgettable. Her bestseller *We and Me* won the Cutting Edge Award (an award de Coster has won three times), and the Opzij Literature Prize, and was nominated for several other prestigious prizes; it sold over 40,000 copies in the Netherlands and Belgium alone. Her work has been translated into ten languages.

NANCY FOREST-FLIER is a New Jersey-born translator who moved to Europe in 1982 and has worked in the Netherlands since 1988. Her literary translations include *The King* by Kader Abdolah, *Dissident for Life* by Koenraad de Wolf, *Gliding Flight* by Anne-Gine Goemans, *Mr. Miller* by Charles den Tex, *Departure Time* by Truus Matti, *Hex* by Thomas Olde Heuvelt, and most recently *The Story of Shit* by Midas Dekkers. Nancy also translates children's literature and has translated for numerous Dutch museums and institutes, including The Anne Frank House and the Kröller-Müller Museum (home to the world's second largest Van Gogh collection).

WE&ME

Saskia de Coster

WE&ME

Translated from the Dutch
by Nancy Forest-Flier

WORLD EDITIONS
New York, London, Amsterdam

Published in the USA in 2018 by World Editions LLC, New York
Published in the UK in 2016 by World Editions Ltd., London

World Editions
New York/London/Amsterdam

Printed by Sheridan, Chelsea, MI, USA

Library of Congress Cataloging in Publication Data is available.

ISBN 978-1-64286-004-7

First published as *Wij en Ik* in the Netherlands in 2011 by
Prometheus, P.O. Box 1662, 1000 BR, Amsterdam

This project has been funded with support from the European
Commission. This publication reflects the views only of the author,
and the Commission cannot be held responsible for any use which may
be made of the information contained herein.

 Co-funded by the
Creative Europe Program
of the European Union

The translation of this book is funded by the Flemish Literature Fund
(Vlaams Fonds voor de Letteren – www.flemishliterature.be)

 Vlaams
Fonds
voor de
Letteren

Twitter: @WorldEdBooks
Facebook: WorldEditionsInternationalPublishing
www.worldeditions.org

'To look life in the face, always, to look life in the face.'
– *Virginia Woolf*

WE 1980

No one comes to the mountain unannounced. Friends always arrange their visits well beforehand. Always, without exception. It's one of the many unwritten rules of the housing estate on the mountain. Unexpected visitors may very well find themselves staring at a locked door, as we say, forcing them to turn away, their goal unaccomplished. Too bad. The residents of the housing estate all lead busy lives. It is in their spacious villas amidst lakes of green grass, protected by trees and six-foot fences, that they are able to unwind. Normal visits are made by appointment. The appointments are written down weeks in advance in a large ledger with sewn signatures issued by a bank—the deluxe edition for good investors—made in the year 1980. Clandestine meetings are moved to highway motels, distant vacation resorts, or private clubs with passwords.

The very idea of casually dropping in at one of the villas in the richly wooded housing estate, just for fun, is out of the question. Friends would never do such a thing, because friends respect each other. There's no reason for that kind of impertinence, say the housing estate residents. No such thing as a neighbourhood committee here, or a charter with guidelines. The men are busy senior executives who already spend too much time at meetings during the day to fill their free hours with more of the same. These are not common labourers who chair their local bridge club, or petty officials whose idea of a good time is to stand in front of a mirror and practise their monthly treasurer's report for the local marching band. Nor do the women of the housing estate see the point of such committees. They have quite enough to discuss with their own families, and they prefer to spend their free time on themselves. Although there's no formal consultation of any kind among the residents, they're in complete agreement on most matters, remarkably enough. Tacit agreement.

The working people who come to the mountain know exactly when they are expected. Gardeners, cleaning women, and manicurists all have fixed hours. Even the procession of Sunday mendicants—black men from Zaire alternating with Jehovah's Witnesses—abide by the resting community's unshakeable schedules and only come on Sundays between the hours of eleven and twelve. The blacks begin their pitch with a broad smile and milk-white teeth, immediately followed by the friendly warning not to be frightened, and in one breath they sing the praises of their little hand-stencilled books containing ancient stories about the genesis of their African tribes, which they are peddling to finance their university education in theology at some unknown or non-existent university in the south of France. Whether it's due to the people's feelings of colonial guilt or to the black men's babbling in a childish kind of French, quite a few books end up being sold. The Jehovah's Witnesses, on the other hand, find themselves staring at a closed door before they've even reached the end of their opening sentence. In the year 1974, when the first villas in the housing estate were erected, a university professor accepted a copy of *The Watchtower* from a Jehovah's Witness. It wasn't long before he and his entire family were conscripted into the sect. Since then, not a single resident has been able to put up with even the opening spiel of a Jehovah's Witness. The door is closed with a vague word of thanks and a resolute nod. No, the front doors here are certainly not flung open wide for every stranger who happens to turn up. What are front door peepholes for, after all?

So it comes as a total surprise to the residents when we make our way along the sunken road to the housing estate on a Tuesday afternoon in April 1980 without anyone on the mountain expecting visitors. We climb the mountain slowly. The road is so narrow here that two oncoming cars cannot pass each other. But there are no cars. Not at this hour of the day. At half past two on a Tuesday afternoon there's no traffic from the housing estate to the real world, or vice versa.

There are only two roads leading to the estate. One of them sets out from the neighbouring backwater as a bumpy patchwork quilt of cobblestones and asphalt, patched countless times. At the end of this road the neighbourhood reveals itself, like the sea to a herd of water buffalo trotting across the Serengeti Plain: home, a final destination, a haven for quenching your thirst. The other way to get there is along the sunken road in the woods. The sunken road is an earthen trench that runs straight through the woods, a former riverbed in which an erratic asphalt road was laid. The road starts in the village and ends up in the paradise among the trees.

Potential buyers of the properties are enticed by the vastness of the lots and the fragrance of pine needles. Building permits are rather lavishly granted here. There's room for large villas with swimming pools and tennis courts at the far end of each back garden. Even horse stables can count on a friendly wink from the mayor.

The families in the lower village still vividly remember how the count sold off the woods and grounds piecemeal to the occupiers up on the mountain. Their clans have been living in the village since time immemorial.

Even before the village had an official name their ances-
tors were here. They were an industrious folk. They set up
butcher shops, cafes, and liquor stores that they passed
on to their children who in turn passed them on to *their*
children, so the only things that had to be changed on
the signs out front were the first names. The villagers
speak a colourful local vernacular among themselves,
with lush tones and heavy vowels that the people on the
mountain can't begin to fathom. There's no direct communication between the two groups. Their only form of
contact is gossip and backbiting.

If a professor from the housing estate should come
down to buy something he accidentally overlooked on
his shopping list for the big supermarket, the villagers
close ranks. When he's just within earshot they tell each
other what for him is unintelligible slander, distilled
from stories from the cleaning women and gardeners
who work on the mountain off the books, fertilizing
lawns and hanging bird houses on tree trunks at precarious heights. The mountain resident quickly purchases a
loaf of salt-free, four-grain bread or a grilled chicken,
jumps into his car, and returns to his family on the
mountain as fast as he can.

Proceeding down the tongue of asphalt that rolls out
of the sunken road, we turn onto the first street of the
housing estate. All we see is one living soul, standing at
the only bus stop in the entire housing estate, a pole
with a minuscule timetable screwed onto it. A golden
retriever lying in an impeccable front garden glances
up for a moment. The smell of pine needles and horse
manure hangs in the air. Somewhere in the belly of one
of the villas a radio emits a news report on the death of
the great master of film, Alfred Hitchcock.

On this calm Tuesday afternoon the housewives creep

even more deeply into their cocoons of calm, drowsy boredom. At number 6 Nightingale Lane, Evi Vanende-Boelens, in an advanced state of pregnancy, leafs through an interior design magazine. Ulrike Vanoverpelt-Schmidt, who lives a couple of houses farther on, takes the ironing board from the storeroom and tackles the enormous pile of laundry generated each week by her husband and three children. The men still have hours of work ahead of them. The children have a little more than one hour at their school desks before the bell rings. Most of the residents started producing children a couple of years ago. The oldest children from the housing estate are now in their first year of school. Their mothers are waiting at home for a report of their day. Evi hopes to give birth soon so she can go back to filling her afternoons with visits to the boutiques.

All the residents of the housing estate are at about the same stage in their lives. They're bringing a new generation into the world, in this paradise that they themselves discovered and developed. They live a respectable distance from each other because they respect each other's privacy. No one can see into their neighbour's bathroom, living room, or conservatory. Only the plentiful magpies see everything.

The dog follows us with his eyes but doesn't bother to jump to his feet. He just lies there in front of his kennel, chained up, his head resting on his front paws. The fresh spring air is dry and every sound carries. It hasn't rained in weeks. A pair of woodland birds break off their song. This is where we come to a halt.

We see the villa on the other side of the road, number 7 Nightingale Lane. There's no avoiding it. The villa is a gigantic, rustic edifice in dark red brick with glazed, blue-black tiles on the weathertight roof and an enormous chimney. It must have taken a great deal of time and an impressive building plan to raise this construction successfully. The house attempts to exude an air of timelessness, there in the middle of a bright green lawn full of tree stumps, oak trees, and daffodils in full bloom. This picture is exactly what Stefaan had led us to expect.

We cross the lane and approach the villa. The hallways in the house must be streets in their own right, the rooms all ballrooms. We plant our finger on the round doorbell. Somewhere deep in the house, metal strikes a gong and we hear the loud reverberation.

It takes a long time. A very long time. This, too, we expected. We know this milieu; we're aware of the time of day. In a neighbourhood like this one it's not unusual for postmen or firemen making the rounds for their annual collection to think they've encountered an empty house. But they're being watched from behind closed curtains and from indoor landings by kneeling cleaning women who are dusting the tubular limbs of the radiators, or by the lady of the house, clad in bathrobe and slippers, as she shuffles her way from the bathroom to the dressing room and looks down through the little window on the landing. The callers know it will be a long time before the locks of the fortified citadels are opened, one by one, and they stand face to face with a human being.

But now it's been a very long time. We ring the doorbell once again. The sound is loud indeed. We've come all this way to congratulate Stefaan. The Vandersandens propagating themselves: that is a happy event that we, too, want to celebrate. Apparently we're too late, or too early. After a third ring and a long wait, when there's still no sign of life, we take a step back and search the front of the house for any movement behind one of the many windows. Nothing.

As unannounced visitors we now commit a double violation. We step away from the path to the front door and walk across the grass, past the windows. You see, there is someone home, isn't there? Sitting in a dark red chesterfield armchair is a squat figure in a flowered robe. It's unusual for someone in the housing estate to sit at the window in an armchair. The street is so far away that you can hardly see anything from the window. And gazing out at the street is the sort of thing old working-class women do. Those kinds of women don't live on the mountain.

You would expect her to be startled by the loud tap on the glass, but the woman in the chair doesn't stir. It's difficult to tell whether her eyes are closed or just sunken into her fleshy, wrinkle-ridden face. Her short legs don't reach the floor but hang in the air, motionless. Is the old woman unconscious, sitting there in the chair? Or is she dead? No, she cannot be dead. To get the old woman's attention in some other way (she may be deaf), we wave at her.

The elderly woman does not wave back. Not even a nod of the head. It's possible that her eyelids moved, like butterfly wings, but that may have been in response to a slight draught. The old woman is slouched in the chair at an angle. Just when we're about to pronounce her dead, her bosom heaves up and down. A sigh escapes from the bellows of her sturdy body. The old woman's heavy head falls forward and is hoisted back up. The head is all we need. Everything is under control. She is alive, her son is alive, and he has been given an heir. We'll come back later.

Melanie Vandersanden-Plottier pushes herself out of the armchair. With great difficulty and loud groaning she slides to the edge of the chair until her orthopedically encased feet touch the floor. The heavy body rights itself. There stands Melanie at full length, far more pitiful than impressive. Stefaan's mother is no taller than one of the rose bushes in the front garden under the bluestone window ledge that is luring the first rays of spring to shine on its buds. The rough-edged little woman is as prickly as the bush and just as uncommunicative. She no longer finds it necessary to reach out to the world around her. Melanie only speaks when she is of a mind to.

Sometimes there are outbursts or brief phases in which she says a great deal. She can give her son a good tongue-lashing when the occasion calls for it, for which her aged body can still work up the energy. Otherwise there's little that disturbs her enough to waste words on. She has a goodly number of obscenities at the ready, though. When she grabbed an open bag of frozen peas from the wrong end recently, strewing peas all over the kitchen floor, her uncouth words tore through the kitchen like a tornado. Down on her swollen knees, she picked up the peas from the marble floor one by one. After the last pea had been swept into the dust pan she disappeared into the cellar, only to re-emerge one hour later, thoroughly subdued, the angry words shaken out and released into the chill of the apple bin.

Her poor vision, bordering on blindness, doesn't keep her from tootling around in her Fiat. Accelerating on the curves and driving down the middle of the road rather than on the right (just to be on the safe side), Melanie cuts her trail through Flanders. Police officers can chase her all they like, but she just keeps on driving—even stepping on the gas if necessary.

She's known far and wide as a first-class grumbling curmudgeon. In all fairness, the gossips do report that there are mitigating circumstances to excuse her dreadful personality: the many tragedies she has endured. She never talks about the tragedies. She saves her peevishness for things no one can do anything about. If the sky is overcast, Melanie has the right to look so disagreeable and accusatory that an outsider will find himself apologizing spontaneously without having any idea why. If Melanie is deeply displeased by something (bird droppings on the window or margarine instead of real butter), she closes up like a clam and pretends to be as deaf as a post for a couple of hours.

And now the woman raises herself from the expensive chesterfield armchair belonging to her son Stefaan and his wife Mieke. Her eagle eye pans the relatively empty, oversized living room. Persian rugs cover the parquet floor, pieces of antique furniture try to out-age each other, and an original Permeke farmer's wife, dressed in her Sunday best, gazes at the interior. What's missing are little figurines for cosiness, a display case for gaudiness, calendars for memory, and a few crucifixes for piety. Her son and his wife prefer to spend lots of money on superannuated antiques, because they're the kinds of overpriced furnishings that belong in a villa of this calibre. The beams over her head come from a demolished mill, the property of Mieke's father of blessed memory. The house is bigger than the parish church, and it also has a gigantic cellar and a crawl space. Even the bedrooms are heated, and all the windows are double-glazed. As if a person actually needed all that.

Anyway, Melanie knows her place. The mother who scarcely speaks two words in succession is waiting in the lovely home of her still living son. He's come a long way: made it to the mountain, with a wife of wealthy parentage at his side. Only now, at age forty, is he having his first child. God, it certainly did take them long enough.

In the meantime the sun has made its way to the other side of the house. Melanie has already been down to the cellar to calm herself and has now clambered back into her pricey but not particularly comfortable armchair. In the chill of the kitchen behind her, the thermostat kicks in. All this time Melanie has been doing what was asked of her: she is keeping watch. She is the house's security guard.

Finally the taxi turns into the driveway. Her son Stefaan jumps out of the car, leans on the doorbell, lets himself in, tears into the living room, congratulates Melanie for her grandmotherhood, and even makes an attempt to plant a kiss on her cheek. She remains seated. She doesn't move a muscle, doesn't even greet him. She doesn't ask Stefaan how it went, or whether it's a boy or a girl, or how Mieke is doing. Nor does she say a single thing about what or who rudely interrupted her sleep this afternoon. Melanie's eyes wander through the living room, making their way toward her son. Then an index finger shoots out of her solid torso. She points ominously at Stefaan's shoes on the living room rug. She has the right to blow the whistle on her son, regardless of the circumstances. It is her intention to keep raising her one living child for as long as she lives.

There are still a number of people in West Flanders who can tell the story of how Melanie brought her oldest son into the world at four o'clock in the morning. She had just enough time to wrap the little one in a sausage of linen and bind him to her bosom before relieving the lowing cows of their straining udders and spending the rest of the day working in the field. Stronger than a workhorse, that was Melanie.

During his first hours of life her oldest son filled his lungs with the moist stench of manure and the sour smell of barley gruel. Eighteen years later he turned his back on the farmer's craft. Stefaan has worked his way up with an industriousness and drive he didn't get from strangers. And now, at age forty, he's a successful manager at a large pharmaceutical firm. He has both a degree in medicine and an MBA from Wharton Business School hanging on the wall of his spacious office. He owns a villa that's still echoing with newness in the housing estate on the mountain.

Stefaan looks exhausted. His cheeks are ashen, yet he's beaming. His dark eyes sparkle, his smile is so wide it almost tears at the corners. Stefaan has been awake for twenty-four hours. Not as in 'not sleeping', not in a slumber setting like his mother. He's as hyperactive as a talking clock. One hour ago he stormed out of the maternity ward of the Sacred Heart Hospital in search of a passing taxi, calling out euphorically to the honking cars. He would never do such a thing in a normal, sober condition, but what has happened here is a wonder of the world guaranteed to make the world instantly forget all its turmoil, all the nuclear warheads and iron curtains.

'Oh, my God,' Stefaan shouts exultantly from the living room. He stumbles over his own words. 'So extraordinary, so unbelievable.' He keeps repeating it, ad nauseam. He wants the whole world to share in the towering happiness that's taken hold of him. Delirious with joy: that's what it's called. A man hugging the sky and momentarily forgetting the dark shadow. From now on, happiness will be on his side. He had already collected the outward signs: wealth and advancing status. Now there's this new dimension to add to them. 'So extraordinary,' he keeps repeating while shaking his head.

'Every birth is extraordinary,' his mother sighs. Her mouth has moved. Words have come out. Four words. She spoke at least four words, one after the other, and she isn't talked out yet. She goes on: 'Extraordinary in its own misery.' His inaccessible mother thinks he can put up with anything. All these years he has been reacting appropriately to her callousness: properly and submissively, because it was she who gave birth to him.

Today Stefaan can hardly hear her. 'A little daughter, Mama. A little girl.' He takes off his loafers, puts them in the shoe cabinet in the utility room, and runs to the ironing room. No running in the house, Mieke would shout if she were here now. Behind the door of the ironing room are a couple of cardboard boxes. He had them ready months ago. He takes the boxes upstairs and goes into one of the seven bedrooms.

He's lived this moment over and over again in his dreams. He goes to the stereo, searches for the right cassette, and chooses the most suitable track by his big hero, Bob Dylan: 'Forever Young'. He wants his daughter to stay young forever. But there's a contradiction there: in order to stay young forever she would have to die. He opens his eyes wide but it's too late; they fill with weary tears. It's all too much for him after such a wakeful night.

In the nursery there's a lovely antique cabinet for linens and clothes, as well as a child's bed that cost three times his college tuition. A royal child from the Habsburg period slept in it. On the floor is a fanciful rug featuring a pattern of purple and red giraffes against a white background. And her desk is where he'll fold the little boxes for the sugared almonds. Follow the instructions on the lid of the cardboard box to fold a compact little house out of rice paper. Stefaan's fingers are definitely not slender piano fingers. They're completely unsuitable for origami, a game played with rice paper that was adopted from the Land of the Rising Sun not so long ago. A Flemish farmer like his father would have blown his nose on rice paper like that.

Last night Mieke went over the instructions with him again, slowly and carefully. She wasn't at all sure it was going to work, yet he soon succeeded in folding a little box with straight walls and a ribbon bow for a roof. His fingers tremble from the effort. He starts in on a second box, and then a third. Stefaan looks with astonishment at how his hands have turned into skilful dancers, daring to perform such perfectly choreographed origami.

He opens a drawer in the table and takes out the felt-tip pen. He and Mieke had had quite a squabble over the felt-tip pen just before her water broke. Mieke said she preferred professional printing to his chicken scratches, an unreasonable demand. Stefaan writes with silver-coloured ink on the outer walls of the boxes: Sarah, 28-04-1980. Sarah. The name they chose for her together, Jewish in origin, the name of a strong, high-spirited woman. It was their shared secret for seven months. They quickly agreed on a first name for a girl. But for a long time Mieke had doubts about the child itself: whether she should go ahead with it or not, whether she and the world really needed another child. These were doubts that Stefaan couldn't relate to. Once they had made the decision it took years before Mieke finally became pregnant. Now their daughter is an indisputable fact. They have everything within reach to make sure their child, more than any other child in the world, has a golden future.

Sarah is offering her father a clean slate. In exchange, he is promising her his total commitment and a hefty bit of cash. Some people are all too eager to dismiss material possessions as something incidental, but Stefaan sees them as a sign of devotion. The most beautiful little pieces of furniture, the most exclusive little outfits, the most expensive diapers—he won't take anything less. Of course he could have had the little boxes folded by someone else, but he wanted to do it himself, just as he refuses to hand his daughter over to the supervision of a nanny. His wife will stay home and take care of her. Everything has been arranged down to the last detail.

He is euphoric. As a doctor he knows the theory behind all this: your hormone curve is out of kilter, your temperature is fluctuating, you observe the world through tunnel vision. He allows himself just enough time to regain his equilibrium before going back to his mother. He looks out the window. There's the lovely back garden, all ready for the child. Yesterday he disentangled the last pulpy winter leaves from the bushes. Stefaan glances over at the little boxes, which are lined up like houses along a railroad track. These boxes are the first trace of his daughter's presence in this house. His daughter. He is her father and always will be, even when he's no longer around. The simple logic of this moves him. He has finally been granted the title of father.

He has always told himself that he must not rest until he has reached that rarefied, precarious point: the top. It's not everyone who makes up their mind one day to assume a leadership position, but such people do exist. These are people who don't take orders from others but deal them out themselves. Arms crossed, shouting defiantly at the world: come on, I dare you.

Stefaan Vandersanden had everything it took to make it big, although he may have let himself be bossed around too much in his early youth. He was too quick to defer to rules and orders. If help was needed with the clean-up at school, he didn't slip through the swinging doors and out onto the playground like everyone else but stood there waiting for instructions, often the only one to do so. A classmate who hadn't finished his homework on time would get the answers from Stefaan, free for the asking. If some roughneck was fixing for a fight, Stefaan would just so happen to find himself nearby. It didn't really help that he was skinny and clever, the usual combination for children who tend to get knocked around. When he was eighteen his father died, and he knew he had two choices: slide into grief or fight to survive. The clever, timid, country boy in wooden shoes from a West Flanders farming village became a respected top student at the great University of Leuven. Unlike his father, Stefaan was determined not to let himself be pushed to the edges of life. He sank his teeth in and held on tight.

Stefaan graduated summa cum laude as a doctor of medicine from the University of Leuven and let the professor who served as his dissertation advisor talk him into spending a year at Wharton Business School in Pennsylvania. Those two diplomas together would open any door, the professor said. Stefaan's preference was to open all the doors himself, the doors to his own company. The day he returned to Flanders he ordered a package of printed business cards. His former sense of inferiority was transformed into one of limitless spunk. He had to start at zero, without a red cent in the bank. He had made some money working in a small print shop during his studies in America, which he had sent home—at least whatever he didn't need himself to survive on campus. He went without meals and wore corduroy trousers in the summer, just to send money to his widowed mother. It was a twisted kind of pride all too familiar to migrants in a strange land. In the print shop he would reach his ink-black fingers into his pants pocket, groping for dimes to drop into the money box to send poor inner-city children to camp. On the day of his graduation Stefaan left this all behind. Now it was up to him. He was going to start his own business, and he needed every dime to invest in his own laboratory. He returned to Flanders, since that's where it was going to happen.

It's amazing how your goal comes right up to meet you as soon as you get it clearly in your sights. Stefaan was always bumping into CEOs, people from the pharmaceutical sector, and investors. And at the least opportunity the twenty-eight-year-old Stefaan would fish one of his gold-edged business cards out of his wallet. He'd corner speculators who liked to play patron and treat them to lavish lunches. No sooner had the aperitif been served than he would make his pitch, without the slightest embarrassment. He knew the rules from the marketing boys at Vlerick Management School, who were beginning to make a name for themselves in Flanders. Their advice was to start out with some serious bullshitting about wines, Napa Valley, and golf courses. Stefaan broke these rules with relish, *and* with success. He saw no point in the unwritten law that you had to begin by discussing trivialities, when both parties knew perfectly well that the reason they had come here to Comme Chez Soi was to seal some cold-blooded deals. Business partners who didn't share the same mentality would never become serious investors. The first three meetings at which he plunged right in with enthusiasm and fervour had taken an average of two and a half hours. Each time, he was able to scoop up more money than he had ever thought possible. He didn't even have to hold a knife to their throats or get involved in any other sordid business.

Stefaan had a plan about the laboratory he was going to launch that was fairly megalomaniacal and rather vague. Dr. Paul Janssen of Janssen Pharmaceuticals had done it before him: immediately after graduating from medical school you start your own company, develop a new medicine, put it on the market, and promote it as widely as possible. Stefaan was well aware of his intellectual capacities. With his expertise he could build up a knowledge monopoly in Flanders and exploit it to his advantage. Many of the big industrial companies didn't have enough in-house knowledge, or their specialists hadn't been properly re-trained in years, and as a result there were gaps in their awareness of the latest developments. This was the hole in the market that Stefaan would take advantage of. With every meeting he had, he could feel the man in the suit opposite him growing more and more intrigued, bending forward, and whispering insistently about what they could do for each other—three different, impeccably dressed, pear-shaped men in their fifties with cuff links on their stiffly ironed dress shirts—until Stefaan almost had to shove them off his lap.

The success of the first three meetings led him to approach the fourth with the utmost confidence. Even if it didn't result in any spectacular commitments, it really couldn't fail. He hadn't counted on the fourth investor being a son of a bitch, a man whose best friend was the CEO of a big pharmaceutical firm. The man let him wait more than half an hour. Pure intimidation, Stefaan knew, and he calmly buttered a second piece of bread. After another hour, and five 'I'm-waiting-for-someones' later, he settled his bill with the waiter and slunk away. The investor's friend hadn't liked the sound of it—an unknown, overly ambitious little doctor, fresh out of

Wharton, wanting to set up an independent laboratory.

The next day the pharmaceutical company's lawyer contacted Stefaan and demanded that he put an end to this lab business immediately, before he had even gotten started. The lawyer threatened to wipe out his entire future by instituting legal proceedings from which he would never recover financially. Within the space of five hours, one investor after another let him know that they were withdrawing their sponsorship. Furious and determined never again to let himself be bullied, Stefaan went to the headquarters of the dictatorial pharmaceutical firm. He was given an interview with the big boss, astonished him with his diplomas and knowledge, and left the building with a top-salary position.

His first years back in Belgium were marked by hard work and assisting his mother every now and then. Melanie wanted to sell the farm and use the proceeds to build a bungalow. After all those years she could no longer bear to look at the high wooden crossbeam from which a rope, along with her husband, had once hung. Stefaan went to the handsome office of the notary on Steen Street in Bruges to attend the public sale of his parents' house. He was wearing a tight-fitting black jacket that dated back to his father's funeral. He pushed the notary's door open, listened to his own footsteps echo in the oak-panelled hallway, and crossed over to a room whose door was ajar. With a boundless lack of interest, and after a full five minutes, the woman who was pounding away on her typewriter finally deigned to look up at him, regarding him with total contempt as if he were something the cat had dragged in. He smiled at her, unable to think of a more suitable response. His jacket creaked as he handed his dossier to Mieke De Kinder. As he recalls she was wearing some kind of dark, severe outfit, but that's not what Mieke remembers. That bit about the look of contempt may have been true because whenever she concentrates, the corners of her mouth always droop automatically. Without a word having been spoken she knew that this was just another man who took her for the notary's secretary. And that may have been why she unconsciously looked at him as if she were about to give him a good thrashing.

After their first brief conversation she came to have a different view of him, as Mieke would tell him once they had been properly married. She no longer saw a piece of filth in a tight, ill-fitting jacket but a shrewd, sharp-eyed man, a serious sort, with a nice, jet black crew cut (no unwashed hippie hair for him) and an honest smile. A good-natured, mysterious man enveloped in an air of melancholy that could just as easily pass for general astuteness. The type that doesn't know his own appeal. It would be exaggerating to say it was love at first sight. Something far more exciting happened to her in the beautiful, oak-panelled, eighteenth-century office of the notary than an ephemeral fluttering of infatuation. It was her husband who presented himself to her on the platter of a banal public sale, although there was a great deal of work to be done on this man. That didn't deter her in the least. She saw it as a project to throw herself into, with all the drive and precision she possessed. She saw the rough basic structure of a man she could knead into the image and likeness of her ideal mate.

A great deal had to happen before the two got closer together, but in any case it was all thanks to the relatively lucrative sale of the farm where he had spent eighteen years of his life that Stefaan and Mieke were able to look each other in the eyes for the first time. She had brought her best friend Elvira along on their first date, but by the second Mieke said with a husky voice that she had no need of a chaperone. Every time he thought she had mustered enough civility to tell him he needn't try anymore, every time he was sure that the next coffee date would be their last, she would nod passionately and suggest something about a concert or an exhibition.

Mieke admired Stefaan because he was so atypical, so modest and dogged at the same time, so authentic and so unmanly, so full of self-confidence and so elusive. She said so quite openly. He let these dubious compliments pass over him and smiled. And even though he learned through the grapevine that she came from a fabulously rich family that he was no match for, he set his heart on her. There was a time and a place for everything, and this was the time to clear a path for the love of his life. So when her family actually welcomed him with open arms, nothing stood in the way of their marriage. Now, more than ten years later, they're the proud parents of Sarah, just when Stefaan had almost given up hope of ever having a child.

Stefaan works a sugared almond out of the box and places it on his tongue. The sugar melts. He gets down on his hands and knees, making himself small enough to fit under the table. As a little boy he loved to hide under the kitchen table at home. It's one of his first memories: being under the sturdy table, his mother above him, changing his little brother's cotton diaper. He looks at his mother's weather-beaten face and listens to his brother's cries until they're smothered on his mother's breast. Stefaan lies down on his stomach, just at his daughter's height. This is how Sarah will crawl through the house. She'll press her peach-soft cheek against the objects in the house to learn about the limits of things and of space, and to familiarize herself with her home.

Downstairs the phone rings. Who knows, maybe Mieke has awakened from her comatose sleep. In his attempt to stand up quickly Stefaan bangs the back of his head against the underside of the table. He laughs at his own clumsiness. He doesn't even feel the pain. Out in the hall, when he picks up the telephone receiver and the insolent ringing stops, he hears a bass voice. The voice sounds familiar but he can't immediately place it. Maybe it's the fatigue, or because the man comes from another world where there are no newborn babies. It isn't until the end of the congratulations that he recognizes the voice of Fernand Berkvens. He and Berkvens studied at Leuven together. Stefaan graduated with honours while Berkvens had to be happy with a simple satisfactory. Now he and Berkvens are colleagues. Berkvens lives in the village, Stefaan in the housing estate on the mountain.

Both of them applied for the same position as director of research and development. Berkvens's wife says it's a beautiful baby, Stefaan hears. She's a nurse in the maternity ward at the Sacred Heart Hospital. Don't nurses have a code of professional confidentiality? Stefaan himself wanted to be the one to announce the good news at work.

'A girl! This calls for a drink,' says Berkvens.

'What shall we drink?' asks Stefaan. He hears the remoteness in his voice. For Stefaan, the line between work and private life is of crucial importance. He guards it closely.

His mother has raised herself from the armchair and is now standing next to him. She takes a dust cloth from her apron and rubs it over the bakelite telephone with its ivory dial, an heirloom from Mieke's parents.

'What shall we drink? A beer at the pub, of course, to

celebrate the birth!' says Berkvens, his colleague.

'A beer,' Stefaan repeats.

Berkvens knows that Stefaan doesn't drink beer. Never did, even before he came to understand that beer is for plebeians. The feeble bubbles and bitter taste are lost on him. After working long hours at his part-time job in the print shop while studying in America, his beverage of choice consisted of several glasses of a bright yellow soft drink.

'I don't know,' says Stefaan. 'I don't know if I have time for drinking.'

His mother is still flitting around behind him. She has strong principles, always has. She won't allow a single drop of alcohol to be drunk in her presence, for instance, no matter what the occasion. Single-handedly she has become Flanders's biggest temperance brigade. She's merciless in her condemnation of the respectable Fleming who joyfully returns to his wife and kiddies with ten glasses of beer in his belly: all the worse for him. According to her theory, alcohol is not only stupefying but it's also very bad for the liver. 'One glass? For the liver that's no different than trying to bolt down a kilo of chocolate. Anyone who doesn't believe me can ask Dr. Verastenhoven.' 'But he's dead, isn't he?' 'Exactly. The drink, you know.'

The last time his mother drank in public in the open air was at a small dinner party she organized following the commemorative mass held for her husband André. She had ordered and paid for dinner for thirty-eight: for the pastor, his nuns, her stone-deaf girlfriends from the retirement society, and her family. At that particular memorial she consumed everything that was left in the aperitif glasses, the wine glasses, the beer glasses, and the hard liquor glasses. At first her customary silence went unnoticed. Her guests never suspected a thing until she dropped the stuffed pear garnish from her serving of quail down her décolleté and, after spooning out the last of the advocaat, proceeded to throw up in the bushes next to the restaurant chickens.

'It must have been the potatoes,' she explained, gasping for air. 'Probably a green one. I'm terribly sensitive to green potatoes.' The establishment was being run by a gang of profiteers who let their filthy, Pamper-clad children run through the restaurant, which also may have had something to do with it, she said.

When Stefaan cautiously suggested it may have been the drink, she denied it up and down, only to toss in five minutes later as part of her sobering-up tirade: 'Marie Brizard, anise liqueur—come on, who drinks that stuff anymore? Maybe the occasional cleaning woman who gets hooked on abandoned bottles when nobody's looking. But otherwise?'

Stefaan sees his mother pulling faces, fishing to find out who's on the other end of the line. He's eager to end the phone call with Berkvens and says, 'Another time.'

'Another time then,' responds Berkvens. 'We'll go out another time. I won't forget, now.'

Stefaan hangs up. Fortunately he doesn't like to go drinking. He has neither the time nor the inclination. He's never shown his face in either of the two village pubs. He also finds it completely unbecoming to hang around in a drinking establishment when you've just been given the most beautiful daughter in the history of humanity.

'How are you, Mother? It wasn't too tiring for you, was it?' He redirects his attention for the moment to his discontented mother.

His mother mutters something. She always seems

angry at him. She is very creative in her reproaches, but they all arise from one underground reservoir of guilt and sorrow.

'Did you see or hear anyone?' he asks.

'No,' she snaps. 'Now that you have a daughter you're going to behave yourself and be happy, is that right?'

Stefaan ignores the caustic remarks that he has come to expect from his mother. 'I'm going to the hospital. I'm taking some sugared almonds, a nightgown, and a couple of towels,' he says. 'But I'm bringing a present back for you. That should make you happy.'

The hours slip past. With a creak in her heavy joints Melanie stands up. She goes to the kitchen and spreads butter on half a slice of gingerbread. She gives herself permission to eat in the armchair, a small indulgence that she hopes will not leave too many crumbs. At some indeterminate point later on, Melanie wakes up with a start that reverberates through all her chins. Stefaan doesn't seem to have been gone for long, although sleeping has caused her to lose track of time. Her mouth feels as sticky as a honeycomb. According to her doctor she doesn't drink enough water. That was eight years ago. Now the doctor himself has died. Her son comes into the room with a carrying case. He zips the case open and takes a video camera out of the padded interior. Melanie's heart skips a beat. Is this the present? It's an ungainly metal hulk with one big, round eye.

'Wouldn't you like to see her?' Stefaan asks.

He carries the camera in his arms like a child. The camera is frightfully expensive, which is exactly why Stefaan bought it. Stefaan wants to spend money on his daughter. He's just itching to replay the scene that he observed with his own eyes through the lens of the camera. Now he wants to see it with his mother. He can also send the images from the camera to the television via a cable, an extra option he has paid a pretty penny for.

'You're not going to tell me ... ' she says. She shifts the fulcrum of her body and raises her right buttock. A loud salvo is heard. Because of her deafness she cannot hear the sound of her own farts. Both her hands grasp the arms of the chair as if her body were about to fly upward, but it abandons the effort under so much weight. She struggles for breath, all the way down to the deepest tunnels of her massive body. The hand that had just been flapping freely lands on her prow, the other points to the unwieldy apparatus that Stefaan is cradling in his arms. Another of her verbal assaults is brewing. ' ... you're not going to tell me ... that the birth is recorded on that thing?' She nearly faints.

'That's right,' Stefaan confirms enthusiastically. He crouches next to the television console and tries to connect the camera to the TV via the cable.

'What will they think of next?' Melanie spits out, along with another handful of words. Her unusual loquacity has to do with an attack on the present age. 'No matter where you turn today, everything is out there for all to see. My goodness, a little baby can't help it if he comes into the world in his birthday suit, but I don't have to see your wife in all her glory, thank you very much. It's become a regular scourge these days—there's an ad for a new gas stove and bang, they have to put a naked lady in it. That'll warm things up all right. Who wouldn't be cold walking around in their altogether? Or yesterday in the theatre section of the newspaper. Yes, they have the nerve to call it theatre, getting undressed down to their last stitch with everyone looking on. To say nothing of that modern art nowadays! It's all an excuse to show off a lot of filth. That guy with his whore and her bare breasts, the two of them in a sculpture. And we're supposed to think it's beautiful? Coarse, cheap, vulgar, too dreadful for words, that's what I say. You can go ahead and call me old fashioned but it's the unvarnished truth.' Then she falls silent and her words hang in the air, until a new fart resounds through the room to conclude her powerful tirade. Stefaan is still down on his hands and knees. He's trying to make sense of the doodles formed by the wires on the living room floor.

'Never mind, I don't need to see it.' Melanie hoists herself out of the armchair and propels herself to the cellar. She walks like a drunken goose. Since her second episode of thrombosis she's had trouble walking upright. In the cellar there are pots, pans, and a whole supply of canned goods. There are also ten-kilo bags of keeping apples that a farmer sells in the housing estate from his old-fashioned pull cart. It's always pleasantly chilly in the cellar, winter and summer.

A cauldron of soup is cooking on the kitchen stove, waiting for the return of the house's inhabitants. It must be said that Stefaan's mother knows something about cooking, at least about everyday cuisine: meatballs in tomato sauce, rabbit with prunes, and pudding with ginger biscuits. He tastes a spoonful so he can compliment his mother when she comes back up from her air-raid shelter. The soup is more or less tasteless. The lack of taste betrays the nervousness she feels about the birth of her first grandchild. He won't say anything about the soup because then he'd have to be honest. That's the way he is: he can't lie, but he can keep his mouth shut.

Mieke can keep her mouth shut, too. When after two months she realized she was pregnant, she didn't share her big secret with Stefaan right away, even though she knew how much he was hoping for a pregnancy. That was something he never quite understood. It offended him somewhat, but as a doctor he knew that when a woman gets pregnant she isn't always herself. The hormones take over. Mieke told him later that she knew exactly when her mind, and not just her swelling breasts, whispered to her that she was pregnant. When she heard the report on the radio about those two East German families who had fled to the West in a homemade hot-air balloon, she wondered whether she had the right to force a child into the world. Before you knew it the dictatorship of the Iron Curtain would spread all the way to the North Sea, and where would they fly then, with a baby, without a hot-air balloon?

For Stefaan there had never been the slightest doubt. It's their job to make sure the child is properly equipped to cope with life's challenges. He needs them to have a child so he can be complete. He can still hear his own overly zealous arguments. Of course we're going to be happy. You're going to feel like a total woman. Our marriage will blossom. Yet Mieke still wasn't sure. She didn't actually utter the a-word, but he felt her thinking it. Then one day he got angry, very angry, and began talking about infanticide. It hadn't really mattered whether he lost control or not when she said there was more to it than that, that his desire for a child was all out of proportion. 'People without children are depressing people,' he said, cleverly quoting her father. He knew that was her weak point. Her father had made his opinions all too clear when they were first married. A few years later the man died of a heart attack. For her mother his death was devastating, and she died soon afterward from the aftershock. 'I know, people without children are depressing people,' she had moaned. 'There's no way back.' She was referring to the crushing responsibility. In a moment of weakness you could get bogged down just thinking about it. Then you'd go crazy and you'd never get around to having a baby.

They got through it together. It took patience and persuasiveness, but she got used to the idea. One month later he started catching her singing little tunes to her unborn child. Her swelling body did have its discomforts, from heartburn and infuriating itchy nipples to swollen ankles, and the enormous embarrassment. She was terrified of losing her slender figure and turning into a blob. She was ashamed of what she called her whale of a body, although the rounded forms made her more of a woman than she had ever been before. She stopped going outside. For the first time she cancelled the six-month check-up visits to the tenants of her properties.

Luckily they have a villa with a large garden. The garden is surrounded by tall rhododendrons. Mieke was able to keep herself well-hidden in the villa during the final weeks. Villas are ideal places for hiding your shame. A house is a body around your body. Would the little one in Mieke's belly be ashamed, too? It was a pointless question, since the little one was still hidden away. Shame presupposes the presence of other people, and she wasn't expecting twins.

During the last week Stefaan's mother came to help out, her face as long as a fiddle. Mieke responded by complaining that she was a prisoner in her own home. The two women avoided each other as much as possible. Mieke thinks that Stefaan's mother is jealous of her own son. When the tension became too great between Mieke and her mother-in-law, Melanie disappeared into the cellar and Mieke took refuge in the bedroom behind closed shutters, with a compress on her forehead and her swollen ankles resting on the footboard of the bed. In both the cellar and the bedroom it was fresh and safe.

'Voilà!' Calmed and even in relatively good humour, Stefaan's mother resurfaces from under the ground while Stefaan has gone back to fiddling with the SCART cables. She's tidied up her favourite spot again, the storage cellar. It needed it, she insists.

'It's got to be clean for when mother and baby come home. The baby may not see much yet, but even a moron can see spiderwebs. You have to keep your house clean, no matter what. Taking a little pride in your housekeeping, that's the basis of all happiness. But a man wouldn't understand that. Yes, indeed, clean in every nook and cranny, especially there.' Melanie takes her handbag from the back of the chair and clamps it under her arm.

'Berta has to be fed,' she says. Berta is her aged dwarf goat. Melanie waddles to the garage under her own steam, reaching out to the cabinets and walls for support. She leaves her beige raincoat hanging in the closet. Without a word of goodbye to her son she closes the door to the garage behind her. Stefaan doesn't know where Melanie got the sudden burst of energy, but he's impressed by the force with which the garage door swings open and the speed with which Melanie drives out in the grey Fiat. He goes out to the garage, which is full of exhaust fumes, to close the door behind her.

Three hours later Melanie is back, honking at the garage door. Stefaan has just returned from the city, where he has bought a necklace for Mieke from Cartier's. Melanie has had time to think. She is offended by the fact that she hasn't been able to see her first grandchild yet because the totally unreliable video player won't cooperate. 'Didn't you take a picture?' She plops down in her trusty armchair. When Stefaan shows her a Polaroid, her first remark is, 'Good gracious, that child is as cross-eyed as an otter. That's going to give you plenty to laugh about, I can see that right now. Just start her off with her knife on the left and her fork on the right.' She holds the photo an inch from her left eye. 'Say, are there six toes on that foot? No? Or am I mistaken? Oh, dear! What a knob of a big toe that child has been blessed with. And that forehead—don't even get me started. I don't dare look at it for fear it'll swell even more. Make sure her clothes are cut wide at the neck. And don't feed her carrots, she's already as yellow as a banana. Well, you can't call her pretty, can you, such a tiny baby. Don't look so disagreeable, tiny babies are never pretty, that's all I'm saying.' There's no stopping her. She maps out the entire naked little body based on defects and curses and deformities. It's done in many countries: a newborn child is made completely ridiculous before being released into the confusing, demanding world. The well-meaning family does it to divert the attention of the Evil Eye from the child itself.

'And you,' she snaps at her son. 'What are you doing, standing there with your nose hanging out? And with a bouncing baby girl, the most beautiful child in the world. I already know what the future holds for Saaaraaah (she pronounces the name like a yawn). Didn't think I would, did you? My own flesh-and-blood granddaughter. But son, that child is bound to be a walking disaster, I can see it all now.'

'A what?' Stefaan is shocked. Even though his mother's frankly absurd, ice-cold reception has prepared him for the worst, even though he knows he shouldn't expect anything consoling from her, this unvarnished, cruel curse is something he hadn't seen coming.

'What do you mean?' Stefaan asks. His voice is hoarse

with fatigue and exasperation.

An index finger flies like a pigeon from her heavy bosom and soars prophetically into the air. She, the oracle, clamps her thin lips together. Her hands land resolutely in her lap. Not another word more.

Stefaan says nothing. He himself knows what his little girl is going to be—a top manager or a top consultant, something at the top at any rate—even though at this point her legs are as crooked as a couple of old pear tree trunks. She may be the eighth wonder of the world but he's not going to tell anyone. Anyone. Even in a stable marriage like his, as well-negotiated as a perpetuity agreement, there are premonitions that are best left unsaid, if only in order to deflate them. They're too fragile to be sent into the world as words. In addition, Stefaan doesn't want to exert any unnecessary pressure on people whose company he enjoys. He knows perfectly well how weighty expectations can be. Against his better judgement he begins regarding this little girl as the coat rack from which he will hang the rest of his life, starting now.

On Friday, 2 May 1980, five days after the birth, Mieke, Stefaan, and Sarah drive up the sunken road to the housing estate on the mountain. They turn into Nightingale Lane. Springtime is raging more furiously here than at the mountain's foot. The avenues are lined with cherry trees in full bloom. Birds hop from branch to branch. A squirrel clings vertically to an oak tree on the property next to the Vandersandens.

In time, Stefaan is going to buy the lot next to theirs so that later on, when their daughter is living in their villa, she'll have an extra big garden. She'll play in the woods, too. Beneath years and years of fallen leaves the forgotten clothing and tents of Napoleon's troops lie rotting. They passed through these woods and camped here for a time. At least that's the story the real estate agent tells each of the buyers, and now they're telling it to their own children. They live on the territory of the smallest punk ever to conquer vast parts of the world.

No sooner does the car bearing the new family ride up the driveway than the dog belonging to the neighbours across the street starts barking. He comes charging out of the villa's open back door. The child in Mieke's arms wakes up with alarm, startled by the fierce noise. Only a few days later the dog will have a new baby to greet in his own villa, for exactly five days after Sarah's birth Emily is born, the daughter of neighbours Evi and Marc Vanende-Boelens, she a former model and former nurse, he a leading surgeon.

More insecure than ever about her own tried and tested beauty, Mieke sits in the passenger's seat. Her ice-cold eyes shoot over the unmown lawn and spot a molehill belonging to the same doomed mole. As soon as Stefaan opens the car door for her, the sunlight begins caressing her blonde-brown hair. With her new acquisition clamped firmly in her arms, Mieke steps out of the car. She begins walking, still rather pale—paler than the baby pressed against her body. It takes a while to get used to the overwhelming open space, but as soon as she sees her mighty round boxwood beside the front door, Mieke knows she is home.

'I could have sworn it was going to be a boy,' she says to Stefaan with a trembling voice. The fact that she has just imparted life to Sarah gives her beauty extra radiance and makes her irresistible despite her loose-fitting dress, although Stefaan doesn't dare lay a finger on her out of pure respect. Mieke plants tender kisses on the tiny girl and places her in Stefaan's open arms. 'Even so, I'm deliriously happy with her.'

Her silken cheeks puffed out in the fresh air, her bright little eyes squeezed shut because the sky is pouring down too much light for a newborn, little Sarah kicks against her fluffy sleeping bag. Beaming, Stefaan carries his daughter across the threshold.

GRANNY 1990

'Hello, Lord, good morning. It's been a long time, but I'm back. Let me begin by congratulating you on your amazing victory in East Germany. I heard on the radio that the Christians there had a huge win in the elections.

'Thank you for this day. I just drank my coffee, so things ought to go well here.

'It seems like I only come to you when I want to ask for something, or when I have problems, or when I want something else done. I realize that. But just look at me sitting here, eighty-four years old. It's already so hard just keeping my eyes open every day that I never get around to the rest. I really believe in you, Lord, even though you don't hear much from me. I want to be clear about that. The fact that I'm here talking to you right now is proof enough.

'I have something to ask you. Something serious this time. I know I've often bothered you with trifles. Far too often, looking back on it. That time when I was fourteen and I had a home economics exam, for instance, it wasn't proper for me to ask for your help. You would have been quite right not to help me. And I didn't even need your help anyway. Such a simple exam. I had the best grade in the whole class. The best of forty-one girls. I can still remember how nervous I was the day before the exam. As soon as I saw the questions I knew: piece of cake. I also knew that I would never be allowed to go any further in school, that's how smart I was. I'm not stupid, you know. How else could I have had such smart children? Thank you for that, God.

'I'm boring you with trifles. I don't want to rob you of

your precious time. You're too busy to listen to a lot of hot air. Imagine if everyone came to you with every little trifle they had. No, that's impossible, you can't work that way. I'll get right to the point, God.'

Melanie Vandersanden-Plottier believes that God can explain everything and that he kneads her fate in the palm of his big, superhuman hand just like a meatball. He has the last word, although he tends to keep his mouth shut. For years he was silent about the deaths of her son Alain, who died too young, and her beloved husband André. Melanie is no hypocrite. She's more a desperate believer, with great pain locked up behind the leaden door of her heart.

It's a grey Wednesday morning in 1990, only a few months after the Berlin Wall came down five hundred miles farther to the east, a few weeks after Gloria Estefan was released from the hospital across the ocean after her accident, and a couple of days after the enormous Hubble telescope found its place in the universe in order to look down on earth, and Melanie is sitting on the toilet in the smallest room in the house. Melanie is a Flemish woman who always flies the lion standard on holidays, a woman who makes deals with God like a Mafioso with the judge of the most supreme court, a sturdy woman who trudges through the wilderness in her head and sees in it a damp, black-and-white Congolese rain forest.

'Almighty God, now you really have to help me. It's an emergency. And between you and me, you haven't been all that helpful so far. If you help me this time I'll forget all that. I mean it.

'I'll forget how you turned your back on my dear little Alain. I remember his birth as if it were yesterday. People didn't know anything back then. I didn't even know what it meant to be pregnant, not the first time and not the second time, either. Chubby as I am, chubby a second time. I've always been a good eater. Everyone said to me: Melanie, we don't understand where you put it all. And I was so proud. I just helped myself to another hunk of bread. After that it turned out I was pregnant. I was going to bring another little one into the world, a brother or sister for Stefaan. During that labour I thought I'd die. I lay there for twenty-five hours praying my heart out. You may still remember that, God. It was such a beautiful spring day, although you may not remember it because of all the births in the world happening one after the other.

'When Alain was born I saw right away that he was a special little man. Those rubbery little hands and feet, just like jellybeans. I was crazy about that little guy. After he was born it took forever for my milk to come in, literally. I had lost blood, towels full of blood. Fortunately I had built up some reserves, but because of the blood loss I didn't have enough milk. I just kept yammering the livelong day: I'm going to die, my baby is going to die. I don't know what came over me, but I just felt like it was going to end badly. Except I didn't know it would take ten years. When Stefaan was born I was just plain happy, and you see, he's still alive.

'Everything was fine for a long time. Too fine. André and I couldn't believe how happy we were with those two boys. They were like two peas in a pod, those two. They did everything together, while most mothers with two sons have to make sure they don't knock each others' heads off. Not them. Big brother and little brother, and no one could come between them. Stefaan was the clever little boss, maybe too smart for this world. He'd let people push him around, and I'd have to say: Stefaan, stand up for yourself. Alain was another story. He was the charming klutz who could never sit still. He was always on the lookout for danger. If he passed a tree, he'd climb to the very top and then start screaming, or he'd only get halfway up because the branch broke off. If he saw a hedgehog, five minutes later he'd be pulling the spines out of his backside. If you let him help you in the kitchen, he'd cut all his fingers at once with the potato knife. There's a big room for worries in a mother's heart.

'Alain was ten years old when he went to heaven to keep you company. We lived on the paved road at the time. It was called the paved road but there was very little traffic on it. Stands to reason, since there were almost no cars back then. There were the farmers' horse carts and mail coaches, that's about all. There was one person in the village who did have a car. Desmet, the brick manu-facturer, with that cigar of his always sticking out of his bulldog mug. And on that horrible, hateful winter day, that car stopped in front of our yard and the door opened. To our utter astonishment Stefaan got out and put an end to our happiness with just a couple of words. Yes, God, I'm telling you the truth. Sometimes I wished I had never been born. Then I never would have lost my child. And the worst of it is: life just goes on. No sooner had Alain been laid in the ground than the neighbour lady came over with sugared almonds. And wouldn't I like to come see her sister's little one, to take my mind off my troubles? Wouldn't that make you crazy, too?

'After little Alain died I didn't say a word for five years. It was not an easy time. Because people begin to think: she's just not opening her mouth, the sourpuss. All she wants to do is sit around and mope. She likes it. But that's not the way it works. I didn't like it at all. I had to do it to keep from doing something worse, to keep from scream-ing. Sometimes I can sit so still that I think it never hap-pened.

'Don't fret so, my sisters would say. You have to talk.

'There's the door, I'd tell them.

'You just can't explain something like that. There you are, literally empty-handed. You hand over the coffin, thank every Tom, Dick, and Harry for coming, and then the next day comes, and the next, and the next. And you say to yourself: Melanie, don't let on how you feel. Just grin and bear it.

'And yes, I cultivated a couple of bad habits to help me carry on. But does that bother anybody, I ask myself. No. And people are less bothered if I keep my mouth shut.

'I hung up Alain's photo. The focal point of our house, which everyone uncomfortably avoided. I burned my eyes on it every day. Even that doesn't work anymore. All I see are the outlines of the frame. No, dear God, grief doesn't wear out. Grief is not a carpet.

'André had such a hard time. He couldn't take it any-more. He was a proud man, my André. You can go ahead and say he was just a peasant, God, but on Sunday you could never tell. At least not when he was still in good shape. Six o'clock in the morning in his three-piece suit, walking through the fields to church in his bare feet, dress shoes in his hand to keep from wearing them out, and his watch in his vest pocket. One of those big, beau-tiful watches, that makes such an impression, you know.

'His fingers might be blue from the cold, he might have tipped over the only glass of beer he'd had in weeks, his child might be dead, but I never heard André com-plain. I mean never. Look, God, I complain too much and I know it's not getting me anywhere, but isn't it possible to complain too little? Isn't that a sin as well, not to do enough bad things? It was his downfall, because he locked it all away inside and it sank like lead until it pushed him down so low that all he could do was follow, into the ground, into the grave.

'Dear Lord, you propose and you dispose and all I can do is resign myself.

'Sometimes, dear God, I'm really afraid for Stefaan. I just can't make him out. He can be so preoccupied and abrupt, even though everything's going his way. With his good looks and his chic, upper-crust lady, with his little Saaaraaah and his enormous villa. Maybe he's had too many lucky breaks, that can't turn out well. Everyone has to have his helping of affliction. Everyone. Except for stars like Michael Jackson, such a cheerful black boy. Yes, well, those people aren't real. It's all plastic, all for show. Anyway I liked the sound of him better earlier on, with all his little brothers.

'But I'm rambling, dear God. I want to talk to you about something else: tomorrow Sarah is going to be ten years old. That's how old Alain was when he died. I know there's some poisonous gift being passed down in this family. It's our fate.

'Now I want to ask you, merciful God: leave Sarah alone and take me. You know that I'm very grateful for the life I've had, at least for a little part of it. Spare Sarah and take me. That's all. It's about time I saw André and Alain again anyway. Look, God, I'm tired, I'm really tired. You aren't planning on keeping me here much longer, right? You don't have to answer me. Just say no or yes. They don't need me here any longer. I can see it every-where I look. In the faces of the people around me who say: how much longer is that bitch going to live? In the mirror that grins back at me with a twisted smile, and in the ridiculous calmness that has crept into my life. There are days that I hardly move at all, or hardly make it from my chair to the kitchen.

'It's not about me. It's about my family. I don't want

them all to bleed to death. All those accidents, they have to stop. All those tragedies and all those deaths, I can't take it anymore. If you have to have one more of us, dear God, then take me.

'I just want to ask you in a friendly way to please keep my request in mind.

'Thank you for your attention, dear God.

'If I might add just one more thing: in the end it's in your best interest as well. If fate visits us one more time, I swear, I won't believe in you anymore.'

MIEKE 1990

Today Mieke has bought white cabbage and vinegar. Sauerkraut has never been on the menu at 7 Nightingale Lane, but Stefaan kept insisting, so she's going to make sauerkraut. Mieke has had to overcome her suspicion of the questionable cheap ingredients, vinegar and cabbage. Sauerkraut—the name itself says it all: a combination of something sour and something that can produce dangerous intestinal gas. A food item that in all probability was invented by some bored fool on an ice-cold afternoon in the unattended kitchen of a lunatic asylum. Making sauerkraut could easily take half a day, she has estimated, but she's been charging ahead due to sheer nervousness. At half past two in the afternoon she's well ahead of schedule. Preparing this peasant German specialty has not been enough to calm her nerves. There's real work that will do that: getting down on her hands and knees, endlessly combing the little threads of the rug in the living room like a nervous house cat scratching a scratching post. It's an aberration that Mieke allows herself when she has worries.

For a woman like Mieke, the world is not a round globe or a flat pancake but a maze with lots of entrances and just one exit that can only be found with the compass of a highly principled upbringing. She learned this during her childhood from her father, a strict man with impressive curling eyebrows that emphasized his wisdom, a prosperous notary of considerable prestige who specialized in corporate law, the proud head of a respectable family with a classic beauty of a daughter, a rebel of a son, and a well-behaved, sweet latecomer to whom they gave the name Mieke. To the great relief of her parents, now more than ten years deceased, Mieke has followed in their footsteps. She is an intelligent woman with class and style, an icon of the values that her parents instilled in her, a radiant beacon of normality in the sea of chaos of 1990.

Mieke's parents were already quite old when they had her. First there was Lydia, the eldest daughter of Gerard and Camille De Kinder, then came Jempy, and finally it took another twelve years for Mieke to be brought into the world. Mieke's sister and brother quickly escaped from their parents' home. Her father the notary, however, was decidedly present throughout her entire childhood. His desk was in the front room of their house. Mieke spied on the many people who came to visit him. People not only came with legal questions but they also brought him their moral problems and dilemmas. The pastor himself felt aggrieved. Mieke had enormous admiration for her father, although her upbringing was a confusing, benumbing cocktail of totally contradictory ingredients. Her father was not only a notary who had a friendly word for everyone, but he was also a dictator who demanded that his children get up every day at six o'clock on the nose, that they keep themselves hidden whenever visitors came, and that they always address him with the same two words: yes, father. At arbitrary moments he was suddenly the loving papa whom they could go to with all their questions, and he surprised his children with extravagant toys. As a child of a father like that you don't have a clock to tell you when such a moment of grace is about to arrive. Mieke developed her own rigid logic that she lowered over all contradictory signals like a bell jar.

In the living room Mieke sinks down onto her latest

acquisition, a hand-knotted Persian rug that took more than three hundred thousand hours to make. She likes her house to be well-ordered and tidy. 'Other people can do as they like in their shacks,' she says, 'but here everything has got to be clean.' Just what her father used to say approvingly to his floor-mopping wife. The word 'shack' does not really apply to the home of Mieke and Stefaan on the mountain. By 'clean' Mieke means: not a single hair is allowed to hang from any of the chair legs, not a mote of dust is given the time to flutter down over the bergère armchair, the residents don't have to keep making arbitrary decisions about where to leave their various things, and all the tassels on the rugs lie straight. The furnishing and maintenance of the villa is a huge job to which Mieke has devoted herself with love.

To keep her shrieking nerves under control she combs the threads of the rug. She combs away Sarah's habit of shrugging her shoulders when Mieke explodes over the spots of India ink on the white kitchen table; she combs away the child's pathological indifference because it drives her wild; she combs away the shrill chords that her daughter tries to coax out of her guitar as if she were, uh, Nana Mouskouri. The combing doesn't fail to have a calming effect. She combs until all the threads are lying neatly side by side and she can breathe a sigh of relief and keep on combing because it does her so much good. Combing rugs helps her the way a glass of wine can help, or stroking a puppy, or covering a baby's bottom with talcum powder. Yes, it's a private thing.

Mieke started her curious hobby after Sarah was born. Determined to work off the mushy pudding belly of her pregnancy, ravenously hungry, she spent many hours on her hands and knees combing the rugs. She ruined her knobby knees with all that combing. The doctor mentioned something about housemaid's knee.

All that rug combing made Mieke slimmer and less gloomy than she had been during the first days of her new life as a mother. No one spoke of postnatal depression back then, a condition that hadn't yet been diagnosed in their circles in the year 1980. Indeed, the word 'depression' was a generic term for lazy people who liked to attract attention by being lackadaisical, nothing that couldn't be cured by a cold washcloth in the morning, extra hard work during the day, and a good swift kick in the backside. And even if the illness had been known, the proud Mieke would never have allowed her affliction to be characterized by such a banal medical term. Postnatal depression or no, the birth of Sarah had shaped the rustic style of Mieke and Stefaan's household interior in any case. A house without tassled rugs was not an option for Mieke. She bought heaps of expensive Persian rugs during the months after the birth and she combed herself silly. She may have gone a bit too far, in retrospect, yet combing was certainly better than lying around in bed, wretched and lazy, like a mussel in its shell.

While she's combing, Mieke runs through all the vexatious possibilities of what can go wrong when a ten-year-old child goes on a one-mile walk. Two days ago Sarah had her birthday, and in addition to a crown and a cheesecake with ten candles Sarah was allowed to pick out a gift. Sarah resolutely chose to go on a journey on foot and without supervision to the village newspaper shop. Her daughter is inventive, that's one thing you can say about her. And Mieke is a woman of her word: front door open, a coin in Sarah's hand, and there she goes to the newspaper shop to buy herself a *Libelle Rosita* magazine. Mieke does not feel easy about this. It's the very first time she's let her daughter out on her own. She curses herself for allowing it. Sarah is far too docile, far too good. If anything were to happen to her, Mieke would never forgive herself. Of course there's no way that Sarah would ever be taken hostage by Palestinians or hit by a car in the silent housing estate, or swept up by hookers from the village. No way. But even so, the most unexpected things are often the first to happen. Especially to a clumsy, innocent child like Sarah, who would give her money away to a moustachioed man in a white van in exchange for a lift.

In this new decade you can't just send your only child out into the minefield of the world. How can she be so stupid, Mieke says to herself, knowing her daughter already made a failed attempt to run away from home at the age of five and tore her dungarees on the barbed wire around the chicken coop. These are the ideas Mieke is combing out of her head, but they don't disappear entirely. It's just like the neighbours. Even if they're not walking past all the time, they're always there and they can pop up unexpectedly at any moment. Her neighbour Evi is forever wiping her feet on the unwritten law that you don't just show up at each other's door whenever it strikes your fancy.

Evi Vanende-Boelens lives with her husband, the top surgeon Marc Vanende, in a hypermodern house with octagonal windows on an enormous plot of land. One year ago they had an English garden installed, complete with labyrinth, in exactly fifteen days. The garden clashes with the design of the eighties-style house, with its conversation pit, open kitchen, countless different levels, and indoor swimming pool. But the Vanende-Boelens family, liberal to the core, think nothing of making whimsical, ridiculously expensive changes every now and then that send shock waves through the Vandersanden-

De Kinder family. Emily is the product of a jovial bon vivant of a father who has been known to hang over the operating table in a shaky state of near delirium but who never loses his concentration, and a devil-may-care mother with the looks of Jane Fonda who takes part in the latest Adidas jogging trends and, with her filthy puff-ball of a dog, fertilizes the front gardens of even the most dignified of the housing estate dwellers at eight o'clock every morning while merrily waving to the passing cars during the daily migration to the city, when any respectable housewife and mother knows she should stay indoors where she belongs. It's one of the fundamental rules that applies to all the housewives in the villas on the mountain: you can sit on your lazy ass all day long, but in the morning between waking up and waving goodbye you're expected to work yourself to death for your offspring. Morning is the only time you really have something to do without having to talk yourself into it. Breakfast has to be cleared away, the beds made, and the rooms aired, and for those who are so inclined it's just a matter of grin and bear it before the first bottle is broken out or the first pack of cookies is torn open, for There Must Be Discipline. This does not apply to the Vanende-Boelens family. Marc is still sleeping it off in bed, Evi is chattering away and laughing, her ponytail bouncing back and forth, and daughter Emily is going about her business. She's been able to prepare her own sandwiches since she was three and she's never lost the knack.

'Mieke, I'm sorry to barge in on you like this, but do you happen to have any ice cubes?' Eyelashes gleaming, Evi is fidgeting at the door and pulling on her short little dress as if she were trying to persuade gravity to lengthen it a bit.

'Ice cubes?' Mieke's eye falls on the sticker she invitingly hung on the doorbell. RAIN OR SHINE, ALWAYS WELCOME, says the flippant little text balloon on an orange background. That has got to go. 'Of course, Evi, just a minute.'

When Mieke comes back to the front door, Evi points down with her diamond-beringed finger to her neighbour's legs.

'Something happen to your knees?' Mieke looks at the red spots on her knees and shrugs her shoulders.

'I knew you'd have ice cubes, Mieke. I can always count on you. Oh, yes, I have a letter here. It was in our mailbox for a couple of days but I completely forgot. Sorry. Who is Jempy De Kinder?'

'My brother. Thank you. And if you need more ice cubes, be sure to come by,' Mieke says with blatant insincerity.

Looking out the bathroom window she watches the neighbour's cat search for a comfortable place among her freesias. The words WHAT CATS HATE rise to the top of her mental shopping list for the garden centre. The neighbours aren't going to teach the cat, so someone else is going to have to set the limits.

Mieke steps into the shower. She never takes a bath. Baths are for lazy people who have too much time on their hands. The Romans took leisurely baths and even had bath houses. It's no wonder their decadence was their downfall. In his letter Jempy writes that he's coming to visit her soon. How long has it been since she's seen her brother? How anybody can live like Jempy does is beyond her, but it's out there in that great beyond that her love for her brother lies. He's like a cat: you don't know where he's come from and whose flowers he's going to destroy, but you can be pretty sure he'll be back, in perfect health and beaming all over. Stefaan is more like a dog. She lovingly keeps him on a short leash. Every now and then he's moody, sometimes even paranoid, and when he's in his basket he licks his own wounds. He's not always Mr. Cheerful, but she values his sincerity. On the other hand, the blindingly white smile of Marc across the street is a perfect example of play-acting. When you take out the garbage cans after sundown and you catch a glimpse of his professional doctor's grin, it can scare the living daylights out of you. As if his fee had something to do with the width of his smile.

SARAH 1990-1991

'How much did you get?' Emily asks. They're walking to the beat of the jingling fortune in Sarah's pants' pocket. It's sixty francs and not a centime more. Sarah's absolutely sure of that. She's even more sure that she's not allowed to walk here with Emily. Excessive contact with other people is not a good idea, Mieke says, even if you just happen to bump into them, even if it's the girl across the street who's like a sister to you and whose mother takes turns driving you to school. Not even then.

For an only child living in a villa on the mountain, the childhood years are a Kafkaesque labyrinth of rules and prohibitions. If you walk down the street you're riff-raff, and if you play music in your room you're committing a major crime because you're making noise.

At the tinkling of the doorbell the owner of the newspaper shop comes out from his dark infernal lair full of children's screaming and televised din in the back. This man, Mieke has assured her daughter, is going to try to cheat her. This upside-down camel, whose humps are hanging out in front, takes his own stupidity for shrewdness and is so stupid that he thinks his customers are stupid and that he can easily put one over on them. He makes a game of it and keeps on trying, over and over and over again, even though he gets caught on a regular basis.

The *Libelle Rositas* are on the camel's counter. All Sarah has to do is take the magazine and count her change. Mieke has told her in no uncertain terms not to look around too much. There's nothing there to interest her, especially in the back of the shop. Some of the magazines there are covered in silver wrapping paper with xxx written on them in black letters. As unusual as those obtrusive letters are, that's how conspicuous and exposed to the real world Sarah feels. She conducts her transaction with downcast eyes, and when no change is forthcoming she turns to Emily, who follows their cleverly thought-out scenario and puts a twenty-franc coin on the counter. 'And Marlboros for my mother,' she says. 'It's three francs too much, but that's all right.' This is too quick for the camel. He puts a pack of Marlboros on the counter and goes to work with his Texas Instruments calculator, but the two girls grab the magazine and cigarettes and rush out the door before he can react.

Behind the town hall opposite the newspaper shop Emily strips the pack of its transparent skin. Sarah takes one of the cigarettes, sniffs it, and places it between her fingers as if she were smoking it. The gesture feels like freedom. Sarah isn't allowed to eat candy because candy makes you fat, and if you're fat you have fewer chances in life. Her mother hasn't laid down any rules for smoking. A car drives past slowly. She quickly slips the sharp-smelling stick of pleasure into the sleeve of her jacket. Pleasure is best done as quickly as possible so you can get on with your normal life.

Along with that thought, an invisible angel of haste comes to perch on Sarah's feathers. A delay of a couple of minutes can be reason enough for Mieke to call the police. It wasn't long ago that she called in the police when a strange man set a ladder against the chimney. The man had come to the wrong house, he explained to the police. It was enough to get her mother to spend one whole hour combing her new rug. Sarah and Emily hasten up the mountain.

At three o'clock on Saturday afternoon Sarah returns

to number 7 Nightingale Lane without any tears in her clothing. She slips in through the back door and goes directly to the bathroom. Behind the toilet, beneath a wooden construction meant to hide the toilet's waste pipe, she hides the cigarette. Sanctimonious Sarah comes strolling into the kitchen. Contrary to all expectations, the one-person welcoming committee (Mieke) is not here to greet her. This is suspicious, since her mother can't be anywhere else but home. What's completely alarming is the pan of spaghetti sauce simmering unattended on the stove. In the middle of the afternoon, inferior food like spaghetti sauce, unattended—in this house that's as unusual as a rhinoceros sitting on the sofa watching television.

Luckily the sound of her mother's unique, high-pitched chatter can suddenly be heard in the living room, alternating with the gravelly voice of an unknown man. She hears the familiar, nervous click of her mother's heels as she rushes into the toilet in the entrance hall.

Mieke usually leaves the door ajar for workmen, but only if there's no other solution than to rely on their services. Mieke may praise the work of the electrician to the skies when he's standing upright in the kitchen, his filthy shoes on a piece of cardboard, drinking coffee from a Villeroy & Boch cup and eating the pralines Mieke has urged on him (and withheld from Sarah for health reasons). But after he leaves she spends days talking about how the man spread mud all over the sheets on the cellar stairs with his ungainly clodhoppers without saying a word about it, how his work crew actually left the cellar looking like a brothel, and how they smeared her light switches with pitch—yes, she swears it, with pitch, which she won't be able to get off in a hundred years.

Something is tickling the extremities of Sarah's nerves: fear and excitement closing in together. Peering through a crack in the door, Sarah sees him. After ten years of life, Sarah beholds the first strange man she's ever seen in this house who isn't a worker. Legs wide apart, backlit, straight off the silver screen: a cowboy, a bad guy in torn jeans.

'No, I won't have it,' she hears her mother say again. She must have rushed through her trip to the toilet. 'You can eat, but then you've got to go.'

'Settle down, Mieke, it spoils your looks. And that's a damn shame for a good-looking woman like you.'

'No, no, I mean it. This time I'm not going to let myself be taken in. You've caused me enough trouble.'

'What are you talking about? We haven't seen each other in ages.'

'Why are you making it so hard for me? Why did you come here to give my family a hard time?'

'Your mother-in-law, who doesn't say a word to you, is welcomed here with open arms, but … '

'Open arms!' Mieke interrupts, sneering.

' … and I get tossed out, even though I've come especially for you. I think that's terrible.'

'If you think it's so terrible, get on your motorcycle and leave. I'm not stopping you. You'll know where to go, or am I your only place of refuge?'

'Mieke, I came here especially for you. You've always been special to me, you know that.'

'Jempy, still the big charmer,' Mieke says in a milder tone. 'The spaghetti should be done, so you can eat. At least if you call spaghetti a meal. I expect Sarah any minute, by the way. She should have been home already.'

The man growls something unintelligible. A heavy cadence can be heard moving from the living room to the kitchen, right where she's standing at the doorway, eavesdropping. When the door opens, Sarah flees to the utility room to continue her spying activities.

This strange man, intruding on a stable family that for ten years has been as unshakable as a sequoia, this daredevil, opens one drawer after another and rummages boorishly through their things. Mieke jumps between him and the kitchen cabinet and fishes a spoon out of the cutlery drawer. He takes the spoon and begins scooping straight out of the pot. Is he a member of a motorcycle gang, and has he taken her mother hostage? No, she never would have let him in. He can't be a Jehovah's Witness, either, because he never would have gotten past the front door. A worker? If he were, the whole house would be eerily covered in old sheets. The only people who ever come here, after much preparation, are Mieke's best friend Elvira and her neighbour Ulrike.

'Oh, please, that's no way to eat,' Mieke laughs. 'Where were you raised, in a pig sty?'

Normally her mother would jump out of her skin. Her lax, tolerant attitude is more than alarming for Sarah, who isn't even allowed to eat an apple whole. This strange man is standing slipperless in the kitchen and scraping a spoon across the delicate surface of the Tefal pan. Who can explain it?

What Sarah reads into this is a passionate soap opera. Her mother is unpredictable, and in her unpredictable logic there's always an explanation to suit her. So it's quite possible that Mieke, who is one hundred percent devoted to her husband, has Another Man. Sarah gulps for air at this offensive speculation. It would be horrible, first of all for her but also for her father, who works so hard six days out of seven, mows the lawn every weekend, and sometimes just sits there staring so distractedly that it makes her blood run cold. If it's true, he'll have to leave the house and there'll be a dreadful fight over her and the lawn mower. Those kinds of catastrophic divorces are common fare for the people in the village, her mother has always said scornfully: the riff-raff who switch partners at the drop of a hat and just keep passing the children back and forth.

The man abruptly interrupts his mechanical eating and slurping activities when he catches sight of Sarah the spy through the crack that gives away her hiding place. His jaw drops, his sauce-filled mouth emits warm air and gasps for the cold. He swallows and calls her by name. Sarah patters shyly into the kitchen. Like a Chinese serving girl on lotus feet, she carries the women's magazine for her mother.

Standing before Jempy is a four-foot-six beanstalk in corduroy pants and a pullover with bright yellow daisies scattered across it like flowers in a green meadow. A large head is doing all it can to hold itself erect on the slender little body. Curious, wide-open eyes stare at him, almost as pitch black as the child's bobbed hair. 'You sure do look like your mother, unbelievable,' says the man with delight as he tosses Sarah into the air like a featherweight package, catches her, gives her a hug and plants her in front of him on the kitchen floor in order to look at her from a distance. 'The last time I saw you, you were just a little thing, two, three years old. What a pretty girl you've turned into. Don't you remember your Uncle Jempy?' Sarah doesn't know what to say, and she stiffens as her cheeks turn crimson. Mieke stands behind her daughter and lowers her delicate hands onto Sarah's shoulders as she would on a piano keyboard. This rare, tender contact clears away the cloud in her head.

'This is Jean-Pierre,' Mieke says to Sarah. 'My brother

and your uncle. He's come to stay with us for the weekend. You may call him Uncle Jempy.' And with this Mieke has supplied all the necessary information. Jempy, the man about whom Sarah has heard so many stifled comments such as 'nail in my coffin' and 'nuisance', is now here in the flesh, right in front of her nose, slurping spaghetti.

'I'm going to stay here awhile, if that's all right with you.' Sarah's uncle smiles at her.

After having tricked her way into the big wide world, the big wide world itself has come to her. It's as if a new person had stepped out of the back room of her tender young life, someone Sarah has never seen before but always knew was there. This cowboy is a member of her family.

Mieke moistens her handkerchief with the tip of her tongue. She goes down on her knees to scrub a drop of sauce from one of the kitchen tiles.

'Where's my change?' she asks Sarah.

'I didn't get any change.'

'Just what I expected! Can you believe it? I told you, that guy from the newspaper shop is a real scoundrel. Cheating children like that.' There's sweat on Mieke's upper lip. 'Get out there right now and start weeding. I'll call you when dinner's ready.'

When Sarah storms into the house after a lightning fast round of weeding, the stove exhaust fan is whirring at such a rate that the curtains are in danger of being swallowed up. The box of Useless Giveaway Presents has been taken down from the attic and all the perfumed candles in it are now lined up and burning in the kitchen, but the smell of cigarettes has penetrated even the most virginal spaces. 'Please, Jempy, if you're going to smoke, do it outside.'

Mieke and Uncle Jempy speak a language full of aspirated letters and amputated words that Sarah unfortunately has not mastered. They talk loud and laugh often. Sarah compares the two family members, combines their silhouettes, and comes up with a hilarious monster: some in-between creature with an agitated babble, roaring laughter, thin wrists attached to hefty arms protruding from shirt sleeves, and the legs of a gazelle in Romika slippers.

'As long as you aren't as naughty as your uncle,' Jempy says, beating Mieke to the punch.

Stefaan works on Saturdays, much to Mieke's displeasure. He's just spent three days in bed with a peculiar chronic fatigue virus, so he's going to have some catching up to do (Stefaan) and he'll still have to take it easy (Mieke). After his Saturday work he slavishly drops in on Granny every weekend. He frequently tries to entice Sarah to come along by promising her cake, and sometimes he even uses emotional blackmail, but most of the time she doesn't want to go. Granny smells bad and she doesn't talk and she always looks so angry (as if she wanted to bewitch Sarah). That's why she's sitting at the kitchen table now, drawing music staffs. While Mieke makes herself presentable, Uncle Jempy takes his things to the guest room.

At seven o'clock Stefaan comes home, just as Mieke is putting the last dish on the table, as usual. He says Granny sends her greetings to Sarah, that she thinks about her a lot and is very proud that Sarah is really doing her best at school. Granny can't possibly have said all that. Then Stefaan shakes Uncle Jempy's hand. Jempy said he's looking damned good, but what do you expect with a wife like his little sister? Stefaan doesn't know how to respond to such a comment. He walks over to the record cabinet and interrupts Chopin's lively romantic piano Prelude, setting Dylan on a long epic journey through 'The Gates of Eden'.

Jempy jumps to his feet. 'That reminds me,' he says, and he runs over to a plastic bag from the Unic department store, 'that I brought a present for you, Sarah.'

He rummages through the bag and hands her a CD from which the cellophane wrapper has already been removed. Sarah sees a comic strip drawing of collapsing skyscrapers with the freaks from Iggy Pop's 'Brick by Brick' swarming in between.

'Oh dear oh dear,' says Mieke. Sarah puts the CD on.

'Not too loud,' says Mieke, 'so we can still hear each other talk.'

The reeking sauerkraut is passed around, and on every plate there's a skinned chicken fillet.

'So healthy,' laughs Uncle Jempy. 'This is sure to give me stomach cramps.' He leans back, hands behind his head, a joker who feels at home everywhere.

'I like it, Mama.' Sarah wants to show her mother that she's grateful—for the food, for Uncle Jempy. Ingratitude, as her mother always says, is the devil's workshop.

'Isn't there any ketchup or mayonnaise, sis?'

Uncle Jempy is waited on hand and foot. He smothers his food in ketchup and mayonnaise that emerge from some secret stockpile, since these leading causes of American and French heart attacks never appear on the table here. Sarah gets half a teaspoon of ketchup, just this once, and she has to make sure she doesn't abuse the privilege.

'The food inside isn't very healthy. Yesterday there was a whole family of worms in my mashed potatoes ... '

'Inside where?' Sarah asks.

'In jail,' Jempy answers.

'Change the subject,' Mieke hurries to interject. 'How's Sonja doing?'

'Don't talk to me about that woman.'

Uncle Jempy eats with relish and is perfectly relaxed. A man of the world.

'Yeah, Stefaan, at least you chose well. If Mieke wasn't my little sister I'd know for myself.'

'Hey! Jempy! What a thing to say!' Mieke laughs.

Stefaan smiles his empty smile. He has to agree with Jempy, but if he were to say so he'd be implicating himself in an indelicate story with incestuous overtones.

After dessert—yogurt with sugar—Sarah stays at the table, sitting silently. She makes herself small and keeps her mouth shut, hoping they'll forget she's there so she can stay up late, like Emily. On Saturday nights she's allowed to take her down comforter to the conversation pit and watch TV for as long as she wants. Sarah wants to learn everything about Uncle Jempy.

'Say, Sarah,' says Mieke, 'we've had enough of that racket. Put some decent music on.'

Stefaan stands up and lets a waterfall of nasally tones roll out of the speakers and over their heads.

'Jempy, come on, you know this one,' Stefaan says.

'"Subterranean Homesick Blues", I'll say I know it,' says Jempy, and he chimes in with the twenty-four-year-old Dylan, 'you don't need a weatherman to know which way the wind blows'.

'That's the beginning of rap music, Sarah,' Stefaan says, his arm draped over the back of her chair. 'Listen to it carefully.'

'I don't know this song,' Sarah answers.

'It's better she doesn't know it,' Mieke says. She refills the water glasses.

'Is the cellar under water?' Jempy chokes out a laugh.

'We have tea, too,' Mieke says. 'Camomile or mint?'

At nine-thirty on the nose Stefaan reminds Sarah that it's time for bed. She gives her mother a kiss and hesitantly reaches out a hand to her uncle, although he says he'd rather have kisses like a real cowboy.

She never expected that her mother would have the same dark blood as a terrorist. The Delhaize Supermarket, where Mieke and Sarah go every week to fill two shopping carts with high-priced provisions, was the target of the so-called Nijvel Gang a couple of years ago. The terrorists mowed down several innocent customers. All of a sudden, the similarities between the world being reported in the news and Sarah's world weren't just superficial points of contact; now the two coincided perfectly. They made the news. She watched the news broadcast and saw the cash registers where she always folded open the brown bags, and the shelves at exactly her eye level that were full of candy, perfumed erasers, and stick-on earrings. *Jail is too good for those men*, Sarah often heard from her mother's armchair. It was all so exciting.

Stefaan kneels beside her bed for a good-night kiss. Sarah takes advantage of his position by firing questions at him. 'Was Uncle Jempy in jail before he came to us?'

'Uh, that's something you don't have to worry about.'

'I'm not worried about it. I just want to know.'

'Yes, Sarah. Uncle Jempy is in jail, but this weekend he has vacation. The director of the jail is letting him spend a weekend home, and apparently he can't think of a better home than his favourite sister's house, where he hasn't set foot for at least six years,' Stefaan tells her.

'Why is he in jail?'

'Mama and Aunt Lydia would rather not talk about it.'

'Is Uncle Jempy a terrorist?

'You watch too much news, Sarah.'

'Why did they arrest him then?'

'Why on earth do you want to know?'

'He's part of my family, he's my uncle.'

'Granny is part of your family, too. She'd so much like to see you again. You have to be nice to old people, Sarah. Before you know it Granny will be gone and then you'll be sorry.'

'But if people are dead, they're still part of your family, right? Isn't your little brother part of the family anymore?' It feels as if she's touched something red hot, something that will hurt her father and leave a mark. She knows very well that this is forbidden territory.

'Sarah!' His lower jaw begins grinding as if he were gnawing on a bone. 'That's enough talking. Time to go to sleep.'

'Papa, you're weird.'

'Go to sleep. Now.' Stefaan doesn't even plant the customary cold kiss on her forehead but simply turns off the light. When he returns to the living room, Sarah goes to the top of the stairs and listens.

'She left me in the lurch, took my own kid away, and now I'm supposed to pay her?' she hears Uncle Jempy say.

'That alimony is for your daughter, birdbrain,' Mieke interrupts. 'To buy her food and clothes and to pay for her school books.'

'My daughter doesn't even want to go to school. It's to pay for Sonja's jewellery, that's what it's for. I worked for her all during our marriage, day and night. If she decides to run off I'm not going to be stuck with all the responsibility.'

'According to the law ... '

'I know you've studied it all, but I don't give a shit about the law.'

'How can you say that?'

'I wipe my ass with the law. You have your principles, I have mine.'

'So you're all locked up and sitting pretty and we're left holding the bag.'

Her mother's sideswipes come galloping up to her while her uncle's bass tones remain submerged under the water of the ceiling like whales. In a little while the refrigerator's built-in freezer door shuts with a click. Would they be eating that bright yellow, grainy, passion fruit sherbet? Sarah and Mieke brought it home yesterday. The cashier at the Delhaize was handing out free products. For Mieke, anything free is suspicious by definition, but she had no choice than to accept the sherbet because it's rude to refuse a gift. Everyone but Mieke has been going out of their way to avoid the Delhaize since the Nijvel Gang held it up. But she won't let herself be scared away. Besides, the last place that the gang would want to attack anytime soon is this Delhaize. What's there to interest them? After the glass bowls have been spooned clean and shoved into the dishwasher, Stefaan announces that he's turning in. Mieke patters to the hallway to lock the five locks on the front door. Preparations for night-time are underway at number 7 Nightingale Lane.

Ten minutes of tooth brushing and make-up removal later the house is sunken in deep repose. After a great deal of foot-stamping, brooding, tossing and turning, and with the distant thunder of hunger in her belly, Sarah still hasn't fallen asleep. She's thinking about her father's little brother. What would it be like if he were still alive? Or if he had only been dead a short time and then came back as a little brother for herself and a friend for her papa? Now there's probably nothing left of the little brother. Uncle Alain has turned into a tiny little person, like all the other dead people. These little people roam the earth endlessly without ever bumping into each other. Her father works with little people, too—viruses, bacteria—but they're bad little people. Maybe Papa thinks his brother was kidnapped by those bad little people. She thinks it's really sad for him, but she's glad Mama has found *her* brother at any rate.

The next day Uncle Jempy is snoring loudly on the sofa when Sarah comes down for breakfast. Seven bedrooms and he sleeps on the sofa, is Mieke's litany. His feet are resting on the ceramic figure of a Chinese warrior. Next to him on the sofa is an empty bottle of Marie Brizard, keeping him company like a shameless lover. He had a go at the liquor supply that gaily decorates the writing desk. As soon as Mieke turns on the juicer he opens his eyes. He comes into the kitchen and pours himself a cup of coffee. Mieke presses her lips together.

'It's Sunday. The weekend is as good as over,' she says. 'Better leave now, then you're sure of not being late.'

He nods, puts his hand on Sarah's head and musses her hair. When he goes outside to smoke a cigarette, Sarah begins to whine: 'Why are you chasing him away?'

'We're not chasing him away,' Mieke snaps at Sarah with the same combativeness that she uses in her exchanges with Jempy. 'Uncle Jempy has to go back. The weekend is over and we've done our duty again, more than our duty.'

On a clear Saturday afternoon in the autumn of 1990 Stefaan has once again been unable to get Sarah to come see Granny. Granny still has her presents for Sarah's tenth birthday, Stefaan said before leaving the house alone. *Ingratitude is of the devil, isn't it, Mieke?* But more than anything else, Stefaan wants to keep his daughter away from Jempy, who's bound to show up at the door again sooner or later. As long as hc can't find an adequate solution for protecting his household from this guy, with his female admirers calling on the phone and the bill-collectors coming to the door (a bailiff!), he'll have to take his daughter away to a place of safety. His appeal doesn't make much of an impression on Mieke. Sarah will just stay at home with her.

Of course Mieke likes to see her brother, but every time he comes it takes an enormous amount of nerve-racking deftness to let Jempy into her house in such a way that the neighbours don't notice. Fortunately he doesn't have penitentiary leave every weekend, his behaviour within the prison walls being far from irreproachable. But once he's in the house it gives her secret pleasure. Jempy is able to shake something loose in her, a kind of playfulness that she can't activate with Stefaan. Even so, it would be better for Jempy to start looking for something for himself. Every time he comes, Jempy assures her he's in the market for real estate, but you can't rush something like that because it's too easy to make a bad investment.

It won't be long before Jempy is released for good, something Mieke can hardly bare to contemplate. If her brother was the only one she was focusing her worries on, she thinks she could manage. But Mieke also has a family, and neighbours. And a mother-in-law who has taken to calling every other minute to talk to her granddaughter. As if that weren't enough, she also has to fob off all the lady friends.

It was Sarah who picked up, that first time a call came for Uncle Jempy from a certain Leslie. That phone call was the first in a whole series, as if the girls were standing in line at the phone booth. All sorts of women call, one after another, twenty-four hours a day but mostly after ten o'clock at night or before ten o'clock in the morning. The girls sound as young as Sarah, Mieke says. The first few times she thought they were Sarah's class-mates calling to compare homework. The sluts talk with a voluptuous undercurrent punctuated by chewing gum, vulgar girls who all ask for Jean-Pierre, Jean, Jempy, their snooky-wookums, their darling. Mieke waits a few seconds and then lets the girls have it, explaining that Jempy has enough problems without having to deal with them, asking them how old they are, how they support themselves, and what they think they're doing.

'Oh, I'm already nineteen, Cindy,' 'I work as a cashier at the Unic, Viviane,' 'Okay, you win, I'm crazy in love, Gonda,' she says, imitating them with contempt. She explains to the girls that her brother Jean-Pierre has a family— Sarah perks up her ears—and that he could easily be their father, after which the air-headed little bimbos start spouting, usually with heaps of self-confidence, that they don't care, or that he's better off with them, or—the coarsest of the bunch—that she 'doesn't need to hear from any sour old bag, but where is Jean-Pierre, goddamn it? You're not finished with me yet. I've got his number now and I'm not giving up until I hear from my guy.'

Mieke fears the floodgates have been opened, she tells Stefaan when he gets back from Granny's. Sarah is sit-ting in the armchair with her headphones on, but the sound is off.

'We never should have let him stay here, not even once. You give them an inch and they take a mile.' That's the way she sees her brother, as a needy child, and that's why it's hard to refuse him. 'With Jempy it's always some-thing. He was no end of grief for my parents, but even they always gave in when he asked for something. In a way Jempy is very special.'

'Very special in the trouble he causes,' Stefaan adds.

'I'm much too good to show my brother the door, of course. But if we don't take control of the situation now, just think what might happen.' Mieke sees her brother being released and moving in with them, setting their house on fire with his cigarettes, 'investing' all their money in the one-armed bandits at the casino, and getting Sarah hooked on drugs while turning her into a smuggler. In her runaway imagination it's only a matter of weeks before Mieke finds the floozies in their sexiest lingerie sitting on bar stools at the living room window and ogling the neighbours. And … and … and are they just supposed to stand helplessly by?

'Calm down,' Stefaan says to comfort her. 'I'll take care of it.'

Nothing seems to have changed when Uncle Jempy shows up again at the door two weeks later. Stefaan and Jempy are drinking port aperitifs in the living room. Stefaan has red cheeks from bicycling home so fast, a blush that heightens his youthfulness. He's put on 'Man Gave Names To All The Animals' from Bob Dylan's conversion album *Slow Train Coming*. It's a happy, childlike tune which he thinks is just the thing for Sarah.

'Iraq,' Stefaan says to Jempy. 'What's going on there, anyway? Saddam Hussein has really gone one step too far.'

Uncle Jempy nods vaguely. The Persian Gulf crisis is not exactly his main concern, but Stefaan goes on while Jempy stares into his glass, surprised that a glass can empty so quickly.

'Anyone who knows anything about the Second World

War will tell you that something like this can't end well,' Stefaan says. 'Saddam has his eye on Kuwait's oil fields, and that's just plain wrong. Saddam's troops and their moustaches rolled into Kuwait one night on their rubber mats. That kind of unscrupulous greed and imperialism is suspiciously similar to the exploits of a certain Adolf so many years ago. The fact that the Americans want to take military action has nothing to do with left or right but with justice, and that's what Bush wants.'

'That's right,' Mieke calls out from the kitchen while stirring the leek soup. 'History repeats itself if you're not paying attention. It's our duty to put a stop to it. The Americans set a good example.' She turns on the exhaust fan, making it impossible hear the men in the living room, yet she keeps rattling on. Mieke can rant with uncommon ferocity about subjects that are so beyond her realm of experience that she can safely vent her own frustrations there. 'Anybody who doesn't want to join in is sticking his head in the sand,' says Mieke contentiously to her daughter.

'The oil fields that are burning there now are an enormous loss,' says Stefaan the scientist. 'Everyone has to do his duty and pull his weight, we all agree on that. And the tragedy that's taking place isn't really so far from us. It's a small world.'

'Yes, it's a small world,' says Uncle Jempy, and he refills his glass.

'But I still wouldn't want to have to paint it,' says Mieke, who has just come in with a silver tray of Tuc crackers.

'Isn't that something for you, Jean-Pierre,' Stefaan suggests as if he's been hit by a flash of inspiration, 'being a soldier? You'll be getting out soon anyway, right? You're a man of the world. A soldier does a lot of travelling.'

'I'd miss my daughter,' Uncle Jempy answers dryly.

'You haven't seen her in a year,' Mieke says.

'I don't have to see her to love her.'

Weeks turn into months. Uncle Jempy stays for the unsolicited pinch of exotic care in the salt-free regime at number 7 Nightingale Lane. No matter how many girls Jempy hits on during his penitentiary leave, his only big loves, he swears, are Mieke and Sarah. His admirers send love letters and stuffed teddy bears to 7 Nightingale Lane, but playboy Jempy himself only sends cards to Mieke from prison, thanking her and letting her know how glad he is to be her brother. He becomes the resident ghost who shows up every few weekends on Saturday afternoon. Sarah can smell the aroma of old soup from the prison on him. She sees how her mother scrubs the traces of her brother from the carpets every Sunday afternoon after he leaves. He's the man who is gradually attacking the family's nervous system and slowly driving them to the abyss of a serious crisis.

'Stuck, stuck,' Jempy grumbles that Saturday afternoon in the kitchen, and he unscrews the cap from a bottle of Tabasco that Mieke's can't open. 'Nobody should ever be stuck with anything. Stuck isn't in my dictionary.'

'By the way, I'm not going to be in your way much longer.' Uncle Jempy tells them he's on a bed of roses. Soon he's being released on parole. And he's gone gaga over a thirty-five-year-old lady and her two kids, who he's going to adopt.

'Roses with thorns, sounds like,' says Mieke. 'So cut the chit-chat. We have to be at Madam Cherry's in the village at three.'

Madam Cherry is a frugal old woman who lived

through the Great War and has a back as crooked as her fruit trees. At five-thirty every morning she mounts a ladder and climbs fifteen feet up into the branches. She'd rather risk her life than let all that magnificent fruit from God's garden go bad or leave it to the birds. Even that pious lady, supermarket bag tied to her head to keep off the drizzle, has fallen for Uncle Jempy's charms. She won't let him leave without one more bucket of sour cherries. Nothing would please her more; he's doing her a favour.

In the kitchen, juice is streaming from the pitting machine. The pits tap against the covered marble tiles like hailstones. The three of them are hard at work, as if together they had formed the conveyor belt of a perfect little family: Mieke washes and selects the cherries, Uncle Jempy runs them through the machine, and Sarah, down on her knees, gathers up the pits that fall beside it. The cherries leave red splashes of blood on the kitchen cabinets, which Sarah must wipe off immediately with a damp cloth. Sarah wheedles her uncle into telling them tall tales. She wants to know what kinds of crimes the other prisoners were in for.

'Sarah, give your uncle some peace and quiet.'

'Yeah, Sarah, how about you tell me something? Or let me hear what you're learning at the music academy. Where's your guitar?'

Sarah doesn't dare. She's much too shy. 'Some other time, uncle. I'm all messy right now.'

'Yes, Jempy, she's right. Leave her alone or my whole living room will be covered in cherry juice. I don't know how she does it, but somehow she manages.' Sarah, who for more than ten years has come to know Mieke's sardonic speech pattern like the back of her hand, is surprised by the cheerful undertone of her mother's comment.

They're all in high spirits. Mieke even makes a joke when she hears over the radio that gangster boss Patrick Haemers is being put under additional surveillance in prison. She says she's going to set an extra place tonight at supper tonight for Jempy's buddy, because he's certainly going to find a way to escape despite the extra surveillance. Fine with her, she says. He looks like a respectable young man, with his blue eyes and beautiful sweaters. Who's going to wash the sweaters, she wonders? In response Uncle Jempy throws a handful of cherries at her head. Everything falls silent. Only the news presenter continues. Sarah looks at her mother. Tears are suddenly streaming down Mieke's cheeks. 'That's not allowed,' she sobs, 'you're not allowed to do that.' Uncle Jempy puts an arm around her shoulder, tries to calm her down, and promises he'll clean everything up. Against all expectations he actually does, wringing out shammy cloths until the water runs clear and the kitchen has lost a layer of paint and is back to being a proper place for preparing the evening meal.

That evening, just as all four of them have swallowed the last of their soup, the telephone rings.

'Oh dear oh dear, who can that be?' Mieke asks. Oh dear oh dear: her life is set to the rhythm of oh dear oh dear. Oh dear oh dear (get a fresh tablecloth) in response to a drop of milk next to a glass; oh dear oh dear (the power of nature) said in astonishment at the sunflowers, which are so abnormally large this year; oh dear oh dear (is that for me?) of silent pride in the surprisingly beautiful bracelet she got from her husband and daughter for Mother's Day; oh dear oh dear as a bell tone (what danger is lurking now?). Oh dear oh dear.

Mieke thinks Jempy should answer the phone, since she's a hundred percent sure it's for him. They don't know anyone so rude as to call during dinner, except maybe Granny, who makes a game out of calling at the most ungodly hours for the most trivial reasons. The last time it was to say that Sarah was ten years and eleven months old. The poor thing is starting to lose it.

'Let it ring,' says Uncle Jempy. 'I'm hungry.'

They're having schnitzel with fried new potatoes and broccoli tonight, something uncommonly unhealthy and festive at the Vandersanden-De Kinder home.

'Please answer it,' Mieke says. 'Then we can have our dinner in peace.'

Uncle Jempy goes over to the phone. He listens for a few seconds and barks a few short phrases into the receiver, such as *how much* and *where* and *now's not a good time but anyway* and *it'll be all right because it's you* and *so close already*. He hangs up.

'I'm going out for just a minute, be right back,' he says, and without further ado he goes out to the hall. The heavy front door closes behind him. They hear an old jalopy come to a halt, idle noisily, and take off again.

Mieke thinks it's rude to start without Jempy. The three of them sit there twiddling their thumbs around the steaming dishes. They can wait for twenty minutes. For two hours even. When the two hours are up Mieke's so mad at her brother she could strangle him, but unfortunately he's not here. He's a disgrace, he's rotten, he's a bad influence on Sarah, a rat, everything that's bad. She thinks it's outrageous and incomprehensible that she still lets herself get mixed up with that prick. They'll never again see that money they lent him, guaranteed. And so forth. And so on. She rushes to the kitchen and starts washing the cooking pots. Stefaan and Sarah pick at the food behind her back. Mieke comes back to the dining room and sweeps the entire evening meal from the table. Before Stefaan and Sarah can utter a word of protest, the cargo from the brimming dishes sinks to the bottom of the garbage can. Shiploads of the most delicious food descend into the depths, just like that, irrevocably lost.

'This has got to stop!' Stefaan roars suddenly. He slams his hand on the table like a peasant in a black-and-white Flemish film from some distant Sunday evening of yesteryear.

If there's something Stefaan can't laugh about, it's this: the food he has a right to, that he's looked forward to after a whole day of drudgery, being picked up before his very eyes and mercilessly tossed out.

'This has got to stop, I said!' Stefaan repeats.

'What?'

'That thing you do, plucking the rugs bare!'

'What are you talking about now?'

'The rugs.'

'Is it that you don't like them? You helped pick them out yourself, so don't come complaining about it now.'

'You spend hours at it. It's just not normal.'

'It's because your daughter makes a mess of my rugs. That's why. She's out of control. I don't know what to do with that kid.'

'Hello, I'm still here,' says Sarah, who's sitting at the table.

'The problem isn't Sarah,' says Stefaan. 'It's not Sarah at all! Any child would get nervous with all that hysteria in the air.'

'That child is just being defiant.'

'Stop it. I don't want to talk about Sarah.'

'Oh, right. That's true, too. How could I have forgotten? We're not supposed to talk about problems in this house.'

'Oh, yes we are. There's nothing I'd rather do. But you

refuse to talk about the biggest problem of all,' Stefaan roars all at once. His voice is loud enough to leave scorch marks, as if the volume had accidentally been turned up to full blast.

'Oh dear oh dear, are you all right? Is everything okay?' Mieke asks, suddenly the very picture of peace, and brilliant in her role of solicitous wife.

'Your brother!' Stefaan explodes.

'Now it's all my fault?'

'Yes, he's your brother and he can do whatever he likes here, wreck the place and toss out our dinner ... '

'He didn't do that.'

'You know what I mean.' Stefaan is gasping for breath.

'What?'

'If he wasn't your brother, you'd call him the biggest piece of riff-raff ever.'

'I understand, Stefaan,' Mieke says, nodding more sympathetically than a therapist with a patient. 'I understand, and I see through your jealousy perfectly. I'm sorry, but it's not my fault that you don't have a brother anymore.'

Stop! We can't just shrug this off. All the colour drains from the room. No one dares take a breath. We'd step in and do something if we could. Stefaan, just let it pass. It happened in another lifetime.

'What do you mean?' Stefaan pants. 'What do you mean? I'm not going to be drawn into this. No, not me.'

'You're right. It's my fault,' says Mieke, who has shocked herself with her cruel swipe.

'That's not what I'm saying. You're also just the product of your upbringing.'

'Yes, thanks a lot,' she says, cloyingly sweet. 'At least I *had* an upbringing, not obedience training like animals on a farm.'

Stefaan snorts like a mare who's just run a race.

'You come home and stick your feet under the table and you don't have five words for me.' Mieke rolls out the heavy artillery.

There's a lather of rage on Stefaan's lips. His voice cracking, he shouts, 'I work myself to the bone and it's still not good enough.'

'How hard is it to be friendly to your wife every once in a while, someone who toils away all day long? Sometimes it feels like I'm living with your mother.'

Sarah watches as her parents take turns placing stones on the scale of love, a scale that isn't made for such weight and soon gives way, leaving two people facing each other, trembling with rage, overwhelmed by the debris of all those complaints, their hearts headed for some unknown depth, quivering, swirling, each one determined for the very last time not to be taken in by this comedy, which has been going on for more than ten years and which no one with an ounce of sense in his head can call a good marriage.

'It's all my fault, all of it,' Mieke cries. 'I should be dead! Where's a gun?'

'Calm down!'

'Just kill me, that's all I ask. Do me a favour and kill me.'

'There's no talking to you.'

'But I am talking, right? I've even come up with a solution.'

It's either the hunger or the commotion, but Sarah suddenly feels faint. She drops down against the wall. She can't get any air. Now she knows for sure: her parents are going to get divorced because they hate each other.

Together they begin howling at the moon, at the stars, at each other's darkest, most hateful, most unbearable shadows and delusions. Stefaan can no longer control himself, and with all the outraged fury and strength he has in him he kicks at the door to the utility room, the only door that isn't made of oak. The door answers with a crunch. He's left hanging in the splintery hole. He begins hopping around on one foot, the other having been swallowed up by the gaping mouth in the door. He isn't able to wrench himself loose.

'Now that's a solution,' Mieke cries.

'I'll take care of it,' Stefaan says, instantly pale and serene. Blood is starting to flow where his ankle has disappeared into the door.

'Oh dear oh dear, you're bleeding,' cries Mieke. She hurries to the kitchen and comes back with a bucket and a sponge. She wipes the blood from his leg and begins to scrub the surrounding floor. Blood, stubborn stuff.

As in the most idiotic slapstick comedy, the front doorbell suddenly rings. Mieke, torn between two places where her presence is required, decides to complete her tasks one after the other.

'Stefaan, everything is going to be fine,' she keeps repeating as she squeezes the sponge into the red water.

Stefaan can't think of anything better to do than smile his eternal smile and say, deathly pale, 'I'm going to deal with this. Everything is under control. You go get the door.' He tries to pull his foot out with a single tug but the door refuses to release its prey from its mouth of splinters.

'Sarah, help me out here!' Stefaan calls out. 'Go get a saw and hammer out of the garage.'

More exemplary than ever, Sarah deals with this moment of crisis by playing the role of obedient child. She goes out to Stefaan's gigantic do-it-yourself arsenal and picks out a hammer and a small jigsaw.

'If that's Ulrike again with more of her penny-pinching, I'll get rid of her fast enough,' Mieke grumbles. Her neighbour Ulrike is extremely well off. Her husband is a professor of economics and sits on dozens of boards of directors, yet Ulrike loves a bargain. For months now she's been trying to convince Mieke to have a sauna installed so both of them can get a twenty percent discount. But it isn't Ulrike. Marc from across the street, not exactly the shy type, slips right past Mieke and walks into the dining room uninvited.

'Marc! What a surprise!' Mieke runs after him.

'Hi, Mieke. I have a question for Stefaan. My regular golf partner just cancelled, and ... '

'I'd go get him but he's in the shower,' Mieke says. 'Sorry, Marc.'

Marc shoots a glance into the kitchen and sees Stefaan struggling at the door.

'Excuse me, Mieke,' and he deftly pushes her aside. 'I'm going to give Stefaan a hand.'

Like a genuine action hero, he forces his way into the kitchen. 'This looks like child's play compared with what I do in the operating room every day.'

'Leave it, Marc,' Stefaan mumbles, but Marc has already grabbed the jigsaw and is skilfully carving his way through the wood until he reaches Stefaan's leg. In no time at all Stefaan is standing with both feet on the floor. Marc looks at his work with satisfaction. After a slap on the back for Stefaan and a wink for Sarah he sails back to the front door.

'Stefaan is in the shower,' he says to Mieke, who has gone purple in the face. Marc now has a cluster bomb of gossip on hand that he can set off all over the neighbourhood. The hole in the door is repaired the next day, but too sloppily to ever meet with Mieke's approval, as if a visible sign were needed of the struggle between two people who will do anything to really see each other. No one in the neighbourhood seems to have heard about the hole in the door.

It's a peculiar coincidence, but on the few rare occasions that Sarah goes with her father to see Granny it's invariably raining. Today, too, the roads seem slippery. Rain in Belgium is like the great leader in a dictatorship: it pops up everywhere. Rain is the starting point of every banal exchange and it seeps into every conversation. You can't do anything about the rain. You can tie a plastic bag over your head like the old ladies and walk around Easter-egg fashion, you can put on a bright yellow poncho that makes you lose control of your handle bars, but these aren't real solutions. You can also put on a sour face, as Granny does so well. It doesn't even have to rain for her to do that. Granny's face is permanently set on bad weather, at least whenever Sarah sees her, and fortunately that's no more than three times a year. Even Mieke has insisted that Sarah go to visit her today. The old woman is so eager to see her granddaughter again, her only granddaughter. This is her eleventh birthday, and according to Mieke she's a big girl now and she can do nice things for other people every once in a while.

Granny is sitting all hunched up in the armchair with a thermos and a cup of cold coffee beside her. On her instructions Stefaan goes to the refrigerator to get a box of pastries and places it on one of the dozen little side tables that are spread out all over the bungalow. When he comes over to her, she squints up at him and asks, 'Is that Sarah?'

'No, Stefaan,' Stefaan shouts. He gives Sarah a nudge, making her stand in front of her grandmother.

'Stefaan?'

'No, now it's Sarah!' Sarah screams.

'Ah, Sarah! My little lamb. My sight is so poor. Every day it gets a little worse. And I can hardly hear anything anymore, either. Say, it's very curious, but you're really starting to look just like your grandfather André.'

The old woman spontaneously starts trembling and crying from all the emotion. Old people can cry when they see a sparrow eating a fat ball on their back porch or a little child standing with their hands on their hips asking where the teddy bear is, or when they get an ordinary friendly nod from the baker, putting his hand on theirs for a second, after they've explained that these days one hard roll is enough to fill them up. The waves of agitation splash about in the little bucket that is still her world. Granny wipes her tears away with a crusty handkerchief and crosses herself over and over again. 'How old are you now, Saaaraaah? Eleven years old, eh? Yes, eleven, yes, yes, eleven, I'm so happy, and then twelve and ... You're going to be a big strong girl. Always eat well—right, my dear?—to make you big and strong. Give her a pastry, why don't you?' Has she been saving up all her words for Sarah's birthday?

Papa and Sarah have been sitting in her parlour for fifteen minutes already. There's a sultry old noise in the background, as if the house had been set to a Russian wartime channel that's still being broadcast from Siberia. Granny stares ahead with glassy eyes and endorses all sorts of obscure things, more to herself than to them. She's already repeated Sarah's name ten times. She's a strange old lady, but maybe the only reason Sarah thinks she's strange is because they don't know each other. What you don't know is always strange. Granny has pressed three thousand-franc notes into Sarah's fist, a precious secret. She knows Stefaan saw her do it; he was too explicit the way he turned his head to the other side.

'Your battery, mother, your battery,' Stefaan shouts.

Granny wriggles a snail out of her inner ear. 'I thought I heard something peeping. You see that? The battery from your hearing aid is dead.' A son takes care of his mother. Hanging on the wall behind Granny are two yellowed photos in wooden frames. Even before she could talk, Sarah knew she was never, ever to say anything about those photos. Mama made that clearly understood. Granny lost a child. That unutterable grief turned her to stone, Mama says, the few times she speaks about Granny without a trace of venom. She usually can't resist adding that there are some people who become more human because of setbacks. Granny has never exchanged a single word with Mieke, that's how heartless and jealous she is of her son's happiness. Even 'hello' is more than she can manage, Mieke says, 'and that is the unadulterated truth, I'm really not exaggerating.'

'Every day,' says Granny.

'What every day, mother?'

'I ask him every day.'

'What do you ask, mother?'

'I ask him to come and take me.'

'Here's a nice one.' Stefaan points to one of the pastries with his fork and places it on Granny's plate. 'One with marzipan, a little pig—you like those, don't you?'

'That child needs to eat well. Give her another pastry. And take one for yourself.' Granny straightens up. 'Eat it all up. Whatever's left you have to take with you.'

'Where are you going, mother?'

'Leave a body in peace for a change. To my own little corner, Stefaan, please.' She walks to the cellar door and pushes the door open. 'I'll be right back. You just eat.'

When Sarah stands up to take a second pastry, just like her father, she looks through the tongues of the sanseveria and sees the foolish face of Berta the goat. Berta is spying on them through the window. She's what gets Granny out of bed in the morning. The ancient goat moved with Granny from the farm to the bungalow. Berta is covered in rough, shabby fur and she has dirty legs, but Granny thinks she has magical powers. She's also immortal.

'Granny is starting to forget things,' says Stefaan to his daughter. 'Getting old like that isn't easy.'

After quite some time a huge box comes into the living room with Granny behind it.

'My heart is at rest now that she's eleven years old. And it's the men in our family that cause all the problems, right, Stefaan? I'm not going to say anything. Listen, son, how are you doing these days? Can I have a little peace and quiet?' babbles the old lady merrily as she starts setting out the contents of the box on her side tables. She presses a knitted octopus into Sarah's hands. And the figure of an angel. And a songbook from twenty years ago. And a mother-of-pearl necklace.

'Don't worry, mother, everything is perfect. Look at Sarah.'

'Too bad I don't see so well,' says the rotund little woman. 'That's my mother's jewellery, Saaaraaah, so take good care of it. Then you can wear it yourself some day ...'

'Why are you giving all your possessions away?' Stefaan asks with alarm.

The most motley collection of junk has found a home in this box: a damaged extension cord entangled in a very expensive necklace, Hummels, Druivelaar calendars still in their wrappers, a green lampshade, pen holders made from toilet paper rolls that she and her girlfriends fashioned in the parish hall. 'We take what the people don't want anymore after they've wiped their bottoms and make something beautiful,' Granny explains.

Granny keeps handing things out and rattling off instructions on how you can use vinegar to clean crystal glasses but not biscuit porcelain. She keeps it up for quite some time before dropping into her armchair, exhausted, and silence descends on the bungalow once again. Her world is a box whose lid is slowly closing.

'That Jean-Pierre,' Stefaan sighs in an attempt to resuscitate the conversation, 'he's more than anybody can handle.'

'It takes all kinds, eh?'

'Mieke's had it with him. I'm going to throw him out.'

'Mieke will do that herself,' says Granny. Outside Berta the dwarf goat bumps her snout against the window pane. 'Our Berta is going to outlive me, poor lamb. And it won't be long for me, you know.' Sarah nods meekly. Surprisingly enough, Granny smells just like Jempy. She has the same wild smell, the smell of a neglected animal.

Granny gropes for another pastry from the plate, breaks it in two like a consecrated host and shoves both pieces into her mouth at once. She keeps shaking her head as a mysterious little smile forms around her mouth, bursting with disbelief in this world.

'Sarah, I'm so glad I've been able to see you just once more. Really, would you believe that I don't have much time left?'

The very last quarrel between Uncle Jempy and Mama wrenches him from Sarah's young life just as abruptly as when he entered it. There's a lot more at stake than the hundred-thousand-franc debt that Uncle Jempy racked up in one night and for which number 7 Nightingale Lane was presented with the bill. This is a war being fought out between continents, a clash of ideologies and genes. Mieke is insisting that Jempy leave at once.

He raises his yellow fingers to his chapped lips as if needing time to reflect on this coup de grâce. 'I'm not wasting my time here any longer,' he finally says. 'Belgium isn't worthy of me. Yes, go ahead and say that Jean-Pierre De Kinder is too big for his boots. Belgium has never given me anything.'

'You've never given Belgium anything, either. It's easy to let yourself go the way you have. If I were to let myself go, there'd be a lot involved. We're made of the same materials, but you've built a shack and I've built a villa. To each his own.'

'Oh, madam is feeling superior again. Everything I've built up has been taken from me. Well, I've seen enough, I'm leaving.'

'So go. I'm not the one who stood here on the kitchen tiles begging to be taken in. For just a little while. Well, that little while was up a long time ago. You've already had your good times here. I have to think of my family, too. We've done our duty.'

'Ça va, ça va. You don't have to put up with me anymore.'

'Okay, go then.' She opens the back door.

'Oh, sweetie, I ... '—the click of a Zippo, the cowboy needs to refuel, to keep up his nicotine level—'I'm starting out fresh. I'm going to launch a wine business in South Africa. Beautiful country, no bullshit. Anyone who wants to work hard there can make it.'

'Will you please not smoke in the house?' says Mieke.

Stefaan is behind her, nodding.

Jempy storms up the stairs and starts making a terrific

racket, but Mieke flatly refuses to rise to the bait and climb the stairs to see what Uncle Jempy is up to. After half an hour he's standing at the top of the stairs with a blue Samsonite suitcase in his hands.

'Well, that's nice of you. That's my suitcase,' says Mieke.

'It's the least you can give to your very own brother. You won't have any more trouble from me. And you're really going to miss me, that's for sure.'

'Give me that suitcase.' Mieke blocks the way to the back door.

That's the last straw.

'No, I'm not giving the suitcase back.'

'What's in it anyway?'

'Don't you trust me?'

She jerks the suitcase out of his hands. The suitcase flies through the air and crashes to the floor. The latches give way. The lid of the suitcase falls open. It's completely empty. There's absolutely nothing in it. Uncle Jempy leaves with the empty suitcase, aching with humiliation and as poor as a church mouse. He turns around one more time, throws his powerful arms around Sarah and says, 'You're going to go far, kiddo. Just like your uncle.' He plants a kiss on her forehead, looks his sister over one more time from head to foot, and strolls out through the back door .

'We did that well,' says Stefaan as they watch him leave. 'We won't be seeing him anytime soon.'

'I don't know about that,' says Mieke with a hint of sadness, 'but our family comes first.' She repeats this a few more times during the evening, as if she doesn't fully believe it herself.

Traces of Jempy's presence persist long after his departure. A registered letter arrives at number 7 Nightingale Lane sentencing Jean-Pierre De Kinder in absentia for fraud. The number of love letters for Jempy that continues to pour in is impressive.

'Go get the letters,' Mieke tells Sarah, and together they light a fire in the fireplace for the first time this season. The Vandersanden-De Kinder family warm their hands on spelling mistakes, exploding golden hearts, and foolish sentences about painless, eternal love.

WE 1991

Stefaan is away on business visiting a daughter pharmaceutical company in China. He left three days ago. Sarah watched her parents as they stood intertwined at the front door and heard the disgusting smack of their kisses.

Mieke and Sarah are managing just fine. When Sarah unsuspectingly hops down the garden path to the rhythm of the lively orchestra she conducts in her head, intent on feeding the cheese rinds and old sandwiches from her lunchbox to her feathered, two-footed friends, she pays little attention to the blooming flowers and insects all around her. But she does notice the humming engine of a blue striped station wagon coming up the driveway—on a Sunday, of all days, the only day of the week when everyone in the housing estate is at home. The station wagon parks there in full sight. Mieke is at the front door in a flash.

She throws up her hands in innocence. 'No idea where Jean-Pierre De Kinder is,' she tells the officers truthfully. She has learned not to lie or distort the truth to men in uniform. If they suspect she's lying, they'll take off their caps during the interminable silence that follows and look straight through her with their myopic little eyes, a trick meant to humiliate her so thoroughly that the truth can be extracted without effort. If she comes right out and tells the unvarnished truth of her own accord, the station wagon will disappear from the driveway more quickly, and the neighbours—those sluggards on the corner, for instance, who lie around in bed until noon—are less likely to have seen it.

'No idea where Jean-Pierre has gone. He said he had business in South Africa. I haven't heard anything from him in months.'

'Neither have we,' says the officer. 'We've come for something else. Is your husband at home, perhaps?'

'No, he's on a business trip in China.'

'Do you know a Mrs. Melanie Plottier?'

'That's my mother-in-law,' says Mieke.

'It is our duty to inform you,' says the officer, eyes downcast, voice lowered, 'that Mrs. Melanie Plottier passed away this morning. She had a frontal collision with a tree. Her seat belt was not fastened and unfortunately her head impacted the steering wheel. All efforts to save her came too late.'

'That can't be true, sir. Granny is deaf and blind.' Mieke is begging them to see that she's right, although she herself saw Granny's Fiat crawling up the driveway like a zigzagging snail only a couple of weeks ago. 'Deaf and blind, I tell you.'

'Indeed it can,' the officer insists. 'We've seen worse than that.'

'How is it possible that someone who can't see a blessed thing and is as deaf as a post is let loose in traffic? It's simply scandalous that such people are allowed on the public roads. These kinds of things should be heavily fined. For years I've been pushing for the mandatory renewal of drivers' licences every other year, *with* a test, for everyone, young and old,' Mieke says belligerently. She seems to believe that by making this speech she can save Granny's life.

As long as she keeps talking and insisting on a reasonable explanation, she can hold reality at bay. The fact that Granny is dead isn't the worst of it. It had to happen sometime. But what Mieke dreads like the plague are the practical implications. All her plans for the coming weeks are thrown into disarray. Not that, anything but that.

'Oh, by the way, ma'am,' says the officer. 'We're supposed to ask you why you sent your mother-in-law out into traffic in her vulnerable condition. But given the dramatic outcome we've decided not to pursue that any further.'

'Is that part of your job description now?' Mieke asks. 'To come and blame people for tragic automobile accidents?'

As soon as the bumbling police have left and Mieke is back behind the closed door, the reality of their message hits her. Granny has never had a word to say to her, never even deigned to look at her. Mieke was too chic, too upper crust, too nervous, too this and too that. She in turn found her mother-in-law a singularly insufferable female. They had tacitly agreed to keep out of each other's way or, at the very most, to limply shake each other's hands in caustic silence if it couldn't be avoided. Nothing can break that silence now. But Mieke is the one who's been saddled with Granny's death. What's this going to involve? To begin with, Mieke will have to notify Stefaan, make a lot of phone calls, dress the child in black, throw together a wardrobe for herself, help her husband, arrange for the funeral, and comb all the rugs. Granny is the last elder to go. Mieke has drawn up a checklist from previous funerals. But even though all funerals look alike, every funeral is different.

Stefaan returns immediately from China, blaming himself the whole time for letting Granny drive the car. As soon as he arrives home, calm and collected, Mieke tells him what one of the police officers had just reported to her on the phone. Melanie had had a heart attack first, which is what caused her to drive into the tree. It was a painless death, if that's any consolation. Utterly silent, Stefaan swallows his words and his tears.

After a day of desolation and phone calls from distant family members, Stefaan wants to have a talk with Sarah. He says this with his back to Sarah while blowing his nose ferociously into a kitchen towel. Mieke sees this and shudders. She feels like pushing his tear-streaked face into the towel like a naughty kitten, but the choking that would produce is palpable enough. The entire weight of all the family tragedies that Granny managed to endure with her peasant strength has now been shifted to Stefaan's shoulders. The weight gets heavier with every death.

'That's what heaven is, Sarah: tiny little bits that search for each other because together they form one whole thing. Those little bits disappear and the later generations push another row upward,' he says to Sarah as if he were explaining Mendeleev's periodic table. He puts his hand on her head, stands up, and walks to the living room. Bob Dylan's 'Every Grain of Sand' fills the air. It's the bootleg version with a German shepherd barking in the background. Sarah knows this song. She hears the docility in every one of the twanging phrases.

Stefaan goes to the bathroom and washes his face with cold water. He peers into the mirror. 'Do you realize that you and Sarah are the only remaining members of the Vandersanden family?' we ask him in chorus. 'The only ones. And it's all your fault.' We point an accusatory finger at him, at a couple of moments in Stefaan's history that were better left unsaid, a list of crude blunders that he cannot undo. He takes down a rough towel that's been dried outside on the line and rubs it long and hard all over his face, as if this can scrub away all his troubles.

On the morning of the funeral a limousine drives past the villa at number 7 Nightingale Lane. This was Granny's wish. A bizarre detail. She has permitted herself this one frivolous act after a life filled with nondescript scenes that were remarkable only in their normality, edged with the black fringe of tragedy.

'The notary is drunk,' Stefaan has said over and over again. 'This can't have been my mother's wish.' But the limousine comes by anyway, just to be on the safe side, since that's what it says in the last will and testament of Melanie Vandersanden-Plottier. In the same will she has also instructed that she be buried with her little son and her husband.

The family of three rides behind the hearse, where the coffin is bobbing around inside. A closed coffin, the undertaker has emphasized. He didn't even let them choose. A limousine is a Hollywood invention, so Sarah grabs her chance to play movie star, just this once, for just a little while. She sits in the back seat, waving at the crowds on the way to the church like a leading lady about to pick up her Oscar. Sarah's not what you would call glamorous in her black nun's skirt, but even so she puts on her prettiest smile.

'A limo and my mother. There's no way that makes any sense. And cut it out, Sarah.'

The one everyone feels sorry for is Stefaan. He spent five long hours last night busily placing service booklets on the chairs of the church and penning a little poem, his last greeting to his sullen mother. At four in the morning he was still in the attic thumbing through photo albums. He also knows perfectly well that his mother wasn't going to live forever and that she quite probably felt her own death approaching, but it's the smell of death that makes his flesh crawl, that throws him back to a place he doesn't want to be. It's cold there, it's bleak, and he hears the cracking of ice.

'It's the death of your little brother, too, isn't it,' says Mieke. 'That's coming back, too.'

'No,' says Stefaan curtly.

Before getting out of the limousine he takes another sedative at Mieke's urging. She's never seen her husband so shaken and devastated. It's not as if it's never happened before, though. Every now and then he has to stay home from work because his nerves are wound too tight. Just lying in bed, brooding and moaning, you'd never see a woman doing that. Mieke reads the brief text he's written as a goodbye to his mother, going over it several times. She's keeping in mind the possibility that she will have to read it aloud to the gathered mourners. Anticipation is her best friend in crisis situations. Half an hour later it's quite clear that Stefaan isn't fit to read anything aloud. The sedative is much too strong; not only does it dull his feelings but it also makes him experience the funeral through a heavy fog. He can barely stumble to the front of the church. Mieke takes him by the arm and leads him to his place, and with a gracious, not too cheerful smile she steps up to the lectern and reads out the corny bit of poetry.

The evening of the funeral they drive past the home of the deceased one more time to appraise the general condition of Granny's residence. The house of Stefaan's mother is not the home he grew up in but a new rudimentary structure full of dried flowers and air fresheners. Stefaan is planning to clear the house out as soon as possible and rent it.

'Do we really have to look at it today?' asks Mieke. 'What's the hurry? It's not on fire, is it?'

'Berta,' Stefaan says. He wants to be strong, as he was after the death of his father. Not letting things slide, but dealing with them. It's Stefaan's strategy for combating grief: fighting back by taking his fate in hand, organizing a game of arm wrestling to see who's the strongest, himself or his grief. Sarah is the first to discover that the stubborn dwarf goat has turned her shaggy back on her allocated bit of grass and sallied forth into the wide world. At her prodding, Mieke searches for a photo of Sarah and Granny with Berta the goat clamped between them. The plan is to cut Berta out, photocopy her picture, and distribute it throughout the neighbourhood under the heading 'MISSING'.

The days that follow are mainly taken up with the requisite driving back and forth to the recycling centre. The glass container gets a bellyful, an entire cellar of freight. Most of it consists of empty bottles of an old-fashioned anise liqueur known as Marie Brizard, a liqueur that hits you over the head like a hammer, so stupefying that you sit in an armchair in silence from morning to night while the world passes you by and your goat comes to look at you through the window every now and then.

Mieke, who has spent days on end doing her very best to resist spewing venom all over Granny out of a sense of decency, and also out of a kind of protective reflex for her badly shaken, grieving husband, gradually returns to familiar territory.

'All those little side tables,' says Mieke, 'with all those glass rings on them. Just like Gustave, the lush, who rented my house in Ghent for only a year, thank God. How could you not have seen them!'

Anyone who's ever emptied out the house of someone who has died has bumped into little things with a long history. A hairpin stuck behind the frame of a photo of her deceased son, a whole supply of Fisherman's Friend breath fresheners, useless bowls full of unused, brittle elastic bands, a comb with only three teeth, modern Adidas sport shoes with Velcro closures that the old lady loved to wear on her home trainer out on the porch. A life that you carry off, relocate, recycle. No one comes away unmoved.

All four of the parents of Mieke and Stefaan are dead. The roof above their heads has been blown away. They're next, Mieke realizes. And who will they leave behind? Sarah. They waited a long time for Sarah. It never seemed to work. And it wasn't for lack of trying. They kept it up to the point of weariness, but there are defects in nature, too. Mother Nature has her forests and her deserts. Mieke was more a rather arid place.

For a long time Mieke has wanted to keep a diary. Now there's only one thing standing in the way and that's Mieke's sense of duty. As the product of an overly Catholic, old-fashioned upbringing, Mieke has to give herself permission to do something that has no immediate purpose. Writing down your thoughts in a large notebook doesn't really do anybody any good. But Mieke excels in convoluted arguments: she finds secret ways to fool herself into thinking that not only should she write such a book but that it is even her duty to do so, for posterity. And that, fortunately, takes all the pleasure out of it. Once again she feels safely constricted in her corset of duties, and under this compulsion she begins keeping a close eye on her daughter, searching for funny remarks and spontaneous (or not so spontaneous) slips of the tongue to give her diary more colour. For an outsider, such an addiction to duty might seem agonizing, but once you're addicted you discover what an exceedingly pleasant and engrossing way of life it is.

Yet sometimes she secretly hopes for a little peace and quiet. Stefaan or Elvira ought to insist that she put on the brakes once in a while because she does everything she can to keep active, to demand the most from herself, and occasionally to reach so deeply into her reserves that when she gets up in the morning she's already dizzy from a whole night of brooding about what has to be done the following day.

Mieke begins her diary like a friendship book, the kind that young girls used to circulate among themselves. What word should she use to describe herself? Say someone asked her who she is. What if her name just wasn't enough? What if someone were to say: okay, fine, Mieke Vandersanden-De Kinder, but who are you really? How can you define yourself in a way that's more or less conclusive?

She would never answer 'a woman' because she's no feminist. Feminists are angry women who want to be men. That's wrong. The world would be in terrible shape with only men in it.

'Sister of Jean-Pierre De Kinder' is something else she would never say, although she loves Jempy very, very much. There's no real reason for it. He never saved her from drowning or stepped in to help her on those dates that never took place behind the church. It's just the fact that for his entire life he's always been his audacious self. What he lacks in resources he makes up for in charm and charisma. But if she were to say all that out loud she'd be tying herself up in knots, because she'd have to explain the whole endless story of Jempy and his adventures. Now he's in South Africa. In all likelihood he's doing well, since she hasn't heard anything from him for a very long time. Unless he's calmly drinking up his whole stock of wine. Oh dear oh dear, could that be true?

She writes 'CALL JP' in her notebook. Jempy is a master of cliff-hangers. That's what she appreciates most about him. At the same time it irritates her no end—that, too.

'Sister of Lydia De Kinder' then? Yes, of Lydia De Kinder, wife of Professor Christopher J. Delaney, engineer, who occupies a chair at Columbia University. His field is materials science, with a specialty in superconductivity (Lydia always drones on). Lydia with her four children. Mieke as sister in the shadows, in other words. No one in the chic town of Ghent, in upstate New York, has ever heard of Mieke De Kinder; she'd bet her life on it.

She could say 'daughter of Gerard and Camille De Kinder'. She honours her deceased parents—that goes without saying—but what did her mother Camille ever do to improve herself? The answer is a terribly sobering 'nothing', except being wife-of. Melanie, Stefaan's mother, was a farmer's wife. She was much more in control. And as soon as she retired, she joined the Farmers' Wives Union to become a surly participant in the card-playing afternoons and homeland pilgrimages.

You're mainly the family that you make yourself, that's what she thinks. 'Wife of Stefaan Vandersanden': that's who she is. So she was never daughter-in-law of Granny Vandersanden. Supposing someone asked her who she was. She'd probably answer: 'First of all I'm the mother of Sarah.' That's what Noor, queen of Jordan, said in an interview recently.

Good, so she's mother of Sarah Vandersanden. But what does that mother of Sarah Vandersanden do? Is she a housewife? Also very degrading. A diary fanatic? Something to work toward. This diary is going to be her project, because she knows enough about herself to realize that she needs something else in her life besides her family. That's a nice insight to begin with. Mieke closes the notebook, puts it away in the drawer of the desk and goes to the living room to remove withered leaves from the indoor plants.

Stefaan longs for a place of his own for keeping his music, his tools, and his heirlooms in order. He demands a hobby room. 'A hobby room?' Mieke sputters. 'Are you going to start inventing hobbies?' When he tells her about the old tools from his parents' farm and how he wants to polish them, Mieke becomes more receptive to the idea. 'You mean a shed, a junk shed?' Stefaan gets her blessing for his hobby shed, to be built at the back of the garden. Before he even has a chance to consider his plan from a broader perspective, she has gone ahead and consulted with Elvira, her good friend and arbiter of taste, and drummed up an architect and a construction firm. An official from environmental planning also shows up, who is pleased to receive a fat tip. For Mieke, a new project has presented itself on which she can direct her energies.

A chain reaction is unavoidable. Now that Papa's getting a hobby shed, Sarah wants a pond. Stefaan is dead set against this 'ridiculous' idea and blocks it with a well-considered argument: 'Out of the question. You like cats, don't you?'

'Yes,' says the unsuspecting prey.

'Cats drown in ponds,' Stefaan points out.

'Squirrels dip their dirty, germ-infested tails in them and infect the whole biotope,' Mieke chimes in. A pond is kitsch and kitsch is the bastard child of style and class. Before you know it there'll be a gnome with a fishing pole on your lawn or a stone frog with a little crown on his head. No, nip it in the bud, that nonsense.

Mieke supervises the work on the hobby shed with

heart and soul. Putting up an extra outbuilding—her father would have been proud to see her carrying out this ancient Flemish custom. It's thanks to her eagle eye and the managerial capacities mastered by every housewife that within scarcely three weeks a miniature house is erected in the back garden with hot and cold running water, electricity, a desk, a sturdy workbench, and a whole battery of tools on the fibreboard walls. Gutters lead the rainwater from the roof to the cistern, and the tiles on the floor form a fleur-de-lis pattern.

The evening of the project's completion, Mieke makes an exception and lets Stefaan drink two glasses of red wine instead of the customary ration of one. For inexplicable reasons she tears into him in bed that night, demanding sex twice without any fuss or wheedling, as if they were a couple of kids—or at least that's how Stefaan imagines that kind of sex to be: turbulent, awkward, deeply satisfying. For a moment the thought flashes through his mind that maybe he's made a new child, but he knows that those days are gone forever.

Stefaan is reborn the first evening he sets a ladder against the outer wall of his hobby shed and climbs up on the roof. He knows that from now on things can only get better. No more valleys, only peaks. Although peaks are also valleys standing on their heads.

STEFAAN 1993-1994

'Would you mind signing these, please?' Stefaan's secretary, Suzanne Rutgeers, presents him with a small stack of letters that all require his signature before they can be posted. She's wearing a light grey skirt, a green, silky blouse, and a scarf around her neck, functional attire for a middle-aged woman with a respectable job. Stefaan always wears a bespoke suit and a shirt with cuff links. It's better to be impeccably dressed if you occupy a position of authority, Mieke always says. He leaves the choice of cut and colour to her. Decorum is her domain.

Stefaan goes to work every day by bike, to Mieke's great displeasure. They've had fights about it. Bicycling is a sport for the riff-raff. No one in the housing estate cycles. He's just got to pick another sport. 'I can't golf or tennis my way to work, can I?' is his usual response. Every morning he goes into the bathroom behind his office, gets out of his inconspicuous warm-ups, and changes into an apparently inconspicuous but very pricey suit. As a member of the board of directors he has a large office with adjoining bathroom. This strikes him as somewhat excessive, but the other executives think it's necessary even though their bathrooms never get used. And who is he to oppose the policy on his own? Once he had had the question placed on the agenda of a directors' meeting, but his secretary tacked it onto the bottom of the list of points, and all the others at the meeting haughtily (and hungrily) dismissed it.

It was years ago that Stefaan took the immense step of crawling out from behind the laboratory microscope and switching to an office of his own as manager. He heads a staff of more than a hundred, negotiates with other directors and managers, and supervises restructuring projects here and in the subsidiaries worldwide. Any man with any pride and ambition would have seized his job with both hands, but they would have been far too authoritarian. Right from the beginning he has developed his own strategy. He likes to make it known that humility and collaboration are important. You have to offer at least an illusion of this to your workers, but you mustn't overdo it. If big changes are in the air, he invites all the department heads from his section to come for a pro forma talk, with coffee and spice cookies, 'to discuss the situation' and 'to identify their vision', even though the changes have long been decided. 'Vision,' he thinks, is a funny word. As if you were gazing into the future with a telescope and could already see what's going to happen. No one knows for sure where we go from here, but everyone likes to use the word. It creates the illusion that you have a high regard for openness and change. If Gorbachev can use it to formulate his slogan, then Stefaan can, too. After about an hour the meeting is usually over and he can thank everyone for their constructive input. 'Thank you, Mr. Vandersanden,' is how they respond. 'We're grateful to you for receiving us.'

Stefaan wants to give the appearance of a gentleman. He's someone who apologizes to his secretary for dumping four urgent tasks on her the minute she comes sailing in late to the office, although he does expect her to make up for lost time immediately. He doesn't just follow the rules, he also follows his personal insights. The human touch increases profits.

Stefaan is known among the company's international partners for his straightforward approach. That, too, is a technique he developed himself. The fact that there's so little scheming and ceremony involved is refreshing for most of the other directors he sits with at negotiating tables in New York, Milan, Copenhagen, and other cities of the world.

His secretary is shoving several more forms under his nose, all of them memos that his advisors and co-workers have drafted for him. Settlements and partnership agreements that have been drawn up by the small army of lawyers and advisors, and have already passed back and forth dozens of times via the pneumatic tube system and the internal post. These are preparatory steps being taken in anticipation of the merger that's about to take place with another large international and that's got the members of the board of directors walking on eggshells. He signs the whole pile of papers almost without looking at them.

There's a thin layer of dust on the frame of a photograph hanging on the wall, which he notices in the late morning light. That picture of the executives has been hanging there for a long time, but he seldom looks at it. Standing beside the sagging CEO with the big rings under his eyes and the hairpiece are a couple of highly motivated men who are steering the company in the right direction. He is one of them. It gives him a warm feeling, the privilege of being part of this team of directors. It's been so many years since he, as a mere kid, had made up his mind not to let this big company thwart his plans for his own laboratory, and here he is sitting in a director's chair and making decisions that influence hundreds of employees. The days of Petri dishes and drug design are far behind him. It's part of your natural evolution in any company not to get stuck doing hands-on work. Sometimes he finds it a bit of a shame, but in the long run it's all about the challenge. He began his job as the director of research & development without having any idea how to go about it, but you could say the same thing about life. You're constantly being challenged.

'Those were all the documents that needed your signature,' says his secretary Suzanne. She straightens the papers with a shake and clasps them to her heavy bosom. The button over her breasts threatens to give way. 'And then I found this note still in your pigeon hole. I have to leave now to pick up my son from his exams. See you tomorrow, sir.' Efficient and discreet, an executive secretary through and through who's been working here longer than Stefaan has. She has a trophy for thirty years of service in her cabinet. She puts the folded note on his table and leaves him alone. He watches her walk away through the glass recess in the wall.

The person who wrote this didn't go to a great deal of trouble. The slapdash message looks up at him. 'It's a mistake,' the note says. The whole thing strikes Stefaan as almost artistic. He's no connoisseur of art. In science, interpretation is limited to correct combinations and observations. Once, at an exhibition in Detroit, he saw a melting block of ice with an object inside that was slowly being revealed. It turned out to be a little lamb. Dead, but lifelike and vulnerable all the same. The eyes of the little animal were open. That's where he saw its beauty, if beauty is a word that can be applied to a dead animal. It literally made him feel cold, although he had seen plenty of little lambs and calves on his parents' farm years before. He can appreciate good art, as long as you, the observer, don't have to go digging for meanings behind the artist's slogans. A few weeks ago he was stuck at the airport on his way to London for a business trip. The only thing there was to read was an abandoned art magazine featuring an interview with the artist Jeff Koons about openness and ambiguity. He didn't understand the man, who came across as somewhat sexually frustrated at best. For a moment Stefaan thinks, conjectures, hopes that what he is dealing with here is some sort of art experiment for the in-house magazine, or a cryptic message from a company oddball. After considering this for barely a second he finds himself staring truth in the face: this message comes from Fernand Berkvens.

Fifteen years ago, he and Berkvens were both in the running for the position of junior manager. Berkvens wanted to compete with him, but that's where he made his mistake. Berkvens couldn't know that Stefaan's entire life is a contest of strength. With every success he books we tell him this: shift up to a higher gear, because what you're doing is fine, but you can always do better. That's what real winners do. It charges us with energy and passion.

Stefaan pulled out all the stops to become manager. Behind Berkvens's back he went out to eat with heavyweights, whom he knew could be useful in helping him obtain his appointment. This sort of thing is not illegal. When Berkvens found out, a quarrel ensued that is still smouldering after all these years. The two men don't trust each other one bit.

Stefaan's promotion was a setback for Berkvens, but he went on to run for the position of union representative. He's never applied for a higher position. He's been working for more than twenty years as a scientific technician in the laboratory where Stefaan once began his career. Every afternoon Stefaan sees him sitting in the employees' cafeteria, where he eats his sandwiches and chairs meetings as union representative. Berkvens and his wife live in a decrepit row house in the village. His wife is a nurse and gave Sarah her first bath in the maternity hospital. That's all Stefaan needs to know about Berkvens. He doesn't delve into the lives of his personnel as a matter of principle.

Because of his 'managerial position' in the union, as Berkvens calls it, he is aware of a lot that's going on. He makes it a point to show newcomers around and to introduce them to their colleagues. He urges personnel services to print people's names on their lab coats. That's not his job, but he does it all the same. Berkvens is the type who livens up the bulletin board in the coffee room with 'Cowboy Henk' comics from *Humo* magazine and replaces them from time to time. A man who can't start work until he's personally wished everyone in his department a good morning.

Last week Stefaan caught Berkvens making a mistake. It may have been absent-mindedness, an all-too-human mistake, a case of one zero too many. Budgeted amounts that were meant for the union ended up in Berkvens's personal account. That sometimes happens when an office party is being organized and a volunteer does all the purchasing. Afterward the expenses are settled, upon submission of all the receipts and invoices. An amount of a hundred thousand instead of ten thousand francs was calculated and made over to Berkvens's account.

Stefaan wasn't glad to make this discovery. For five minutes he even pretended he hadn't seen it and went on with his work. You're wrong, he said to himself. Now *you're* making a mistake. He looked at the accounts once again. It was a mistake, all right. As soon as Stefaan was sure of the error he took action, without wasting too many words. Don't beat around the bush, that was his approach. He drew up a memo and had it delivered to Berkvens. In it he asked Berkvens to repay the money with late payment interest.

'It's a mistake,' it says on the note in a sloppy hand. What a feeble excuse.

The last people from his department have gone home. The strip of glass in his office bothers him. The openness, it's too much. Why should the employees be able to spy on the boss and check up on him? It doesn't make any sense; it's excessive. As his mother used to say: *the world is changing, no one's in charge any more, children have stopped obeying their parents.*

'It's a mistake.' Is that all that Berkvens has to say? Is that his message, a simple mistake? If Berkvens had any brains there would have been no note and he would have transferred the money without hemming and hawing. This message looks suspiciously like a provocation. Stefaan sent a memo and asked for prompt action, and all he gets is a wad of paper. It's crude and completely uncalled for, but he does understand it. When a police officer fined him for running an amber light because it really was impossible for him to step on the brake, he cursed every cop on the beat. He blurted out something like, 'Oh, really? I didn't know. I didn't even see it.' It's pure self-defence. No one likes to be stripped of his dignity.

How does a fair-minded manager react to something like this? This is what he's paid for, to make decisions. So he decides: Berkvens will have to admit his mistake and redeposit the money. End of story.

It's already after half past six when Stefaan lifts his bike out of the loop in the bike rack and swings his leg over the bar. When he looks up he sees Berkvens standing next to him, grinning. It scares the wits out of him. For a moment Stefaan considers nodding goodbye and biking away quickly, but for someone with his status that simply isn't done. His mother taught him that he should always talk to workers the same way she talks to her seasonal labourers and her pigs. He should show the same respect for everyone, since they're the ones who put the bread on the table.

'Good evening.' Stefaan bows forward to turn on his bike lamp.

'You should wear reflectors,' says Berkvens. He points to the luminescent strap across his rounded belly. 'One lamp isn't enough. The cars will sweep you right off the road.'

'Yes, I'll have to do something about that.' Mieke, too, has told him this repeatedly.

'Come on, let's bike together.'

'Fine, then you ride on the outside with all your flashy lights,' Stefaan says. Berkvens also has strips on his shoes and a lamp on his head like a mineworker's.

'I'd gladly get run over to protect my boss.' He laughs crudely and gives Stefaan a chummy slap on the back.

'Working overtime, Berkvens?'

'A preliminary meeting with a couple of guys from the union to get ready for the staff party next week. So I thought: I'll just hang around a little longer until the boss is finished with work and I can light his way home.' He takes the bidon from his bike and squeezes all the water into his mouth. Has this man been drinking? He doesn't smell all that fresh in any case. It may be his moustache, a hotbed of germs.

'Shall we?' Stefaan clicks his feet into the pedals and shoves off down the hill.

Not a car passes without Berkvens naming the updated model with all the extras. Every passing car gets a seal of approval.

'Christmas? We're staying home,' Berkvens says. 'You're probably going skiing. Davos is the place to be, I've been told. We drove past it once but the crowds turned us off. We just kept on driving, and believe it or not only ten miles farther on it was all peace and quiet. When are you packing your car?'

Stefaan and Mieke have never hit the pistes in their lives. Mieke is afraid of fractures, and of osteoporosis later on. But he figures that's none of Berkvens's business. He attaches great importance to a strict separation between private life and work.

'We're staying home,' says Stefaan.

'Home? That'll be a change. On Sunday I happened to bike past your house with the guys from the cycling club. What a castle. Nice, huh? Nice, gorgeous. Have you ever gotten around to visiting all the rooms?' Berkvens shakes with laughter.

'Yes, we did once.'

'We go biking on our vacations. We love skiing. What a great way to live it up.' Berkvens is standing up on his pedals, ready for a sprint. 'Come on, Stefaan!' Stefaan doesn't like being addressed by his first name by people beyond his most intimate circle of friends. It happens in all the American companies, during church services, and while waiting in line at the bakery, but it irritates him. *Keep your hands off my name!* he wants to say.

At the foot of the mountain they bid their hasty goodbyes. Stefaan races up the mountain with an ease that surprises even him. During the zucchini soup, Mozart is playing in the background, pulling out all the stops. Mieke is doing all the talking, and during the chateaubriand with peas and potatoes she casually asks how it was at work today. 'Everything under control,' is his standard answer, as it is today. Mieke nods and clears the table. 'Everything under control with me, too,' says Sarah just like that, to the great delight of herself and of Mieke. Stefaan sometimes feels like a boarding school child who shows up at the table at fixed hours but is so shut up in his own little world that he can't laugh along with the other children.

Mieke says they're going to build a traffic circle in the city, which will mean opening one end of the shopping street. It's really going to be something with all that mess. Suddenly the thought strikes him that Berkvens wants to involve him in some dirty little game. Without realizing it Stefaan has agreed to play along.

'That'll make the cars look charming,' Mieke continues. 'Especially when it rains. Whose bright idea was this, anyway?'

After washing up, Stefaan, Mieke, and Sarah sit down together to watch the current affairs programme *Panorama*. The broadcast today is devoted to the Vatican. A desiccated priest is describing the pope's abstemious eating habits: white bread with cheese spread for breakfast, soup made from seasonal vegetables with more white bread and salami for lunch, and in the evening he eats with the nuns and has a glass of wine. At half past nine it's Sarah's bedtime. Stefaan supervises as she brushes her teeth. When he was a child he brushed his teeth far too little. On the farm it wasn't such a big deal. Now he only has seven of his own teeth in his mouth, with a whole lot of metal bridgework and dentures.

Stefaan tucks Sarah in, creeps out of her room, and leaves the door ajar. He sits down next to his wife and reads a bit from the *Financial Times*. Everything is proceeding in a streamlined fashion according to the same pattern, just like every other day. At ten o'clock Mieke has already fallen asleep in the armchair. He shakes her awake and tells her she should go upstairs, that she looks very tired. He has learned to skip the time-to-pack-it-in jokes. He kisses Mieke good night and promises to set the alarm when he comes to bed. Now he's going to his hobby shed for a little while. There's a clammy hand of uneasiness on the back of his neck. He sits down at his desk and begins to write, filling entire sheets of paper with his scribbling. He picks the pages up, examines them from a critical distance, shakes his head dejectedly, and starts all over again. A quicker mind would be able to jot down a whole series of valid points at one go, but not Stefaan. He searches in vain to connect with an unknown, amoral genius to correct his plans and help him further. As dawn begins to break he takes the stack of papers, stores them away behind a couple of old canisters, and goes to bed.

The next morning, according to custom, Stefaan slips his attaché case under the straps of the ultralight rack that he has had mounted to the back of his racing bike. He inserts his feet into the pedals and rides into the autumn morning, dead tired. One of his most precious memories is of his father rooting for them whenever he and Alain organized bicycle races around the farmyard. His father would stand on a tall bale of hay and shout, holding his cap up to block the sun, squinting with his weak eyes in order to focus better. His father was a cycling fanatic, but he himself had no time for racing. A farmer in West Flanders during the fifties and sixties worked himself to the bone. That was his deceased father, whom he had not paid enough attention to when he was young. His own daughter wasn't exactly overflowing with interest for him, either. One day Sarah can be friendly, maybe out of a kind of compassion for the hard-working breadwinner, and the next day she makes fun of him. Raising his only child is not what he had expected. He has to put up with it, though, pretend everything is fine, and leave for work the next day as usual. It takes a while before he realizes there's a man biking behind him. It's Berkvens. Speeding along, without even standing on his pedals, Berkvens catches up with him and passes him by. Stefaan takes up the challenge. Berkvens is wearing a bona fide cycling outfit that's stretched too tightly across his hefty paunch. Stefaan breathes in the misty morning air. Berkvens's little game is a contest of strength. Contests of strength fill him with anxiety and propel him forward. The last thing he's going to do is give up.

He and Berkvens have known each other a long time. They have a common history, a ghostly presence that sat beside them on the university benches, stood at the hospital dissecting tables where they both worked as interns, then followed them to the same growing company that was all too happy to recruit them both, and witnessed the duel they fought for the managerial job and the quarrel that followed. The ghost knows there's more going on here than a matter of unpaid money.

Berkvens rattles on non-stop during the entire ride, makes comments, asks questions, and anticipates the answers if, like last night, he thinks Stefaan is a little slow in responding. What's wrong with pausing for a breath between words, especially when the words aren't all that memorable? Berkvens is most likely searching for an elegant or suitable way to introduce the topic of his so-called mistake, but the strong current of his own babble keeps driving him further away from the subject.

When Stefaan drops into his desk chair he sees that he has beaten his own record for getting to work. So at least some good came out of the ordeal. He spends the rest of the day working on plans for the possible merger. There's a lot riding on this. The turnover for the past year was not exactly brilliant. Only higher management is aware of the tentative first steps and the laborious negotiations. The companies are like two dogs sniffing each others' backsides.

Stefaan does his very best to stay focused. Between two of the meetings he calls in Suzanne. He wants to ask her to check and see whether Berkvens's transfer has been made yet. When she appears in the doorway he changes his mind. The fewer people who are involved in Berkvens's slip, the sooner it can be forgotten. He tells Suzanne he didn't need her anyway.

You can't improve on silence, said his mother on one of the rare occasions that she spoke. Not coincidentally it's one of the most popular aphorisms in Mieke's arsenal as well. She can deliver sermons like a priest, interspersed with *thou shalt not, it would be better if* and *if only everyone would just*. His rosary of certitudes. He enjoys them even as he rolls his eyes. Mieke knows the secret of a normal life, and she shares it with him. In the winter his wife buys him woollen sports socks for cycling. When that difficult season arrives she leaves the fatty edge on his pork chop, a small but heavenly pleasure. She heaves him up out of the melancholy that descends on him in those dark winter nights.

He saw it coming. Every morning and every evening Berkvens intercepts him. Berkvens is hounding him with his bike. Stefaan has to push his body to the limits. He knows he can rectify things with a couple of simple words, but he has his status and his powerful pride.

Berkvens jabbers away, and as he does he wants to hear Stefaan's well-founded opinion about the Oslo Accords, the new King Albert II, the past grape harvest, and the football matches that Stefaan never watches. The man never leaves room for answers in his remarkable monologues. Stefaan is constantly on his guard for words that Berkvens seems to use with abnormal frequency in his inane discourse, such as 'deception', 'sneaky', 'terms of employment'.

There's never any room for personal outpourings but all the more for stupid jokes, Berkvens's way of venting standard annoyances about company cutbacks. Are they going to save the company by depriving the employees of their free daily can of soda? That would mean more savings for the bigwigs and even bigger net profits.

Stefaan knows perfectly well that he shouldn't let himself be taken in. Isn't it up to him to confront Berkvens? Berkvens is probably just waiting for it. 'Take the offensive, buddy,' he says to himself, and he tries to arouse his inner tough guy, but the inner tough guy is in hiding. When a Chevrolet flashes past them one morning, Berkvens can't get over the fact that Stefaan doesn't know which rich person is behind the wheel. 'All those directors up on the mountain know each other, right?' he claims. And by a few circuitous conversational routes he ends up sighing, 'Boy, I sure would like to go to America one day and kick up some dust with the little woman.' A snot bubble escapes from his right nostril. He loudly snorts it back.

'Do it, Berkvens. Do it.' The autumn cold is burning Stefaan's nose as well.

'Yeah, yeah. Pretty soon. I'm going to take all my overtime and go on vacation.'

Stefaan asks for Berkvens's personnel file and studies it thoroughly. Just as he expected, Berkvens has no overtime. Stefaan hoped to stumble across the next serious slip-up, such as Berkvens tampering with his extra hours, but he finds nothing.

One month later the money still has not been returned. Wait a bit, Stefaan thinks, wait a bit. Berkvens is the kind of man who slowly musters the courage to fight against the injustice of a just ruling. It's as exasperating as pulling out nose hairs. Soon he'll be forced to dismiss him. There's sufficient grounds for it. He'd easily be able to justify such a move to the board of directors and the personnel service, especially now that the purse strings are being tightened. But why does such a simple man need so much money anyway? His racing bike is an old wreck and his clothes are nothing but rags. Even Stefaan can see that, although he's no sartorial expert. There are people who need money to be happy but don't do anything with it. They put their money in the bank. Every week they go to the bank to get a statement, which they can spend the next week scrutinizing. They watch their money grow. That happens as fast as watching your own child grow. It takes love to do it.

Maybe Berkvens has given himself the raise he'll never otherwise get in his dead-end job. He's been promoted to his highest level of incompetence, and after that 'the only way is down,' as a charismatic American manager once put it at a conference in Bern. It's bound to happen. Berkvens is already on the downward slide, whether Stefaan lies awake at night thinking about it or not. And yet, Stefaan has been lying awake for several nights now.

Dismissing people is no picnic, despite what they suggest on the news. He's already had to let staff members go, which he did entirely according to the rules. It was never a pleasant experience. After one case in particular, the dismissal of a female lab technician, he ended up with a heart arrhythmia. In those days his subconscious visited him regularly and alerted him to the woman's natural curves. Stefaan was terrified that at some unguarded moment he would gaze at her too long or touch her with a single finger. A broom closet full of thoughts like sticky spiderwebs, which he only walked past but never entered. She was an ambitious young woman who could overwhelm everyone with her technical explanations, only to lapse into silence, pick at the fluff on her dress, and thoughtfully swirl the fluid in an Erlenmeyer flask while waiting for an answer that never came. So he simply couldn't imagine her getting down and dirty in the conference room with one of his researchers, in the dark of the oncoming twilight when they thought everyone had gone home and Stefaan thought he heard mice above the ceiling panels.

Then, too, he had lain awake for several nights in his chilly bedroom with the window open. He made a connection with his young daughter. Some people are egocentric and see everything in terms of themselves, but what do you call people who see everything in terms of their daughter? He saw in the lab technician a future version of his little girl. What kind of brute would fire his own daughter? But he also saw his daughter in the cashier, which may explain his blunt, disappointed reaction to her feeble greeting and her total lack of helpfulness when he tried to open a flimsy little bag with his fat, sausage-like fingers. He couldn't bear the thought of having to throw the talented lab technician out because of her reckless behaviour. Finally he just decided to get it over with and fired both the lab technician and the researcher on the spot. When he got home he got out the drill and ladder and screwed a little birds' house onto the trunk of the tall oak tree, which caused the tree to bleed resin.

This kind of thinking isn't at all useful. He's seen it happen more than once in the emergency room, where overworked, exhausted interns handed out sleeping pills like candy because they craved them themselves, or with the anorexia patient in his student digs who baked cakes non-stop, preferably using the richest recipe, so she could enjoy watching other people cram the calorie-laden mass into their bodies. Vicariously—that's how the world often works, but it's never a good solution. Finally he decides not to be irritated by Berkvens, because who knows, to do so might betray an even greater irritation with himself, his management style, his own slip-ups.

There's something scratching on the inside of Stefaan's head, something that has come crawling out of the crack between his work and his domestic life. At half past twelve he carefully slinks out of bed. Downstairs he turns off the alarm. It's pitch-dark outside. His heart is pounding loudly. He walks out to his hobby shed. Above his workbench he notices a spot. It's varnish that he's spread on the wall to test the discoloration. He stares at the spot so long that he wishes he could disappear under the layer of varnish and end up somewhere else.

He goes outside and climbs up on the roof to remove the rotten leaves from the gutter, inhaling lungfuls of oxygen until he can breathe normally again. What a pleasure to feel the dark sky above him and to look at the universe dressed in black, the brightly illuminated streets of the village below, the deck chairs, the sauna cabins, and the tennis courts. The neighbours, in their modernistic house full of corners and slanting windows, are already in bed, except perhaps for Marc. The surgeon is probably cracking open a new bottle of wine right now. The swimming pool of the next-door neighbours is brightly lit, as usual, a chalk line on the dark blackboard of the night. Night birds swing into action. A pair of tawny owls leave their pellets on the neatly trimmed lawns, grey balls of crushed mouse bones and other indigestible bits from their owl stomachs that they don't know what to do with. Stefaan shivers suddenly and realizes he's cold. He climbs down the ladder. When he turns around he sees that there's a light on in Sarah's room. She's standing with her little face to the window. He waves to her.

At the office he gets himself a double coffee, although he might just as easily have called the coffee lady. It's still early in the morning and the cafeteria is sparsely populated, all of them people whose faces are vaguely familiar. No one exchanges greetings. It's morning; people have yet to get fully energized. He's just at the point of asking Berkvens: aren't you even a little grateful that I've let you keep your job, even though you haven't done a lick of work in years? Even though you paper the walls of the coffee room with your stupid jokes and waste everyone's time with your endless blather and your attention-getting little meetings?

After he's finished his coffee and gone to the bathroom he comes to the carefully thought-out conclusion that he's going to ignore Berkvens completely for the time being, until his dismissal. He won't give him any more evaluations or briefings, either. Stefaan has already been taking a different route to and from work for a week now. Berkvens will have to come to Stefaan's office and go through the secretary to find out what's going on.

His secretary Suzanne comes in and lays a file in front of him, along with a folded-up note. He waits until she's closed the door behind her and opens the note.

'Forget it,' it says this time, written in Berkvens's same childish handwriting on lined paper. The message has a radioactive impact. Is there something else he's supposed to forget, or can the company kiss the repayment good-bye? What do these two words mean? He shoves the note into his pocket.

At home Mieke is conducting a successful experiment in the kitchen. She happened to run into Berkvens's wife today at the broccoli section in the Delhaize. The woman spontaneously shared a broccoli recipe with her. They didn't know what else to talk about.

'It's really not all that complicated,' Mieke warns, 'except for one secret ingredient. Guess what it is!'

Sarah and Stefaan are the guinea pigs. He takes a bite. He can taste the flavour of soap, or something unmistakably chemical. What if there's poison in the vegetables? He really has to get a grip on his paranoia. This is getting out of hand. Even so, he spits it out. Sarah likes it.

'Ginger!' Mieke says triumphantly. 'Did you know, by the way, that Fernand Berkvens and his wife have split up?'

'Berkvens is playing the old two-coat trick,' Elleke reports out of nowhere. Elleke, the brazen new IT specialist, talks a lot and parades through the whole department in high heels and with pursed lips. The company invests heavily in desktops for its personnel. They've taken on a couple of experts to help people with all their computer problems. Elleke deals with everything, even problems that fall outside her competence. Stefaan has asked her to keep an ear to the ground on the work floor. She's overheard from more than one person that Berkvens has two coats in his locker. He takes one coat and drapes it over the back of his chair. Then he says good morning to all his colleagues, and if he's of a mind, he goes out for a few hours in his other coat. When people ask for him, his colleagues think he's somewhere in the building because his coat is hanging over his chair. Apparently his closest colleagues have been aware of this for a while, but no one has felt the need to tell Stefaan. He ought to understand this, since snitches are never popular.

Today the board of directors is convening a meeting with the union representatives. Soon the matter of the merger is going to be introduced, and good relations can be helpful in that regard. These are the nineties. The unions still reign supreme. Their champions are hotheads who have been demoted or have just never risen any higher but are tormented by a longing for power and prestige. They want to count for something, come what may. It doesn't matter what a union leader has been up to; the man is a kind of god within the corporate hierarchy, a spiritual leader who keeps morale high, a man people can rely on and complain to. The executive personnel of a company are much less important. Stefaan is aware of this when he walks through the corridors or stops for water at the SipWell machine. Most of the employees would do anything not to greet him. As he bends over the water fountain he can see how they walk past him without saying a word. He can't count how many times he's said 'good day' to the water fountain. It's part of his job as manager. You learn to live with what you can't change; you find other ways. Mieke is right. It's very difficult to divvy up the money and get on with the masses. The masses can be stolen from him. All great ideologies have wrestled with the masses and looked for a way to get along with them. It's tough going.

It's partly his fault. For too long he's put off visiting the shop floor. He opens the large closet next to the door and takes out his lab coat. With his lab coat draped over his arm he goes to the ground floor and walks to the research wing. A couple of heads pop up above the low partitions in the large open rooms when he comes in. There's a faint mumbling here and there. They're excluding him from their territory, that's it. They can never forget that he has authority over them. On the contrary. That's why they don't want to see him here. As far as they're concerned his place is in the observation tower.

His former lab partner, Steven, comes around the corner, nods to him, and tosses a twenty-franc coin into the Coke machine. Even Steven doesn't stop to chat. Has someone been gossiping about him or has he always been far too passive? He almost never takes the initiative for small talk. He twists a can of Fanta out of the machine. He's not thirsty, but he doesn't want people to wonder what he's doing walking around here. With the soda in his hand he goes back to his office by way of the stairs. He thinks about his scrawny father, how he climbed the ladder to the hayloft so long ago with his back straight as an arrow, a picture of dignity.

When he gets back to his desk he has his secretary call Berkvens in.

'Come in,' says Stefaan. 'Sit down.'

Berkvens stands on the other side of the oak desk, looks at him, and frowns.

Maybe he didn't make himself clear. 'You may sit down.'

'Why did you call me in?' asks Berkvens.

'What are you going to do?' Stefaan asks brusquely. 'Reimburse the company or not?'

'What do you mean?' Finally Berkvens sits down.

Stefaan does his best to ignore the ringing in his ears. 'You hardly do any work, you steal money from the company and you refuse to pay it back. I could have fired you long ago.'

'It's not true.'

'I have it in black and white. You stole money.'

'That was money for the union.'

'Ninety thousand francs was mistakenly deposited in your bank account. Are you planning on paying it back?'

Berkvens shrugs his shoulders.

'What do you need the money for anyway?'

'I like to keep my private life and my work separate,' Berkvens says.

'Shall I give that as the reason when I ask the personnel services to dismiss you? I'm curious to see if it makes any difference.'

'The union will protect me,' says Berkvens, his moustache in the air.

'Ah, the union is protecting you? People like you destroy unions. You steal and you lie. You know that an industrial tribunal will approve of your dismissal in one second after they see the file?'

'Ha ha,' says Berkvens. 'Not true.' He smooths his moustache with his thumb and forefinger. Why isn't anyone walking past? Is it something they've all agreed to? He's sitting in a glass cage, the very picture of openness and transparency. Usually his employees are glad to make use of this, to catch a glimpse of their boss. It's six minutes past eleven in the morning, which apparently is the only time of day when everyone is screwed down to their chairs. There's no movement at all along the local hunting paths.

'The file is full enough to fire you on the spot,' Stefaan repeats.

'Interesting.' Berkvens chews on his lower lip. 'Things are different the way I see it.'

'Okay, and how do you see it then?' Stefaan asks mockingly.

'The merger.'

'What do you know about a merger?'

'I have my sources.'

'What do you want?'

'Justice. You're not the right person to be occupying this position. For you—and for the rest of your pals on the board of directors, by the way—only three things matter. Profits, profits, and more profits. You guys are ruthless when it comes to profits. How many were there in China again? Let me see.'

Because a pharmaceutical company is not a bank, there's no red emergency buttton to push. And because this isn't a movie, there's no trapdoor on the floor that snaps open when a scoundrel grabs you and sprays flakes of saliva all over your leather desk top.

'You listen to me.' Stefaan is almost whispering. 'What happened in China was an accident.'

'An accident? If you bleed people dry year after year and have them working overtime for starvation wages, yes, then accidents do happen.'

'The families were properly compensated. The working conditions in the factory have been improved enormously.'

'A factory burned to ashes. One dead, five severely wounded.'

'What do you want?'

'It was your fault, you son of a bitch. You went to see that company. You knew how deplorable and dangerous the situation was there, yet you didn't lift a finger.'

'What do you know about it?'

'If this gets out, it sure doesn't look good for that merger. I don't think our big boss is going to rush to support you. It would be much easier for him to throw one little element overboard than to let the whole board of directors go under. Brutal, huh? Now you know how it feels to be an employee in a company that only thinks about profits.' Berkvens leaves and closes the door behind him.

Usually he knows how to conduct himself, even in cases of panic. Like that time the deep fat fryer burst into flames. He quickly threw a damp mop over the whole thing and carried it outside without a moment's hesitation. Then he and Mieke both stared at the wildly sputtering gunk that had almost burned their villa down. This time he didn't act fast enough, not fast enough to hurl a damp rag onto the whole smouldering mess.

He's been unmasked by a good-for-nothing. Stripped to his bare skin by a fool. What does that make him? His colleagues, Mieke, Sarah, all of them are going to find out that he's not the big man who effortlessly kicked his way to the top, but just the little boy who got out of the car to bring the bad news to his parents. The man without a job: here he is, his butt still planted on the leather manager's chair. There's a little coffee left in his cup. His false teeth chatter against the plastic rim. His male member is stiff, a fear response common to all mammals. He has lost everything. Stefaan comes out from behind his desk and opens the window. Fresh air always helps. He sits down again with difficulty and stares at the fluorescent green letters on his computer screen.

Stefaan arrives home completely winded. He wolfs down the meatloaf with carrots and potatoes. Sarah tells him about the St. Michael's Agreement and what its consequences are for the Belgians, who since then have been living in the federal state of Belgium. Mieke gives him a look as if to say, 'My brains or yours? Or maybe a combination of the two?' This is it, this is what he has to cling to. This is what he's fought for: his family. As long as he can keep his family safe everything will be fine, no matter what he has to sacrifice to do it. Mieke comes up with a remark she's overheard about her brother Jempy. Her voice drips with contempt. But hidden beneath her disapproval is a certain admiration for the man's sheer audacity: *her* brother, who plunges from one adventure to the next without giving it a moment's thought. Hitchhiking from Cape Town to Russia—no problem, certainly not with that sea between them.

After supper Stefaan goes into the garden. The faithful night owls are waiting there, ready to turn their heads toward the dome of heaven. He looks through the bars of tree trunks and the foliage of the slender, recently planted fruit trees and sees the light around the neighbour's swimming pool. The surface of the water is covered with a thick crust of leaves, a treacherous invitation to walk across it. He sniffs the housing estate's forest air. Then he grabs the handle on the oak door to his hobby shed and jerks it open, steps inside, and stands facing his collection of tools, his legs wide apart, as if to see which will be the first to wake up, the first to jump down from the rack and do him a favour. Here the objects are waiting for him: a whole arsenal of hand saws, fine-toothed hacksaws, jigsaws that Sarah borrowed during her third year of school to cut out a clown for Father's Day, an axe for splitting blocks of wood for the fireplace, a steel drill, and a mean-looking wood saw with big teeth that has left ragged traces on the inside of his left hand. The saw that he uses only on rare occasions, for really serious jobs, is under the lean-to at the back of his shed, covered with a heavy plastic shield to protect it from rain and rust. It's a monster with a row of deadly teeth, a charcuterie slicer for wood. It effortlessly cuts a railroad tie into slices of ham.

He removes the protective covering from the big, surly electric saw, which is now silent, but five seconds later, with one push of a button, it starts howling at the stars. He places stump after stump against the iron blade. Look, this isn't a man without work, he's always busy. It's one of Mieke's complaints about him: never a moment's rest. Mieke is standing on the patio in her bathrobe, shouting. Has he gone completely crazy? she wants to know. A couple of weeks ago she was standing there as well, yelling that under no circumstances did she want a disabled husband, because what would she do then? He'd spend whole days sitting at home and he'd have to live on benefits from the Public Centre for Social Welfare, which would just about cover Sarah's school books and a bowl of oatmeal. 'Stefaan, what's going on, buddy?' she said then, ending her roaring good-naturedly, laying her words on a cushion of kindness.

But now she keeps on screaming. Stefaan lowers his hand into the atmosphere surrounding the blade. He touches the spinning air, the heat of the razor-sharp, rotating knife, and pulls his finger back at once. It's been decapitated. A terrible gash, a deep flesh wound. He gasps. Mieke starts shrieking again. He feels a jab of pain, of nauseating, paralysing pain. He barely has the presence of mind to turn the machine off with his left hand. The blocks of thought click back into place in his head, his observations are all lined up once again.

'Everything's fine,' he calls from a distance, like a King Lear raging at the elements. 'I'll be right there.' Panic echoes through his voice, but he hopes the distance will filter it out. A whip shoots through his body and drives the endorphin up to his head, which suddenly feels very light and lucid. He walks out to the garden path, where the lights turn on automatically. Bent down over his finger, he sees the bone standing out against the horror of the torn flesh. 'Fucking idiot,' he says, cursing himself, and he sniffles with self-derision. Mieke drags him into the house, pulls out a long strip of paper towelling from the holder and presses it tightly against his amputated fingertip. 'Now what have you done?'

'I'll take care of it.' Several minutes later Stefaan notices with relief that he is not going to bleed to death, although the tip of his finger is really gone for good.

High from the pain, he lies down on his back in the darkness of their cool bedroom. He can't sleep. Mieke shakes a pillow, burrows into it, and within a minute rolls into the deep ravine of slumber. He can't restrain himself. He shakes Mieke awake and asks, 'May I say something?'

Mieke often tells her husband that most people would be twice as interesting if they said half as much, but that he ought to try saying a little more. She turns toward him, snuggles up to him, and with a low voice that clearly indicates her desire to wander back into a deep sleep as soon as possible, she asks, 'What is it, buddy?'

Once he starts he can't stop. He bleeds words when he tells his story about Berkvens, the irritating business with Berkvens. The man who follows him on his bike. The man who stole money and now won't pay it back. He drowns Mieke in details, but he doesn't say anything about the threat that Berkvens made earlier in the day.

'I'm glad that's happening to you for once. The small irritations are the worst,' she says. 'Take today. I was making soup and I accidentally mixed in a dirty potato peel. You can never get it out and you can taste it anyway. Terrible.'

'He's stopped now—following me, I mean.'

'Thank God. I saw that tub of lard Berkvens biking

past recently in a kind of sausage skin cycling outfit. Do me one favour, Stefaan, and never wear a cycling outfit. This Berkvens can wear them if it makes him feel good, but not the manager. No, Stefaan, you make yourself look ridiculous in a nylon stocking like that. And I know that everyone has the right to make themselves ridiculous, but you're not everyone. You're my husband. If you start showing off, it rubs off on me. So it's my job to keep you from doing anything stupid.'

What Mieke is offering him is anything but a solution. She doesn't even seem to grasp the heart of his problem. She also yawns incessantly, but that often happens in bed. Stefaan is lying there dying of pain. She hasn't got the faintest idea what he's going through.

Stefaan feels the rage welling up within him. He's angry at himself, he's angry at the world. It arouses him. He starts kissing his wife, moving down to her belly, and then between her legs, and he's surprised by her receptivity. While he's kissing her he strokes her belly vigorously, her buttocks, her breasts. The blood throbs in his decapitated finger and in his bare member. He's as hard as a rock but won't allow himself to enter her. He wants to stay hard, throbbing hard. 'Come into me,' Mieke orders. Suddenly she feels an intense urgency, there isn't a second to lose, she can't wait. He lifts her pelvis up with his battered hand and thrusts himself into her. Lifting her is painful, entering her is painful. He pants like a wounded animal. And behind that blazing pain, which spreads and burns the entire field of his body to cinders, he also discovers a diabolic joy. He attacks his wife and pleasures her until both of them are unable to go any further. In bed they become different people, two strangers who want to go to bed with each other on impulse, two strangers who trust each other through and through. They lie for a long time in each other's arms in the dark, on the journey back from somewhere they've never been to before. He loves her, in all her guises, with all her masquerades and her slightly inflammable convictions.

He spends the rest of the night tossing and turning. It keeps running through his head: always in retrospect, when it's too late. He knows he should have pushed Berkvens out earlier on. Thirteen years ago, after that first quarrel. He blames himself for that. What's going to happen now? He'll lose his job, and who will benefit from that? Would the Chinese workers want him to be fired? No, of course not. Since the accident they've never had it so good, and that's his doing.

At breakfast a totally different Mieke, his lawfully wedded wife, reports to him that his salary has not yet been deposited. She monitors it scrupulously. Even though half his salary is nibbled away by the gluttonous Belgian tax service, the remaining half is more than enough to maintain his family. With his assiduousness at work, as well as Mieke's inheritance, they can allow themselves this luxury. For Mieke, luxury is not an extravagance but a living standard. She needed the carpets, the built-in halogen spots, and the new kitchen with an induction cooking unit. It's her payment in kind for being a housewife. Say they'd moved into a row house in the city or a ground floor apartment on the outskirts. Mieke would have sold part of her patrimony anyway in order to buy a villa up here on the mountain. After all, they want to live in a house that looks a little like that of her late parents. For her, luxury is a question of tradition.

'Are you going to look into this?' The tone of her voice makes it clear that the previous night was from another, far-off era. People are different in the morning, and different laws apply. On the radio two constitutional experts are disagreeing about the Brussels-Halle-Vilvoorde voting district. Sarah is crumbling her sandwich.

'All right, all right,' he mutters.

'*All right, all right*, that won't get us very far. You have to assert yourself more.'

'It's only the third of the month. Tomorrow the money will be in our account. You know how long banks take to do this kind of thing.'

'You let them walk all over you.'

'I do not!'

'Or ask them to skip a month.'

'What difference does it make?' Did she get her period all of a sudden, or is she smelling a rat? He has to be on his guard with Mieke. She always finds out in the end.

'Remember that month when you just turned it over to Van de Meulebroeck, as a gift?'

She's right. The first month after his promotion he had not been paid. He didn't dare inquire about it because he didn't want to seem too greedy.

'If I hadn't pushed to get it straightened out you'd now be a manager with an advisor's salary.'

'I'll take care of it.'

'And see a doctor about your finger.'

'I *am* a doctor.'

Stefaan doesn't even know if he's going to work or not when he jumps on his bike and takes his usual escape route through the woods in the hope of avoiding Berkvens. There's no one in the woods. It's so quiet that you can hear the magpies discuss their booty from the top of one pine tree to the next. Suddenly someone comes biking up behind him, breathing loudly. Stefaan accelerates; he doesn't want company. The panting builds. His blood flows faster, but he tries to ignore the cyclist until the very last minute.

He doesn't look to the side but bikes on at a brisk pace until a heavyset boy comes cycling up in his right field of vision. He's leaning over his handle bars like a yeti, propelling himself forward with every scrap of energy he can muster. A moronic smile slices his face open and reveals an overabundance of teeth, pressed into gorilla gums. There's something childlike and curious about him. Stefaan smiles affably, because you can't go wrong with a smile. The boy returns his smile.

He's the kind of boy who used to be put to work ploughing the field, even though a farm horse was out there doing the same thing. A big guy with unbridled energy who you had to stuff with stacks of sandwiches, but in return he would move mountains. They used to have a fellow like that on the farm at harvest time. This boy is better cared for, though. His clothes and face are clean.

It's out of pure curiosity and thirst that Stefaan gets off his bike in a clearing in the woods. He tries to prop his bike up on its kickstand, but it sinks into the soft leaf mould. The bike tumbles onto the forest floor. The boy rests it against a blown-over tree trunk, into which many love messages have been carved. He turns his body stiffly toward Stefaan.

The boy comes closer and places a massive, hefty paw into his outstretched hand.

'I am Xavier,' says the boy courteously, with far too much moisture in his mouth. He slurps on the end of the three words to keep his saliva and his tongue inside.

'And I am Stefaan,' says Stefaan. 'You sure are a good biker.'

'Pfggahghhnaaa,' says Xavier very slowly, and he nods vehemently to indicate that he is in full agreement.

They get back on their bikes and, urging each other on, they race together farther and farther, panting and laughing. They go through swaths of woods and open fields until they end up once again at the bottom of the mountain. There they stop. The boy looks at him, happily surprised, and shakes hands before vanishing in the direction of the village.

Stefaan knows perfectly well that he has to face up to the truth. Like those men in the movies who lose their jobs and take the train to the airport every day to waste hours waving at the planes, he's too paranoid for such a thing. He's willing to bet his whole sawn-off hand that Mieke will find him out, in her own inscrutable way.

That's why the next day he steps through the revolving glass door at half past seven in the morning, to let himself be ground to bits in the managers' room and, with bowed head, to accept his letter of dismissal. The question is whether it will be given to him or whether he'll ask for it himself. Another question is why he hasn't noticed anything unusual. His secretary continues to inundate him with work. She has laid all the files neatly on his desk. If he takes one day off without prior warning it's unpleasant for his staff at the very most, but he never gets a reprimand.

Even before relieving his desk of the files—something he normally starts the day with at the office—he goes downstairs. Berkvens shares an office with six of his co-workers. When they're not working in the lab they write their results and analyses here. He hasn't been in this room in a long time. It strikes him how drab and boring it is: the white lacquered desks and cabinets that are supposed to exude an air of professionalism, the expensive desk lamps that are recommended for companies operating around the clock, the identical mesh wastepaper baskets. Here and there he comes across a rare personal detail: a porcelain cup with 'Sweetest Mom' written on it, a metal canister of bonbons, and on Berkvens's desk a red lunchbox with an open lid, and inside a white bread sandwich of sweating salami. Berkvens comes in. Without being thrown off balance, Berkvens hangs his coat over the chair, carries out his first round of greetings, and bids Stefaan a friendly good day. Stefaan asks Berkvens to come upstairs with him. He didn't want to send his secretary out to chase him down. It's something between the two of them, without the intervention of outsiders.

For the first minutes nothing happens. The men stare each other down like two Mafiosi who take each other for traitors. You don't have to be a genius to realize that they'd both be better off under an oath of secrecy. Stefaan breaks the silence and puts a proposal on the table. Berkvens will keep his job and keep his mouth shut in exchange. As for the 90,000 francs, Stefaan expects to see the money back in the company account within the year. As Berkvens stands up and is about to shake Stefaan's hand, he notices the bandage. Stefaan sees Berkvens's undamaged fingers and turns around. 'You can go,' he says.

For the first brainless hour of relief, Stefaan feels like a winner. Firing Berkvens would have cost the company tons of money anyhow, even if it were possible given his union status. And if he were to fire him, Berkvens would drag Stefaan down with him, a possibility that has now been foiled. Two coffees later his brain is back in working order, and a simple, sober analysis teaches him that actually he's coming away empty-handed. Berkvens has been advanced a serious sum of money and otherwise nothing has changed. Berkvens will still be able to blackmail him. The pain in his fingertip intensifies but he refuses to take any painkillers.

For the rest of the working day Stefaan makes phone calls till he's blue in the face. He confers, confirms, double-checks, punches in numbers, and signs documents. He goes to more meetings than he can count because they're at a critical point in the merger negotiations.

Now he and his fellow managers have to sell the merger internally to the personnel, who are already grumbling and ready to organize picket lines if the rumour gets out that three people will be swapping offices. If this merger goes through, the company will be bigger and more powerful than ever. The fight for the limited number of top-level jobs will erupt with greater ferocity. New people will arrive who will be even more intent on sawing off the legs of his chair.

The merger has given rise to a flurry of constant arrivals and departures in the management beehive. Both companies have agreed to a thorough screening by an external auditing agency. As his colleagues produce more and more new files, Stefaan keeps quiet. He bobs around to the steady rhythm of files and meetings while treading water and fearing he could drown at any moment. There isn't a single demonstrable reason for that fear.

Berkvens celebrates his birthday by treating everyone to homemade waffles. Buttered waffles, Stefaan notices when the coffee lady sets the plate in front of him. Thick dollops of white sludge, cement, ensnared in the little indentations of a limp waffle. Who made these waffles and spread them with butter? And who's trying to get rid of him, shuddering with horror from behind his desk?

Winter has left its first glassy fingerprints on the windows. His secretary asks him if he wants to sign Sarah up for the Sinterklaas party this year, but he tells her that at thirteen she hasn't believed in the good saint for a long time now, 'but thanks anyway'.

A few years ago, large signs were posted along the highways of Flanders that said FAST DRIVING IS AS DUMB AS FAST SEX. It was a traffic safety slogan that did not go unnoticed, since sex back then was still considered taboo. And it was a stupid slogan that all of Flanders could heartily laugh at, Stefaan included. Why shouldn't he go fast? When he's on his bike he's in charge, and he can put on speed with abandon. He hears the sports reporters zooming by on their motorcycles. They shoot past his racing bike, dangerously close, but he remains focused. He's concentrating on the finish line and he knows his strength. He knows how far the caloric value of his sandwiches can take him. He has no need of attendants, only those little voices in his head, spurring him on. He remembers them from his youth, when he still had little buddies to play Rik Van Steenbergen, Briek Schotte, or Fausto Coppi. They raced against each other, and they were triumphant. 'Theeeeerrrrre he comes, theeeeerrrrre he goes. Just look at that agility, ladies and gentlemen ... ' This is how he eggs himself on, in the bawling words of the sports commentators. All through the ride he's in the lead, alone, bent over this steering wheel, the wind in his face. He straightens himself up and stretches his hands into the air as if fifty thousand fans were standing at the finish line, cheering ecstatically, with another million screaming at home.

'Take it easy when you bike,' Mieke tells Stefaan after he gets home, puffing and sweating, his face bright red. 'Don't the people on your staff ever say anything about it, showing up at work like a steaming bull? They must say something, the guys at least. What's the point anyway, for God's sake—biking yourself to death. You going to a fire? Supper isn't even ready yet.'

It's started to snow without let-up. While war is raging in the outside world and children are being kidnapped, Stefaan is sitting indoors. He never could have expected that starting a family would make him both happier and lonelier. Gradually he's beginning to understand the position of black men in New York. Recently he read that seventy percent of them abandon their wives and children. African-American women usually raise their children alone. Maybe the father is supposed to leave as soon as his task is accomplished. That's more in line with nature. This causes unspeakable convolutions to form in his mind that in many other people would lead to a violent outburst sooner or later. Recently the father of a family in New Orleans went into a Wendy's restaurant and emptied his Smith & Wesson. He then got into his parked Ford and dutifully turned himself in to the police.

He gathers up his records to move them to his hobby shed. His fingertip is itching. He sees Mieke suddenly straighten herself up near one of her rugs. He doesn't say anything (what had they agreed to?), but he stares down at the pattern on the floor. You can lose yourself in a repetition like that. The weavers must go loony—they'd have to. He'll end up loony, too, given his own family pattern: his little brother was too wild for this life, his father was too sensitive for this life, he is too weak for this life.

None of us has ever insisted that a person should

always walk around with a wristwatch, but you do have to make sure that the past doesn't catch up with you. A rough sketch of Stefaan Vandersanden would look like this: someone who has fled to the room adjacent to life and can't find his way back. Leave the moaning to us, Stefaan, we'll take care of it. You have some fighting to do, even though you complain about being so tired, so dog-tired. You're a modern-day survivor.

Since March, Sarah has been studying classical piano on Saturday mornings at the suggestion of Elvira, Mieke's friend, who has heard her tinkling away on the Steinway in the parlour and can make out a few skilled sounds in the fog of false notes. Her first exercise book contains songs like 'When The Ship Comes In'. As a true-blue Bob-Cat, a hardcore follower of the religion of Bob Dylan, Stefaan is completely satisfied with the lessons as well as with the teacher, a pale, ageless crow who extends her bony hand to him at the front door every weekend to let him know that she expects him back in a good hour. During that time it is presumed that he will conduct himself like a modern family man, something that doesn't come easy to him. To make sure that both of them use their time more efficiently, Mieke has asked him to go shopping during that hour. He drives to the nearby Delhaize. He steers the cart through the super-market with one hand; in the other he holds a list he's trying to decipher. Shopping costs him an arm and a leg. See how monstrously expensive a steak is, not to men-tion all those breakfast cereals, the individually pack-aged gingerbread, or that product that's supposed to get wine stains out of clothing and rugs.

When he's three quarters of the way through his list, he parks his shopping cart at the far end of an aisle. He'll carry the rest of the items back to his cart a few at a time. Stefaan disappears into the aisle with heaps of Popla toilet paper and cuts across to the dairy section. He hastily grabs a strip of Actimel drinks from the open cooler when he notices a familiar lumpish figure. He and Berkvens haven't seen each other in weeks. Stefaan was seldom in his office because he had to attend so many meetings in Luxembourg and London for work. Thanks to Berkvens he's still got his job. Thanks to Stefaan this guy is still twiddling his thumbs in his own meaningless little position. Something that could have ended in a catastrophe has become a win-win situation for both of them.

'Seems to be good for the intestinal bacteria, right?' Berkvens is talking to him. He points to the Actimel.

'Yeah,' says Stefaan. 'Who are we to contradict the doctors?' They share a hearty laugh.

'Hey, I'll let you go,' says Stefaan, who can see from the corner of his eye that someone wants to push his cart aside to grab the empty space in the row. 'See you soon!'

Later that afternoon Stefaan goes to his hobby shed and cleans his drill chucks to the music of *Nashville Skyline*, a Dylan album that he has to listen to on a regular basis. It's a pure country album that's shocking in its choice of genre, but with such refreshing and lively numbers that you forget what a silly record it actually is. Stefaan doesn't feel good about having interrupted Berkvens and then walking away. The man was just trying to be friendly. After all, he is Berkvens's superior and Berkvens has kept to the agreement, so it's up to him to show him some respect as well. He locks up his hobby shed and goes outside. Then he looks up Berkvens's number under the B's in the phone book.

'Who are you talking to?' Mieke asks as soon as Stefaan

hears Berkvens's voice. She's just come into the house wearing her gardening gloves. She's been out on the sun porch running grapevines through the strings on a wooden rack.

'Berkvens,' he says, not unashamed of his charm offensive. Mieke grabs his nose between her plastic fingers and pinches. He slaps her bottom and motions for her to keep still. A couple of years ago her brother Jempy sat here for entire weekends, driving a wedge between them.

'Berkvens, this is Vandersanden. I've got a proposal.' Stefaan asks Berkvens if he feels like a game of squash. He remembers that Berkvens is a squash fanatic, and he isn't too bad a player himself. They're probably quite well matched.

Like a politician who goes to football matches to show his affinity with the people, every executive should take the initiative to engage in sports with a union man every once in a while in order to stay on friendly terms. They agree to meet that very afternoon at the sports centre at four o'clock to play squash.

One by one their cars glide into the concrete tower of the large industrial building on the canal that houses an outlet store, a garden centre, and a sports centre, all based on the American model. Each man has his own racquet, but Berkvens has to rent shoes. He may not enter the squash court in his coloured soles.

Stefaan feels good about this right from the start. He's bursting with energy and he easily gives Berkvens a run for his money. After the first set he calls for a timeout. Although his head is pounding from the excessive strain, he keeps on going. But now his bladder is acting up. A soaking wet Berkvens thinks it's a good time to order an Aquarius at the bar.

Stefaan walks through the fitness complex. The stairwell is utterly silent. This is where the storage rooms are located for the cafeteria, the haunt of many Saturday drinkers whose excuse is that they're waiting for their offspring to finish with their sports. After drying his hands Stefaan looks outside. He sees a solitary canoeist paddling up the canal with a languid stroke, as if he had already covered a long distance and was effortlessly topping it off with a few more miles. Stefaan watches him until he's out of sight. It must be glorious to keep on going until you're unable to stop, until you've sailed through all the countries and all the seasons without encountering any obstacles, until you forget time entirely, until time no longer exists.

Voices in the sauna complex tear him away from his dream. He splashes water on his face and goes back. They resume their game. Berkvens is serving. He lets the little dark blue ball roll along his fingertips and looks at Stefaan defiantly. Stefaan grins and nods to let him know he's ready. Every time Berkvens hits the ball at a clever angle Stefaan receives it. Every time he makes an impossible shot Stefaan returns it with ease. He feels all-powerful. Berkvens plays out the second set stoically and racks up loss upon loss. Stefaan spurs him on, shouting loudly. It's in his own best interest. What he wants is an exciting match. With a speed and flexibility that he himself finds astonishing, Stefaan returns even the most difficult ball with inordinate skill. But then Berkvens begins gaining ground and sets off in pursuit. He scores point after point. The air is thick with sweat. They discuss lines and bad serves with the gravity of professionals. The world shrinks to a glass cage, an over-heated little rubber ball, and two men.

It's Stefaan's turn to serve. He jumps up and down like a basketball player about to make a free throw, turns his head to the left and to the right, and gazes at his opponent with steely eyes. The serve he opts for is razor-sharp and low. Tock. Berkvens rushes forward. More by happy accident than by intention, the ball just barely hits the strings of Berkvens's racquet and bounces above the lowest red line. Stefaan sprints forward in response, and with a powerful stroke he sends the ball to the opposite corner. He lets his racquet swing in a broad arc, and feels some resistance. The racquet has hit his opponent full in the face.

Stefaan has split Berkvens's upper lip with his racquet. There's also a broken tooth. This is no laughing matter, and Berkvens is trembling with rage. The barkeep comes running out from behind the bar with a pack of ice. Stefaan offers to drive Berkvens to the emergency room because he can't go home like this, but Berkvens hisses at him to make himself scarce. Stefaan insists, but Berkvens only shouts, 'Go away!' He slinks off. Deeply abashed, he closes the glass door of the squash court behind him. He feels an intense pressure in his chest.

He drives home, shaken and trembling in his saturated sportswear. He takes off the salty clothing in the garage. Then he goes to the attic to stow away his squash racquet forever. It's much too dangerous an instrument. He turns on the light and sees Sarah sitting there.

'What are you doing here in the dark?' he asks.

She isn't practising her guitar as usual but is down on her knees in front of a bulletin board covered with torn-out pictures from magazines. A tealight candle is burning.

'Kurt is dead.' He sees photographs of the dead guitar hero, Cobain. Since yesterday, 5 April 1994, when he was found dead in the attic above his garage, the whole world has been talking about him.

'The man didn't want to live anymore,' says Stefaan. 'He couldn't handle it all, so many fans and so much money.'

'He was murdered,' Sarah spits out.

'Sarah, he put a bul ... '

'Leave me alone!'

Stefaan keeps the rest of his comments to himself and leaves his daughter with her adolescent grief.

Downstairs Mieke is doing the ironing.

'Your face is so red,' she says. 'You overdid it again, didn't you? Apparently squash is a pretty gruelling sport. One of the most exhausting there is. Go take a quick shower to cool off.'

The cool water does him good, but the swing with his racquet continues to torment him. If he were being interrogated under duress, a revolver pressed against his ribs and a fluorescent light shining into his wide-open eyes, he would not be able to swear that it was purely accidental. Nor can he be sure that he didn't have it in for Berkvens right from the start. It's something in his head. A point when the machinery starts misfiring, a point when somebody else takes over. In a burst of anger Stefaan kicks the wall with all his might. The merger is not going to take place. He's going to be fired anyway. He's blown it, just when he wanted to make amends.

SARAH 1997

It's eleven o'clock at night and Sarah is standing in the tiny little shower stall of a seedy hotel in Palma de Mallorca. Palma de Mallorca is the frivolous final note to the school trip to Spain during the summer vacation.

Sarah has waited for everyone to be finished in the bathroom so she can shower undisturbed. Unlike her classmates, Sarah prefers to undress without an audience. She murmurs words of encouragement to the paltry stream of water while groping around in the soap dish. The bar of soap slides out of her hand. One minute she's bending over to pick up the fallen soap, the next minute she's stretching out her hand to break her fall. Fifty kilos is more than the rickety door of the shower stall can bear. The door falls out, followed by Sarah.

She lands on the cold tile floor of the bathroom, stark naked. Her three classmates come rushing in.

'Small breasts,' someone says. 'Spindly legs,' says someone else.

Emily asks if she's okay, if she's broken anything. The classmates stifle their laughter in cups of Batida de Coco. Sarah is certain that all her bones are broken and that she's going to spend the rest of her life in a wheelchair. Yet the shame is even greater. She's never going to have girlfriends again. Never, she says to herself, just before her consciousness shifts down a notch. With vacant eyes staring at the grey-white ceiling, she returns to a scene from a few weeks ago.

Sarah was biking home in high spirits after a long day of eight periods at school. The physics teacher had demonstrated the existence of charged particles. This time Sarah had the feeling that she had really discovered something. Even from the furthest seat in the back she had been able to follow the lesson perfectly as the teacher rubbed a glass rod with a cat skin and then held the statically charged rod to the hair of Cindy, the outraged cat lover, so that it stood out straight. As soon as Sarah began biking up the driveway at number 7 Nightingale Lane her mood changed. It wasn't that she had decided to be bad-tempered; it was just a thing that had been happening recently.

'I know what you need,' Mieke said in an attempt to cheer Sarah up. 'A girlfriend party.' Mieke had stopped browsing through *Sweet Homes*, her interior design magazine, and looked at her daughter expectantly. He reading glasses were balanced on the tip of her nose. 'I'd like to see who you hang around with. That interests me as a mother ... Gee, there's less and less in these magazines. Why do I buy them, anyway? Look at this, I've gone through the whole thing and there are maybe two articles that I want to read, that's it. Boxwood has to be insulated in the winter: even a little child knows that.'

'They make it all up,' Sarah answered.

'Yes, I think you're right. The two of us should write something like this someday, and this is a magazine.' Mieke tossed the periodical onto the coffee table. 'Seriously, Sarah, make a list of all the girlfriends you want to invite for your seventeenth birthday.'

'Mama, I already had my birthday last month.'

'Exactly. So it's about time. Everyone is welcome here.' Her mother didn't mean a word of it, or she meant it but failed to see how she herself nipped potential friendships in the bud and chased everyone away. It all began with her nineteenth-century greeting: 'Good day, young lady. Whom do I have the honour of addressing?'

Sarah distrusted her mother's longing for her to have girlfriends. She did have girlfriends, but not the kinds of friends she herself would have chosen if she had had the final say. There were two of them, three if you counted Emily, but Emily didn't count. She was almost family for Sarah. Emily's increasing height was marked on the inside of Sarah's closet with lines and dates. Emily was the one who automatically grabbed Sarah's hand during those dreadful dancing lessons that were part of the gymnastics curriculum at their girls' school.

The two other girlfriends had put themselves forward, oddly enough. They were girls whose names she probably wouldn't remember later on. The girls had a great desire to be near her. Their round, innocent eyes followed her through the school corridors. Their wardrobes were even more appalling than hers. Each one had decided on her own to worship Sarah. It was exhausting to always have to distance yourself from them in public. One of the two sent Sarah an unvarnished declaration of love in an envelope with a swan on it. It contained a flowery description of friendship with frankly pornographic overtones. When the other girl found out, a war broke out between the two that so engrossed them that they forgot Sarah altogether.

'You do have girlfriends, don't you?'

'I don't want a birthday party, Mama. That's for little kids.'

'That's impossible,' Mieke said. 'Not wanting a birthday party? It's abnormal.'

'I don't like to invite girlfriends to do things.'

'Are you ashamed?'

'You don't invite any of your girlfriends over, do you? The only ones who come here sometimes are Elvira and Ulrike.'

'That's different.'

'Everything is different.'

'You're getting awfully fresh. Papa and I hope you get stricter teachers next year.'

'I'm going on the school trip to Spain like a good girl, right?' She could never explain to anyone the logic of living in a family headed by a dictator disguised as a slave.

Sarah is aware of the drops running down her eyelids. The shower head is still leaking. How long was she out? A second? A year? The shame, along with her consciousness, branches off at lightning speed, and her body fills up again. She reaches for a towel. The foaming shower water flows to the drain in the navel of the stall. Sarah sobs silently into a large bath towel that's as stiff as cardboard. She doesn't seem to fit into the time in which she's growing up. Her parents are nothing like any of the other parents of the nineties. She has to watch out or she'll get swept along into their world.

After jumping into her clothes she accepts the drink from Emily. Sickeningly sweet Batida de Coco: the only way she sees of getting through the evening without dying of the embarrassment she's suffered. The bottle makes the rounds at a brisk tempo. Soon the world becomes one irresistible joke. Caught in a timeless no man's land, she and Emily jump from one absurd thought to another until their roommates start yawning in turns and announce that they're going to sleep. No sooner do they clamber into the bunk bed and turn their backs to Emily and Sarah than the two start imitating them.. 'Shut up,' shouts one of the girls. 'That's enough of that,' shouts the other. Sarah can't stop laughing. The more they mimic the girls' speech, the more hilarious it gets. Halfway through 'that's enough of that' they both bend over double.

The others get so annoyed that they threaten to call in the teachers. They whine that they just want to sleep, goddamn it.

'If you swear like that, then I won't be able to sleep,' Sarah giggles.

'Look, I'm really lying down now.' Emily throws herself on the bed and drops her head onto the flat pillow. 'Me, too,' Sarah says. She lies down next to Emily. The bed linens are filthy. The air in the no-star hotel is so stuffy that you can hardly walk through it without coughing. Her mother would never set foot in a room like this. Sarah is still wearing her sweatpants, which in this heat is a bad idea. The pants stick and scratch her skin. She kicks off the down cover, sits bolt upright and looks around the room in the semi-darkness. It's as quiet here as it is in the house at number 7 Nightingale Lane at night. The night paints a black edge around her thoughts. Cobain's widow picks up her note pad and writes down the lyrics to a new song in the dark, grieving for someone she doesn't yet know.

The next day they start the journey back by bus. As they board the bus, each of them is given a half-frozen donut. Sarah suppresses the urge to gag and offers her donut to Emily. 'Oh, Montignac is going to be so angry,' she says with a smile full of sadistic joy and powdered sugar. Today, a few centuries after Rubens, all normal women are too fat. At least that's what the fashion world would have them believe. Heroin chic is in. But in Flanders, skipping a meal or pushing a piece of cake aside is simply impossible. It's an insult to the host or hostess. For many well-mannered, overweight, desperate women, the knight in shining armour is Michel Montignac. He forbids carbohydrates, but he's a boon to the butchers' guild and the fat producers. Butter, cream, chocolate, bacon: all diet products, according to the revolutionary Montignac diet. An exemplary diet meal now consists of a juicy beefsteak with mayonnaise and Béarnaise sauce, all in unlimited amounts. The first doctors and beauty specialists approach the diet with scientific suspicion, but later they give it the green light and shovel in the food. Emily's mother—a doctor's wife, no less—is also a Montignac disciple. She's glad there's finally a sound diet that her daughter can follow.

Sitting next to Sarah on the threadbare bus seats, Emily claps the sugar from her hands. She's dead tired. The plan is to cover the entire seven hundred miles back to the homeland in one go, with short breaks along the way. After forty minutes the toilet is overflowing. After forty-five minutes the toilet door is locked because Cindy has thrown up next to the commode.

'She's pregnant! By a Spaniard with a moustache!' come the shrieks from the bus. Fifteen minutes later the bus is pulled over by the Spanish highway police. They have to stop at a highway restaurant and wait for a replacement for the driver. The man had already been driving thirty-eight hours straight. The girls are all given free drinks. The restaurant personnel are told in English to keep it alcohol-free, but it turns out they only understand Spanish. One of the employees disappears with Marijke, the biggest slut of the year. They go to a storage room in the back.

A couple of hours pass and no replacement has shown up yet. The quarrels and annoyances that have been smouldering between the classmates are ratcheted up into existential crises. Buckets of tears are shed and serious oaths of vengeance are sworn because of the treachery committed in the allocation of seats, and earlier in the allocation of rooms, and because they're all worn to a frazzle. When the bus pulls out five hours later with the same driver, Sarah is suddenly stricken by raging homesickness. She's desperate to be home and alone. She doesn't want to invite any girlfriends over. The fact that no one ever comes to visit except Emily is her choice entirely.

Emily is lying next to her, sound asleep. Her mouth is hanging open. She keeps encroaching on Sarah's half and exhaling her peanut breath into Sarah's face. Emily wakes up with a start and snort when the bus makes a turn and suddenly stops. She discovers the spot of drool on her own shoulder and looks at Sarah reproachfully, as if she had been the one to slam on the brakes. The twenty-two-hour bus ride is torture.

The coup de grâce comes at their final destination, the Brussel Noord station. The girls stagger out of the bus. Crying and needling each other, they say goodbye as if they were being torn apart forever by cruel fate, personified by their parents. Through their tears the girls turn to their parents and nod: 'Yes, those are my suitcases.'

Dead tired, ill-treated, evil-smelling, close to exhaustion: that's how Sarah feels. 'Oh dear oh dear. No staying up late tonight,' says Mieke at her first glimpse of her daughter. Sarah hands her mother the dirty backpack and follows her to the car. 'Carry your own backpack. Anyone who can go on a trip can also carry her own luggage.'

Sarah dumps her backpack in the trunk and pulls the back car door open. She sits down on the back seat and tries to stifle her tears.

The parents' cars take off in all directions, driving through the acid rain of Belgium.

'We've got to get up early tomorrow ...' Mieke pauses for a moment of dramatic silence to arouse Sarah's curiosity. Her words evaporate into the void. Sarah is mute in her comatose twilight zone.

'... tomorrow we're leaving for America!' Mieke announces exultantly.

A sniff is heard from the back seat, like the sound of a small dog. In the rear-view mirror Mieke can see Sarah's entire sweaty, cumin-smelling body react with a jolt. There it is again, the sadness that flows beneath the surface of life and crops up in Sarah with a certain regularity.

'Seat belt!' Mieke says.

Sarah grabs the seat belt mechanically. She clicks it into the black slot. Although she wants to stop crying, she can't. She isn't cried out yet. Her body is tired. Otherwise everything is fine and dandy, except for the fact that she hates everybody, especially her unpredictable mother.

'Boo hoo,' Sarah blurts out.

'What's this? What's with her?' Mieke asks out loud to someone out of the picture. The windshield wipers make it hard to see. She's bent way over the steering wheel in an effort to complete the journey home in safety. 'Anybody else would be jumping for joy!'

'I don't want to go,' sniffles Sarah.

'We're going.'

'I just got back.'

'I can't make any sense out of you. You ridicule us because we hardly ever go anywhere ... '

'I don't like to travel.'

'You ought to thank your father for working so hard for you. The merger is almost finished and he's been given a bonus, so he's insisting that we take a trip. He's all happy and cheerful for once, and you're going to sabotage the whole thing, right? I can't believe this.' Mieke brings her fighting spirit into play. 'You are going!'

Why can't she get over something as banal as being tired? Half the planet is walking around tired and the other half is dazed from malnutrition. But they haven't just come back from a gruelling school trip. Sarah wants to roll up in a ball like a hedgehog, in the winter of her own pink bedspread. She's a small child in adult packaging.

The next morning Sarah is sitting buckled up between her parents in the first class section of a Boeing 747. Together with four hundred other passengers they take off for the West Coast of the United States of America. When the airplane engines start rumbling and the plane lunges forward like a wild animal, leaping into the air, a primitive power awakens within Sarah. She's never going to be like her parents. She's never, ever going to get married. She's going to move to a foreign country and perform everywhere there and get rich with her music. Uncle Jempy will be proud. Finally she's reached clarity about what she wants to do and they've only just taken off. For the remainder of the flight she sleeps under the blue airline blanket.

They're going to drive down the West Coast in a big rented car. While Stefaan and Mieke test the air conditioning in the parking lot and arrange the water bottles in the trunk, Sarah plays on her miniature guitar. She juggles with various chords until a new number slowly emerges. Back in the car she keeps on practising. After a couple of hours silence is imposed on her. Mieke takes the earplugs out of her ears in order to repeat the safety instructions in case fire should break out.

Stefaan shoves CDs into the CD player, and for the hundredth time he tells them about Bob Dylan's religious period. He also knows a lot about the chemical industry in California. He's virtually unstoppable. The stooped man who used to pace through the house is gone, and in his place is his energetic, silly-joke-telling twin brother. 'We'll let him get away with it, won't we, Sarah, with a merger like that?' says Mieke, laughing. Sarah even forgets to be irritated by him, just as she consistently strolls fifteen feet behind her mother on this continent so they won't be seen together.

Without any outside observers they function just like a model family. The three of them are floating on a cloud of familial satisfaction. Mieke allows a twenty-minute margin into her schedule. Every time they take their seats in a restaurant and start leafing through the menu, Mieke sighs how wonderful it is not to have to do anything. 'Enjoy this trip while you can,' she exhorts her daughter. 'Other children don't get such a chance to see the world.'

On the beach at Carmel, Sarah writes a postcard to Emily. Emily is spending the summer in the south of France. Sarah writes about her mother's nagging, the masses of cute, interested boys, and her plan to earn tons of money with her totally original, freshly composed songs.

Stefaan wants to have an adventure in the Grand Canyon, a three days' drive from here, but Mieke has objections. There's no way she's going to risk her life in that horrible gorge, where it's probably swarming with irresponsible tourists who are fighting each other for the best view so they can go back home with some trite bit of video. After a discussion that lasts for miles they strike a deal. Mieke agrees to visit the Grand Canyon with Sarah and Stefaan, but she's not going on the adventurous hike in the small canyon farther on, the least touristically exploited canyon in the entire state. 'Make sure you take two litres of water per hiker,' Mieke reads aloud from the travel guide, which she consults several times a day. The air conditioning in the rented car is running full blast. Mieke also implores them not to deviate from the paths, not to pick any wild plants, not to touch any carcasses. 'Helicopters cannot come to rescue you. Do me a favour and stick together.' The guide has marked the hike as 'simple'.

Stefaan and Sarah descend into the canyon. Chasms and fissures in the ravaged face of the earth give way to a deep red-brown wound, gaping and abandoned for centuries. Nothing is growing here, and it doesn't seem possible that any animal could live here. This place knows no mercy. The sun underscores that with its most fluorescent yellow. Stefaan walks with his backpack in front, sun visor on his head. Sarah follows in his footsteps. She becomes hypnotized by the simultaneous thudding of their shoes in the sand. They walk on as the world of brown earth passes by.

'Let's take a break,' says Stefaan after an hour. 'We have to make sure we drink enough water.'

Stefaan and Sarah drink greedily. They let the water flow from the corners of their mouths like babies. 'This is how Moses walked through the wilderness,' says Stefaan cheerfully. He screws the cap back on the bottle and sets out again at a brisk pace. He's almost running.

'You wouldn't be able to maintain that speed for forty years,' says Sarah. Sweating profusely, she tries to keep up with him.

'You would if you were running away.'

They haven't met a single tourist or any other living soul. The deeper they penetrate the chasm the less likely that is to happen. Her eyelids begin caking together from the salt and sand. Her legs are filthy. Suddenly Stefaan stops dead in his tracks.

'Listen.'

Sarah stops. There's nothing to hear but her own heavy breathing. She stops panting and hears nothing. Less than nothing.

'The big nothing,' Stefaan smiles. 'The deepest silence in the world. Nothing nothing nothing.'

Sarah doesn't see what there is to smile at in this gothic environment. She dares not think what would happen if the light bulb of the sun were to be turned off and they were left standing here.

Stefaan starts singing. 'Nothing nothing nothing.'

Is he serious with this chorale? 'Papa, Jesus. Don't be so childish.'

Sarah is dying of embarrassment, although it helps her to realize that there's no one here to see them. She hears the wisps of sound blowing in the air, she notes the biting of the teeth on the 'n', the mighty bridge of the 'o', the cavernous formulation from tongue tip to throat in 'thing', and she feels the distance growing between herself and this man.

By the time the first of their two bottles is emptied they've already made quite some headway, Sarah walking in her father's wake. He comes to a halt at a spectacular view: a hyperrealistic hologram of rocks and tufts of green. Like a large-scale landowner indicating the extent of his holdings, he waves his arms around with exaggerated sweeps. He points to the big rock in the distance, which is where he wants to walk.

'Can't do it, Papa. According to the map we have to go straight ahead here.'

'Give me that map.' He jerks the map out of Sarah's hands. 'From this point we'll follow the grey stripe.'

'No, we have to follow the blue path. That grey stripe isn't a walking path.'

Stefaan rubs the tip of his shoe in the dust. 'And what if we call this a path?' he says with a smile.

'No, I'm not going with you. You go, I'll wait here.'

'Saaraah, we promised your mother we'd stick together. Trust your papa just this once. We're not going to die, you know,' he hisses. 'Those travel guides are always incredibly careful about making people like your mother feel that they're being taken *au sérieux*.'

Stefaan descends the steep slope, past a thorny bush. Sarah follows him down the twisting path. He's moving so fast, he's so eager, that she feels like a little old grandma who can't keep up. She totters down step by step and holds her arms out protectively to break her fall in case she should trip. 'You have to bounce through your knees,' she hears her father shout. Luckily there are nasty dry bushes growing close together that would break her fall. In her haste she slides and scrapes her leg against a piece of rock.

'Papa, where are you?' she calls.

Why is her father doing this? Why does he exasperate her so? Why is he pushing her over the edge? She could die here, she really could. This isn't some little fantasy out of a book. Sarah calls her father and gets no response. She howls like a hyena. He's just gone. The reality that descends on her is piercing: her father has left her here.

'Papa!' she hears herself shout again. 'Papa!'

All the difficulties she had predicted multiply like lightning. It's going to get dark. Birds of prey will smell their next meal. A bush shakes and is cleft in two by the figure of her father. He's standing there grinning. 'Found me.'

'I hate you, Papa.' She turns around and scrambles back up. 'You always have to ruin everything.'

'It's nothing, it's nothing.' He keeps repeating this the

whole way back, to calm himself more than her. Her father is demented. A normal father would never do such a thing, right? 'Don't say anything to Mama, okay?' he says imploringly when they walk into the lobby of the Grand Inn, a hotel in the park.

The next morning they drive, air conditioner lowing, from the monumental desolation of the canyon to the fata morgana of Las Vegas, a one-day journey. For the first time during the entire trip Mieke does not take out her can of spray disinfectant upon entering the hotel room of the MGM Grand. In every hotel they visit she normally cleans the toilet seat, the telephone receiver, and any other breeding ground of fatal illnesses. The floor is covered in wall-to-wall shag carpeting. Mieke squats down and strokes the carpet like a newborn lamb. 'Feel this, Sarah. This is what not having to do anything feels like.'

On the way to Los Angeles, with Las Vegas disappearing behind them like a sketch in the rear-view mirror, Mieke insists that she's glad to be leaving that madhouse of decadence, although she doesn't sound entirely convincing.

One day later they park the car outside Los Angeles in a much too spacious parking lot along a strip, where the outlet stores are lined up like multicoloured blocks played with by giants. The mega parking lot is almost empty. No grand tour of the West Coast of the States is complete, Stefaan thinks, without a visit to a mammoth Walmart supermarket. Mieke has barely set foot in the Walmart when she claims to have become physically sick. She's going to look for a toilet somewhere else and then drop into the Le Creuset shop farther down the strip.

Sarah follows her father into a Walmart as big as an

airplane hangar. She lets herself be carried along past the wreckage of Western civilization. Jeans so big you could re-stitch them into hot-air balloons; terrifying stuffed animals that are bigger than people; sets of pots and pans you could start a restaurant with; sixty different kinds of pasteurized, deathly-pale cheeses; greeting cards for domestic pets, fewer debts, and amicable divorces; seven million pairs of purple-flecked rubber boots; teabag dryers; buckets of chicken bouillon; billions of packages of baking powder, butter, Béarnaise sauce, baloney, butterscotch, beans. Stefaan takes her along with him to the drugstore, all the way in the back of the supermarket. There her father questions the head pharmacist about the brands of medicines he stocks.

'Listen to that, Sarah. They sell the entire line of medicines produced by my company.'

Sarah wants to escape from this insane, oxygen-depleted biosphere. The pharmacist invites them up to the roof, where the view is unique.

Followed by the red-ringed eyes of washed-out Walmart employees, they climb the metal stairs to the roof. The view is no less than astonishing: a plain trampled flat by the giants of Walmart and turned into a canvas that the sun uses to test all its tints of yellow and red.

The manager's beeper goes off. He has to leave. 'But you're both welcome to stay and enjoy the view.'

Sarah and Stefaan walk carefully to the edge of the asphalt roof the size of a soccer field. Down below they see Mieke walking to the car with a big cardboard box in her hands.

Here we stand, all of us together on a roof in faraway America. We join Stefaan and walk over to his daughter.

'I hear you've made enormous progress with your

music lessons.' His hesitant attempt at conciliation.

'I'm writing my own songs now, and when we get back home I'm going to ask Emily if she wants to form a group.'

'That sounds like a good plan.'

Do it, Sarah, we say encouragingly. We're big rock 'n' roll fans.

'I want to stand on a stage as big as this roof, with thousands of people at my feet. As soon as I play the first note, they'll all start screaming.'

'That's a nice dream. Go for it, never give up,' Stefaan urges his daughter.

Never give up sounds rather defensive to us. If there's one sentence that typifies us it's this: at every setback we step on the gas.

Back downstairs, Stefaan and Sarah hear music coming from a lonely pickup truck in the parking lot. Behind the steering wheel is a man slumped down in his seat and smoking a cigarette.

'Sometimes you have to admit that it's bad, or at least that it's not so good,' says Stefaan cautiously.

'What do you mean?'

'I think Bob was drinking back then. Every time he releases a new CD everybody says it's his worst, but in this case it's really true, I'm afraid. *Down in the Groove* from 1988. I even feel a little embarrassed for him. What do you think? Do you think this is any good?'

'I'd rather listen to grunge and electro,' says Sarah.

'But after that he had a comeback,' says Stefaan, as if she needed to be comforted. 'Bob never gives up.'

On the way to school on the first day of the term, Emily gives a flippant description of her vacation in France. They had rented a house there with a swimming pool.

Suddenly her voice drops an octave. 'It happened,' says Emily in a whisper. She went to bed with a good-looking surfer. He lives in the coastal town near Nice where her parents had rented the house. One morning her parents had gone out for croissants, but three hours later they still hadn't come back. The surfer came to the door. He offered his services to clean the swimming pool. She let him in. As he began cleaning the pool, she sat and dangled her feet in the water. He carefully put his equipment on the ground and came to sit behind her to give her a massage. And that's how it happened. On a deck chair next to the swimming pool. In the full sun. Then she took a shower and he went on to the next villa. Fortunately her parents stayed away long enough at the outdoor cafe where they were hanging out. Sarah dishes up an adventurous version of her trip to America and holds forth on the five songs she completed.

The legendary duo of Marie-Hélène and Suri are in Sarah's class this year. Marie-Hélène is from a noble family and an insufferable bitch besides. Sarah can see this at a glance. Suri is a mysterious Asian who walks around with a parasol to protect her from the sun. Marie-Hélène and Suri are inseparable.

If you're going by physical appearance, Suri is by far the more striking of the two. It's not just her angular face with her light blue eyes (coloured lenses). She's also very small and delicate. You'd easily overlook her if she didn't radiate such a relentless beauty and if she didn't have such a striking wardrobe, which consists of a mixture of rags dragged out of the gutter and sleek designer clothing.

Marie-Hélène is the one with the big mouth. During every lesson she makes her lack of interest perfectly clear right from the first minute. She's the type who is thought to be too clever to ever amount to much, because she'll probably end up making a big mess of things along the way on account of her nonconformity. When Marie-Hélène is asked to come up to the blackboard to solve a matrix equation, for instance, she writes out a whole new problem that even the teacher has to wrestle with.

Sarah is having a very hard time getting herself psyched for the new school year. As a girl you're expected to be full of admiration for the miracle of nature, but according to Sarah there's a lot not to admire. Her body has lumps, her nipples hurt, and she had to lie on her back in bed to fasten her jeans. At the most unexpected moments her body will give her a blood red indication of her unfertilized condition. You can't appear in public with such a body, but it's impossible to make her mother understand this. They never talk about bodies. Every day she gets up with hope in her heart. She can only hope that an extra vacation day has been added for the death of Lady Di, that the underground atomic testing has gone terribly wrong, or that an unlikely flood has hit Nightingale Lane and the water has come right up to her window. But Nightingale Lane is not in Bangladesh. After this she hopes for some kind of physical defect, a vague pain in the stomach, maybe a virus that would keep her out of school, an imaginary migraine attack. Sarah's body refuses to go along with her plans, however; it does not break down. In fact it frustrates her at every turn by insisting on being in perfect health, despite a freezing cold shower, seven tablespoons of coarse mustard, and an onion under her armpit.

Sarah avoids the mirror more and more. She hates the bulges that are appearing all over the place. She wants to be the way she was before. She's jealous of her younger self. It looks at her from a photograph: wiry, in full action, tennis racquet in hand. Mieke says she's finally there, and that every day she's a little bit more of a woman. A young version of Granny, that is. Something within her that's ready and waiting, pushing outward like a branch of a tree.

Sarah goes with Emily to the back of her garden. Behind the big chestnut tree they share a cigarette and smoke it as fast as they can. Flocks of birds rise up from the cornfield that borders on the garden. A few children are chasing each other, screaming and pelting each other with unripe ears of corn. A batch of new families has moved into the housing estate recently. Emily tells Sarah about the invitation from Marie-Hélène and Suri. They've asked them to come to their music studio for a jam session. Two children's heads pop up among the cornstalks and duck back down when they see they've been discovered. Emily puts out the cigarette and buries the butt.

Marie-Hélène and Suri heard Emily and Sarah play at the school party last year. They threw together a provisional group that included Mireille, who is a horrible bore but who can sing surprisingly well.

'Don't expect too much of this,' says Emily, handing Sarah a King peppermint. 'Tomorrow at five at Marie-Hélène's. Oh, yeah, we're supposed to say MH.'

Sarah hurries home. Chances are she won't be able to go. Mieke's house rule is that appointments must be made at least two weeks in advance. If they aren't, Mieke doesn't recognize them and they don't get entered in her big appointment book.

Mieke's current reading matter is lying on the kitchen table: Emile Zola's *Germinal*. Old writers don't use dirty words. Sarah browses through today's newspaper, which was already folded up and stacked on the old paper pile.

Sarah's words are lost when Mieke opens the door of the dishwasher. Hot steam hits her in the face. Mieke unloads the white plates. She sets the table for breakfast early tomorrow morning.

'No, Mama. There's no hidden agenda here. I'm just going to play music tomorrow with Emily.'

'I have to wonder what you're keeping from me. Why don't you tell me anything? Why is this whole house laden with secrets? You're just like your father. He doesn't talk about anything, either. Why not, for heaven's sake?'

'Because all my life I haven't been allowed to do anything!'

'Now what are you saying?'

'It's true. I'm never allowed to go anywhere. I always have to stay at home.'

'All you need is the wherewithal. If you let me know two weeks ahead of time you can do whatever you want. Everyone has a right to their own lunacy. You can do anything.'

'I can never do anything.'

'What a fresh mouth,' says Mieke as she takes the glasses out of the dishwasher and polishes them again with a dry cotton towel. 'Where did you learn that? Did you learn it at school? I should have known. My mother warned me. It's my own fault. I should have had you tutored privately at home. I should have listened to her.'

'So you used to be disobedient?'

'A private tutor,' Mieke continues, following the same track. 'That would have been best.' Something else she can sincerely blame herself for.

'And then lock me up in a cellar somewhere.'

'You know what the problem is?' Mieke asks, more to herself than to Sarah. 'I raised you too liberally. That's it. I would never have spoken to my parents that way or I would have been sent straight to the cellar. Oh, well, no use thinking about it. You've had it much too easy, that's it. Everything was handed to you on a platter.'

'I work too, don't I?'

'If you do, you're darn good at hiding it.'

'We're going to Marie-Hélène's house to make music.' A strategic argument.

'Ah, Marie-Hélène, the daughter of the count who was killed in that accident. So you're going to her house?' Mieke's voice shoots up.

'Yes, tomorrow from three to nine at her house.'

'The poor girl, losing your parents just like that. What kind of a girl is Marie-Hélène?'

'I don't know. Just normal.'

'Now that's what I call beautiful, that someone from a noble family can act normal,' says Mieke without a hint of irony. 'There, you see, people with standing have the simplest way of acting. They don't need to be showy, they just act normal. Distinguished. You don't have that with all those nouveaux riches.'

'I'll find out tomorrow. If I can go, that is.'

'It's fine, as long as your grades don't suffer. That would be the end of all this going out.'

A couple of weeks ago, Ulrike the neighbour lady revealed the whole story of the castle while Sarah was within earshot. Everyone in the village and on the mountain knows that the count's children have moved back into the castle. The castle is located in a secluded part of the woods between two villages on a large estate that's completely walled in. Noble families are the butt of many jokes in the nineties. Almost all of them are flat broke, and they stopped having servants or maintaining their bastard children a long time ago. They can barely afford hay for their horses, and they give the animals away to *manèges*. Valuable antiques and china services that have been in the family for centuries are auctioned off. Whole families cluster around one heater in one room in the castle. Sad. Most of them have pulled down the shutters on their castles and fled to apartments in the capital or left for Switzerland with their hoarded treasure. No one even looks at the castles anymore.

That impoverishment does not apply to the higher classes sitting on large family fortunes, and it certainly doesn't apply to the nobility who are still very active in businesses where there's good money to be made. The modern count helped lay the groundwork for the compact disc and thus amassed a huge fortune, but he also must have had unimaginable capital and connections. A celebrated architect was called in for the swimming pool and for general modernization. He was the only one who succeeded in reconciling the modern and the historic during the seventies. The architect used sustainable materials. He more or less restored the old castle to its former glory, but the dusty windows suggest that the count never actually lived there. Most of the time he shut himself up in the caretaker's lodge in the garden, which had been converted into a music studio. Endless nightly recording sessions took place in the lodge. Limousines drove back and forth. Legendary musicians were spotted in the village cafe. The large caretaker's lodge had a nasty reputation. The police from the neighbouring city had already broken in a couple of times with sniffer dogs, and the dogs had barked their heads off, Ulrike added.

Then in Switzerland the count met the woman who would become his wife and who gave him three children. They all lived together in the castle until ten years ago. Then one day there was a death notice in *De Standaard*. The count and his wife had 'unexpectedly passed away in Tibet'. No one in the village or on the mountain knew what he was doing in Tibet. There were some who wanted to give the impression that they were buddy-buddy with the count, but none of them was sufficiently convincing, their only evidence being smudged black-and-white clippings from the newspaper. Everyone knew that the count had been an eccentric, decadent society figure. He was always headed for someplace else, galli-vanting all over the world. People are only too glad to fill in the blanks and make insinuations. He was ahead of his time, and had even taken a course in Tibet with the Dalai Lama, or he travelled back in time there once with George Harrison for the recording of a new CD. Anything was possible, according to the lore kept alive by the neighbours. In any case, after the death of their parents the two girls moved in with a distant aunt and the boy was sent to an institution. Now that the oldest girl is twenty-one, she can act as the official guardian of the two younger children. The three of them live together in the castle.

Every villager and every resident of the housing estate has had at least a glimpse of the castle. A pair of brothers who own a little private plane fly over the village every year to make aerial photographs. The photos are eagerly snatched up by the inhabitants of the villas on the mountain who have just had swimming pools installed. You can see in the photos how large and well maintained their domains are. The brothers also take annual photos of the castle and its grounds, which are then hung in the town hall among the pictures of the other pearls of the area. The photos show that behind the castle there's also a swimming pool, a large caretaker's lodge, a pond, and a gigantic garden house. In the fantasy of some of the vil-lage women this is a huge closet with seven thousand pairs of shoes. Not true, Ulrike says, who is no gossip-monger.

Mieke wants to take Sarah to the castle by car. Then afterwards they can have a lengthy discussion of the tiles in the entrance hall, the fragrance of the flower garden, and the painting of the gutters.

'Suri's mother is taking us, it's all been arranged,' Sarah says.

'Don't make it too late,' says Mieke as she stores the vacuum cleaner away in the utility room. 'And not now either. It's time for bed. I'm going upstairs myself. No use waiting up for your father. By the time he's finished pottering around, or whatever he's doing in his shack, I'd be sound asleep anyway, so I might as well go up now.'

When the noises in the bathroom die out, Sarah goes upstairs in her stocking feet to listen to music in the attic. There are plenty of other rooms in the house where she could listen to music, but in the attic she feels most at ease. It takes at least ten minutes to climb the steel fold-out steps without making any noise.

At the far end of the large attic, in a sea of fibreglass, there's an old wicker cradle, lampshades, and couple of boxes full of notebooks and photographs. On a small table are Sarah's collection of scribbled song lyrics. She kneels down next to the spherical radio-CD player. It glistens in the semi-darkness like the eyeball of a fly. Tethered to the six-foot cord of her headphones, like a goat grazing in circles in the musical meadow, Sarah listens to a compilation CD. After half an hour she gives up. It's hopeless. There's no way she's going to be able to brush up her musical knowledge in one evening. Suri and MH are undoubtedly walking musical encyclopaedias. She's going to have to do her best to hide her limited knowledge of grunge. If she survives one round with

MH and Suri she can consider herself lucky.

On the roof of the hobby shed she sees a point of light. Her father is standing in the solitude of the housing estate, smoking a cigar. Ever since they stood together on the roof of the Walmart he has become withdrawn and silent again. He's that strange, distracted man who irritates the hell out of her, especially when he eats, or rather: when he noisily dumps the food into his cavernous maw. Sarah knows that at his work he's a man of authority and prestige, but at home she never sees any sign of this. Whether it's the dissatisfied building contractor, the tax inspector, or his very own daughter, he always lets Mieke do the dirty work. He's a coward, a gutless bastard who does weird things in his hobby shed. What does he ever do for her? Does he help her in any way? He takes her to music lessons, he pulls up his chair at the table, and they pass each other in the house, but that's it. She even has serious doubts that he's her real father (that dry cough, that shy, shifty smile, those bad table manners). Maybe she was switched with another baby in the hospital, or her mother had an affair and all those childhood photos were simply doctored.

The next day during the second period after lunch everyone is sitting at their desks dozing in the autumn sun. The voice of the French teacher is grating. Last month she didn't waste much time on words of welcome. After two introductory statements in broken Dutch she switched to elegant French. Since then she has spoken French exclusively and expects her pupils to do the same. Today they're discussing the *passé simple*, a totally overlooked tense reserved for archaic and literary texts. The French teacher asks if anyone has heard of Jules Laforgue, a decadent writer. His favourite tense was *passé simple*, as the teacher would have them believe. She asks if anyone knows what decadent means. For the first time in her school career MH raises her hand. MH says in flawless French that she is inspired by the Decadents and by Gainsbourg.

'Gainsbourg comes later,' says the teacher in French. 'Much later.'

'But Gainsbourg wrote a song about it,' MH protests. Twenty-five mouths begin to chatter. '"Décadanse." 1972. About anal sex.' She has most of the class braying with laughter. With the triumphant nonchalance of someone who knows everything, she begins scribbling in her new notebook while telling her neighbour what the rest of the song is about: a woman who is made to bend over. The chaos in the class increases. The teacher calls a couple of names. MH turns to Sarah: 'Emma says you're coming tomorrow.'

'Emily, you mean,' says Sarah flatly. 'Yeah, yeah.' The first commandment says that overly tempestuous joy should always be tempered. You must beat the exclamation point down to a bland announcement.

'Sarah et Marie-Hélène, dehors!'

They stand up and go outside. MH is wearing a white lace dress, the very picture of decadence. There's an enormous tear yawning in the bodice. A lace bra is peeking out at the daylight, and at curious eyes. Mrs. De Decker, the homeroom teacher, already warned her about it this morning. If she wears that dress tomorrow she'll be suspended.

'Bass guitar?'

'No, regular guitar.'

MH's hand disappears into a pocket of her dress. She takes out a little metal box and walks away toward the grotto, the former place of pilgrimage for the nuns and now the clandestine smoking den for the pupils.

Whenever school closes unexpectedly early, Emily and Sarah like to bike into town to hang out and do a little shopping. Sarah always has to rush like crazy in order to get home on time. Today they go to a second-hand shop where Emily talks Sarah into buying a dress for next to nothing. To her surprise, the Victorian children's dress of black velvet fits Sarah like a glove. Emily encourages her to make the purchase.

The next morning Sarah wears the new dress to the breakfast table. Mieke, loudly clearing her throat, makes it all too obvious that she has decided not to react to her daughter's velvet dress.

'Wow, that's tight,' says Stefaan, with the subtlety of a man at the head of a company. After years of carrying out efficient policy without any flirting and with a profound fear of sexual intimidation, delicacy has gone by the wayside. 'A little too warm, wouldn't you say?' Sarah could strangle him.

Emily and Sarah make their way cautiously down the muddy driveway, Sarah with her guitar on her back and Emily clutching a case containing her drumsticks. They have great expectations with regard to the castle in the distance: a forest of lilies at the entrance gates, burning candles with immense wicks on the steps, a butler who waits for visitors day and night, polishing the brass lions' heads until he can see himself in them, a coach house with a fleet of antique cars, and everywhere the impassive busyness of garden personnel and lackeys. It becomes increasingly clear that what she is walking toward is a big, dilapidated facade. The castle strikes her as languishing and sad. The houses in the housing estate are nowhere near this big, but not a single villa is so neglected. The gutter is sagging, and green streaks made by copper pipes are running down from the roof. There are large damp spots on the outer walls, and plastic is flapping in the battered eye sockets of the window frames.

An eye-catching, bright yellow sports car is parked facing the crumbling stairs. It's a classic English Bentley, with lots of glistening chrome and a gleaming little horse on the trunk lock.

Emily rings the doorbell. She looks around somewhat uneasily in the gathering autumn darkness. It's a good thing they waited in the woods for half an hour. You should never arrive exactly on time; it isn't cool.

Footsteps are heard in the castle passageways. There's a stiff breeze. It's as if the double, wooden entrance doors had been opened by a single gust of wind. Before they quite realize it they're being piloted into the house by a blonde woman.

'Jules,' she says, introducing herself. She is obviously related to MH, but this woman has climbed higher out of the gene pool. A top model from the nineties: lean and tall as a giraffe, hollow-eyed, at home in another world of gruesome fairy tales.

'We've come for Marie-Hélène,' says Emily.

'She's in her studio in the garden.' She has a rasping, sleepy voice that betrays lots of cigarettes and long nights. 'Come with me.'

There are large bags filled with rubbish in the entrance hall. They look up at a very large painting of an important man from long ago. He's wearing tight white riding breeches and a blue velvet jacket with gold buttons. His fingers grasp a walking stick. He looks despondently around the room as if he could step out of the frame at any moment. He could be one of those men who die of grief, just like her grandfather. They enter a ballroom. The late afternoon light is streaming in on two sides of this ship, which is being propelled into an endless garden. Rising from the parquet floor is a grand piano and the four curled legs of a massive oak dining table with only one chair beside it. Three other chairs are lying on their sides like wounded soldiers and are connected by pieces of cloth, kitchen towels, and bath towels. The tent camp is held together by clothes pins and is pitched in the middle of the heated, airy space.

'Xavier!' Jules calls, and she looks under the sheets.

Lying on a mountain of pillows near the double patio doors are magazines and a book with a cracked spine next to a bottle of red wine and a bag of Cheetos. An extremely expensive wall tapestry is hanging askew on the wall. Damsels dance stiffly around a squirrel, in brown autumn colours. Below the tapestry is a can of red latex paint with its lid off. Mieke would kill for a tapestry like that.

The music is turned up so loud that the gigantic crystal chandelier in the ballroom is almost singing along. The good-looking woman drops onto the mountain of pillows and immerses herself in a glossy magazine, *Les Inrockuptibles*. She makes annotations in a CD review with a red felt-tip. Sarah isn't sure if she's deliberately pretending not to see them, or if she's just the type of person who lets the whole world go down the tubes while she concentrates on whatever it is she's doing. She doesn't even look up when an older, heavyset woman comes in with the hose of a vacuum cleaner draped around her neck, the way her mother does at home.

From now on Sarah is one small, trivial, but nevertheless significant step ahead of her mother by entering the world of the true aristocracy, the aristocracy who don't care a whit about status.

'Very ordinary people,' she'll say to her mother. 'Very

normal. They also have a housekeeper. And their rooms are quite a bit larger than ours, of course.'

They have to wait a very long time. Emily has already lit a cigarette, as has the good-looking woman. The cigarette is almost finished when the woman suddenly looks up from her magazine and says, 'Marie- Hélène is in the studio, the building behind the swimming pool and the garden. You'll find it.'

Jules sits up. Her head is nodding to the music. Squatting down next to the towel tent, she pulls one of the towels away and shouts, 'Come on, Xavier, you've been sitting in there long enough. Come on out, lovely boy.' Suddenly her voice takes on a cheerful tone. Whoever or whatever is hiding in there is not going to get punished.

Sarah and Emily go into the garden to look for MH. The back of the castle is as luxurious and well-cared-for as the front is dilapidated. It's as if the front were turning away from curious distant glances and showing off its ugliest side. The caretaker's lodge is quite a distance behind the swimming pool, next to the large pond. It looks like an enormous country house from a southern state in America, one of those houses that overlook the vast expanse of a cotton plantation. The door of the caretaker's lodge is open. A whole row of framed golden records are hanging in a place of honour in the entrance hall. Sarah and Emily walk cautiously toward a room from which the monotonous drone of a vacuum cleaner is issuing.

The enormous studio is packed with musical instruments and a disorderly hodgepodge. A sitar is seeking support from the pleated skirt of an accordion, seven classical guitars are all lined up and ready for use, a triangular guitar with flames drawn on it has hung itself by its own ribbon from a nail on the wall. Stacked on top of several layers of carpets and animals skins are some Mexican suitcases, an enormous silver candlestick with one arm missing, animal skulls, and a tower of vinyl records with Howie B. on top. Lying in a chaise longue right next to a speaker from which the monotonous sound of Daft Punk is booming is MH. As soon as she sees them an unintelligible sound escapes her lips. Then from behind an armchair on the other side of the room, Suri pops up. She nods. She's drawing Arabic-looking letters on the wall with a brush full of orange paint. MH reaches into a nearby bag and takes out a handful of breadsticks, which she shoves into her mouth like little swords.

After the tepid reception, Sarah takes her guitar off her back. When MH rolls a joint, Suri comes over to sit beside her on the sofa. Suri snuggles up to MH, who gently strokes her black hair. Sarah sits down on the floor just as she does at home, where she prefers to avoid the chairs. The chance that one of them might get dirty, and that mother's nerves might snap, is greater if you sit in them. For at least an hour MH then cross-examines Sarah and Emily with regard to their musical influences. Titles of albums and bizarre groups fly back and forth. Suri comes up with the strangest names. After a dispute between Suri and Marie-Hélène over the singer from Massive Attack, they decide to jam.

Suri straps on a massive bass guitar that almost throws her off balance. MH shuffles to the middle of the group and snarls something into the mic. What is expected of Emily and Sarah? Communication is reduced to gestures, shrugs, and chords. Sarah breaks into a spontaneous smile when she plugs her guitar in and rams along as background accompaniment to the scraps of Rimbaud that MH is singing, alternating with a couple of blood-curdling shrieks and a hand-knitted, one-word scarf of pure emotion. She has an outstanding voice for the kind of music they're making.

Somewhere in the distance a church bell rings over and over again. In a flash of paralyzing panic, Sarah imagines her mother now swinging into action. She looks at Emily urgently and taps her wrist, where there is no watch. Emily stops drumming and lets the others know that she has to leave.

'Yeah, let's go,' says Sarah. 'I'll let you hear my new numbers the next time.'

'We'll see,' says MH. Suri has already tuned in to *The Real World* on MTV and is no longer responding.

Their heads spinning, Sarah and Emily wander through the evening air. Sarah gratefully accepts the King peppermints that Emily offers. She gives Emily a poke.

'We,' she says with a laugh, 'are going to make it.'

MIEKE 1997

'No luck?' Mieke asks. Stefaan comes sauntering into the parlour. He's been working in his shed for scarcely ten minutes. He smiles cautiously. Long ago, in the notary's office where they first saw each other, he smiled at her in the same way. Back then she thought he was just shy. Mieke doesn't know why he's giving her that wordless smile now. She doesn't see the humour in what she's doing: arranging chocolates in three levels on a silver tray. She had to reach deep into the cabinet, behind the gold-rimmed plates and the heavy box with the silverware, to bring the tray out into the daylight. The tray is too beautiful and too impractical to use very often.

'You try keeping it clean and polished if you have a whole family, a flower garden, and masses of antique rugs to look after,' she says to Stefaan. 'And where's the cake server gone to? It's unbelievable—just when I need it. Would Sarah have run off with it?' She knows that Sarah purloins the mascara and tweezers from the maternal sanctum, so why wouldn't she steal a silver cake server?

'What's happening tomorrow again?' Stefaan asks with a smile. Is he excusing himself by smiling? She can tell him the same thing a hundred times but he doesn't seem to absorb it. When he does the grocery shopping he's sure to forget at least one product, as if forgetting was on the list as well. Sometimes he'll suddenly storm into the hallway, only to come back after thirty seconds muttering, 'What was I going to do again?' She sometimes wonders what planet he lives on.

'Elvira's coming tomorrow for coffee.' She's said this to

Stefaan at least twice. It's been a long time since her bosom friend Elvira dropped in, busy as her life is.

'Ah, Elvira, of course,' says Stefaan. 'I read that you can have your name changed for five thousand francs. You might tactfully mention that to Elvira.'

Even when they were together at boarding school 'Elvira' was considered an outdated name, but the choice of name probably had something to do with her origins. Elvira comes from very chic people, Mieke explains. Her husband doesn't understand that kind of explanation. He starts poking at the mirror with his thick fingers.

'The mirror really isn't clean,' he says quietly. It's the antique mirror inherited from her parents, who were given the mirror by Baron Courtier. Her father did a lot of notarial business for him. The spots that Stefaan thinks he sees are flames in the copper background. A man can't see such things.

'Get away from that and help me here. Go get the step ladder and give me that blue Val Saint-Lambert vase,' says Mieke, standing next to the big antique cabinet in the living room. 'I asked Sarah to polish it. Now I'm curious.'

Stefaan grabs a chair, stands on it, and stretches as far as he can. 'Stefaan, please, standing on the chair in your shoes. Have a little respect for our things.' With a great deal of difficulty he succeeds in hooking the crystal vase with his forefinger and pulling it toward him. He hands it down to the anxious Mieke.

'Just what I thought,' says Mieke, turning the vase around. 'As filthy as a cow's backside. You really have to do everything yourself.'

'Shall I give it a wash?'

'No, never mind. You've helped enough. I'd rather you looked to see if the chickens have enough water. The poor things aren't being treated properly here at all. You really should pay more attention to them. If you have animals you've got to take good care of them. At least that's what I think.'

The house is her domain. The hobby shed and the chickens are his. She keeps her house up in her own way, preferably with as little interference as possible. Mieke spends the next hour working up a storm behind the closed doors of the kitchen and living room. Sarah is in her room practising new guitar chords. The gnarled chords play havoc on Mieke's nerves, as if someone were sounding an alarm in code. Fortunately she has a vacuum cleaner to drown out the ghastly music. On she works, polishing feverishly, as if she were trying to keep ahead of Elvira who could walk in on her any minute with a big telescope to observe the secret preparations.

'Stefaan!' she shouts an hour later, running out with a red face. 'Stefaan! We've been burgled!'

'No!'

'They took the cake server.'

'Boy, you really scared me.'

'But they stole the cake server!'

'That's impossible.'

'Well it's true! The cake server is always in the same place. You know I'm very consistent about that. Sarah doesn't have the cake server either. I've already asked her.'

Theft is the only other logical explanation. Mieke begins formulating a profile of the perpetrator. A very special kind of thief has broken in, a thief who isn't interested in the safe in the office cabinet hidden behind a whole bunch of binders, who also doesn't care about the expensive art nouveau Horta vases or about all of Mieke's twenty-four carat jewellery, but a thief who is interested in only one thing: a cake server.

'That silver cake server is an heirloom from my father's mother's mother. Of course thieves would be interested in it.'

The thief went about his work so artfully that he managed to outwit the high-tech alarm system. It's a balanced alarm system with fifteen all-seeing eyes mounted at crucial locations near entrances, garage doors, and windows that register the least bit of movement, such as the eyelash of a passing bat or a human being who unsuspectingly gets out of bed to go to the kitchen for a glass of water. Immediately, faster than the speed of sound, the alarm goes off at the Securitas surveillance company and the police station. Within a millisecond both the police and Securitas are at your front door. In the meantime, the alarm system is lowing like five million cows whose udders are being kicked.

Her husband and Sarah are mobilized to search for fingerprints and footprints belonging to the thief, who presumably was so clever that he struck during the day, thereby sidestepping their ingenious alarm system.

She prods her lethargic husband to call the police. His attempt to calm her down just adds fuel to her fire. After increasingly impassioned counterarguments from Mieke, the head of the household shambles reluctantly to the phone in the hope that Sarah, his offspring, will hasten to help him by uttering the liberating cry that the cake server has turned up. Just when Stefaan has explained the situation to the police in the most shrouded terms as 'a possible break-in', and they have said that they aren't going to come out for a missing cake server and they wouldn't even do it for the queen, and after Mieke has wondered out loud—so loud that they can hear it on the other end of the line via Stefaan—why in God's name the people on the mountain have to pay handfuls of tax money, given the fact that government services refuse to help people, at that very moment Sarah calls out from the cabinet where the cake plates are kept: 'Found it!'

Now Mieke remembers: she made a mistake when she put everything back five weeks ago. Her neighbour and German scholar Ulrike was *paying a call* (not: had dropped in for a cup of coffee) and had brought a not excessively large Javanese cake.

'Good thing the police didn't come,' Mieke says, relieved and still shaking. 'Those people have better things to do anyway. Everything always turns out for the best!' She waves the cake server around triumphantly. Within a minute her composure is restored. The oxygen has made its way back to her brain.

In the kitchen, ironing the tablecloth a second time, she sees Stefaan standing on the roof of his hobby shed. He is her husband, essentially unfathomable. That's why you stay with someone, because of all the question marks and surprises that remain despite the familiarity. That's why, and also because of the lifelong promise to stay together for better or worse, of course. She looks at her quiet, unobtrusive husband.

At ten o'clock that night, as they stand side by side, each at his or her own sink, brushing their teeth, Stefaan asks, 'Why are you going to so much trouble for Elvira? She's just your girlfriend, isn't she?'

'That's exactly why,' says Mieke. 'I want to give her a proper reception.'

'It looks as if you feel inferior.'

The friendship between Mieke and Elvira goes way back, all the way to the fifties at boarding school. Through all the intervening years, their friendship has acquired an irreplaceable depth, even though they only see each other a couple of times a year, if that, and though their conversations may strike an outsider as superficial.

Stefaan clicks the bridge out of his mouth and runs it under the tap.

'Ew, do you always have to show off that disgusting set of teeth? Isn't it time for a replacement?'

'Would you rather I didn't wear it?' he laughs, opening his gaping mouth wide. 'That bridge is going to outlive me.'

'If you intend to die just to be mean, I'll kill you,' says Mieke, and she kisses him on the shoulder. 'And for the hundredth time, dry off that toothbrush!'

He smiles his toothless smile. He lost those teeth on the farm, where they took excellent care of every living creature except the human ones.

The next day, at exactly two twenty-eight, Mieke is sitting in the flowered armchair, in the sleek, uncompromisingly vacuumed showroom interior that is her living room. The subject of Elvira's divorce will be carefully avoided, as usual. Whether Elvira is really divorced from that German, and exactly what her marital status is, Mieke dare not ask. Mieke's whole life is contained within the facets, nuances, and shadows of the verb 'to dare', especially its negative form. Not true, she says to Stefaan in her own defence when accused of a lack of daring; it's not a question of daring but of tact. The word 'tact' is something her father drilled into her. It's constantly ringing in her ears. Every time she hears someone ask a young childless couple when they're going to start their family, every time she senses a shred of heartache in her friend Elvira, the word 'tact' begins resounding in her head. It's her job to receive Elvira tactfully. She cannot place any stumbling blocks on the path of their friendship.

Being discreet is so undervalued these days. Discretion is a sign of deep respect for Elvira. That's why Mieke never asks about the details of her life, such as her relationships. Each time they're together she can see how appreciative Elvira is. Any angling for juicy bits is strictly forbidden. It's a deprivation of freedom. Shoving a painful question under someone's nose is like holding a pistol to their head. She cannot ask Elvira why her relationship with that blue-eyed German is on the rocks, or if there's any truth to the rumour that he has a child locked away in an institution somewhere. For her part, Elvira is the only one who has not asked Mieke any questions about her brother Jean-Pierre. She's probably already caught wind of the stories that he was involved in all kinds of unsavoury business, that he did time in prison for refusing to pay child support, that he's a womanizer who tears through life in a permanent state of drunken mania and collapses every now and then, only to wrestle with a minor depression. Elvira never asks, parenthetically and ever so delicately, what so many others do: *What's happening with that brother of yours, anyway?*

Mieke licks her index finger in order to turn a page of the *Home Country* magazine lying in her lap when the doorbell rings. It's not at all unexpected, yet she jumps out of her skin. Mieke runs through the afternoon in her head at top speed and smooths out her skirt.

Elvira travels the world over with the fabulously rich. She's accustomed to a bit more than a humble abode like this one with a cup of tea, a Marcolini bonbon, and a slice of cake. There hasn't been any discernible movement at her rose hip-encircled villa a few streets away, not for weeks—not even for months, according to Ulrike. When Elvira isn't travelling she's only too glad to switch from the housing estate to her apartment in the European district of Brussels. It's her proving ground for new conquests, Ulrike claims rather tastelessly.

The doorbell rings again. Oh dear oh dear, she's too slow, she's too deep in thought. Through the peephole she sees a bouquet. The spring roses sail in toward her as soon as she opens the door. Then from behind the blushing bouquet Elvira comes into view. Stefaan was the first to notice the similarity between Elvira and Mieke's sister Lydia: both are strikingly tall, slender figures, close to emaciated, like a drawing in a fashion magazine consisting of a single willowy line on the page. Elvira is a woman who wears Chanel and gets away with it, even better than Coco Chanel would have herself. To tell the truth, Mieke has to admit that Elvira sometimes appears too fashionable, which may be why she attracts the attention of the wrong men. On the other hand, Elvira has it all: that worldly-wise yet distinguished look, the well-timed compliments. The pants suit she's wearing today fits her perfectly; only she could bring it off.

The two women kiss each other warmly. Of course Elvira wastes no time in complimenting her on the impatiens growing in the front garden. Mieke attaches great value to this exchange of formalities, proof of their years of attentive friendship. Elvira looks a few years younger than the last time they met. At that time she walked in with a furrowed brow and stiffly folded arms, and the conversation was particularly painful.

'Don't mind the mess,' Mieke says.

Mieke and Elvira make quick work of their tried and tested scenario: commenting on the weather, road construction, and each other's clothing. Barely seated, Elvira confides in Mieke that 'yet another relationship is on the rocks', as if she were talking about a relationship between two unknown individuals she was observing from a distance. Mieke is ruthlessly strict when it comes to marital fidelity, but that doesn't apply to Elvira. Elvira is different. She's the victim of men who fall for her money. She falls for their charms—or rather, she has a need for vast amounts of love, but the men would rather grope around in her pockets while she murmurs in their ears that the whole world adores them, just to get a compliment in return, just one, just half of one. At dinner parties with couples, Elvira has wisely been showing up alone more and more often in recent years, after having coaxed a couple of idiots to accompany her and probably having read pitying disapproval in the eyes of her girlfriends.

Elvira tells her about her latest conquest, Orlando. He made a vast fortune in the world of commercial art galleries by snatching up a whole roomful of Dubuffets when they were still going for less than five thousand francs per picture. This Orlando kept Elvira dangling for so long that that she finally showed him the door out of sheer misery.

'Yes,' says Mieke, 'they really can string you along.'

'Orlando,' says Elvira. 'God, how could I not have seen it? He spent more time in front of the mirror than I did, and that tells you a lot. He blow-dried his hair every day. Those bracelets, those little gestures—it's all right as far as it goes, but then going out with all those young guys, it was just too much.'

'Oh,' says Mieke. She's thirsty; she needs a drink. 'I can understand that. That was just too much.'

'It's a setback,' Elvira concludes. 'I'm a whole lot happier without him, without all those lonely nights of waiting. It's much better to go through life alone than with a man who doesn't give you what you deserve.'

Mieke can agree to that one hundred percent. 'It's never simple.'

'Men,' Elvira sighs. 'Wouldn't it be much easier if you and I were to live together, for instance? It can't be that hard, can it?'

Mieke's heart turns somersaults. She searches Elvira's face. She needs a reaction so she herself can react. Elvira laughs heartily; together they laugh heartily.

'I think the same thing sometimes,' Mieke confesses. 'Women are so much easier.'

In the middle of the conversation, as Elvira is drinking the glass of water she asked for, Mieke suddenly remembers the beautiful bouquet of flowers. Leaving the flowers to perish on the counter in their transparent collar is most ungrateful. She jumps to her feet.

'How can I be so inattentive,' she stammers. 'The flowers.'

'I'll keep you company in the kitchen.'

While Mieke frees the flowers from their translucent cellophane in the spotless kitchen, Elvira lets her eyes wander across the lawn and the austere beauty of the bare trees. Mieke fills the waiting blue Val Saint-Lambert vase with water from the tap. She has caught herself smiling. She can't help it, it just makes her happy, every time Elvira comes here to her house and finds satisfaction in the paltry things that are offered her.

'What a stunningly beautiful garden you have,' says Elvira. 'I ought to spend more time in my villa up here. Believe me, you really miss plants in an apartment. And that boxwood at your front door, that's a thing worth seeing all by itself.' It's true. Sometimes people come to a stop just to gaze at the lovely, dark green boxwood, gleaming with health, as big as a giant's head. They don't realize the superhuman attention that such a bush requires. Fortunately gardening is one of Mieke's favourite activities.

On Wednesday mornings, before school is out, Mieke often drives to the garden centre, where she buys out half the contents of a greenhouse with the help of her credit card. Nature may not pay much attention to her, but she certainly pays a great deal of attention to her country garden. She laid it out herself, rooting around in the soil to drive the weeds from her primroses. She'll have nothing to do with the Greenpeace hooligans; Mieke is green *avant la lettre*.

'I ought to spend more time out in nature,' Elvira resolves.

'Oh, Elvira, I've seen your patio in Brussels, and the next day I went out and bought the very same terracotta pots. If you look carefully you can see them there next to the boxwood, but they don't have anywhere near the same effect as yours. Here they look like thimbles.' Now she's indirectly insulting Elvira, she thinks.

'Gosh, how gorgeous,' Elvira sighs.

'No!' Mieke cries in an attempt to hold Elvira back. As if Elvira were being magnetically drawn by the oak tree, she walks right up to the long window in the dining room, behind the open kitchen. How could Elvira be heading for the only spot in the house that Mieke didn't clean this morning, not even with the vacuum? To divert her attention, she puts the kettle on the stove. 'Please, Elvira, have a cup of tea. Go sit down and take a piece of cake.'

'Mieke, do you have anywhere else to go this afternoon?' Elvira asks over her shoulder, mesmerized by the tamed forest outside.

Mieke is aghast. Elvira doesn't want to leave already, does she? She can't, that's not possible, that's never happened before. Her legs are trembling. The silver tea pot she's holding trembles with her. She hears herself emit noises that sound like the babbling of the Indian woman in the film Sarah used to love. 'Uh, uhm, uh.'

Elvira comes over to her. 'I'm glad we're seeing each other again. Shall we just relax and have a cup of coffee?' She places a hand on Mieke's trembling forearm.

'Coffee?' squeaks Mieke. 'So no tea then?' She's bought five different kinds of terribly expensive tea from the new tea shop in the city. She was assuming that Elvira was still in the caffeine-free phase, as she was the last time. 'What is it?' Elvira asks, as she leads her to the living room and helps her into the armchair. 'You're so tense. Are you all right?'

'I'm perfectly fine.' There are so many reasons to be tense. It's not that she wants to be tense as such, absolutely not. But there's so much work. It never stops. There's never a moment when she can lean back and say: now my work's done, that's that.

Elvira, on the other hand, has it easy. She has no steady work. Not that Mieke wants to put Elvira down. For someone with her background, the work she does is astonishingly humble. With her fortune Elvira could just as easily lounge around on a desert island, but she doesn't do that. She chooses to lead an active, useful life. She has saved a couple of historic buildings from destruction. No one asked her to come to the defence of those buildings; she just did it, out of pure love for the collapsing facades and the miserable interiors. In her own words: she wanted to restore to those rooms something of their former greatness. Blenheim, the British country estate and home of the Churchill family, who were living beyond their means, was consigned to the National Trust partly through Elvira's intervention. She was at the White House when the First Lady organized a dinner to benefit the restoration of a White House wing. Every year she opens the doors of her parents' mansion, now renovated and classified as a monument, to a small select group of underprivileged children. They're invited to spend an entire day looking around and singing. In the evening they're served a candlelight dinner. It must be an enormous job organizing something like that.

'Why are you so nervous?' Elvira asks.

'I'm not ... I don't know.' It's a machine she can't shut down. The gears keep turning, even when she sleeps.

'Do you give enough thought to yourself?' asks Elvira.

'Yes!'

'You would come to me if there was something wrong, wouldn't you, Mieke? Whatever it is, I want to help you. Is everything all right between you and Stefaan?'

'Stefaan is a good man. Everything is fine.' Mieke is almost choking.

Elvira leaves to go to the bathroom. When she comes back, she launches into an elaborate speech about building preservation. Mieke is so restless that she can barely acknowledge Elvira's description of the new foundation, whose goal is to raise funds from private sources. There are so many buildings that can use their help. Of course they can't save them all at once, but they're going to go about it systematically, supporting a couple of projects each year. Elvira sees something grand and international.

'There are businessmen in Shanghai, Boston, and London who would like to help restore buildings. The new organization will help their companies free up the necessary capital. We help people put their money to the right use. It's still embryonic,' Elvira tells her. 'I'm still in the exploratory phase, but I wanted to sound you out to see if you'd be willing to assist us with your legal expertise. We could make good use of your persistence as well. It's a foundation, so we won't be making any profits, but all expenses will be covered. What I wanted to ask you, in friendship and without obliging you in any way: would you take on the job of treasurer? I'd be very honoured.'

Mieke glances at Elvira from the corner of her eye, at how she pats her lips so meticulously and looks at her with an encouraging nod.

'What do you think, Mieke?' she asks quietly. 'Are you in?'

Half of Mieke, the extremely sceptical, self-protective half, is insulted and thinks: forget it. This is a question meant to snap the poor little housewife out of her lethargy. We're not falling for that. But her other half literally starts growing. As if the flowers in her armchair were growing along with her, that's how she suddenly feels, elevated high above the living room. She's ready to go over to the new personal computer in the office right then and there and draw up the first draft of the foundation's statutes.

So Mieke assumes a cautious expression and bites into a bonbon. 'I'll have to think about it,' she says finally. 'But don't worry, your plans are safe with me.' Asking Mieke to be discreet is like asking a drop of water to be wet.

'Mieke,' Elvira whispers. She bends forward and tries to catch Mieke's attention with her big, brightly made-up, almond-shaped eyes, 'it's time you started thinking about yourself.'

'Yes,' Mieke laughs shyly. A childless woman can only advance so far into her world.

'How'd it go today?' Mieke asks.

'Nothing special,' says Stefaan. He stirs his soup vigorously. It makes a whirlpool. 'Restructuring is coming up. There's a lot of uncertainty but everyone's trying to cooperate—except for the unions, of course, as usual.'

'Is that why you have to play with your soup?' Mieke asks nervously.

'We want to record a demo,' Sarah tosses in.

Mieke serves the Brussels sprouts and meatloaf. She grumbles about the power of the unions. They've single-handedly created the vast safety net of the Belgian state. The Belgian state, where a person can get benefits from the Public Centre for Social Welfare just like that, after years of not having done a lick of work, and where civil servants at the Ministry of Administrative Garbage Collection sit with their feet up on their desks and cling to their permanent positions, only to demand early pensions and then to enjoy a cushy old age while working illegally off the books, chopping down trees in the Sonian Forest and selling the firewood for a small fortune to people who live in the villas, where they also charge you an arm and a leg for painting your shutters, while their wives get their health insurance paid for them because they've been declared disabled as nurses due to a painful toe, and in the meantime their children keep repeating the same year at school over and over again thanks to scholarships paid for with money from people like Stefaan and her, who themselves get zero-point-zero francs from that safety net even though they've worked hard, too, and have chipped in more than their fair share. It's all the fault of the socialists. That's Mieke's clear-headed analysis, and no one at the table dare contradict her, because she's right.

'What's for dessert?' For someone with a sweet tooth

like Stefaan, dessert is the main course.

'There is no dessert,' says Mieke.

'Why not?' asks Stefaan.

'I don't need any dessert,' says Sarah stoically.

'I've decided to start taking more time for myself,' Mieke answers.

'Me too,' says Sarah.

'Why?' Stefaan asks.

'Why?' Mieke almost flies at his throat. 'Don't I have a right to it? What about when Sarah goes off to college and I'm living here alone with you? Am I supposed to take your laziness as my role model? I don't think so. I'm taking time for myself. Period.'

Stefaan stammers something about of course you should, and so on and so forth. It's hard to use words to straighten out what's crooked, especially the crooked things in Mieke's head. She's eager to start making up for all the time she's lost, all that well-intended, poorly spent time.

'What are you going to do then?' Stefaan asks.

'That's for me to know and you to find out.'

'Whatever Elvira's doing, probably,' says Sarah.

Mieke thought she had figured out years ago what to do with the time that's left after cleaning the whole house like a maniac, dusting the vegetables, reading the magazines from A to Z, and double-checking the shopping list. She made a conscious choice not to cultivate a dependence on drink, like half the housewives in her neighbourhood. She writes in her diary. Yet more and more often she's seized by the feeling that it's not enough. Something is missing.

'Time to start thinking about yourself,' that's how Elvira put it, although Mieke would argue that it's more complicated than that. She's not a victim hiding out in a villa in the woods. She writes that in her diary. And she's not a parasite, although she realizes that she spends entire days in this house thinking about herself and doing everything she can to make herself happy, or at least to keep everything under her control. She sees herself reflected in everything, but doesn't every woman do that?

Actually, she's not worried about anything. Well, there's Sarah, who's unmanageable, and Stefaan, who walks around like a beaten dog. But that's a path in her head she'd rather not take or there'd be no stopping her and she'd make herself a nervous wreck.

What if she could see her daughter and her husband apart from herself, she writes. Sarah as a girl who dresses too warmly in the spring, who's too reserved when she goes to the village shop and too cheeky with adults, but who's actually a fairly decent, clever, pretty girl. Stefaan as a good-looking man for his age who's too self-effacing and who works too hard so his family always has what they need (although Mieke, simply because of her inheritance, has more money than he could ever bring in).

STEFAAN 1998

The woman is angry. She's standing next to him and she's shouting. There are tears in her eyes. He was about to merge into traffic, but a car came racing up at such a speed that he had to step on the brake at the last moment. He heard a tap against the trunk. The woman behind him had bumped into his Audi. Before he knew it she was standing in front of him. At first she was able to control herself, but now that she's about to fill in the collision form and her pen doesn't work, she's getting angry. Her heel glances off his hubcap.

'Calm down, ma'am,' he says, shaking. 'Calm down, we'll take care of this.'

'How?' she sniffs.

He gives her a pen with the name of the company on it. They exchange information, fill in the forms, and part company. She's still muttering but she keeps it civilized. It's not so bad; he's come away with only minor damage. If he had been riding his bike he'd be dead now. The traffic in the last few years has become too dangerous to risk commuting by bike.

He drives away with a dent in his trunk. The metal is irreparably damaged; the dent is permanent. Yet it could have been worse, much worse. He did not apologize, even though he did brake quite abruptly. The traffic regulations are clear: whoever drives into another car is at fault. He drives at a snail's pace to the restaurant where he has a lunch date with the CEO of the company, Mr. De Corte.

He hadn't driven the car at all the previous week. He spent most of his time either in bed or watching a cycling race. On Sunday, while sitting in his armchair staring at the screen, he heard the housing estate being torn open by a car honking *Rodania, Rodania, Rodania* and followed by a swarm of Sunday runners. He's paying for all those years of walking on eggshells, Mieke says. The merger, Berkvens's dismissal, the restructuring, the daily stress, it mounts up year after year and it wears a person out. The doctor had prescribed a couple of weeks' rest, but he noticed that after one week Mieke was at the end of her tether, so he decided the one week would have to be enough. She's not used to sharing the house, a house big enough for five children. The house is a sound box in which every sound is amplified. Even from his bed he could hear what room she was in and what she was doing. A few mornings ago he lay in bed in the rarefied no man's land between wakefulness and sleep when the doorbell sounded at number 7 Nightingale Lane. *Who can that be?* he heard Mieke ask a non-existent house pet in her work-room. She was giving her books a good dusting. Sarah was at school. It couldn't be the mailman come to deliver a package, because the mail slot was made big enough to accommodate a sheep, as a precautionary measure. The persistent, impatient person at the door rang the bell again. Mieke dashed out of her room. Stefaan tried to picture it: Mieke sprinting to the front door, her clean-ing apron lifted over her head, giving her hair a once-over as she passed the mirror.

He looked out the window. He couldn't see the person at the front door, but he had a good view of the Vanende's domain across the street. Their garage door rolled open. The blind, ancient dog crept out from under the crack of the garage door and stumbled over to the plants, while Evi and an attractive young man who was not her hus-band came into view. They were close together, caught in the frame of the garage.

'Yes, it's me,' he heard a woman's voice say in the entrance hall in response to a delighted scream. 'Joan!' Joan? Joan Baez? Joan Collins? Then he remembered. Joan, Jempy's daughter. Joan De Kinder, her niece, was standing there. The little thing with the chubby, pudding legs whom they had last seen a good eighteen years before, during a relaxed Saturday afternoon at Jempy's. How happy he and Mieke had been back then as newlyweds. He'd never be that carefree again.

Mieke had a whole series of family members who were united by deceased parents, a motley collection of aunts and great uncles, godmothers, great-nieces, and great-great-nephews. As the years passed, Mieke's family contacts had waned. Jempy ended up in jail and then went abroad to seek his fortune. Lydia in the States had her hands full with four children and now more than eight grandchildren. But on that one Saturday afternoon they were all together. The contrast between that clan and his own fizzled-out family was shown in high relief. It was one of the reasons he wanted children.

Mieke's adorable little niece Joan walked back and forth between the swimming pool and the pond on the expansive grounds of De Kinder Meat Industries, carrying swimming pool water by the bucketful and pouring it into the pond to give the *frogs a bit more to drink*. Humming in the background were the stationary cold storage trucks, always filled with dozens of carcasses. At a time when stamps were still easy to counterfeit and inspectors drank their way through their working hours, her brother Jempy enjoyed the heyday of his career as a meat dealer. It was a time *when friendship still meant something*, to quote Jempy himself. Jempy and his wife Sonja had built up a meat processing imperium in no time at all.

The girl ate a slice of strawberry cake with the whole

gang, then threw her little arms around Mieke's legs with delight. He was sitting nearby and he looked over at Mieke's legs. After the cake and another pousse-café they had planned on going home. At the last moment (they had already said goodbye), Mieke had exchanged a few heartfelt words with Jempy. The two always communicated by way of bickering and squabbling. Jempy dragged his wife and young daughter along on all his journeys throughout Europe. According to him it was because travel was good for the general development of wife and child; Sonja insisted that she went along because she didn't trust Jempy any farther than she could throw him.

Mieke thought it was irresponsible. That afternoon Mieke offered once again to take care of the little girl while the two of them criss-crossed Europe distributing their meat products. But for some unknown reason, Sonja and Jempy were unyielding. When Mieke and Stefaan were about to leave, Sonja let her know why, her speech slurred after many glasses of wine: 'We don't want our Joan growing up to be a goody two shoes like her Aunt Mieke.' After that revealing comment the relationship cooled.

Jempy's downfall set in as Mieke and Stefaan began their upward climb: they moved, Stefaan was given one promotion after another, and they finally were expecting a baby. Mieke had had very few opportunities to see her niece, although she kept asking for photos whenever she saw her brother. As his imperium moved closer to the abyss, he no longer replaced the photos of his daughter that he kept in his wallet. So for years Mieke was shown the same well-thumbed amusement park photo of Joan with her head stuck through a wooden panel that had cowboys painted all over it and an opening for children's heads, her eyes squeezed shut against the sun or the flash of the camera.

Stefaan looked across Nightingale Lane and watched Evi's caller pick up the dog in his strong arms. Evi opened the car door for him, walked around the car, and stuck her hand in the air. Caught by surprise, Stefaan waved back. Her vision was apparently twenty-twenty. His own vision was weakening, but he didn't have the energy to say anything about it. His mother had been as blind as a bat at the end of her life. He was gradually moving in the same direction. Evi's car vanished around the bend in the road. Now she probably thought that he was spying on her. He had been caught doing something that he wasn't doing. He didn't care what the neighbour did or with whom, but it bothered him that she now wrongfully took him for a spy.

He put his bathrobe on, an article of clothing that he only wore when he was sick at number 7 Nightingale Lane, and then only as evidence of illness. He went down the stairs. In the entrance hall Mieke was hanging up the coat belonging to the feverishly gum-chewing woman. Mieke's relative looked old and exhausted for her age. Deep wrinkles were carved into the skin around her eyes.

He and the woman who claimed to be Joan shook hands. He was just about to explain the reason for his being there, his illness, when Mieke came to his assistance and said that he had the flu but was now on the mend. She directed them to the living room. He, the helpless man, had an illness without a name that was going undercover as the flu. His illness was the illness of the age: he had strained himself from too much egoism, had a fracture caused by staring at his own navel, was dying of envy for the stronger members of his kind, was suffering from a total and irrational fear, was always on the run. All of society creaked and groaned in the waiting room of the great world hospital, all of them in Villa Europa were working themselves to death and being treated like children, stimulated and stupefied, mortally ill and hypochondriacal. If you wasted away long enough in the waiting room your problems became chronic and you began suffering from bedsores. That's what was wrong with this continent. He had seen with his own eyes how the companies in other countries were much more dynamic, but did anyone ever listen to him?

'How's your father doing?' Mieke asked Joan.

Stefaan took cover behind the newspaper. This was a matter between his wife and her niece.

'Why the interest?'

'I'm always interested in Jean-Pierre, *and* in you.'

'Which is why what you'd really like to do is to show me the door. This Jean-Pierre just so happens to be my father, and he just so happened to have run off on us many years ago. I want to know where he is,' said Joan. Her raven black eyes scrutinized everything in the living room that was valuable and glittery.

'He's my brother, dear, not my husband. Portugal, that's all I know. He calls me every now and then, always totally unexpected. He claims to be doing fine.'

'As long as he doesn't have to make any payments, the cheapskate.'

'Cup of coffee?' Mieke asked diplomatically. 'I can also offer you a piece of cake. It's from yesterday, but rice cake keeps quite long. You really ought to eat more, dear. It'll give you strength. Eat well and sleep well, it does wonders.'

Eatwellsleepwell, the recovery motto. Stefaan's mother always said the same thing when he was sick as a little boy.

'I'm going to turn my life around,' said the girl. 'I want to find a job. But to do that I need money.'

'You need money to find a job? Good gracious, how odd.'

'You don't work, so you don't know.'

'What? I certainly do work, a great deal, in fact.'

'I need money to buy a boring suit. Otherwise no one will believe that I have a college degree.'

'What did you study?' She displayed a solicitude and patience for her niece that she had stopped showing for Stefaan centuries ago. Aggrieved—he was that, too. A chronic lack of attention. He always felt cheated, even though it was undeserved. And he could also feel guilty about that. He certainly had a lot to brood about, the man without any apparent problems.

'Marketing,' Joan replied. 'Although I would much rather have studied classical languages. But there wasn't any money for that.'

He heard Mieke thinking that Jempy never should have married an uneducated woman. It pulls you down. Joan wasn't dumb, not by a long shot, because a De Kinder isn't dumb. And if she'd just make herself up better she might even pass for pretty. If she had grown up somewhere with a minimum of parental guidance, or if she would just try a little harder herself, she'd go far. He bet anything that tonight, lying on the electric mattress, Mieke would say the same thing. She believed in weak and strong, black and white, life and death.

'I thought I'd found the man of my life,' the girl said scornfully, 'and it turned out to be an exact copy of my father. Lied to, cheated on, and he stole from me right out from under my nose. He just did what he liked, but every time he made up it was all compliments and sweet talk. Or are all men like that?'

Stefaan's newspaper rustled. Just the way the newspaper rustled in his father's dirty hands. Calloused fingers with traces of earth and printer's ink that wouldn't let go, no matter how hard the man scrubbed.

'What I don't understand is: where did his inheritance go to? That must have been a pretty sizeable amount?'

'Oh dear oh dear, I fear the worst. That money is long gone. I'm glad your grandfather didn't live to see the day. The entire fortune was squandered before it could even be invested.'

The women discussed the niece's problems in confidential tones. They both sipped their coffee in exactly the same way, pinkie in the air. They talked as if he weren't there, his wife with a maternal inflection, the niece a grown-up child. She hung on Mieke's every word, lapping up her good advice. He was nothing but air, air when the two drank their coffee, air when they gossiped about distant family members, air when the two recognized each other's family grievances, and he was still air when Mieke decided all by herself to get her check book from the office and fill in an unknown amount without any consultation.

When they said goodbye, Joan gave Mieke a kiss and shook hands with Stefaan. She repeated her promise to Mieke to look for a job. 'And eat more,' Mieke reminded her. 'Scarecrows don't get hired.' Giggling, Joan stepped outside. Mieke shut the front door.

Stefaan was too tired to start an argument. He brushed his teeth, but there was a sticky taste in his mouth that wouldn't go away, as if he had just eaten fatty cheese. As long as Mieke kept her hands off the money he had saved for Sarah. His savings contrasted sharply with everything she owned. She doled her money out to whomever she wished while he saved for their daughter.

The red light won't turn green. The tip of his finger begins to twitch. He can't be late. There are a couple of eating establishments near the office, but De Corte has insisted on going to a Japanese place outside the city. De Corte is a man of the world, and he likes Japanese food. Stefaan is sure to be sold on it, too, as soon as he's eaten his first piece of sushi, as De Corte has tried to convince him.

Finally the light jumps to green. He drives between the cow pastures. There are arrows pointing to the restaurant posted along the side of the unpaved road. Their cars arrive simultaneously in the spacious parking lot of the Osaka restaurant.

Entering the dark interior, they take their seats at a reserved table near the window, sitting across from each other like a couple.

'I've never eaten Japanese food,' Stefaan confesses. In San Francisco, in Hong Kong, and in other cities where they tried to press sushi and related delicacies on him he always politely refused and opted for the most Western cuisine.

'Always a first time for everything,' De Corte says with a wink.

De Corte asks if all is well on the home front. Stefaan distrusts such questions. What are they talking about anyway? What does De Corte want to know? It's just an attempt at small talk. He shouldn't react with such irritation. He's been so easily irritated lately, as if he were walking around holding a full glass of water in his clumsy hands and not being allowed to spill a drop, while everyone is pushing him.

'Glad to hear that everything's fine,' says De Corte. 'Then it can only get better. Let's talk a little about the restructuring.' De Corte picks up the steaming towel from the bamboo dish that the lady presents to him.

Restructuring. Just hearing the word makes Stefaan yawn, and he feels an irresistible urge to crawl into bed and not come out for the next few months.

'We'll have a boat for two, a sushi and sashimi combo,' De Corte tells the lady, who has been waiting for them to order. Stefaan has no idea what to expect from a boat. 'We can be glad we've been freed of a number of weaker elements, although that Berkvens cost us a pretty penny in severance pay. I really don't understand why you didn't edge him out earlier. Well anyway, I'm glad the matter has been taken care of. There's no longer any room in the company for screw-ups and freeloaders. Quality over quantity.'

De Corte asks the lady for a piece of paper.

'What is this restructuring going to involve in concrete terms?' De Corte asks rhetorically while accepting the piece of paper. He takes a ballpoint from his inside pocket, a pen from the new Guggenheim Museum in Bilbao, Stefaan notices. De Corte is an *Uomo Universale*, although he doesn't realize that such a thing has simply become impossible at the end of the nineties. The grand view is gone, and there isn't a search engine in the world that can rake up every scrap of information. De Corte leans forward and draws something on the paper. Here we go, Stefaan thinks. A shudder passes through him. He's nervous about the boat, about the news, about his nerves.

The new, privileged route that they've mapped out for Stefaan is just what he's cut out for, De Corte tells him. Stefaan is the bridge builder, the man who makes connections between the company and the government. He points to the paper showing the indicated route, and a couple of arrows and crosses.

De Corte reminisces about Stefaan's audacious job

interview all those years ago. He's never forgotten it, the hotshot who thundered in and gave the old, entrenched system a good shake. Everyone was talking about it. It wasn't a question of hiring him or not. The question was what position to start him out at. It can be quite nice watching someone work his way up, nicer than watching someone waste away at the top.

Stefaan smiles. The lady, who has arrived at their table with a big wooden hulk, smiles back. She places before them a large rudimentary model boat made of blonde wood. The boat is full of raw fish, just fished out of the sea (i.e. the kitchen). The pieces of fish are resting on a bed of crushed ice.

'You can regard this as a reward,' De Corte entreats him. That sets off an alarm in Stefaan's head: the man wants to console him, in a good-hearted way.

'Ma'am, ma'am,' Stefaan calls to the lady hastily as she walks away, 'may I have a fork, please?'

De Corte laughs merrily and clamps a piece of white-veined salmon between his chopsticks. He fills his square plate with lumps of rice and fish, and motions to Stefaan to do the same.

'I may be mistaken,' De Corte says, mixing the bright green clay through his soy sauce, 'but isn't it time for something different anyway? Are you actually comfortable in your department?' Now it's De Corte's turn to smile, a big, broad smile. 'What did you call it, a battery cage?'

'Did I say that?'

'Elleke says you did.'

Stefaan is silent. It's true. He did use the term 'battery cage' during a conversation with Elleke, in the build-up to their incident. A battery cage, he couldn't describe it any better. For a battery cage, his office is scandalously beautiful. He's right in the midst of all the other cackling chickens, however, although he has no contact with them. He scratches a few files together, but whether he does it or not, his salary is always deposited in his account and his feed is delivered promptly. Any other battery chicken could just as easily sit in his place.

Elleke didn't agree at all, as she told him. Elleke always had a valid reason to drop in. If it wasn't to install a new virus scanner on his computer, then the Dutch IT specialist had a new program she wanted to show him, or she was searching for a data cable. A couple of weeks before she had appeared at his glass door and knocked. 'The battery cage is open,' he had joked. She had had a good laugh over that one. They had gone on talking about battery cages and their own chickens. Elleke had two English hens that wouldn't lay. She just kept on talking. 'I have to get back to work,' he had said when she began hanging over his desk. Her pushiness was intolerable. She really overstepped the mark when she warned him about pain in his shoulders if he kept working at his desktop bent over like that, after which she stepped behind him and started massaging his shoulders. She *was* attractive, in that sturdy, energetic Dutch way. She forced herself on him. He let it happen for just a little while, and then for a millisecond a short circuit occurred in his head. He turned around abruptly and gave her a jab with his elbow. It was a little push, but she grossly exaggerated it. His own wife would never have screamed like that over such a little push. It had been an awkward manoeuvre, certainly, but he could not have foreseen that her foot would get caught on a leg of his desk and that she would end up with her face down on the windowsill.

She scrambled up, looked at him in shock, and with a face contorted with rage she shouted, 'You brute! So they were right. You *are* a brute.'

'What do you mean?' he stammered.

'Everyone knows it,' she said. 'You're totally deranged, you just sneak away, you never say hello to anyone, you always shut yourself off. You hit an employee in the face. Everyone knows it.'

Brute. He certainly wasn't the brutish type. But you don't push people, that was certainly true. He had let himself go for a brief moment, but she shouldn't have called him a brute. 'Now you've gone too far,' he shouted after her. 'You can't get away with this.'

'Brute!' she echoed. He watched her through his glass walls as she sprinted to the elevator.

'Eat something. You haven't eaten anything, Stefaan,' De Corte says.

Stefaan hoists a few pieces of dark red, raw fish onto his plate and pierces one with his fork. He feels rattled. He has to eat fast so he can get out of here fast. It's urgent. Despite feeling rattled he's also dead tired. His eyes hurt. The white ice is shattering his eyeballs.

'You like it?'

'It's quite unusual,' says Stefaan. He's chewed the ball of fish three times at the most and swallowed it. 'An unusual taste.' It doesn't taste like anything. De Corte is sitting across from him feasting on the Japanese food. He deftly drags the fish through the soy sauce and tosses the chopstick with his catch into the black hole of his mouth, like a fisherman with his pole. The Japanese muzak sounds like the braying of a donkey.

He can't distinguish De Corte's chatter from the music. Stefaan stabs another piece of dark red tuna with his fork. His eyes keep falling shut, always momentarily, power naps of no more than three seconds, while at night he's unable to sleep at all. Apparently it's normal for a man of his age to lie awake thinking about life. He looks at the ice that's been scooped into the boat. A sleigh, he thinks. A sleigh full of ice. A memory is awakened of the days full of snow that he spent with his little brother. They were deliriously happy with the new sleigh and the first heavy snowfall. They played outdoors for hours and didn't even feel their wet pants and their hands, so flimsily protected from the cold. On the slope near the river they shoved snowballs in each other's faces, down each other's necks, under each other's clothes.

'Do you get what I'm saying?' De Corte asks. 'Don't be afraid to ask any question. Everything is negotiable. And buy yourself a new suitcase, because this big guy is going to travel the world. What do you think?'

Stefaan has just shoved a large chunk of raw swordfish into his mouth. He brings his hand up in front of his face like a fan and nods violently.

Maybe it really is a good idea to distance himself a bit from number 7 Nightingale Lane, in order to calmly take all this on board at his own pace and to heal. When he thinks about the years ahead, the first image that comes looming up in his mind's eye is a bull as big as the building he works in, surrounded by flames and scorching smoke, pounding in the end times.

The Japanese lady comes to take the boat away. They haven't eaten the entire catch, but many pieces of fish are gone.

'I'll have a Fujiyama,' De Corte says to her, and he looks over at Stefaan. 'That's a Japanese ice cream dessert.'

'Yes, the same for me. But wait just a minute, ma'am,' he says, 'and I'll finish up the leftovers.'

'I knew you'd like it!' De Corte says.

The woman places the hulk back on the table, between the two of them.

'How's your daughter doing, Stefaan?' While Stefaan forces himself to eat all the remaining pieces of sushi, hastily, with revulsion, gobbling it down like a wolf, De Corte keeps talking.

'Fine, fine.' Stefaan gasps for breath between bites. Loathsome pieces of raw flesh cut from animals. 'Last summer we went together to the West Coast of the United States. She's getting big.'

'That's what they do.' De Corte suppresses a burp. He picks up one more large shrimp on rice between his thumb and his forefinger. 'Little girls get big.'

It's been a long time since Sarah wanted to marry her papa, in defiance of every known law and taboo. Out of the cocoon that was once his chubby little daughter has crept a long-legged, slender woman, her recalcitrance wrapped around her like protective barbed wire.

In the wink of an eye the boat is replaced by the ice cream, a two-scoop sundae right under his nose.

'Red beans and green tea,' says De Corte, identifying the flavours. The ice cream doesn't really have much flavour. It's not sweet enough to be worthy of the name ice cream.

'I'm glad we could have such a good talk,' says De Corte in the parking lot. 'Congratulations! From now on you're the International Relations Manager.' They shake hands. That terrible feeling creeps up on him once again as he slides behind the steering wheel. He failed to ask after De Corte's children.

All the way to the office Stefaan worries himself sick. With the new millennium right around the corner, it's urgent that something be undertaken worldwide to prevent the precipitous collapse, the humiliating downfall. That much is clear to him. He listens to Bob Dylan's *Time Out of Mind*. Stefaan ties his own fate to that of the master, the soothsayer who lays his cards on the table and points the way. There he is again, Dylan, more depressing and better than ever. The song 'Standin' in the Doorway' is unadulterated masterful heartache. The whole record is a cross section of this modern, disjointed age and at the same time a biting picture of a disintegrating love affair. Stefaan has only had one great love. Bob Dylan has had hundreds of women. How much pain can one loss inflict? It's nothing compared with his suffering.

One week later he's on a plane to Namibia, feeling rather dazed. In his briefcase is a folder about exciting bicycle trips through the desert. Looking through the little airplane window he has visions of African desert villages. He dreams of endlessly cycling through a desert of clouds, propelled by the wind.

SARAH 1998

The Lady Di's have closed the curtains to banish daylight from the studio. Five days ago they worked together writing the lyrics for their new song, 'Waterfront'. It was like a dream that's vivid, exciting, and meaningful the minute you dream it, but afterwards none of the Ladies can understand much of what it's about. At the insistence of Sarah the Adrenaline Bomb they practise another song. They've rushed through almost all her songs this afternoon, but not a single one is good enough to be recorded. The other Ladies think she's too critical and that she exaggerates things.

They had already resigned themselves to the fact that first they'd have to invest all their time and money in making an expensive demo before any of the record companies would beg them to sign a contract. That's how it was with the Seattle grunge scene, too. But thanks to all the contacts that MH's sister Jules has in the music world, a short cut has opened up to them. Tonight a real producer will be paying The Lady Di's an unexpected visit. This is what they were working toward all those months; this is why they've been rehearsing twice a week at the castle.

Jules is a shining example for all four of them, the expert who knows how to act around the record company fat cats and at the interminable parties where the deals are made, the unofficial Lady who's never afraid of expressing her frank opinion about the official Ladies. She tells Emily that a thick layer of make-up to make her skin look smoother wouldn't be a bad idea. She tells MH that she'd be much prettier if she dropped half her weight. 'Fat isn't cool. Meat Loaf is fat.' She advises Suri to trade her fairy-tale rags for a sleek suit. Jules can say anything she likes because at age twenty-two she's already built up considerable experience, and mainly because she thinks the Ladies should leave the song-writing to Sarah.

They're wild, fragmented, tormented, shabby—just what the nineties dictates. Their music bridges the gap between grunge and electronica. Sarah's father has come around three times with chord diagrams for Dylan songs, but Sarah will have nothing to do with them: insipid human-rights guitar-strumming folk music, eighty planets removed from the world of The Lady Di's.

They have everything a group might need to make it. Sarah and MH come up with absolutely brilliant lyrics and musical finds. Suri is the creative daughter of Björk; she drags in empty cheese containers and old toy pianos and magically produces the most original sounds with them. And even though Emily has a little trouble keep-ing up with the hyped-up rhythm of the drum section, chaos is part of their world.

'Come on, let's do the first lines one more time,' Sarah urges MH. Normally her voice is like the blow of a sledge-hammer, but today MH is almost incomprehensible. She keeps fidgeting with her left ear lobe. A couple of days ago Suri jammed a hot needle through MH's ear ten times to produce ten little holes. Instead of ten earrings MH now has ten infected red lumps on her ear. 'Relax, Sarah,' says MH. 'We've been practising all afternoon. The producer isn't coming till tonight.' MH licks a ciga-rette paper and rolls a joint, of which Sarah definitely will not partake. 'Hey, Emily, how was that date with Lars? Is there anything we ought to know?'

'It was okay,' says Emily evasively. 'Listen, I think my mother's fucking the dog-sitter.'

'Good for her,' says MH with a laugh. She passes the joint to Sarah.

'What makes you think so?' asks Sarah, handing the joint to Suri without taking a toke.

'It's just true. She's getting more dolled up than usual and she's being excessively friendly to me. She can't stop the chit-chat. It's unreal. And more than anything else: she's losing all this weight without dieting.'

'If she just starts losing weight then it's a sure thing,' says MH.

'And she thinks I don't notice. That guy is as old as I am.'

'Underage, you mean. That's against the law. You can blackmail her and make loads of money.'

'Do it!' gurgles Suri. 'We can invest the money in outfits and instruments.'

'Does your father know?' Sarah pipes up.

'Not yet,' she says. 'But he will when my mother tells him she's pregnant.'

'Is your mother pregnant?' Sarah can't believe what she's hearing. She absent-mindedly takes a toke from the joint, which has made its way back to her.

'I hope not.'

'Why not?' asks Suri. 'Little babies are super cute.'

'Hello. I don't want any little sister or brother.'

'Sure you do, as a mascot for the band,' says Suri. 'We can put it in this birdcage.' Suri holds up the wooden birdcage that she filled weeks ago with tiny mouse bones hanging on nylon threads.

'A variation of the "Smells Like Teen Spirit" baby.'

'And then we'll teach the baby to whistle, for during the performances.'

'And we'll hang the cage from the ceiling of the hall so our fans can see the baby dangling over their heads.'

'Good. I'll tell her she has to keep the baby,' says Emily in a column of smoke.

'And explain to her some time how the pill works.'

'Yeah, she could use it. Because after being married to my father for twenty years ... I bet those two haven't had sex since they made me. If she tells him she's pregnant, he'll smell a rat, the loser.' The joint continues its journey.

'My father is nuts,' Suri blurts out. 'A massive midlife crisis, if you ask me. And then he thinks I don't know what's going on.'

'My father is a total vegetable,' says Sarah. Everyone looks at her, full of expectation.

'Is your mother having an affair, too?'

'No!' Sarah could never even imagine such a thing. She takes a long toke on the joint, which has ended up with her again.

'That means yes,' says MH. 'It's always the holier-than-thous who do the nasty.'

'Your father should get together with my father. He's in his old-fart adolescence, too,' says Suri. She's mixing paint furiously on her improvised palette, a piece of heavy cardboard.

'How old is he?' Sarah asks Suri.

'Right now? I'd say twelve. He drinks protein shakes and he's taken up boxing. He tears around on his motorbike and now he's a peroxide blonde.'

'So they don't have sex anymore, your parents?' MH picks up the thread once again.

'No,' says Emily.

'I wouldn't have somebody like that around for long,' says MH. 'Somebody who doesn't want to have sex or who screws it all up. Like that Alexander, Suri—remember?

That loser we got to know at Rock Werchter. He had e He all this stuff with him and then, while we were in bed, lying on top of each other, he forgot that something else was supposed to happen. Out cold, the moron. I kept his weed but I kicked him out of bed. No, at least Barend is a real guy.'

Shit, I didn't want to smoke, Sarah says to herself, stoned out of her mind. She concentrates on swallowing. She keeps trying to swallow this big lump in her throat, at least five times in a row. The problem isn't so much that she's going to throw up as that the others would see her throwing up.

The hash has crept into their bones and propped them in the armchairs like dolls. They only have enough energy for chattering, at least the others do. Sarah has already noticed that her body sometimes responds in exactly the opposite way; coffee makes her tired and apples make her hungry. This hash, or whatever mind-constricting shit it is, has sealed her off as hermetically as if she were a canning jar. All she can do is tough it out and do her best to act normal. Right now, acting normal is limited to sitting in a corner and not saying a word. Her thoughts flash past at the speed of a Concorde jet. There's so much she wants to say, but it barely gets to her mouth before some other demented idea or interesting thought pops into her head. Sarah is silent, just like the little girl who used to stare down at the tiles with lowered eyes or make a run for it. It was the only response she could think of when someone spoke to her.

Her thoughts caress all the good people around her. She is genuinely moved that they've allowed her into their circle. It's quite possible that the hash is making her feel incredibly silly, but the truth is that she owes a lot to MH. Thanks to MH she's not sitting at home feeling annoyed by her apathetic father and her neurotic mother. She's discovered that she really does have a talent for music and she wants to go further with it. If she hadn't bumped into MH, she'd probably be combing the rugs with her mother. MH is the best outsider ever. She can call Sarah at home without Sarah having to worry about it. She's able to strike the perfect tone with her mother if Sarah's in the bathroom or momentarily indisposed.

Actually, if Sarah had been a better daughter she would have asked her mother to come pick her up from one of her castle visits and let her walk around the two front rooms, which are now fully restored. How Mieke would have enjoyed a censored peek behind the castle walls. But look, she doesn't allow her mother even that much. She's a bad daughter.

She sniffs vigorously to keep the tears from trickling down her cheeks. She tries to focus on the lively conversation the other Ladies are having. They're surfing over the music, shouting louder when Soundgarden demands it and mumbling when there's a pause between numbers. Her attention zooms in. She ends up back among the Ladies.

'Do you have any idea when the producer is coming?' Sarah asks MH as they walk through the garden toward the kitchen. The fresh oxygen does her good. 'We have to know when we can peak, right?'

'Scott was supposed to come at about eight o'clock, Jules said. Just enough time to have a leisurely bite to eat.'

An unknown dog with a stubby snout and little red eyes emerges from the bushes. The dog greets them with hoarse barking. Sarah can't say she's afraid of dogs. It's more like she loses all control at the sight of such a monster. But that's all right. Blood-curdling fear is only a feeling and she has to learn to overcome it. 'Barend's Rottweiler.' MH strokes the dog. He walks away and disappears into the dark bushes.

Barend is MH's brand new boyfriend. He's an older man with a passion for vehicles, and in his free time he tinkers with motorcycles. An incredibly good-looking man, according to MH, whose only fault is that he's a civil engineer, but you wouldn't say that to see him. The other Ladies haven't had a look at him yet. They're walking past the small pond that Jules had dug last week for her koi fish from Berlin. Every time Sarah comes to the castle, a truck or van pulls up to deliver something. Gradually the abandoned rooms are being re-occupied and decorated with designer furniture, packed to the rafters with hats, accessories, exercise balls, first pressings of records, a hand-carved, life-sized giraffe, and thousands of garments hanging on racks. Jules has money in abundance. Where it comes from—whether it's royalties from records the count produced or a share in the sale of every CD—Sarah has never found out, but what difference does it make? The koi fish gulp noisily for air. They look at Sarah with their little mouths gaping in surprise, as if they were prim and proper English ladies.

In the majestic castle kitchen, MH empties a jar of gleaming frankfurters into a pan. The candelabras look down from the sky-high ceiling and shed their yellow light all over The Lady Di's. MH eats the way she talks, from one thing to another, from sandwiches spread thick with chocolate paste to bolognese chips, rolling from one association to another, perhaps following a greater plan or a hidden logic that no one can detect. She walks outside on impulse to give the koi fish a piece of frankfurter. The others follow her. Suri says koi fish eat yogurt, not frankfurters. She empties a small pot of yogurt between the pursed lips of one of the fish.

By the time they get back to the kitchen the frankfurters are dancing in their pan on the eternal flame of the Aga stove. Anxious about Scott's unexpected visit, slightly paranoid from the hash, Sarah refuses to eat. She hears the distant growling of her stomach, but her throat is all choked up as though a wad of paper were blocking the entrance. She takes sips from a can of Coke and swallows painfully just as Jules whirls in through the open door.

Jules looks breathtakingly cool in her black leather catsuit. The difference between them and her—between the little quartet and the expert, the inexperienced misfits and the woman of the world—is phenomenally vast.

'Have you heard anything from Scott?' Sarah ventures to ask. 'Are we really going to record a number?'

'Of course,' says Jules. 'Scott. A fantastic guy. Always lots of fun with him around. Be careful what you say, though, because he can explode, and when he explodes … you don't want to be there. He stripped his hotel room in Zurich right down to the wall-to-wall because somebody apparently said to him that he liked fat beats.'

'Sounds likely,' says MH, and she bolts down the last frankfurter.

How can they stay so calm? Sarah wavers between delirious happiness and extreme desperation. It's impossible to sit calmly in the kitchen when they're about to lay their future down on a track.

'Munchies?' Jules casts a glance at all the comestibles Marie-Hélène keeps pulling from the cabinets. Jules herself takes a can of Perrier out of the fridge. 'Every pound that goes into your mouth sticks to your ass.' She gives her sister a resounding slap on the backside.

'You said Scott was going to be here at around eight,' says Sarah.

'With Scott you always add a couple of hours.' Jules clamps a cigarette between her lips.

Sarah's heart skips a beat. She already had to nag her mother endlessly for permission to stay until eleven. If this Scott doesn't show up on time they won't be able to record the song and it'll be her fault that The Lady Di's don't have a demo and consequently fail to have an international breakthrough.

Back in the studio MH says they have to do some more brainstorming to come up with a better name, something more grungy or more electronic, or drum 'n' bass to mix things up, another option.

'Let's practise a little more first,' says Sarah.

'We've already practised really hard today. Really, really, really hard,' Emily yawns.

'Are you guys unionized or something?' Sarah laughs out loud but no one gets the joke, which she heard from her father.

'I'm already working hard. I'm making the cover for the demo,' says Suri. She's making little knots in nylon cords with her slender fingers.

A heavy hand suddenly lands on her hip, and Sarah jumps. She hadn't seen Xavier come in. He latches onto her and lays his large head on her breasts. She pushes him away. Sarah is curious to know what's wrong with Xavier but she doesn't dare ask. It's not a neutral question but a judgement, as if she were implying that there's something the matter with the family's entire aristocratic gene pool. If she were to say that she thought his being handicapped—no, differently abled—was cool, she'd look just as stupid. In a certain way, such as the way he's standing next to her now, Xavier looks quite remarkable. He's unique, completely himself. Jules often calls him *beautiful boy*, without a trace of irony.

Sarah is about to pull Emily out of the chair she's sitting in and stick her behind the drums when the same bloodthirsty dog they saw before comes wandering in. He stares at her intently without making a sound. He doesn't even blink his vicious eyes.

'Come here, doggie, come here,' says Xavier. Curious, the dog comes closer.

'No!' shouts Sarah. The dog's teeth glisten. A large drop of slobber falls from his blunt, rosy chops. There's something in her scream that sounds like her father's car alarm. She covers her face, which would be the first thing such an aggressive beast would fly at and consume. Then Xavier walks over, stands in front of Sarah, and grabs the dog by the collar.

Suddenly heavy footsteps are heard on the floor. Now of all times, when she's banished any thought of the producer from her mind, he shows up in the studio. Sarah pushes Xavier away, Emily jumps to her feet, and both of them roar 'Hello!' in unison.

'We're so glad you're here,' Sarah gushes. 'We'd love to play a couple of numbers for you. They're not completely finished, but they'll give you a good idea of our work.' The man looks at her quizzically.

'I'm sure that's true,' he responds, and he turns to MH. Suri and MH burst out laughing.

'Hey, Barend.' MH rolls out of the chair. The man walks up to her and kisses her full on the mouth.

'Stay away from my ear,' MH says.

Barend exchanges a few words with MH and continues on his way to help out a couple of musician friends.

After one more deep French kiss he walks out the door with the Rottweiler.

What would it be like to be overpowered by a bear of a guy like Barend? What would it be like to surrender yourself entirely and throw yourself into the arms of— of who?

'That's a man, at least,' MH sighs. 'Those little boys? Not for me. After school we're taking a whole year to go around the world together.'

'And what if we go on tour? We said we were going to conquer the world. I'm not going to sit around and wait a whole year.'

'In a couple of months the Ladies will be in New York,' Suri adds. 'I swear it.'

'And then a night in the Chelsea Hotel,' says Sarah dreamily. If the producer comes, that is. It's already late. She really does have to be home by eleven. Otherwise there's a real possibility that her furious mother will come racing to the castle, tires screeching, honking like a maniac, to give Sarah a good going over.

'And what if we split up during the year you're gone?' Emily asks.

'Of course we'll keep seeing each other. We're going to the top, right? Don't you forget it.'

Xavier looks at them one by one.

'Then let's agree that in ten years we'll come back here to the rehearsal shack. Remember that: March 5th, 2008, at five o'clock. Leave your husband and kids behind and get yourselves over here.'

'If I even have a husband by then,' says Sarah. 'Or a couple of husbands.'

'At Jules's summer party we have men for the taking,' says MH. Sarah hopes The Lady Di's will be invited to Jules's party. Who knows, maybe they'll be asked to perform? And there'll be lots of people there from the music scene. *That's* where their chance lies, not with a producer who's too lazy to show up and who they've never even heard of anyway. If it had been Rick Rubin, the greatest producer of all time, they'd be making a voodoo doll of him by now to put out their cigarette butts on. But the unknown Scott is too insignificant.

The robot arm of the B&O installation changes CDS from Mudhoney to one by Tricky. The opening strains of *Maxinquaye* ring out. MH pushes the cork out of the neck of a bottle with Suri's thick number 12 knitting needle.

'To the Ladies!' says MH, taking a hefty swig. They're working on their career and their image, and drinking is part of it. They aren't wimps like those other girl groups, who are enough to make you puke—fake sugar candies in a commercial box, put together from a couple of fashion catalogues and selected on the basis of ankle thickness.

Suddenly Jules is in the studio, having glided in on the threadbare Persian carpets that absorb the sound of footsteps.

Suri holds her bass guitar in the air like a theatrical Slash hurling defiance at the stadium. All eyes are on Jules, who's standing in their midst. 'Uh! Hello! We're working here. You're disturbing us!' MH roars at her sister. 'Where's Scott?'

'He's not coming,' Jules answers.

'Hey, I thought you were asleep, gorgeous.' Jules puts her long, slender arms around Xavier and nestles her head on his sturdy shoulder. Remarkable how Jules's beauty shines even more brightly next to his imperfect body. 'Keep playing. Don't mind us.' Arm in arm, Jules and Xavier look over the titles of the CD covers. Emily steps on the pedal of her drum kit to start jamming but the sounds go every which way. They're all more attuned to what Jules is doing, the litmus test for their brand of cool.

A few more people come traipsing into the studio unannounced, three friends of Jules: a surly, plump brunette with a mile-long scarf wrapped around her neck and two guys in sunglasses who propel themselves on horribly scrawny insect legs. One of them is wearing a leather monkey jacket, the other a Billy Corgan-type skirt. Sarah pretends not to notice.

Their playing founders utterly. Emily even drops a drumstick and rummages around under her drum kit with her left hand while tapping the cymbals with her right, out of time. Marie-Hélène makes an attempt to sing 'Silver Spoon', their most finished number, with a Marianne Faithfull-like depth. They look more and more pathetic the longer they play.

After a brief inspection of the studio the three take to their heels.

'Who are they?' MH barks into the mic.

Jules shrugs. 'Bad musicians. Bavarian peasants. You guys are a hundred times better than them. Just keep it up.'

The air crackles with electricity, and magically the four Ladies, without anyone giving a signal, come in together at the same moment for the refrain of 'Silver Spoon'. 'The handmade blade / the silver spoon / I forgot more than you will know soon.' The gravity and dedication with which they sing, wrenching every ounce of strength from their instruments, surprises even them. They keep it up for a very long time, half an hour, perhaps, or an hour—who can say?—screaming themselves hoarse and urging their instruments on long after their audience has disappeared.

MIEKE 1998

Mieke is organizing the files of the foundation, which is under the protection of her majesty the queen, placing them in little stacks. For an outsider it's hard to believe how much is involved in sprucing up just one historical building, or restoring it to its original condition.

Shamefacedly, she herself has been forced to admit that she seriously undervalued Elvira's work. All that time she thought of it as a fine and noble diversion that mainly gave Elvira the chance to do a lot of travelling. Now when she looks at Elvira's busy schedule she considers herself lucky to be able to operate from home as treasurer (and partly also as secretary). Elvira is in Boston on work for the foundation, and this afternoon she's scheduled to meet with an interested, cultivated businessman. Where does Elvira get the time to eat a decent meal? How does she manage to always walk around so stylishly and impeccably dressed? You'll never see her twice in the same outfit. Where does Elvira get her worldly wisdom from?

From the world, of course. Two cappuccinos and fifteen proseccos in Milan, wine tasting in Rome. Mieke tapes the receipts from the trip to Italy onto a large sheet of paper. She notes them in her ledger according to the amount and date. Two pasta vongoles in Turin, two ossobuco in Aoste. Stefaan has already tried sitting her down at the personal computer on the other desk in the room. She'd be able to input and save everything very nicely in the computer's memory. The data can even be saved on a disk. She's tried it a couple of times with Stefaan's handwritten instructions on her lap, but the letters on the screen make her nervous. They flicker so much; they can't be trusted.

She stands up to get the stapler from the cabinet just as the phone begins its merry ringing. She lifts the receiver from its cradle with an equally merry 'Good afternoon, Vandersanden-De Kinder here'. It's Elvira calling from Boston. The people from the Historical Society are a bit disappointing. They barely listened to her speech, which they received with tepid, polite applause. Historians who cannot be aroused by a story about the historic importance of building preservation are people she'd rather not have much to do with. But the good news is: this afternoon Elvira had lunch with Ron Hoffman.

Mieke begins a feverish inventory of her memory. Ron Hoffman, she's heard that name before. Yes, it does seem to ring a bell. But what bell? For all those years she spent as a housewife she did far too little thinking, and that's why the answer isn't springing to mind. Elvira explains that she knows Ron Hoffman personally from when they went to parties together in New York. The gears click into place. Mieke's memory begins working again. Ron Hoffman, Jewish businessman, has lived in New York for years, the last great love of Jacqueline Kennedy, the unforgettable Jackie Kennedy. Mieke's regular habit of buying and reading *Royal* every week has finally paid off. Hoffman stood by Jackie Kennedy with such moving loyalty when she became ill, until she died of cancer in 1994. Hoffman and Jackie were both crazy about the antiques and interiors designed by Maison Jansen. Jackie devoted her whole life to the restoration of public buildings, beginning with the White House. Mieke jumps on board; she's in.

'He's well disposed toward the foundation, surely, with his love of antiques?'

'Yes, Ron is a great admirer of our work. He told me confidentially that he and Jackie had plans for a similar foundation.' Elvira perfumes her sentences with a hefty splash of good cheer. 'It wouldn't surprise me at all if he were to give us a substantial shot in the arm. Oh, Lord, my taxi's waiting. Let's talk again soon! Bye!'

'Bye!' Elvira's optimism is infectious. Mieke takes a whiff of her orchid plants, blissfully happy. Full of disbelief, she looks back on the Mieke who acted so foolishly a couple of months ago and said she'd 'have to think about' Elvira's offer to become her right-hand woman in the foundation. Together they went on to convince German scholar Ulrike to join them as well, so she can be responsible for the project descriptions.

Mieke is now part of a cultivated club of women who are trying to talk their manager husbands into securing sponsorship money. An organization under the protection of her majesty the queen—what respectable company can refuse to support that? It's for a good cause, a neglected cause. Children in Africa are suffering from hunger, everyone knows that. There are hundreds of organizations dedicated to that cause; they do terrible work and the money disappears into their own pockets. That won't happen with this foundation. These women are involved in a modest effort to make the world a more beautiful place and to give all those abandoned buildings what they deserve: attention and rehabilitation. It may be a modest goal, but the women's dedication is palpable. With her hand on her heart Mieke can truthfully say that no one puts any money in their own pocket. On the contrary, they're all making personal contributions, one more than the other (Ulrike).

One week later, while having coffee in the city, Elvira confides in Mieke that she had more than a friendly relationship with Ron Hoffman. The relationship ended quite some time ago in his home base in Boston. The affair is anything but shocking to Mieke. She has always harboured so many suspicions and imagined so many scenarios that even the most improbable outcome seldom comes as a surprise. A disappointment, yes. She doesn't know what to make of it because she doesn't like to pass judgement on Elvira.

She considers herself fortunate that Elvira keeps her so well informed regarding her trips. That way she can travel with her in her imagination.

'Mieke, I have to go back to Boston soon for the Paul Revere Housing Project. How about coming along? It would be such fun.'

'Boston?' Oh dear oh dear. She hadn't seen this coming (she had hoped for it, though, between the lines of her diary). Mieke's in seventh heaven. This is her chance to go on a business trip. Would she consider it? Stefaan is constantly travelling for his work these days. Sarah would like nothing better than to see her mother disappear for a while. It's a fabulous fantasy, but the scrupulous Mieke from the olden days cannot make room for the reborn Mieke of today. Not yet, she says.

'Two is better than one,' says Elvira.

'What do you mean?' Mieke asks, much too harshly. She would never leave her family to fend for themselves while she went off with Elvira to Boston, even though the invitation alone does plenty to fuel her daydreams. Emphatically denying her escapist fantasies to the outside world is all part of it, of course.

'Take your time and think about it.'

'Homemade lemon cookies with bits of lemon peel? Fantastic!' Mieke accepts Ulrike's cookies with a bouquet of thank-yous and takes her coat so she can join Elvira in the parlour. Who would ever think of imitating Ulrike and showing up with homemade cookies? Another stingy bitch who doesn't want to part with any money at Neuhaus, most likely. Mieke is holding an informal meeting with Elvira and Ulrike at number 7 Nightingale Lane. She has offered to host the meeting in her home. That's how she was in grade school: the first to raise her hand when the teacher asked if anyone had room at home for a dwarf rabbit.

'*Lemon zest* is what the Anglo-Saxons call it,' says Elvira. 'Grated lemon peel.'

'And the Chinese?' Ulrike asks. A family photo on the windowsill attracts her attention, the family in their Sunday best at Mieke and Stefaan's wedding anniversary several years ago. 'Wow, Mieke, your daughter looks so much like you.'

Until a year ago Mieke heard this so often that she didn't know how to respond. Now none of her girlfriends could claim that the little girl in the photo, leaning awkwardly against the patio railing and exposing the gap between her two front milk teeth with a grin, still bears a striking resemblance to Mieke. Where has that darling little girl gone? She's been standing there forever in the sun, the focus of attention. Despite Sarah's frequent protests, Mieke continues to display the photo ostentatiously on the windowsill.

'Isn't that Les Tuileries, the restaurant with pretentions of being Versailles?' Ulrike has changed since her divorce. She still has the same unattractive looks but she tends to speak her mind more than she used to.

'You look a little like Jackie Onassis in that photo. Remember that we called you Jackie O in boarding school?' Elvira asks. At boarding school Jackie O was Mieke's big idol, her modern version of the Virgin Mary, a woman full of depth and love. A woman with many faces, too, a grieving widow scarcely fourteen years older than herself.

'The resemblance isn't all that far-fetched,' says Ulrike. 'You still look exactly like her.'

'If only it were true,' says Mieke, beaming.

'It is true!' the women insist.

'Although,' says Mieke in a panic, 'she hasn't been among us for four years now!'

The others laugh. Mieke fails to see the humour. 'Poor Jacqueline Kennedy, she fought the cancer battle and lost.'

'I mean: she was a woman with rare class,' says Elvira. 'No one would deny that.'

Mieke imagines herself a real president's wife. 'Yes,' she says shyly, accepting the compliment. Her girlfriends are expressing their admiration for that strong American president's wife who showed character and style like no other and dared to be different.

'Jackie O's long line of men, we could have done without that,' says Mieke to scale back the resemblance somewhat. 'But everyone has their faults.'

'She must have been desperate for love,' says Ulrike, not yet officially divorced from a professor of economics and overextended collector of seats on various boards of management, 'and a president like that doesn't have a minute to spend on his wife, of course.'

'Oh, come on,' says Elvira sympathetically, 'everyone has his shortcomings.' She shifts in her chair and smooths out her chiffon dress. Whenever Mieke sees Elvira she thinks of Ron Hoffman. Even when she doesn't see Elvira she thinks of Ron, who personally assured her yesterday on the phone that his promised contribution was on its way.

'Just between us, I think it's a bad idea, dating a man for his money,' says Ulrike resolutely. 'It didn't make her any happier, in any case.'

'I don't think I agree with you,' says Elvira.

'Money is a way to keep people small; it's abuse of power.' Ulrike's former sporadic sympathy for the working man has taken a one-hundred-eighty-degree turn toward socialism.

'Her last husband was a tower of strength for her,' says Mieke, 'and it just so happened that he was well off.'

'Just so happened,' Ulrike sniffs.

'Is that any worse than going out with a man for his looks or his brains?' asks Elvira.

'Cookie, anyone?' Mieke asks.

'Mmm, yes,' says Ulrike, and she grabs one of her own homemade cookies from the plate.

'Delicious,' is the unanimous praise for the lemon cookies. They're very crumbly. Mieke goes to get the little dustbuster and kneels down to vacuum a few crumbs from the rug.

'How do you make them?' she asks from her knees.

'It's very simple. I'd be glad to tell you later on,' says Ulrike. 'But there's something else I wanted to say: I think marrying a man for his money is a form a prostitution.'

'Aren't you going a little far?' Mieke interjects.

'For the looks, for the money, for the brains—I don't see why one is all right and the others aren't. Frankly, I think it's quite common for a woman to go out with a man for his money,' says Elvira.

'That's not always true,' says Mieke enigmatically. 'Or haven't you heard?'

'Who's been gossiping about me?' Ulrike asks sharply.

'It's not about you, it's about Evi Vanende,' says Elvira.

'She's having an affair with the dog-sitter.'

'Well, what do you expect? She spends the whole day at home and doesn't even stick her nose out the door. Except for other men, apparently.'

'And not only that, but she's pregnant by him. I don't want to gossip, but last week she was spotted at the abortion clinic.' Elvira takes another cookie and nibbles on it sparingly.

'If she was spotted it isn't gossip. There's also such a thing as facts.' Ulrike pops a whole cookie into her mouth.

'Terrible,' Mieke declares. 'Abortion is murder.'

'Aren't you exaggerating a little?' Unashamedly Ulrike brushes the crumbs off her lap and onto the recently purchased Varamin rug, the queen of carpets.

'A foetus already has a life.' Mieke sits up straight and takes the dustbuster in hand once more, vacuuming the crumbs from the rug.

'The lemon in these cookies had a life, too,' says Ulrike.

'Please don't make it ridiculous, Ulrike, that's a totally different matter,' says Mieke, waving the dustbuster around.

'No it's not. All those people who go on and on about life, they all eat meat. They don't have any problem with letting living creatures be slaughtered in terrible ways for their own pleasure.'

'I just don't think it's right, abortion. It's almost become a form of birth control these days. That's terrible, isn't it?' She returns the dustbuster to its holster with a firm snap.

'Not at all,' says Ulrike. 'There are just way too many of us. I read somewhere that soon we're going to pass the six billion mark. Do you two realize how many people that is? It's the source of all our misery. How are we going to feed all those six billion mouths? There's already so much hunger in the world. It's enough to make you depressed, the more you think about it.'

The conversation meanders as only conversations between women can. All three of them effortlessly follow the trail of associations.

'Depression,' says Mieke sharply. 'Now that's what I call a sign of weakness. Letting yourself go, hanging your head. It's a disease of civilization.'

'It's hereditary.'

'I don't believe that for a second. Then abortion is hereditary, too. It's free will,' says Mieke. Polite courtesy has been pushed aside. The curtains open for an increasingly honest discussion. Not a quarrel. It's quite possible to disagree in a civilized fashion without one of the parties walking away in a huff.

'It's the spirit of the times,' Elvira says soothingly.

'Is there such a thing? Show me where to find it,' Mieke asks.

'You can't make me believe that everything used to be better,' says Ulrike. 'I saw the film *Daens* this weekend about the abuses in the Flemish textile factories at the end of the nineteenth century. It took place in our very own beloved Flanders. Right here.' Ulrike presses home her argument by stamping her foot—right on top of the last of her lemon cookies, in a worst case scenario. Ulrike has changed enormously in the last few years. She's worse than socialistic. She's become both communistic and blasé. Under those circumstances you can't stay married to an economics professor, of course, since he knows better than to believe such naive claptrap and to eat tofu at the same time.

'Children today don't have good manners, there's no denying it.'

'Nobody's taking the trouble to raise them.'

A recent discovery has been made to deal with the child problem: the nanny. When Sarah was little there was no such thing. Not that Mieke would ever make use of one. She's raising her child by herself, entirely alone. By contrast, the new women in the neighbourhood are not raising their own children, nor can they be accused of excessive domestic activity. Causing problems, yes— gossiping and stirring up trouble, that they do in spades. But otherwise? That's the problem with this neighbourhood: too many people with too much money and too little taste have found their way to the housing estate on the mountain. Nouveaux riches have installed themselves among the old faithful, erecting their palaces of kitsch. Many of the parvenus don't even speak proper Dutch. A Ron Hoffman would stand out here like a sore thumb.

'So they don't know their children anymore and can't see when they go off the rails.'

'Although I'm not sure it's always the parents' fault,' says Ulrike.

'I think it is. *If the children go off the rails, the parents have made a mistake*—that's what my father always said and I think he was right,' Mieke says. Stefaan is conspicuous by his absence. That's also a mistake.

'I wouldn't be too quick to judge, Mieke.' Is Ulrike now putting her in her place?

'Those nannies do good things, too, you know,' says Elvira indulgently.

'By the way, have you heard the awful story about those kids and their drugs?' Ulrike pauses to let the silence take over. She wants an audience that hangs on her every word and begs her for details. Mieke is obliging and lets the pause take effect. Stories have priority over conflicting ideologies. The coffee pot makes another round.

Ulrike tells them about four kids from the neighbourhood who were arrested for theft and grievous bodily harm. They managed to get hold of some Viagra (unknown to Mieke) and other kinds of pills, not just one pill but entire strips of them. They jammed them down the throat of a mentally disabled boy. The hospital had just enough time to pump out his stomach or that would have been the end of him. How the kids got all those pills is a mystery.

It's a good thing Mieke's parents no longer have to witness such perversities of the modern world. Her father would have grabbed his hat from the hatrack and gone after the owners of the pills to teach them a lesson. Yes, he liked to stick up for the underdog. He would have called the entire neighbourhood together for a crisis meeting.

'Do you ever have that with Sarah, that you feel shut out?' Ulrike asks Mieke, casting Elvira a sidelong glance. Elvira leans forward, closer to the hostess.

'Oh, no,' Mieke says airily with one eye on the clock, which is telling her that Sarah is already forty-six minutes late. 'I have absolutely no complaints in that regard.' She is strictly opposed to candour and only opens up at moments of her own choosing. After all, the news presenter Martine Tanghe doesn't spontaneously break down in tears every night at the showing of gruesome images, does she? At the most you might suspect something, a flicker of discomposure, but even that can be handled professionally and enacted, even by such formulaic means as 'Thank you for watching and have a very pleasant evening.'

That's why Mieke inevitably refutes any form of criticism of her family. It's one thing to suffer the disintegration of a family that had never been perfect but is at least surviving in the midst of all the new family-type constructions. It's something else to hang out your family's dirty laundry. This is something Mieke's father drilled into her. Even though she finds family life so suffocating at times that she can barely catch her breath. It makes her feel like a fish that has fallen out of its aquarium and is flapping its gills in misery. Everyone thinks it's applauding but actually it's choking to death. Fortunately the foundation is giving her a bit more breathing space, but somehow she'll keep applauding no matter what the circumstances. She'll keep her facade intact until the end of her days.

Mieke stands up and invites Elvira and Ulrike to come with her to the dining room, where she's set the table for their meeting.

There's a folder for each of them containing all the necessary documents, with a ballpoint pen clipped to it bearing the name of Stefaan's company. 'Enough chitchat. Let's get on with the project definition.'

When Ulrike takes her leave, she turns to Mieke and, with an exaggerated, somewhat masculine wink, she says, 'Finally, a woman with character. I really enjoyed our differences of opinion.'

Mieke doesn't know what to make of this. The new Mieke laughs with the poor, run-down Mieke and her rug obsession. Which makes her think that her rugs could use another thorough going-over. She can't let herself slip into the other extreme and neglect them. That wouldn't do anyone any good. What if Ron were to attend one of the meetings here?

Mieke has spent a week in intensive reflection, thinking about the trip to Boston and weighing all the pros and cons. That evening she puts the question in all seriousness to Stefaan, a question she has already answered. He's between two business trips and is finally spending an evening at home. There are never too many answers if you already know the right one.

'What do you think about my going to Boston for the foundation?' she asks her husband.

He looks as if his whole head were stuffed full, like a small garbage bag that weighs far too much and could burst open at any moment. And then that tormented look. It's a slow-motion ordeal for Mieke. What is the matter with this man?

'What do *you* think?' he asks. His face is ashen. His Mona Lisa smile is unchanged. Even on his death bed that smile will still be on his lips, Mieke says to herself.

'Boston is far away, but ... '

'If only I could stay at home,' Stefaan interrupts with a sigh.

'Can't you arrange to do that instead of walking around like you're under a cloud? You're working yourself to death. It's inhuman. You're badly in need of a vacation.'

'A vacation like our trip to America last summer,' he says. 'Why don't we go to Israel some time?'

'Stefaan, what are you talking about? Israel? What would we do there? Tanks? Accidents?'

'The Jewish culture is fascinating.'

'And very dangerous. Those Jews are only too glad to give it up. That's why they're going to live on the land of the Palestinians. What you have to do before anything else is take some vacation time. It's almost spring. You can clean the gutters. There are cracks in the tiles in your shed. I don't even dare to go inside. It's probably not clean, either, judging from the smells coming out of that place.' The sparks of her irritation rain down on him, but he's a steel Faraday cage.

'Staying home,' says Stefaan, untouched and listless. 'What bliss.'

'I thought so, too,' says Mieke with a kind of masochistic obstinacy. If her husband doesn't encourage her to break free of her surroundings then she'll stay inside, forever. She'll throw away the key to her cell and limit her world to the square feet constituting this lot and the cubic feet of air inside this ponderous house. There's still so much for her to take in hand at number 7 Nightingale Lane, so much to be cleaned with her unobserved, grim industriousness.

'I'm staying home,' she announces, as if it were her own choice.

One evening a week later, Mieke winds up the bookkeeping for her properties. It's a huge job, making sure that all the rents have been properly paid each month. Stefaan's monthly salary has been climbing higher and higher, but the yawning gap between gross and net income is steadily increasing. It's enough to make you scream for revenge, how little concern the state shows for its valuable human resources. Managers always take a beating. As the clock strikes ten she shuts the filing cabinet with the key. Then she goes to the kitchen, fills a glass with water from the tap, and swallows her fish oil tablet with difficulty.

Mieke is home alone and is enjoying the humming silence she's become so accustomed to over so many years that music often disturbs her, like a scratchy, overly warm blanket around her shoulders. Sarah can come home any time now. Stefaan's return will not be immediate, since he has a business dinner tonight with a couple of Indonesians who only eat Indonesian food and like to take their time, a whole row of spicy dishes consisting of thick chunks of meat, copiously sauced, alternating with yogurt full of chopped chives and stale herbs. Stefaan takes no pleasure in such food because it takes him three days to digest it. She's not looking forward to it, living with a husband at death's door.

Suddenly alarm bells go off in her head. For a long time she's pushed her sputtering marriage aside to concentrate on the state of the world, projected onto the big screen of the world stage. It's all very well to devote yourself to a foundation, but your housekeeping mustn't suffer as a result, and your marriage shouldn't become unglued. A marriage is something you have to work on. A marriage crisis can be solved if you have the good will to do it. She is the only one who can turn off the alarm. The time has come to take the responsibility that politicians are always talking about. She is not the kind of woman to stand with her hands behind her back and watch the ship go down. She has to surprise her husband because marriages thrive on surprises; at least that's what Queen Paola said in a heart-warming story in *Royal*. A surprising new hairdo or delicate lingerie, you won't catch her doing anything like that; it's just not her style.

What you would catch her doing is surprising her husband on his own turf. Mieke decides that for the very first time she's going to enter Stefaan's most precious two hundred square feet on the planet, his hobby shed, and straighten it up. She can't remember the last time she was there. Of course she knows enough not to touch his things, but she has enough energy for two, and a good round of cleaning never hurt anybody. If that doesn't make him grateful, she doesn't know what will.

Armed with a bucket, yellow rubber gloves, Vim, and another whole battery of cleaning products, she goes outdoors by way of the utility room. She never does this sort of thing. No, not even once has she ever ventured forth after ten o'clock at night to clean anything. Take it as a sign of love, she says to Stefaan in her mind. When she reaches the newly built deck the lights flash on. But from the garden path onward she's plunged into darkness. Inch by inch she shuffles along the stones. The tablet of fish oil is repeating on her. The wind sends tremors through her bushes and crocuses, which are now blooming in the spot where Sarah had planted a mini vegetable garden as a child. Every spring her little daughter would persistently flood her scrap of earth. With great dedication she'd screw the garden hose to the chicken coop tap and drag it to her garden. Sarah had wanted to plant a rice field until Mieke introduced her daughter to rhubarb, an undemanding plant that did well in Sarah's patch. Sarah was crazy about the prehistoric plant. She expected a tiny dinosaur to stick its nose out at any moment. On warm summer days Sarah and Emily would behead the rhubarb and Mieke would wash the stalks. The girls would suck on the rhubarb along with a cube of sugar, their faces contorted from the sour taste.

The dark soil has a strong smell. There's nothing like living in the housing estate, a mixture of healthy outdoor air and city refinement.

She stands in front of the wooden door of the shed where her husband goes to regain his equilibrium. The house is her terrain, where he feels for the chalk marks with his fluffy slippers. Here she finds herself facing his world. She feels proud of his imagination, which comes here for shelter, and proud of how good she was to grant her husband this space, even though it's been difficult recently to muster any sympathy for him. She trusts that she'll be able to recover the love that's hidden so deeply under all the layers of irritation—dig it up, dust it off, reuse it, and rehabilitate it. She taps the side of her bucket, an incentive to repress her anxious premonition and get it under control.

She pushes the creaking door open, which could use a bit of oiling. The smell hits her immediately. That there are secrets hiding here is something she takes for granted. Anyone who might accuse her of being naive is sadly mistaken. She even hopes that her husband has something that is intrinsically his and his alone, that no one else has to know about (as she has Ron). Mieke knows exactly what's going on; it's just that the details haven't been coloured in yet. Stefaan has his mind on someone else. She can hardly blame him. Their daughter, who is loitering in the waiting room of real life and thinks she's going to conquer the world with her guitar tunes, is a source of greater concern to her, truth be told.

His hobby shed is a shambles, just as she expected. *The universe is also an organized chaos*, is how Stefaan defends his junk. The workbench in the back is covered with paint cans, brushes, and all sorts of stain removers, polishes, and varnishes. It looks almost unreal, like the laboratory of a blundering professor from a children's series that can blow up at any moment. She leaves that part of the hobby shed undisturbed; Stefaan can take care of that mess himself.

Mieke takes her dust cloth and goes over a row of books, his entire Dylan collection consisting of surviving cassettes from the sixties and well-thumbed vinyl records as well as CDs, and a stack of paperwork pressed into an advertising folder from the Gamma do-it-yourself store.

Like a fairy rising on her tiptoes from a great flowery feather duster, she taps logs and removes dust from tools and cigar boxes. Even the ceiling gets a dusting. Taking the path of least resistance, sheets of paper whirl down from behind a coffee can filled with rusty nails. The sheets of paper are covered with scribbles just waiting to be read.

Having a sealed envelope in her hand, and a whistling kettle on the stove eager to lend its steam to loosen the glue, could make her die of curiosity, but she will not act on it. She would never even think of checking the numbers on her husband's angrily summoning beeper, or inspecting her daughter's drawers. Her honour is a precious commodity.

As a legal expert she knows that confidentiality of the mails is inviolable. Article 29 of the Constitution on the Belgians and their rights. But if these papers happen to be exposed, like a newspaper on a very old wall where the wallpaper is being removed, she can hardly avert her gaze. Does that make looking a legal offence? Eyes can do nothing but pick up stimuli and signals; that's what they're made for. Mieke's eyes are just too good. That is her great misfortune.

Mieke starts to read, gleaning a strange sort of story. She can't make out very much from the stops and starts, the sketches, the words inside circles with arrows shooting off to other circled words, snippets that she kneads together into one incomprehensible whole in her overheated brain. Dislocation is literally what she feels. Her own powers of reasoning are shaken loose, *manu militari*, by the whipped-up hostile soldiers whose boots are stomping loudly over the cobblestones in her head.

It's not as if these scribblings were of earth-shattering importance. In fact, after looking at two of the sheets she's ready to stop and turn away. But the soldiers press her against the wall, pushing the letters into her eyes and ordering: Read!

Her husband's handwriting is a barbed wire of flat lines with sharp, piercing points attached. It contracts and billows, sweeping from left to right. Alain, Sarah, André, Mieke, Melanie, Jempy, Berkvens—the soldiers drag one name after another into the torture chamber and wait for them to crack. Who is the guilty one? they cry out in unison. Bewilderment, repugnance, and uneasiness are all closing ranks and surrounding her. She gathers the papers together and shoves them into the Gamma advertising folder along with all the others, pushing the folder hard as if to crush them.

Mieke trusts him the full hundred percent and loves him with everything she's got, sometimes to the point of despair, these days often out of habit. But the fact that he doesn't seek her out when there's something wrong, that's what she cannot understand. That he's endlessly slapping down frightening words on paper, that's creepy. That he would rather do that than come to her is downright selfish. She continues with her cleaning. *A window requires no more than hot water with a splash of ammonia and a spotless cloth. Simple tricks do wonders. Mix bicarbonate of soda with lemon and you'll never need bleach again.* That's what she's thinking. Only that. She says the words out loud to keep from admitting the disgust she feels.

When she's done, Mieke gathers her cleaning materials together and goes back to the kitchen with a heavy heart. The sensors above the patio flash on to light her way. Loneliness accompanies her into the house, sits down at the kitchen table, and makes itself at home. For the rest of her days loneliness will occupy this big house, and she'll have to spend her time alone with him here when Sarah leaves the nest and goes off to college.

The ringing of the phone makes her jump. She's almost sure that Stefaan is trying to reach her. She won't answer; the shock is too fresh. It nauseates her just to think about it. As if she's being enlisted to accomplish something that no one has explained to her. She shouldn't have read all those scribbles. The phone keeps ringing. She stands and picks up the receiver. She hears the thin little voice of Sarah, who's calling to say that she's leaving MH's house now. They were practising a new number that they just couldn't get the hang of, which made them lose track of time, but now she's coming home. It's already ten-fifteen so she'll be at least fifteen minutes late.

Sweet of her to call, Mieke says to herself.

This time Sarah didn't even make an attempt to get permission to stay overnight. Mieke herself has never slept in a castle without paying for it. Who knows, maybe she can coax Sarah into organizing a party at Marie-Hélène's family's castle? She pours all her thoughts into that gutter of shallow thinking so there's no room left for anything else. In any case she has to organize a party where she can see Ron and focus all her attention on him.

After half an hour of torment, staring into the eyes of Loneliness, her new lodger, Mieke wakes up. A car comes careening around the corner and deposits Sarah at the door. Mieke calls to her from inside the front door and tells her to come around back, since all the locks on the front door are locked and it's such a huge job opening them again.

'Hi, Mama,' Sarah says at the back door while pulling off her shoes. She's carrying her guitar on her back. 'Sorry I'm so late. We're practising for a gig and I lost track of time. I'm going to have a glass of milk.'

'Of course,' Mieke says hoarsely. 'Drink something

before you go to bed. And eat a Betterfood cookie, too. You could use it. Do you eat well, there, when you're playing with the group?'

'Sure, we eat fine,' Sarah chirps. 'There's a cook at the castle.'

There's a sound of rattling at the front door, then the bell. It's Stefaan, who can't get in.

'I think all the locks on the front door are locked,' he shouts.

'Of course they're locked!' shouts Mieke, back in her role of conscientious housewife. 'Come around the back!'

She goes to the kitchen to keep Sarah company. Sarah takes the carton of skim milk out of the refrigerator door and pours herself a large glassful. With her narrow back to her mother, Sarah waits the sixty seconds of warm-up time at the microwave. Mieke lives in a house with two strangers, one of whom she bore herself. Two people who don't hesitate to deceive her with their secrets. She can put up with a lot, but if there's one thing she can't stand it's deception. She refuses to be deceived. She doesn't want to beat around the bush, not tonight. Mieke asks her daughter the burning question that's been on her lips for so long. 'Sarah, have you had any contact with drugs?'

'Yes, Mama,' Sarah says. She looks at Mieke, her cheeks glowing from the cold outside, her eyes glassy with fatigue, and takes a swallow of milk. 'I even deal drugs. Haven't I told you that yet?'

'No,' says Mieke slowly. It takes a fraction of a second for her to step into her daughter's little drama. 'But have you got quality merchandise?' Mieke has kept herself informed. As a modern-day mother you can't let yourself be ignorant about these things. On Thursday afternoon, when she had an hour to kill, she bought a book about narcotics and hallucinogenics, from amphetamines to morphine, from whisky to Xanax.

'Want to try some hash?' Sarah asks.

'I'll stick to cocaine, preferably without the ground glass.'

An idiotic conversation develops, with Sarah staring in disbelief at her mother's extensive knowledge of drugs, not only about rolling joints but also about hard drugs and varieties she's only heard about through the grapevine. Mieke is reassured that her daughter is still a child who enjoys a glass of milk.

'Papa, Mama is a housewife who cultivates drugs,' says Sarah in an effort to draw her father into the conversation. Stefaan has silently seated himself at the kitchen table and is ensconced behind *The Economist*.

'Shh, Sarah, that was our little secret,' hisses Mieke with a laugh. She's pleased with his paper shield. She doesn't have the courage to look him in the eye.

In all these years he hasn't told her anything; he has shut her out, humiliated her. Now the light has turned green and she's ready to do what she's always been longing to do, without scruples.

'And what did you eat tonight, Papa?' says Mieke, turning her attention provokingly to Stefaan.

'Huh. What do you mean?'

'Didn't you eat that delicious Indonesian pigswill you're so crazy about?' Mieke asks. Sarah laughs and almost chokes on her milk.

'Hey,' Stefaan asks, falling back to earth, 'what is this? What are you two talking about? What's your problem?' He stands up, goes to the closet to get his scarf, and walks outside to his shed, in the dark. He's smelled trouble. As soon as Sarah is upstairs, Mieke also goes out to the garden. She closes the back door quietly behind her.

Relationship in nature is the logic of the transitive: the one wolfs down the other, and the other is nibbled on, skin and all, by yet another, who then flies into a rock and is smashed to pieces, after which a bird of prey gets him in his sights and happily enjoys a fresh evening repast. Human beings consume each other, too, skin and all.

Yes, she went through his things. There are no apologies. Nor does she have any intention of apologizing to her husband. On the contrary, she's afraid of him, but she's not going to let on. She's going to go on the offensive rather than be forced to her knees.

The door of the shed is ajar, as if he were expecting her. When she goes in he jumps out from behind the door, where he's been oiling the hinges. Mieke pushes him with his face to the wall. Roughly, without mercy. He doesn't know what's happening; she doesn't know where her inspiration will lead. She pushes him harder against the wall, his cheek pressed flat against its surface. The power of fifty horses is concealed in her wiry body, just enough to clasp his body so hard that he knows he needs her.

'You're mine,' she whispers in his ear. She repeats the word. 'Mine.' She attacks him. She beats him on his back, on his buttocks. Her ring rebounds off his spine. He turns around and looks at her. Fully aware of how cruel and severe she is being to her husband, she goes further. He deserves it. For all these years, he has cheated not only himself but her as well.

The wooden door rattles in the wind. His erection is solid. She sits down on his desk and pulls him toward her by the ends of his scarf. With her eyes fixed on him she commands him wordlessly. She gives a tug on the scarf around his neck. If she wanted to, she could cut off his air supply and choke him. She squeezes his throat shut with the scarf. She's so angry about all that silence, all the consolation he deprived her of, everything she could have done for him. She wants to love him, but he won't let her in. 'Look at me,' she says, and she keeps pulling on the scarf. He looks at her with wide-open, terrified eyes, choking. He's at the very point of toppling to his death, without oxygen, finished. 'We are your family. We.' He hides his face in her neck while they tear each other's clothes off, and he starts fucking her standing up. But she feels this less—his penis inside her—than she feels the painful distance bristling through their two bodies.

'I'm totally lacking in life experience,' Mieke writes the next day in her diary in a trembling, panicky hand. 'I've been married for years to a man I don't know.'

STEFAAN 1998

When was the last time anyone asked him what happened to his finger? Stefaan looks at his fingertip with its missing piece. He's become so used to it that he rarely notices it at all. If there's a thunderstorm or a heavy downpour, he feels it in his finger. It's as if the world were using his finger to warn him, as if he had contact with some other system.

He's staying off season in a vacation hotel on the outskirts of Istanbul. The whole place is abandoned and empty, except for a few faded kiddie cars and buckets in the sandy back garden. After arriving at the hotel at eight in the morning he immediately went to his room. He locked the door behind him and dropped onto the bed, fully clothed. After an hour of tossing and turning in the irritating light that pierced through the net curtains, he gave up and called room service for breakfast. He was lying in bed when he heard a woman place a 'Turkish breakfast for one' outside his door, sighing loudly. She knocked. He jumped up, opened the door and looked into the corridor, but there was no one to be seen. At his feet was a tray with a fake silver pot of tea and a plate containing a piece of white bread, oily black olives, and a thick slice of feta cheese.

Yesterday he was still in Dubai. He stayed in a super-deluxe suite the size of a soccer field, yet he still couldn't sleep. He can't sleep at all anymore. He'll never again be free of the burning eyes, the marbles rolling around in his head, the spinning world beneath his shaky feet. It's not for lack of trying: valerian drops, big glasses of whisky, two hours of power training, a hot water bottle, milk before bed, a footbath with a soothing bath fizzer. Mieke keeps coming up with new remedies and tricks, but nothing helps. What still helps best is not talking about it. Whenever Mieke calls to ask how he slept, he nods vaguely.

'I can't hear you,' he says. 'I can't hear you. There's static in the line again. I'm going to hang up.'

The plane that took off from Dubai had an eight-hour stopover in Istanbul. Instead of hanging around the airport or making a useless flash visit to the city, he went to the first hotel he came across on the way to Istanbul. He has to get some sleep or he'll collapse. Yesterday afternoon a meeting had been scheduled in Dubai with the government representative. At the very last moment, five minutes before the talk was to take place, a veiled secretary with crimson lipstick came to announce that the thing had been cancelled. The same meeting was supposed to have taken place three days earlier, and yesterday it was rescheduled for today at the selfsame time, ten o'clock, but he couldn't stay in Dubai a minute longer. He heard from an offended partner of the sister company in Italy that the Arabs make a game out of jerking Westerners around.

All that bright white in Dubai, with the sun beating down on it, was driving him crazy. He left his air-conditioned suite, with its sparkling fresh dates and pineapple slices, and went out to the terrace. The desert had seen him coming. He heard the djinns calling into the wind: *Go away*. He doesn't believe in ghosts, but he felt so miserable that he scraped together what was left of his energy and got one of the ubiquitous hotel staff to drive him to the airport at top speed. He fled from the gaping maw of the desert, ran away from the inhuman, loathsome, gaudy buildings that prove for the umpteenth time that humanity is doing all it can to make itself impossible. In the middle of the desert, bushes and plants are brought in every day and irrigated continuously by means of complicated watering systems. At the opening reception of the conference there were dozens of ice sculptures, proof that man can overpower nature. Stefaan has no respect for such things.

He stares at the slice of white cheese on his plate. The cheese doesn't melt, despite the intensifying heat. He takes off his shirt. A pair of black trousers and a white sleeveless undershirt, that's how the men here appear in public. He saw it when he was in Istanbul last month for some negotiations and was given an unsolicited tour.

A sip of tea, that ought to work. Sweet tea. All his life he's had a sweet tooth. He takes the little glass, pours the tea in, and spills some on his white undershirt. A green-brown stain spreads across his belly. He looks at it. He'd like to react, but his system is blocked and threatens to seize up entirely. He negotiates with himself, he begs: do something, curse, laugh, cry. The last time he laughed was when the CEO recently told him about the upcoming split. He burst out laughing, only silently. First they all almost risked their lives for the merger, and now the whole thing is being split up again. It's just like a family where you do everything you can to keep your child well-protected, only to let her go eighteen years later. It's a circular movement whose only benefit is that the split-off part will repeat the same pattern.

You have to mix more with people or you'll lose touch with reality. That's what Mieke says. It's true. You aren't an island. Or a country, or a city, or a flagpole. Don't talk to yourself, Stefaan. Read the welcome brochure. Enjoy these lovely surroundings, with their many assets and free bus service to the city. There's lots to experience for the adventurous tourist. Or is shopping more your cup of tea? Istanbul is a shopper's paradise. There's something here for everyone.

He calls Mieke. He tells her that the plane has made a stopover in Istanbul.

'Istanbul? I thought you had to be in Dubai until Friday.'

'The meeting was cancelled. I'm trying to book a flight for tomorrow so I can come home. I'm in a beautiful area here. There's lots to see and free bus service to the historic centre.'

'What's the name of your hotel?'

'I don't know myself, but it's a regular paradise here.'

'You sound strange. Is anything wrong?'

'Caught a cold from the air conditioning.'

'Take good care of yourself. And keep me posted.'

He nods.

'It's hard to understand you,' she says. 'There's static in the line again. I'm going to hang up. I'll see you tomorrow. Let me know when your plane lands.'

He's doing it for Mieke, travelling from one side of the globe to the other, to give her the oxygen that he himself hasn't been able to breathe for such a long time. As if a cork were stuck in his bronchial tubes.

The only thing you have is your family, he realizes, but you don't know them. You're a bystander with a ringside seat. You can't go back to that bourgeois life where nothing is happening, but you can't run away anymore either. You're the right man, and all for nothing. It's your own fault. It's been going on for years and you haven't wanted to do anything about it. Unlike Mieke, who sits down at the table with her inexhaustible optimism and tries to comfort him: 'We let them walk all over us. We have to learn to say no. Really, Stefaan.'

He can say no. He's done it plenty of times. Like that time he came home and found Sarah and the neighbour girl Emily diving into the bushes along the edge of the garden, next to a mud puddle, even though the garden was such a big beautiful paradise to play in. Usually he was very quiet at home, just like his mother. Only occasionally did he open the door to his innermost world. He rarely hollered, but when he did it was completely spontaneous. If he were to see a lab technician with a coffee cup leaning over a specimen, his roar would burst forth as unexpectedly as an avalanche in the mountains.

When he saw that the silver forks were just lying there, drowning in a mud puddle, and that his daughter and the neighbour girl were leaning over the puddle like giant swimming pool attendants, it took all the effort in the world for him not to roar with outrage. The silver forks and knives that he had paid for, for which he had wolfed down nauseating salt-free paté sandwiches and slurped hot coffee every morning to the tune of the Radio 1 jingle, for which he had pushed himself to give his all, all day, every day—those forks didn't belong in a puddle.

'What are you doing?' he asked. It sounded incredibly loud, and even he was shocked at how many decibels he could produce.

'The backstroke!' Sarah said. She didn't look up.

'Oh, no you aren't. Those forks were made for eating,' he roared at his daughter, 'not for doing the backstroke!'

'Hi, Stefaan,' said the neighbour girl Emily insolently. 'We're having a contest.'

'Oh, no you aren't,' he repeated. He raised his foot and let it drop like an elephant's foot in the middle of the mud puddle. The mud spattered all over the leg of his trousers. Dirty water dripped down his leg. His foot was wet.

'Mama says it's okay,' Sarah said hastily. There he stood, one foot in the mud.

'They're old forks, Papa,' Sarah added. His mouth was full of dry rags. The girls continued to sit next to the puddle, giggling and playing with the old forks they had gotten from Mieke.

He knew he shouldn't have lost control, because that was the persona he had assumed. His wife's authority towered over his on the home front. That had been their tacit agreement. He had his work as manager, where he could invest all his energy, and Mieke's sphere was at home. There she ran the show. Actually she's the one who works twenty-four-hour shifts.

Somehow he manages to pass the time. He leans list-lessly against time, slowly kicking it down the road. He hangs out, he lies down, he looks out the window, where sand banks up like snow in a fierce winter. Fortunately he's able to blame the objects here for his sleeplessness: mattress too thin, travel alarm clock too noisy, a strange droning in the old air conditioner, a tremor that comes right through the walls.

The next day he calls Mieke to let her know that something has gone wrong with the booking of his flight. What did you say? he asks Mieke. Yes, he's going to try to get it straightened out today, so he can come home tomorrow. What? Yes, his cold is better. Now I really can't understand you anymore, Mieke, say it again. She shouts why he never asks how she's doing.

When he gets home, he's going to take his wife's hand and say: we've got to get to know each other again. He can already hear her voice: what are you talking about?

It's nobody's fault, but his strength is waning. When he was younger, after his father's death, he drank an elixir that for a number of years made him a big strong man. That elixir has gradually worn off; he's lost the formula. He's sitting on the imitation leather chair in his room and his pants itch. He stands up, takes his pants off, and folds them up. It's important that he eat something. No matter what your ailment is, eating always helps. *Eat well, sleep well.* His breakfast tray is outside the door. It may have been there for hours. Stefaan sits down with the tray on his lap. Now his legs are caught between the sticky imitation leather and the wooden tray.

All the grief that has been building up over all those centuries has accumulated in you, and you let it happen. In fact, you made it worse. How easy would it be to close your eyes now and wake up in a hundred years? He read Sarah the story of Rip van Winkle. Rip fell asleep and woke up a century later in a completely different world. He didn't recognize anything anymore. What a relief it would be if he could advance time a hundred years.

A telephone rings somewhere in one of the hotel rooms. Someone is searching for someone else. No one can call him here, no one even knows he's in this hotel. If a murder were committed here he could just walk away, a Turk among the Turks in his get-up, and no one would single him out. He'll slip onto the plane and fly home.

The phone has stopped ringing. He hears a woman's voice in the corridor. It's probably the cleaning woman chatting with someone. She has many more rooms to clean, interminably more rooms. Although there are almost no guests at this time of year, her work is assured. Rooms have to be constantly maintained. His bathroom floor is covered in linoleum, thin from years of wear and tear. The shower smells of bleach and the grooves between the tiles are encrusted with filth. The woman has years of work ahead of her.

Stefaan stands up. He puts the breakfast tray on the

windowsill because he doesn't know what to do with it. He can hardly lay it on the moustachioed face of Ataturk, who is staring up at him from a picture book on the nightstand. The cleaning woman will certainly see the tray on the windowsill. Or won't she? He's hardly eaten any of the bread. Will she be offended? He sticks the knife in the slice of cheese and wiggles it back and forth. Now the cheese is broken up. She'll see it: the cheese is broken up but none of it has been eaten. This is not respectful. He has to hide the cheese. There are a couple of tears in the window screen that separates him from the open air. He jabs the knife into a piece of cheese and pushes it out through a large tear. It falls down into the withered bushes. One small piece remains stuck to the screen. It could easily be a piece of fuzz.

Somewhere in the hotel—it's difficult to tell exactly where; the lack of sleep has made him somewhat dizzy— the cleaning woman keeps on chattering. He leaves his room and wanders languidly in the direction of the sound. His legs are pale; he can see that now with the endless movement of left leg in front of right leg, over and over. The woman's voice is coming from the downstairs corridor. He goes down the stairs, which descend in a spiral. It's impossible for two guests to pass each other. One would have to wait until the other is off the stairs. At the bottom of the stairs he can hear her more clearly. She's on the phone with the manager or with her husband. The door of the third room on the left is open. He walks up to it and stands in the doorway. She utters a series of little sounds; she's probably listening to instructions. Run the vacuum at half speed, check the swimming pool for corpses, don't give anyone a room after ten o'clock. It's a good thing the man at the other end of the line is attentive, he says to himself. He could just as easily have been a man with base intentions. There are so many of them. It's too much for any woman.

He is prudent enough to wait at the threshold. He is no intruder. He raises his hand to the cleaning woman as if to ask her a question. She's aware of him standing there but ignores him for quite some time. He feels sorry for the woman. All that work awaiting her. The woman finally says goodbye and hangs up.

He holds up his damaged finger, like a fortune teller testing the atmosphere in search of the right answer. The woman utters a little cry.

Yes, a little piece of his finger is missing, a tiny little piece, the very tip. But does a fingertip serve any purpose? The woman stares at the grown-up E.T. before her.

'Can I help you?' The same sentence she used to welcome him when he arrived, a second-hand English sentence that she may not even understand.

He feels dizzy, as if he were looking down a spiral staircase on the thousandth floor into the heart of a whirlpool. You have to look into my eyes, he wants to say. That's where the entrance is.

The woman exudes a revolting anguish. She takes a step backward. Her husband Hamid hasn't lifted a finger all day. She comes home after a hard day's work at the hotel and he demands to be fed, or to be sexually serviced. Stefaan shudders to think of such men. As a man it fills him with shame. Men can feel deeply ashamed for the behaviour of their fellows. He must apologize, to make clear that not all men are like that.

He takes the woman by the hand and leads her to the chair. She can rest a bit there. He himself sits down on the bed, where there's only a mattress and a mattress cover. The woman looks surprised.

'Look, my finger,' he says to her, and he holds his finger up again.

The woman turns her dark gaze to his fingertip.

'Ouch,' says the woman. She bites her lip and swallows her words. Doesn't she dare say anything?

'You can ask me anything you like,' he says, to put her at ease. She shrugs her shoulders and points to her cart full of cleaning materials. He shouldn't have said what he did. It's up to him to entertain the woman.

Begin at the beginning. Give her something to drink.

'Would you like something to drink?' he asks. He takes a bottle of Coke from the mini refrigerator. 'Coke?'

The woman nods slightly. He opens the bottle and gives it to her. He's determined to talk with her. Talk for the sheer pleasure of it, talk to fight the drowsiness. But this is where we raise our objection. Enough of this messing around. Only when that misery, that attack on us, has been transformed into sentences and ejected from your system—only then can you go further. Speak, Stefaan, open your mouth. We demand that you tell her the true story of your brother Alain, who was never aware of any evil or danger.

It had snowed, and Stefaan and his little brother wanted to play in the snow. That was all right, as long as he took good care of Alain, because that boy was a little rascal. They were allowed to play in the field as much as they wanted, but they mustn't go near the river. He promised his mother he would do what she said. After an hour they began to grow tired of the field and went over to the river anyway. There were more slopes there and the snow was thicker. It was the very best place for sledding. They climbed the hills endlessly and sledded down at lightning speed. At a certain point the sled slipped away from them, onto the frozen river. For a moment he thinks he's telling a fairy tale. A Thousand and One Nights. A Thousand and One Sleepless Nights. His little brother wanted to go get the sled. 'Okay, go ahead,' he had said. 'You go, since you're the lightest.' The fat ducks could walk on the ice without any problem, Stefaan reasoned, suspecting, not being at all sure, that the ice could bear Alain's weight. It was a gamble with a tingling, uncertain tension. When Alain had almost reached the sled he suddenly dropped down, as if a rope had come out of the centre of the earth and had begun pulling hard on Alain the marionette. He fell through the ice. A black hole yawned open. Stefaan wanted to pull his brother out of the water, but as soon as he set foot on the ice he felt it crack. In a blind panic he walked back home. They never found Alain. He never dared tell his parents that he had given his brother permission to go out onto the ice, knowing full well that the ice could crack. That's the way he is.

'That's the way I am,' he said, and falls silent. The woman pushes herself up out of the chair during his brief pause and nods. She wants to leave. He stands in front of her and says, 'Is this getting through to you? Do you understand what I'm saying? I caused my brother's death. My fault. But you're acting as if it were nothing. Unbelievable.'

'Thank you,' she says. She puts her empty bottle on top of the refrigerator, pushes her cleaning cart forward, and disappears from view.

Stefaan stands up and walks back to his room. He looks at his finger. If he were to cut off one fingertip for each person dead or wounded or hurt, like a Mafioso, he'd run out of fingers and toes. He clips into his damaged fingertip with his nail clipper. The searing pain does him good. It casts a light on his life. Be honest with us for once, Stefaan. You do it on purpose. There's no end to the accidents and the stupid mishaps. Not only do you experience them but you also plot them, you set them in motion. You act as if you were helping other people, but actually you're obliterating them. The Chinese workers, Berkvens, Alain, your wife, your child, the children you haven't made yet. You're your own worst enemy.

'Mieke,' he says on the phone. 'I'll be flying back home later on.'
  'What did you say?'
  'That I'll be ... that it's very beautiful here.'
  'All right. But why don't you come home now? Sarah is beginning to wonder how many meetings a person can attend.'
  'So am I,' he says. 'So am I.'
He looks down at his sunken stomach beneath his white undershirt. He can't imagine that other kinds of garments actually exist. He knows in theory that the bazaars, the supermarkets, and the boutiques are bursting with clothes, that at this very moment garments are being put together in sewing factories, that haute couture is being shown on the catwalks, just as he knows that somewhere there are human beings, but not here.

That woman needs comforting. She works here alone in this deserted hotel. Some people have trouble with loneliness, especially women with children. Does she have children? He'll go talk to her again, even though he finds her a bit frightening with her gypsy eyes and her sullen mouth. But she is a human being, so she can talk. He picks up the phone and orders a light lunch. Then he stands at the door until he hears her footsteps, her creaking joints, a plate rattling on the tray. Just before she's able to drum on the door he pulls it open. This is your moment, Stefaan. You don't know it yourself, but we do. An opportunity is presenting itself and you cannot let it pass. There are only two bodies here. The woman drowning in her work, and you.

'Wait,' he says. He holds up his hand like a policeman. She's free to take a break. He's the only guest in the hotel. He takes her cart and rolls it across the lumpy wall-to-wall carpeting, into his room. A bit of fluff wafts past. He leads the women inside and locks the door. She looks at him with wide-open eyes. Big brown eyes in a round brown head. He waits for an answer, a yes or a no. He wants her to contradict or confirm something.

'Yes?' he asks.

She nods unwittingly. She pretends not to understand him. One simple word, is that too much to ask? Does she want his company or doesn't she? She closes her eyes. He's doing his best, isn't he? He gives her a Coke, he gives her an excuse to take a break from her cleaning, he lets her rest in the chair he paid for.

'What is it?' he whispers softly. He's being friendly to her, isn't he? The woman covers her face with her hands. Is he such a monster? Is he so horrible to look at? Is that the problem? He grabs her by the shoulders, straightens her out, and shakes her as if she were an oversized pillow. If you ask us, there's something wrong with *her*. She's not responding like a normal person. Don't let yourself be taken in, Stefaan. This woman is taking advantage of your good nature.

He tears the thin, cheap fabric of her dress and pulls it from her body. Finally she cries out. She's calling for her husband or her god, but they aren't here. It's just the two of them in one room. He clasps her wrists firmly. She's brought at least one child into the world, he sees. Her body is made of rubber, light brown and drooping from the hips. He bites her rubber breasts.

'Children?' he asks her shaking body. Now that the

woman is standing naked before him, it occurs to him that he urgently needs to call the company. They need him. It's quite possible that he won't be getting to London on time.

He doesn't desire her, not in the least. He just wants to get her talking. He brings her wrists together, holds them tightly with one hand, and moves her mouth with the other. 'Look, these are your lips. When you move them, you can talk.' He doesn't give up, although she is not proving compliant. He throws her on the bed and falls on top of her. He opens his underpants and shoves his penis inside her. A protuberance, a branch disappearing into the earth. The woman utters the same cry that she did on the phone.

With his eyes closed, and while clinging to that rigid body and trying to penetrate her deeper and deeper, he thinks about a blue Volkswagen. The car had stood for weeks in the parking lot near the woods, not far from the castle, its windshield shattered. Some young people had gone joyriding and had left it there, as if it had been used for a robbery. All the proof of identity had been removed. He and Sarah happened to bike past it. They stopped near the car and saw the ding in the windshield, and both were struck by the same feeling. Destruction calls for more destruction. Sarah bent down and threw a handful of pebbles that clattered against the body of the car. Scratches appeared on the dirty blue flanks. Together they took a large cobblestone and hurled it in through the back window. When another car appeared in the distance they jumped on their bikes and fled away, the adrenaline coursing through their bodies.

He comes. It's painful. The pain awakens him; it does him good. He slides out of the woman, stands up, and pulls the sheet up over her as she sobs. He takes his wallet from his pants pocket, removes two hundred dollar bills, and throws them at her. He's a walking cliché: the businessman who goes on a business trip in order to indulge himself. He pulls his pants on and stuffs all his things into his suitcase. Without even looking back he rushes out of the room.

Stefaan, this is a secret between you and us, we tell him as we charge down the stairs together.

At the reception desk there's a glass bowl filled with dirty potpourri. The purpose of the object is to brighten things up and to fill the area with a pleasant fragrance, but for him it's just the opposite: a gathering place for all the filth hanging in the air.

SARAH 1998

The boy jumps over the low wall along the dike and disappears among the beach houses and the beach's many sun worshippers, running with every ounce of strength in his body. Sarah follows him with her eyes. The farther away he is, the smaller he becomes. Now he's no bigger than a matchstick.

This morning, while her mother was out shopping, Sarah seized the opportunity to run off, without saying a word and without turning on the alarm system. She did leave a brief note on the table. 'I've gone to the castle. I'm staying there overnight, as we agreed. S.'

MH had called Sarah at home. Yesterday Jules had been sent the keys to Gregory's vacation house on the Belgian coast by courier. Gregory is Jules's Swiss acquaintance and Celine Dion's producer. MH made retching sounds when she uttered the singer's name, but she and Jules immediately left for the villa on the sea, along with Barend. Xavier stayed home because he was still a little sick. The cook promised to take care of him, but if he was better today Sarah and Suri could bring him along. Sarah had now become aware that Jules was not really the type who could go very long without an entourage. The queen liked to surround herself with a whole swarm of buzzing companions.

Now that Sarah had completed two driving lessons, MH thought she could come with the yellow Bentley, which was languishing away in the castle's gigantic garage. Just watch what you're doing, MH had said, because the car isn't insured. Sarah put on the long leather coat that Suri had picked up in Brussels and from which she had burned out whole pieces by hand. According to one of their vague, half-communistic, half-sectarian rules, Sarah was wearing the jacket now, and next month she'd pass it on to Emily.

As soon as she turned the key in the yellow Bentley's ignition the engine began roaring like a tormented beast. She was doing something that was forbidden and was taking pleasure in the transgression. If you were young and you were a Lady, then committing misdemeanours was something you just did. Misdemeanours like getting picked up for driving a yellow Bentley without a licence and without insurance looked very good on your cv. It gave pleasure knowing you were breaking the law.

Xavier, alarmed by the roaring engine, came storming out of the castle and jerked the passenger door open, throwing himself onto Suri's lap. Suri screamed in protest. Xavier was like Emily's old golden retriever, who thought he was a little lap dog. Sarah laughed herself silly.

With the radio turned up as high as it would go, the ever-present cigarettes in their mouths, and all the windows open, they drove down unknown roadways. It went quite well, as well as can be expected for someone who has just learned how to start a car and how to shift into first and second gear.

Quite by accident they noticed the arrows pointing in the direction of Oostende. From there they made their way to Knokke, when Jules's brick of a cell phone began ringing from the glove compartment. Suri clamped the antenna between her teeth and pulled on the phone to extend the antenna as far as it would go and create a relatively good connection.

'Jeez! You've only just left? Bring some eggs, would you ...?' and a whole list of other unintelligible orders. Lurching off the highway, they slid under the canopy of a gas station where Sarah noticed a particularly good-looking guy. 'And don't forget Xavier!' MH commanded.

When they got to the gas station pump, the blonde god walked right up to them. He was about twenty years old. He asked for a lift, didn't matter where to, and crawled into the back seat without waiting for an answer. He pulled out a six pack from his backpack and began passing cans around.

'Your little brother wants one, right?'

'No, better not.'

Suri rushed to fill the tank with gas and get back in the car, and, forgetting the Ladies' cool aloofness, she began showing off. She turned all the way around, facing the back seat, and consumed the boy with her eyes, even though he was clearly flirting with Sarah via the rearview mirror.

Slowly, and with many stops and starts, the Bentley sputtered through the rush hour traffic toward the coast. Sarah got a wink from the boy and that was good enough for her. Let Suri sweat it out, she thought, let her try to keep up a faltering conversation. Go ahead, toss your hair around and laugh your head off. The boy was bending forward now and hanging between the two front seats. Xavier began to grumble because he had to go to the bathroom, an undertaking that in his case could take quite some time. They stopped at the next gas station.

'Bring some beer back, will you?' the boy asked a reluctant Suri.

'We have plenty of beer,' Suri protested.

'And chips.'

Muttering, Suri accepted the assignment and went into the gas station shop with Xavier. She moved forward with heavy steps, Xavier leading the way. The boy sat down in the passenger's seat and talked nonstop about his wanderings through the country as he carelessly stroked Sarah's arm. She held her breath. As soon as Suri and Xavier were in sight, she shook her arm loose. Suri came up and stood at the door on the passenger's side, where he was sitting. Her eyes flashed.

The boy quickly jumped out of the car and crawled back into the back seat. For the rest of the ride Suri refused to say a word. She picked morosely on the lip of her beer can and used the butt of her cigarette to light the next one. All Sarah could do was smile broadly, tingling from head to toe. When they got to the sea she parked the car amateurishly on the dike, taking up two spaces. Although it was still early in the year, it was a beautiful, warm day.

The boy took his leave rather abruptly. He jumped over the low wall along the dike and disappeared among the beach houses and the beach's many sun worshippers, running with every ounce of strength in his body. Sarah followed him with her eyes.

Warm and tipsy, and with all the time in the world at her disposal, Sarah keeps replaying the scene of the good-looking boy's departure as she lies on a beach chair listening to MH's Discman. It's three in the afternoon. They're in no rush to go to the villa and be with MH. Serge Gainsbourg starts panting into Sarah's ear, as if he might plop down in the sand with them at any second, aviator sunglasses flashing, cigarette in his mouth, threadbare jeans, denim shirt unbuttoned.

The question is how to hold onto this happiness with both hands. This is the life that suits her, not that succession of cheerless days and nights of which she's had too many, endlessly shuttling between the house on the mountain and school. No one can keep that up. Even her mother has taken to stacking the magazines up on the coffee table instead of fanning them out for display. After spending an afternoon with her little club, her mother has been known to serve lasagne from the supermarket catering service. *As if a whole salt cellar had fallen into it* is her mother's standard reaction, a fanatic follower of the salt-free diet.

Squinting her eyes, Sarah can just make out her father lying on a beach chair, licking an ice cream cone. What a shock. It's no surprise to see him eating an ice cream cone because he does have a sweet tooth, but lying on a beach chair at the seashore is simply out of the question. He would never have the patience to lie on a beach chair without having anything to do but lick an ice cream cone and stare at a view that makes him close his eyes: hundreds of half-naked bodies on a long stretch of sand. Yet she recognizes how stiffly the man is lying on the deck chair, not completely at ease. His pale white face letting itself be comforted by the sun and his hand shooting up into the air for a second to push his sunglasses back up his sharp, Jewish nose—these are the unadulterated characteristics of her father.

Xavier comes tearing out of the cold water, dragging a tangle of seaweed behind him. In one fierce move he throws the wet tendrils over Sarah and Suri, lashing their deck chairs and dumping them over. In itself this would be funny if he wasn't so strong. But he's torn off Suri's bra and destroyed it and almost obliterated a beach chair, and now he's pulling Sarah by the arm to invite her to play. She's startled by the sudden contact between his warm, moist arm and her body. She hasn't had anything to eat since that one bowl of Cocoa Krispies with skim milk. The only drinks she's had have been coffee and beer, and she's smoked half a pack of cigarettes. Her head is spinning. She clutches onto Xavier and leans heavily on his massive body. His warm breath blows against her cheek with the power of a hairdryer. Like a Madame Bovary swooning for the umpteenth time, she collapses. The light of the sun above her darkens for just a moment, the bulb is replaced, and the sun goes back to shining in the sky at full strength. By the time Sarah decides to walk over to her father she notices that the beach chair is empty. Fortunately she didn't go up to the man; it could never have been her father.

A man carrying a pair of black shiny shoes, socks in a knot, comes walking up to them through the sand and says the taxi is here. He's come to pick them up and take them to the villa.

The taxi takes them to the spacious vacation house half a mile down the beach, nestled among the dunes in a rare wisp of untouched nature on the hideous Belgian coast. The utter pointlessness of driving that half mile in the taxi is the loveliest thing Sarah can think of. When she has oceans of money, not just the inheritance from her parents but mostly money she has earned herself by making music, she's going to take great pleasure in thinking up ways to spend her money as pointlessly as possible every day.

Barend is sitting at the overcrowded kitchen table drawing enlarged doodles, while an English boy, who introduces himself as Mike, is bent over the stove. He's slowly stirring melted butter in a pan, which he will use in making a space cake.

'Did you remember the eggs?' asks Barend. Of course, they've brought a dozen eggs.

There are many subjects that The Lady Di's never tire of talking about in the studio: David Bowie, their demo, weed butter, clothes by Stilus in Brussels, whether to put Maltesers or M&M's on their rider when they go on tour. But when boys are around the conversations stagnate more quickly, opinions change without warning, and the average IQ of the Ladies drops by half. Suddenly they act like toddlers who don't know a thing. It makes Sarah sick to her stomach. She takes her notebook and goes outside.

The evening blows its surprisingly warm spring breath between the villas. The seasons are all discombobulated. Suri says they can tell that the year 2000 is coming soon. Sarah's father will be happy to hear that a small minority are not entirely brushing aside his warnings of a major crisis. Humming as she works, Suri paints Japanese characters and a bleeding '2000' in red paint on a large sheet that will serve as the background for their performances. She's in a phase in which she finds Miro hideous and hackneyed, yet she incorporates a suspiciously large number of elements from his work into hers.

Suri and Sarah are a perfect twosome. She could actually live with Suri. Next year Suri is going to study fashion at the prestigious La Cambre in Brussels. Sarah herself doesn't yet know what she wants to do. When they were small, Emily and Sarah swore they'd go to college together, live in the same house, and always tell each other everything. Sarah can't help it, but Emily has been making her very nervous lately when she says things like: *you never would have said that before*, or: *would you really do that now?*, even though she herself is going to horse camp, for crying out loud. Sarah writes all sorts of unrelated ideas in her notebook, the raw materials for new songs. She uses metaphors—I'm yesterday's news when you're gone—in the hope that someone in the crowd will pick up on it and apply it to their own experience, like a blanket with just the right dimensions.

'You guys hungry?' Barend comes to ask. Sarah and Suri barely look up.

'There's no way you can't be hungry,' MH snarls, and she and Barend go out to the kitchen. Suri has an insatiable hunger for candy, but other than that she has a dormant metabolism that doesn't seem to have any cravings at all, except for her own humming, her gumdrops, and more kitschy candy. Arms laden with food, Barend and MH come back outside and sit cross-legged on the patio.

'Hey, Sarah, want to try one of these?' MH holds up a pack of cookies in a Scottish tartan wrapper. 'Jules brought them all the way from London.' MH reads the label on the package out loud: 'A hundred twenty calories per cookie. Times eighteen. That's almost two thousand two hundred calories. Shit, I can't eat anything else today or tomorrow. Now I know for sure: I'm pregnant. And if I'm not pregnant, I have bulimia. Even my tongue is fat,' MH complains. 'Say, there are still a couple of cookies left. You guys take them. Come on, Sarah.'

'No, I really don't want any,' Sarah says. She's chewing on the end of her pen.

'They eat so little because they have no love life,' says Barend guardedly.

'Or they have no love life because they eat so little.'

'Isn't it time for you two to have sex?'

'Good idea. Come on, Barend, let's go burn some calories.'

Half an hour later they're back, red-scrubbed cheeks, providing audible commentary on Suri's brightly coloured designs.

At ten o'clock that night it suddenly occurs to Suri that she hasn't yet called her parents. 'I can't really say when I'll be back,' she says nonchalantly over the phone. 'At least before Sunday, I think.' Sarah has definitely decided not to call her parents. They've agreed that she's going to spend the night at the castle. They just have to trust her. If she were to tell them now that she's actually out on the coast, the sparks would fly through the phone. Thanks but no thanks. Now it's up to her to educate her parents and to teach them that they have no longer have any hold over her with their bourgeois habits.

Mike is greeted with loud cheers when he appears on the patio with the space cake. Sarah nibbles at a piece cautiously; after recent experiences she's just about had it with drugs and their little friends. She decides to go get the Bentley, which is still taking up those two parking spaces. At eleven o'clock at night the chilly sea air is a godsend to her slightly burnt face. The black sea is doing its best to creep up on the land. A melody is resonating in Sarah's head, an unfinished song that she allows to undulate, up and down.

When she arrives at the Bentley, she sees the good-looking hitchhiker from this afternoon sitting on the bench next to the car. He comes ambling up to her. Without saying a word he pulls her to him. His warm hands free her, easily and full of trust, from her leaden suit of armour. He asks for the keys, opens the door, and invites Sarah to get in. They snuggle up together on the back seat. She has no idea what is expected of her. The boy strokes her face and kisses her passionately on the mouth. It's so unreal, there in the Bentley parked on the beach, but it's also so real when she feels how wet she's getting. He slowly inserts one finger inside her. She lets it happen. It's the first time she's given a stranger permission to touch her. All resistance drains out of her. He moves her hand to his crotch, and for the first time in her life she feels the hard bump that MH is always talking about. For a moment she recoils. She has to talk herself into taking the next step. *You can't go through the rest of your life as an idiotic virgin. Do it now, get it over with, then you won't have to think about it anymore.* 'Help me,' he asks, breathing heavily. She opens his pants and strokes the beast rising in her hand. He throws his arms around her waist and pulls her onto his lap. She entwines her body with his to close the awkward distance between them. His enterprising hands put her at her ease; she's being lusted after by someone who knows what he's doing. This is the world where only the two of them exist, two bodies exploring each other's contours, two bodies that fit together, although not with the greatest ease in the world. Gaining experience demands physical pain, but triumph outclasses everything. *Now my life can begin.*

After it's over the boy promises to write to her: '7 Nightingale Lane, I won't forget that.' She barely hears him. It's happened, she rejoices inside. He gives her one last kiss and disappears into the night. Sarah knows full well that she's never going to hear from the boy again, but she doesn't care. She starts the Bentley and drives back to the villa.

Still in a jubilant mood, she goes inside. Everyone but Jules is asleep. Jules is typing a letter on her desktop. Even though she's completely exhausted, Sarah doesn't want to go to bed yet. She doesn't want this day to end; she wants days with more than twenty-four hours.

'Why does everything have to be so clearly defined?' Sarah asks Jules, who's sitting bent over the computer keyboard. Jules turns around to face her.

'Nothing is defined in and of itself.'

'What do you mean?'

'Definitions only exist because there are people who need them, who wouldn't know what to do with their lives without them. A definition gives structure to life, a kind of rhythm. But fuck the rules. We have our own rhythm.'

Jules talks and talks. It might be due to the sickly sweet space cake, to her no-longer-a-virgin status, or to the late hour, but Sarah senses exactly what Jules means, even though she only hears half her words. Yet they help her understand why she so often has the feeling that she jumped into the air when she was born and came down right next to where she was supposed to be.

Jules comes over and sits down on the arm of the chair, next to Sarah.

'I know about that life on the mountain. I know how things work there. The only control mechanism parents have to keep their adult kids in line, the only means of blackmailing them emotionally, is money. You get it in dribs and drabs, but only on the condition that you behave yourself, that you go to college like a good girl, and that you take their place later on. Most people stay in that little matchbox world and think up all kinds of rules to keep from bumping into each other all the time. You have more going on upstairs than that.'

Jules bends forward. She puts a finger under Sarah's chin pulls her face toward her.

'Get rid of those idiotic rules,' Jules says softly. 'Real life is bigger than a matchbox.'

She takes Sarah's head in her hands and kisses her. To give wings to her prophetic counsel, because there are so many different kinds of love, or for no reason at all?

Sarah falls asleep curled up in the chair, her notebook in her hand and a guitar at her feet. That night in the house on the sea, she dreams of an endless trail of sleep-walking children, dressed in their pyjamas, their hands on each other's shoulders, marching along the water line. The whales that have been washed ashore want to return to the sea, but they don't dare break through the line of children. Sarah runs up to the children to wake them. She taps one of them on the shoulder. The child turns his head toward her. The face that looks up at her is the face of her father.

MIEKE 1998

Anger makes a damn good girlfriend as far as Mieke is concerned. The two of them have already been through quite a lot together. Spending two days sitting on your lazy butt in a castle, that's fine with Mieke. She has no objections whatsoever. Doing something like that in a group, with the so-called best friends you finally have—it's music to Mieke's ears. In fact, *as long as my daughter is all right* has always been her motto. But if you can't find half a second to call your mother and tell her you haven't been kidnapped, drowned, or raped and left for dead, if it doesn't occur to you just once to make that magic phone call, then you're a horrible little shrew of a daughter and you've pushed your mother so far that she's ready to be institutionalized. Despite the port, the meaningless calming efforts of her husband, the amusing phone calls from Elvira, and the human robot of a policeman who says that's just the way teenagers are, her nerves have snapped like electric cables when an oak tree falls on them during gale force winds.

Accompanied by her best girlfriend Anger, Mieke drove to the deserted castle. She almost got stuck in the endless mud of the driveway and came across a few Polish workmen on the castle steps who naturally didn't understand a word of Dutch. So she walked into the castle on her own initiative, but there wasn't a trace of Sarah or her girlfriends to be seen. Mieke raced home at breakneck speed to give herself plenty of time to prepare the welcoming speech for her daughter, alternating with fervent appeals to a Supreme Being for her safe return. The worst thing is that later that day, while delivering her tirade, she hears herself repeating—and even repeating verbatim—the same words her father used when he laid into her. But this is different, isn't it? She never pushed her father to such extremes. Sarah just stands there, staring indifferently at the pattern on the wallpaper.

'I'm just telling it like it is,' says the woman on the other side of the Formica-topped desk.

'Of course, and you're right to do so,' says Mieke. 'Thank you, and have a pleasant evening.' Mieke thanks the homeroom teacher for telling her that her daughter is unmanageable at school, that she smokes, that she's obstructive, but that unfortunately she's still getting good grades.

'I'm not finished yet,' says the woman in the roughly knitted purple pullover. Her black beady eyes take Mieke's measure. 'I'll spare you the details. But ... ' The woman suddenly straightens herself up, stands on her tiptoes, and casts a glance over the translucent interior window. She taps her watch and holds five fingers in the air, gesturing to someone hidden from view. There are other people waiting after Mieke on this parent-teacher evening.

'I'm taking up your time, ma'am. I'm sorry.' Mieke stands up. Her chair scrapes across the classroom tiles. 'I'll talk this over with Sarah this evening.'

'Please stay a few more minutes,' says the homeroom teacher. 'We have something else to discuss.'

'I'll take Sarah down a peg,' Mieke says, sitting down once again on the hard chair. 'At her age they think they can do anything they want.'

The woman twirls her Bic between her fingers like a majorette's wand.

'It's true. Sarah is … not an easy child.' The homeroom teacher shakes her head, as if it hurts her to have to say it. She squeezes her black eyes shut. 'Not easy. She's always argumentative, she takes every opportunity to go on the offensive. She's always got something to say.'

'Hypercritical. She's had that all her life.'

'We have to think about the other pupils, too. The other pupils also have their rights, like their right to the truth,' says the homeroom teacher stiffly.

The truth has nothing to do with rights. Anyone who's studied law knows that. But try explaining that to a homeroom teacher who hasn't been doing anything for twenty years except rattle off the same math lesson. The woman's eyes flash at her like two little black holes, glowing with a disconcerting emptiness.

'And now I'm getting frequent complaints from her other teachers as well.'

'And now?' Mieke asks.

'What?' The unmistakable smell of drainage drifts across the table every time the woman opens her mouth. It makes Mieke think of the bathtub. When was the last time she cleaned the drain?

'You teach her too, don't you?'

'She keeps strictly to herself, along with a couple of girlfriends who aren't what you'd call a good influence, either. She never takes part in the lunchtime activities, for example.'

'She's never told me about that, the lunchtime activities. What activities would they be?'

'Track and field, volleyball, painting on silk,' says the homeroom teacher. There is a spotted silk scarf twisted around her neck, Mieke now notices.

'What else?' Mieke is absolutely not accustomed to letting herself be barked at.

'Let me think ... Russian camp, cards.'

'Really?'

'Yes, we offer all these things.'

'All these activities?' Mieke asks.

'And cooking, if you sign up on time and you're technically inclined.'

'Sarah is not technically inclined.'

'No, so cooking is out then.'

'To be honest, ma'am,' says Mieke, 'I wouldn't get involved, either. Is this a school for teenage girls or a kindergarten? What can you possibly learn from slapping down some paint on a scrap of silk?'

'She doesn't do much to promote the general climate, either,' says the woman, unruffled, 'and that really is important.' She keeps on talking.

Mieke nods to the undulating rhythm of her interminable chatter. It's like a draining bathtub, a slurping noise that gets louder and louder. 'Is the climate a condition for learning? Is that part of the new pedagogy?'

The woman snickers. 'No, not literally, but ... '

'Oh,' says Mieke. Sarah hardly ever tells her anything, but she has said that this creature before her is a dreadful person. For once she believes her daughter implicitly. 'If climate had been something modern, a new concept to guide and support the learning process, then I would have regarded it as Sarah's duty to contribute to the climate.'

'But climate is very important.'

'What does this climate do? Can you clarify that for me?' Mieke asks sharply. She shows not a single visible sign of involvement. An old-fashioned psychologist would have described her as the prototype of a refrigerator mother, all impersonal and goal-oriented.

'The worst thing of all,' says the homeroom teacher, 'is

that she acts as if butter wouldn't melt in her mouth when I take her aside. It's as if the real world isn't getting through to her.'

The image of a mouthful of butter is more than Mieke can bear. She can't waste another minute of her time here.

'I thought I was having trouble raising my child,' Mieke answers curtly, 'but thanks to you I am disabused of that illusion. You haven't got the slightest idea how to deal with young girls. I'm sorry.' Again Mieke pushes her chair backward.

'Just a moment, ma'am.'

'You may have all the time in the world to test the climate and conclude that there's something wrong with it. And to look for a person to blame, who could be anyone but yourself. Well, I don't have that kind of time.'

'Then there's something else,' says the woman imperturbably. 'Sarah's hygiene. To be honest, it leaves a lot to be desired. After gymnastics class the girls have the chance to take a shower. I have the impression that Sarah never showers.'

Mieke has no intention of answering, or so it seems. She just keeps her lips pressed together. She bends down to pick up her diamond-shaped Delvaux handbag by the handle and leave the classroom. Then her eyes fall on a bucket of blackboard water.

'That's right. We don't have running water on the mountain,' Mieke hears herself say. 'Even so, thank you for your willingness to receive me.' Mieke's manicured, bony hand shoots across the table toward the flabbergasted teacher, who shakes it half-heartedly and is about to stand up. 'Don't bother. I'll show myself out. Have a nice evening.'

The bucket is filled with the dirtiest water imaginable,

a mould culture at least one school year old. What Mieke now does is so brazen that it etches itself in her memory, in the middle of the lobe of her brain where shame grows like weeds. The teacher has plopped her bag on her lap and is rummaging around inside it, searching for a pack of cigarettes. Just when she becomes aware of something over her head, a dark cloud, all she can do is watch powerlessly as a curtain of dirty water cascades down upon her.

Mieke flees. Mothers are doomed by the birth of their children. Like Cassandra, Mieke has an unerring ability to detect any disaster. There is such a thing as the maternal instinct; no one can try to convince her otherwise. She knows her own child. It's entirely unnecessary to let herself be humiliated by some frump who has nothing but contempt for her daughter. What just took place in that classroom is something she'll never get over. She comes to that decision in the car on the way back. The easiest thing is to put it out of her mind. She never went to the parent-teacher evening.

Suddenly she understands why Stefaan is always so quiet and why Granny never opened her mouth. Talking only makes things worse, and bigger. Repression is the rock on which the Catholic Church was built. To keep the future open, to make sure that shame is kept within bounds and doesn't start to fester.

When Mieke slips into the house and bumps into her daughter, who is also prowling around in the dark of the kitchen, she notices from the way Sarah takes a glass out of the cabinet that something fishy is going on.

'So. Did you have a nice evening?' Against her better judgement Mieke tries a cheery tone with her teenage daughter as opposed to the cool-robot-tone and the girlfriends-together-tone, to see if it goes down better.

'I'm tired, Mama,' Sarah drawls. She puts the glass back in the cabinet and plants a hasty, perfunctory goodnight kiss on her mother's cheek. Groping her way along the dark walls of the unlit kitchen and hallway she flees upstairs. She bumps her hand audibly against the banister and stifles a cry of pain. Her limbs have grown too long, her self-confidence is bruised.

A tap is turned on in the bathroom. Would Sarah be crying in front of the mirror? Why is she shutting out her very own mother? Why is she acting just like Stefaan? Is it in their blood or is it her? Since the discovery in the hobby shed Mieke has been in a permanent state of vigilance. She tries talking to Stefaan but there's never a good moment. Or he has to entertain foreign visitors at some restaurant, or he's too tired, or he doesn't understand what she's driving at. He shrugs his shoulders, tosses her his Mona Lisa smile, and vanishes. She's thought about making an appointment with a psychiatrist for him, but that's like stirring a stagnant pool. You dredge all the filth up from the bottom and muddy the waters. Why would she want to do that? She doesn't want to even think about dirty water.

Cool and composed, Mieke climbs the stairs. She drums on the wooden doorpost lightly to announce her arrival and pushes the bathroom door open.

'I have a right to an answer at the very least, or you can start looking for another hotel,' she explodes. With exaggerated enunciation, stressing every syllable, she repeats her question: 'Did-you-have-a-nice-eve-ning?'

Even before she can put one foot in the bathroom, Sarah begins to scream hysterically, demanding that she go away. The screaming immediately shifts into an entreaty to leave her alone, but it sounds so desperate that it could easily be interpreted as just the opposite.

This has never happened before. Mieke recoils. She keeps looking at her daughter. She registers the words 'I hate you', but lets it pass. Mieke wants to tell her it's nothing. It's not so bad, even if you've been rejected, even if you've never felt so miserable before, or if all your hopes are in tatters, it's not so bad. This house is solid, it's here for you.

The profile of her daughter, toothbrush in hand, is outlined against the white bathroom wall. What's that red on her hands? Is it red? Is it blood? Mieke can't help it. She's not crazy, is she? That's blood, isn't it? Where is the blood coming from?

'What?' Sarah looks at her defiantly.

'I just want to have a chat with my daughter. Is that asking so much? Is that so difficult? Why is your hand bleeding?'

'You've been to see that bitch De Decker, haven't you?'

'Are you listening? Pull yourself together. Let me take care of your hand.'

'Pffff.'

'I knew it. What have you been up to out there at that castle? Those people may be nobility but that's no guarantee of good behaviour.'

'And how about you, talking to that Ron on the phone all the time while Papa works himself to death. Is that good behaviour?'

As if they had been practising for it, mother and daughter, in a perfectly choreographed exchange: just as the five fingers of Mieke's right hand land full on Sarah's jaw, Sarah shouts, 'Go away.' That was it, a work of art, and it's over in a second. Blink your eyes and you would have missed it, aside from hearing the two-word wail, underscored by a slap.

Afterward Mieke writes in her diary that she could

have put up a better fight, that she should have taken her daughter by the shoulders and said: 'Don't start hating me, it's not my fault. Even if you think it is, even if you firmly believe that I want to see you unhappy, just the opposite is true. I only want the very best for you. Just don't shut me out. You're part of me. You're my daughter and I'm your mother, and nothing can change that. Even though I've hit you for the first time in my life, and even though that's an absolute no-no according to the modern handbooks, you pushed me so far that for that one second I couldn't answer for myself. Don't you dare hold that against me, ever. A judge in such a case would pass the only fair sentence possible: suspension of punishment on account of overwhelming duress.'

The next day Sarah acts as if nothing had happened. She simply says, by way of veiled apology, that she had been 'a little bad-tempered' the previous evening because she had written a bad song. The red fluid wasn't blood, by the way, but paint from Suri's never-ending paint experiment, which she had fallen into. She absolutely refuses to go to the annual memorial mass for her paternal grandparents, and there's no changing her mind. Mieke registers her protest. Sarah claims that Mieke is abusing her daughter; Mieke calls the claim parental abuse. Sarah says she's prepared to settle the matter amicably. She wants fishnet stockings.

The timing couldn't be worse. Mieke decides to ignore her daughter's rebellious behaviour and come up with a suitable punishment later on. But she's going to give it some thought first, since Sarah is too clever for her by half. Right from the beginning, the child has always wanted her own way. And if she didn't get it, she'd bite her way through. Mieke remembers vividly how Sarah bit a piece out of the seat of the car after having been told that they still had one hour left to drive, which is how long she'd have to wait to get her juice.

'Just do it for your father. He's already having such a tough time.' A couple of years ago Mieke had to bend over to talk to Sarah; now she has to look up at her. She brushes a bit of fluff from Sarah's pullover, but there's no end to it. It's a moth-eaten fabric shell. Take an optimistic view, she admonishes herself: normally you wouldn't want to sit next to your daughter if she were wrapped up in rags like this.

'I'm having a tough time, too,' says Sarah. 'Papa's not. He travels all over the world and does whatever he likes.'

'You shouldn't say that,' Mieke corrects her. You can make assumptions, but as the daughter of a very wise notary, Mieke has learned that you should never betray your partner in front of your children. What you *can* do is never speak to him again.

'You're sabotaging me,' Sarah roars. 'I want the address of Uncle Jempy. I'm going to live in South Africa!'

Mieke looks over at Stefaan as he knots his dark blue tie, standing beside the built-in wardrobe on his side of the conjugal bed. Her husband looks much older than he did a year ago, many years older. Aging is a process she cannot control. Suddenly you're next. You're powerless. All that your friends and neighbours can do is watch, or buy night cream.

Mieke pushes the pause button. The husband she has now is different from the one she thought she had married. Although he's as faithful as a hound, and although he needs all her love and devotion more than anybody else's, there are times when she simply can't give any more. Mieke doesn't blame herself for this. She just puts up with his moods, something for which she can give herself a pat on the back.

Without any outside advice, she knows that the best thing would be to take a pause in her marriage, a marriage that has produced an ill-mannered daughter for whom she prays every night to an indiscernible divinity, asking that she not follow in her father's footsteps, that Sarah be immune to the destructive despondency that laid her grandfather low.

She isn't going to throw her husband out. That's out of the question. But she's succeeded in separating herself from the electrically charged field of Stefaan's despondency and Sarah's pig-headedness by following the Ron Hoffman escape route. She feels stronger than ever. She gets through the memorial mass with flying colours. She even manages to shed a tear for the terrible loss of half of the Vandersandens. Then she tucks the Kleenex into the sleeve of her Valentino suit and straightens her back on the hard church pew. Lovingly she places a hand on the trembling thigh of her legally wedded husband.

Everyone has a couple of high points in his life. The most obvious are marriages, births, and elevations to the nobility. For some it's the day they discover they love fly fishing. Others derive endless pleasure from the memory of a night under the open sky with a horny one-night stand. And for people like Mieke, a high point is waking up on the day she's going to meet Ron Hoffman after so many extremely pleasant phone conversations.

At first Ron was purely businesslike and professional, but now he calls her more and more frequently for some trifle, a transparent excuse for a chat. He sounds like a gallant, extroverted man who has no time to be dragged down by the existential gravity of existence. She cannot believe—and so she doesn't believe—that such a man is showing interest in her. But it does make a delicious breeding ground for her fantasy while she's lying awake at night, or when she rolls out of bed, drenched in sweat, and sits down on the ice-cold toilet seat in anticipation of the foundation's benefit chamber concert.

At five in the morning on the day of the concert she's lying wide awake, romping around in her fantasy world, while Stefaan gets out of bed beside her to catch his flight to Berlin. As soon as she hears the front door click shut she gets up. She folds up his pyjamas and presses them between his pillow and the mattress. Then she shakes the down duvet and folds it double, to air out the bed. The indifference of the objects in the room surprises her: the steadily ticking alarm clock with its big, red, digital numbers, the eye drops on the marble top of Stefaan's nightstand. The objects do not respond to her. She's spent the whole night moiling with agitation like something nocturnal, but the house gives no sign of life. Nothing can stifle her excitement. After downing a dry, wholewheat sandwich and a cup of black coffee, she goes to work. Her sense of guilt even adds excitement to choosing the right perfume and putting together the ideal outfit.

She's self-confident enough to know that a man like Hoffman might find her appealing in a silk dress by Natan, purveyor to the royal household, but that an ultra-short lamé dress in flashy apple-blue-sea-green would go over just as well. As long as her jewellery says she has money but isn't flaunting it, and as long as her perfume conveys class and a hint of seduction. She finds Chanel N°5 a bit hackneyed but a safe choice, just like her blue Armani dress with long sleeves and built in bra, which is especially flattering for her bosom. Quite intentionally she opts for reliable safety. If she were to sit there in a short skirt, gnawing on her nails and squirming with discomfort, she could forget about making an impression on Ron.

More than two hundred people have signed up for the dinner, to be followed by a chamber music concert. The event promises to be a great success for the foundation. She's seen to it that in the table arrangement she'll be seated next to Ron. Elvira and Ulrike are scattered among the other guests.

She's already there one hour ahead of time. She wanted to beat the traffic and make sure she wasn't too late, and she drove at a snail's pace, probably the first in a line of bumper-to-bumper traffic that formed behind her, which she hears reported on Radio 1 as she opens the car door in the parking lot at Genval castle. Mieke makes use of the extra time to check the table arrangement for the dinner, since trusting Elvira's promise is fine but verification is better.

On the other side of the large room she sees a small man make an inconspicuous entrance. He's short and rather spherical, but he looks tanned and healthy. An active man, nodding warmly. This can be none other than Ron Hoffman, the man she's only had the privilege of seeing in a couple of Elvira's group photos. He guesses immediately who she is before she's even opened her mouth. This sort of man has engaged in polite chats with hundreds of men and women in his lifetime. He's spoken with strangers over wine at embassy tables as everyone sat there waiting for the main guest, the drawing card, to give his speech. At airports and in bars he has greeted personnel and strangers alike with the same amiable smile and heartfelt handshake. Before taking his seat at the negotiating table he spends a few minutes amicably running through the golf results with his business partners. When he meets people whom he wants to go further with, to ask a question whose answer may really interest him, he raises his right eyebrow. During his talk with Mieke the eyebrow doesn't move.

An industrious table setter interrupts them to ask if she can interrupt them, and if she is the madam treasurer. The best fish shop in the country has just called. The order is ready, but they can't deliver it because the delivery truck has broken down. What should they do, call a taxi? Even before Mieke can roll her eyes with irritation, Ron proposes that they go to the fish shop together to pick up the order. He's arrived too early anyway, quite by accident. She laughs, caught by surprise. Enterprising, but nonchalant and surprising as well; Mieke makes a mental note. A man who takes his ambition seriously without being crippled by it.

Mieke nods furiously. She wants them to pick up the fish together. Bewildered by the operation of her own mind, she does her very best to suppress the memory of last night, the incredibly brutal sex she had with Stefaan. He had turned her onto her stomach and stuffed a corner of her pillow into her mouth. The intimacy of that anonymous, rough, downright crude sex had made her writhe and shudder as never before. She lay there, frantic and spent. She wasn't born yesterday; that sudden change in his behaviour indicates something. Never thought she'd think such a thing, but in her head she gave him permission to think of someone else last night, in exchange for letting her do the same. That made the whole scene even more perverse and exciting. She didn't ask him if he'd had someone else, nor does she want to hear the answer.

Never before has a man deigned to pick up lemon sole and salmon fillets with Mieke. Courteously, Ron Hoffman sweeps the back door of his BMW convertible open for her. He walks around the car, sits down beside her, and gives the chauffeur instructions. He's so flippant about it all, as if the chauffeur and the luxury don't even exist, or in any case play no role, for he's giving her his undivided attention. Whizzing down the highway toward Brussels he wants to know everything about her, especially now that she's told him how crazy she is about gardening. He loves nature, too, he says. He takes a photo from his wallet, not a picture of children or of an attractive actress but of a vast lake full of reeds with a heron standing on one leg at the water's edge. 'My patch of land, bought to keep it untouched. It's too beautiful to turn it over to developers.'

All that Mieke longs for is an oxygen pump. Or a kiss from the man who, objectively speaking, isn't much to look at, but who has a personality that blows her away, a man who connects with her on every level. She's glad to have met him at this phase of her life. Too late to be sure, but anyway, imagine what her life would look like now if she had never met him at all?

One touch of the hand is enough, and then that kiss to top it off, the pinnacle of all gallantry. The bag of fish between them doesn't bother her; they both love nature. It's true that she's had this unbridled longing before. Thirty years ago, in her uncomfortable desk chair in the notary's office. That's when she first became acquainted with fiery desire, and because of that she's able to detect more gradations this second time around. Nothing wrong with it. This is completely separate from her marriage, she keeps telling herself.

She and Ron play a game at the table. They act as if they've never spoken to each other, and they exchange calling cards. He plays the game so convincingly that for a moment she fears he really has forgotten her already, like a busy goldfish in a bowl full of identical goldfish who no longer remembers whom he swam a lap with three seconds after he's done it. After all the back-and-forth glances between them she plucks up her courage. This is why she loves decorum so much: she enjoys the theatre, the sentences spoken over and over again that acquire a certain sparkle when actors find each other beyond the script. They eat fish, talk to the other guests, and imitate normal life.

After having acted their way through the main course, it requires a superhuman effort on her part to keep the flirting civilized, to keep from making it too obvious to the waiters and the cellist sitting next to her that she's entered a new phase in her life. She stores his calling card like a golden key in her new Louis Vuitton handbag, purchased especially for this occasion. She presses the bag close to her heart during the interminable chamber music concert.

STEFAAN 1998

You can still clearly remember how your little daughter used to come knocking on the bedroom door, scared to death. *He was back*, she'd say with her pouting lower lip. The monster who walked around in the attic and would come down the creaking collapsible stairs. He was back, and at any moment he could eat her up. You had to help her, because you were her papa. You tried to reassure her by telling her that monsters didn't exist and that no monster would want to walk on the fibreglass in the attic anyway. You even showed her the next afternoon: *feel it, it stings*. Your attempt to comfort her didn't work. As you stood there with that trembling little body in your arms, you knew that it wasn't the monster she was worried about. You wanted to promise her that nothing bad would ever happen to her, but you couldn't do that. When you were small, you often prayed before going to bed that everyone would be all right: Mama, Papa, your little brother, and yourself. You made a tent of your sheets and prayed that prayer, whispering, with your fingers against your lips so you could feel the words, while you could hear the rumbling noises in the next room. A basin of water was being filled because your father had another headache and your mother was laying belladonna compresses on his forehead.

It's Easter vacation and you've decided to spend these days with your family. You've cancelled all the appointments in your datebook. The reassuring everydayness of bedroom slippers, daffodils, and lawn mowers awaits you. Everything is very familiar, but you have changed.

The breakfast table is richly decorated. There are hard-boiled eggs, *pains aux raisins,* and chocolate spread. Although it isn't Easter until tomorrow, Mieke would like to celebrate the Easter feast with the two of you today. Later her sister is coming by and she won't have any time for such things. You see your daughter sit down at the breakfast table. You see your wife bite her lip to swallow her criticism of Sarah's clothes and appearance. On the radio the news announcer is talking about a study that has shown that aggression among young people is increasing. 'I wouldn't want to be young today,' says Mieke, and she means this as a bit of encouragement for her daughter. A couple of birds are singing outside so assertively that Mieke wonders whether they're having a fight. Sarah laughs. This is the impetuous child again, not the recalcitrant teenager. With an appetite you don't usually see in her, Sarah bites the ear off a chocolate rabbit that Mieke placed on the stiffly ironed tablecloth one hour ago, next to her cup of milk. Sarah makes no secret of the fact that she's childishly pleased with the attention. She also gets an envelope containing money to buy something for her room. 'Because if I buy it you'll just think it's ugly,' says Mieke.

A heavy antique atlas is pressed into your hands, full of maps of these regions as they looked during the Middle Ages, faithful reproductions of the originals. It's a gift. You haven't even thought about gifts. Where has your head been? The three of you look for the place where your house would be located if you had built it in the Middle Ages. Apparently your house would be right in the middle of a brook.

Sarah jumps up and looks out the window, searching for traces of the brook. Your daughter is all skin and bones. You really ought to do something about it.

It's a disease that many girls from her social background are suffering from. You see them, totally emaciated, biking up the mountain or jogging for hours in their baggy clothing. They're nothing but stick figures, on the verge of collapse and always digging up excuses for not having to eat. Ambitious young women, every one of them, growing up too slowly in overprotective environments. They're looking for ways to handle the immense pressure they live under. Everything they do is measured against what their parents have already achieved. Growth without end, climbing higher and higher, until you find yourself adrift with no point of reference. In your case it was a bit easier to outdo your parents.

Mothers bear an overwhelming amount of the blame for this. They keep a close watch on what their daughters eat, especially what they don't eat. They reward them if they pass up dessert. They lead them to believe that fat people get fewer opportunities and are basically inferior. Self-control is the key word. How can you ever get as far as your parents if you can't even skip dessert? Or one meal? Or two?

And you're guilty as well. You ought to protect your daughter, but you don't. You fall short in every respect, and you know it. It's a thread running through your life. You let people bring disaster on themselves. These last couple of days you've been disguising yourself as a normal family man. It's costing you all the strength you have. You're already an outsider. You stand there looking in through the window at the world of number 7 Nightingale Lane.

Your wife can do it: live a more or less happy life, full of worries but single-minded. It seems to follow a certain law. The more energetically she makes her way through life, the less power you retain. The more enthusiastic she is, the more aloof you become. When she caught on to the fact that she could no longer count on her husband, and she realized that he didn't give a damn whether she dished up packaged soup for him or homemade soup she'd spent half the day working on, the scales fell from her eyes. She decided to put herself first, and that increased her happiness considerably.

Mother and daughter have no need of anyone else. It's a fair exchange: Mieke can keep a close eye on Sarah within the grounds of number 7 Nightingale Lane, and in exchange Sarah can have uncontrolled mood swings, ups and downs that switch and overlap in the spring of her life like rain falling while the sun shines. When you see those two bent over your atlas, you know your role has been played out.

Your sister-in-law Lydia is coming to visit from New York. 'Lydia and her professor doctor engineer,' Mieke has been saying for years when referring to Lydia and her workaholic husband, Christopher J. Delaney, the professor of materials science. Lydia and her husband enjoy the elaborate meal Mieke prepares for them. Mieke spends three quarters of her time in the kitchen, so you're left with the job of trying to converse with your sister-in-law and her taciturn husband.

The next day Lydia throws an improvised party for her Belgian friends in a rented commercial hall. She dumps cans and jars of food onto plates and plunks them down on a row of tables in imitation of a buffet. Mieke cries shame. Her sister Lydia is swimming in money but won't spend a franc if she can help it. The hem is hanging from her skirt and her husband is missing a canine tooth.

'She's just not interested in those things,' you say.

'Tut-tut, that's no excuse,' says Mieke.

There's one more obligation to be met that day. In the

Dennenhof Rest Home, cake is being served in the room of Mieke's great-aunt. The lady is the sister of Sarah's grandmother. She's very interested in Sarah's 'music makery', as she calls it, and she's so charming and sassy that Sarah is incapable of maintaining her surly, cool appearance. You're too tired to sit up in your chair and too nervous to stay in the small, overheated room. After a while you volunteer to take the cake dish and the coffee back to the cafeteria. Your wife goes to the visitors' toilet farther down the corridor. You pause for a moment at the door. The old woman asks your daughter to turn up the radio. Apparently the station selector has been frozen at the same old folks' station for years. A tango hurls itself against the walls of the sweltering little room, which are covered with photos of deceased loved ones.

'Would you like to dance with me?' the old woman asks your daughter. At first Sarah pretends not to hear, but the woman asks her a second time, louder now: 'Would you like to dance with me?' Your daughter complies. She takes the frail woman by the hand and dances a slow dance with her. The woman dances with her eyes closed, thinking back to earlier days when she danced the tango with her husband on Sunday afternoons in their winter salon.

We, too, dance along. We pirouette gracefully around the dancing couple until we get dizzy.

They shuffle through the room. The fragile old woman dances with her wrinkled little head against your daughter's shoulder. Walking on tiptoe, you leave the room to keep from disturbing the scene. You see Mieke approaching from far down the corridor. You dive into a side passage.

Your getting acquainted, engagement, and marriage—those steps followed each other so matter-of-factly.

Looking back, each step could be perfectly predicted. First living together in a small apartment that could qualify as modern. Curtains with big orange flowers on a brown background, wall-to-wall carpeting right up to the bathtub, and an intercom system: those were the items that made the rent respectable. Mieke wanted a minimum of comfort, after all; you agreed to whatever your wife wanted, certainly after both of you had made the joint decision that Mieke would pursue the most honourable but least valued calling in the world as soon as you had had a baby. As a housewife she would be able to devote herself to everything she had neglected for so many years. There were so many unnamed things that she hadn't learned, so much she had done without in her protective home environment, with a dominating, capricious father and a submissive, highly respectable mother. Who knows, she could even take tennis lessons. The two of you built an enormous villa, tried for years to have children, and then finally Sarah was born. You had the hope that she would raise you up, but gradually it began to dawn on you that you were growing smaller and smaller.

This is the last necessary step.

It's all so logical. You go back to the room where your daughter is dancing with the old woman. There's your daughter, there are we, standing in the midst of life. And you, you're already gone.

SARAH 1998

On a sunny day in April, during French class, there's a knock at the door. The girls look up from their old, thoroughly gouged wooden desks and dimly make out a female form through the milky glass.

Almost immediately there's another knock at the door, this time more emphatic. Without waiting for an answer the door is opened onto the din of class 6B. All heads swivel automatically to the doorway at the front of the classroom. Antonia trips in. She's a lanky, friendly, but rule-conscious lady from the secretarial office with reading glasses hanging from a gold chain on her bosom. According to stories, she's been working here longer than anyone else, even longer than the headmaster. She peers into the classroom but doesn't immediately see the pupil she's looking for.

'I'm interrupting you,' she says to the teacher.

'Say it in French or she won't listen!' someone shouts.

' ... Sarah Vandersanden is to come with me.'

Sarah looks around at the rest of the class from which she is now being called forward. She stands up, only too happy that Antonia hasn't come in with her mother in her wake carrying a lunchbox, as she did two years ago. Sarah got so angry back then that her mother more or less admitted for the first time that what she had done was excessive, although it was important that Sarah eat a healthy meal.

'There's a phone call for you.' Sarah walks through the silent corridors at Antonia's side. Who knows, maybe there's some incredible news for The Lady Di's. The bell in the distant tower strikes three as Sarah walks into the staff office behind Antonia. A pupil is not allowed to enter this room unaccompanied. Antonia's desk is full of freshly made photocopies that she is collating in stacks and fastening with staples. Probably more guidelines for caring for the plants in the corridors or a repetition of the ban on playing volleyball in the school building. Antonia from the secretarial office is unceasing in her attempts to focus the pupils' attention on trifles; that's her job. Who in God's name would want to speak with Sarah so urgently? MH, Suri, and Emily are all sitting at their desks. It can't be her mother, because she would just come straight to the school. It must be some producer.

Lying on top of a stack of papers is the telephone receiver, an ivory-coloured thing that hundreds of people have spoken into.

Antonia says she can take the call. She turns away from Sarah ostentatiously, as if doing so puts her outside the room and certainly renders her incapable of listening in. Sarah can't imagine why she was chosen to hear the news, but it's a huge compliment in any case. She'll limit the conversation to one-syllable answers to keep Antonia in the dark.

'Hello?' Her own voice sounds thin and jittery.

'Sarah!' She hears a voice that she doesn't recognize right away because her guesses are so far off. She hasn't even allowed for the possibility that it might be him, her father. One second later she's disappointed because her daydream of a record contract and a flight to London— Now! Today!—has collapsed.

'Sarah, is it you?' her father asks.

She's shocked to hear how loud her heart is pounding. Her father doesn't call out of the blue for laughs, or to tell her a bit of news from Sri Lanka. Her father, like everyone who's bad at small talk, is a disaster on the phone. Sarah can't remember ever having had a real phone conversation with him. Once on a class trip she had spent two insuperably long minutes on the line with him because her mother had gone grocery shopping. They never got any further than *how are you, fine, and how about you.*

'What is it, Papa?'

'It's important to me, I don't say it enough: I'm proud of you.'

'Papa, I'm at school, you know.'

This declaration of love from her father is so unusual that she's forced to look somewhere else for a cause: in alcohol, for instance. She's never seen her father under the influence before. Her mother always puts a stop to it. After two glasses of wine the cork goes back in the bottle. She supposes he's been staring into his glass too long in Sri Lanka and is calling her for fun, not fully aware of the five-hour time difference.

'I just wanted ... Never mind. I'm sorry I disturbed you, honey.'

Sarah listens closely, since maybe there are background noises that might indicate where he is and why he's calling her at school for the first time in her life. And who takes the phone number of his kid's school on a business trip anyway?

'Is that why you're calling me?' she asks. Behind her, Antonia from the secretarial office pricks up her ears.

She doesn't understand what he wants. Her father is a mystery. There's nobody on the face of the planet she understands less than him. She can easily come up with five qualities that characterize this Antonia of the secretarial office, but she knows next to nothing about her own father.

'Looking forward to seeing you,' he says. She imagines him standing in the corridor of a big hotel, in a phone booth near a conference hall. There was so much servility and confusion in his voice that it makes Sarah uneasy. What prompted him to think she could cheer him up on a boring business trip? Her father has already hung up. Sarah does the same.

'I hope it was something important,' says Antonia of the secretarial office. 'Ask your father not to make a habit of it. You can go back to your class now.' As if she were speaking to a kindergartener. The woman returns to her desk and begins stapling at high speed to make up for the delay. The phone call has kept her from her work.

Sarah goes to the playground and takes the longest possible detour to get to her class. Distant teachers' voices can be heard from the classrooms. Out on the athletic fields a workman is climbing a ladder in order to fiddle with a loosely hanging basketball hoop.

MIEKE 1998

The telephone rings at number 7 Nightingale Lane. Mieke is in the kitchen patting dry some oyster mushrooms. You must never run oyster mushrooms under the tap. They're sponges that absorb every bit of moisture. Once they come in contact with water you might as well throw them away because you'll never be able to sauté them properly. The paper towels that Mieke carefully places on top of the mushrooms keep sticking. She suspects the man in the poultry and game shop of having dampened them. You can charge quite a bit more for oyster mushrooms that way because it triples their weight. Her fear is that she won't have enough of them for her dinner with Elvira tonight.

She stares at the fleshy mushrooms in her hands and lets the importunate telephone keep on ringing. The composure that she has tried to force on herself for weeks with regard to Ron has yet to take effect. On the contrary, every encounter is a scene from a movie that she plays over and over again in her head as she falls asleep. It never loses its clarity. She has an infinite capacity to remember every word they've ever exchanged. She turns Ron's words every which way and looks at them from every angle, like diamonds she can endlessly admire. There's little to admire, however, about Sarah's categorical 'no'. That 'no' was a direct response to Mieke's question, asked in the silkiest tones, as to whether Sarah might sound out Madam Jules concerning the possibility of her mother organizing a party—a prestigious party to benefit the foundation that, by the way, would not cost Madam Jules a single franc—at the castle where

Sarah spends more time than she does at home. Her daughter barked out the 'no' before she was even finished talking. That's a hard one to swallow. Especially if you've already piqued the attention of your girlfriends at the foundation by describing the whole setting, and you've already explained to them that your daughter is the best friend of the nobility who now inhabit the domain. No one has a child as difficult as hers. No one.

Sometimes she has a strong urge to drive to Brussels, to Rouppe Square (or wherever it is that the reporter Jan Balliauw does his stories about riots and drugs), and to pick up a substantial supply of drugs and give them to Sarah. 'See how modern I am? I'm not as backward as you think. Here, have fun.' After which her daughter would stare at the life-threatening stuff in her mother's hands with her eyes popping out of their sockets, turn the little Ziploc bags over and over again, conclude that it was all genuine, gasp 'Mama, don't use this!', promptly throw it all in the toilet, and flush. In every one of these fantasies Mieke sees herself triumphant. Unfortunately she doesn't like to drive the car in a dangerous, hectic metropolis like Brussels.

'Haven't you ever had the feeling that you're the maid?' Ulrike asked her yesterday. 'The maid who's supposed to just keep her mouth shut, and certainly not ask any questions. All sorts of things happen when those kids get together. You stand there watching them, but you have no idea what they're talking about, and you can't make head nor tail out of all those hand gestures and those so-called dance steps.' Ulrike dunks a homemade cookie in her coffee, where it breaks off and sinks inexorably to the bottom like a submarine. 'And then that gloominess. Wearing black, can't stand even a ray of sunlight, getting their kicks out of blood and hacked-off limbs, and those horror files about serial killers. Brrr. I still remember that in my day I was happy with a flowery dress and a day at the beach.' Mieke's thoughts flit from there to a stolen hour with Ron on the virginal beach at the Zwin.

Mieke grabs the hare by its sinewy legs and removes it from the greaseproof paper. The dark red, lean flesh is invisibly riddled with shot. The animal was shot on one of her own properties. Every year the tenants give her a pheasant or hare they shot themselves as a gesture of sympathy. Her tenants are the children of the tenants her father knew so well. It's been going on like this from generation to generation, without a single problem.

The phone won't stop ringing. The clock on the wall says it's exactly three in the afternoon. It's six hours earlier in Boston. Three minus six is nine o'clock, she calculates. She's almost sure it's him, Ron Hoffman. She lets the phone ring, since she doesn't want to give him the impression that she's always home.

For the very first time she's serving store-bought croquettes instead of homemade, a bit of tomfoolery that she now allows herself. Stefaan says it's not a waste to buy ready-made, it's just a bit of pampering. The pitiful objects she encounters in the aluminum tray emblazoned with a wild boar, the logo of the poultry and game shop, are disappointing: most of the bread crumbs have fallen off and the croquettes themselves are dented. Her definition of pampering does not include dented croquettes.

The phone has been ringing long enough. There are limits. Mieke tosses the croquettes into the fodder bin for the chickens and picks up the receiver. 'Hello, Mieke De Kinder,' she says. When there's no answer she repeats the desperate, futile 'Hello?' All she hears is the murmur of a distant sea.

WE 1998

A black Volkswagen turns into the street. Like an uncertain beetle it moves past the properties by stops and starts, feeling its way along the house numbers on the mail slots (never on the fronts of the houses themselves). When it reaches the Vandersanden's imposing mail slot the car comes to a halt. Safety belts are clicked open. The reflection on the windows makes it difficult to see who's inside. There are two of them, a man and a corpulent woman. Before getting out of the car they put their caps on their heads. Two arms of the law in timeless dark blue, the uniform colour they share with cloistered nuns and mail carriers.

A white bolt of panic flashes before Mieke's eyes as she opens the front door. The powers that be have sent a female police officer and not just a policeman. A woman communicates better, has more empathy. It's part of the strategy, although it might also be a coincidence. They've come to get her; she's being punished for all her illicit fantasies or, who knows, even for child abuse. Once again, she's gone five steps too far in her disaster scenario. Calm down, she exhorts herself. The policewoman tries to meet her gaze. Chestnut brown eyes pin her down, a friendly nod. Mieke nods instinctively in return.

Eschewing niceties, the two bombard Mieke with a series of questions whose answers they already know. Whether Stefaan Vandersanden lives here, whether she is his lawfully wedded wife, whether it is true that they have a daughter named Sarah. She fights against the moisture that has suddenly welled up in her wide open eyes, totally out of nowhere. Breathe, look, register. The police uniforms for women are none too flattering. Especially for a buxom little squirt of an agent who's trying to strike an attitude. The policewoman asks if they might come in for a minute. Mieke is too overwhelmed to hide her honesty; she'd rather they didn't.

The policewoman insists. They'd prefer that Mieke sit down. She actually says this. Mieke takes a deep breath, balls her ice-cold fingers into fists, and asks politely if they would please tell her what they have to tell her without beating around the bush, and if they would then leave her property. In one brief moment of consultation the two officers exchange glances. Then the policewoman begins speaking. Barely three minutes later the officers are compelled to take to their heels. With heads bowed they get back into their black car.

Ulrike knows that they also send policemen to your house in cases of serious tax evasion. Well, that could never happen to the Vandersandens, of course. She's with Evi on that point. There's no getting around it: Mieke can use their help, since an uninvited guest in a blue uniform is enough to scare the living daylights out of you. They're both ready to come to Mieke's assistance. Marching in step, Ulrike and Evi cross the street to number 7 Nightingale Lane.

Immediately their eyes fall on one alarming detail. The Vandersandens' front door is open wide but there's no one to be seen. Ulrike calls out the name of her neighbour, her girlfriend, who has either forgotten to shut her front door or has fled the house.

They hear a stifled moan, an animal sound, an emotionally starved cat who threatens to scratch if the little girl stretches out a hand to pat it.

'Mieke?'

The moaning is coming from behind the eight-foot

boxwood. No one in the housing estate has such a boxwood at their front door. Some have normal ones; some
get a tiny new one every year, as Evi does. This plant is at
least twenty years old. The care it requires is not insignificant: one winter of inattention, one night of close to
freezing temperatures, and the boxwood dies a quiet
death.

Evi keeps quietly calling Mieke's name. The moaning
sounds more stifled in response. The woman who is pro-
grammed to never make mistakes is not at all herself.
Something has happened beyond her control. If you hear
a woman moaning with agony you tend to double up
yourself. Ulrike and Evi are overcome by a rapidly bifur-
cating pain.

'Mieke, please answer me.'

Mieke is hiding behind the boxwood. Ulrike and Evi
worm their way into the narrow passage between the
front of the house and the boxwood plant, the trench
where Mieke is squatting down.

Mieke becomes aware of a presence. Evi's voice pricks
through a little hole in the black surface of her percep-
tion. Suddenly she comes to. Mieke holds up her nose
and sniffles. Because not a single weed is growing around
the plant, she begins rooting around in the soil.

She didn't know it would be like this. In every human
life the days are strung together, forming a cord you
never would have designed yourself. But this is something she had not allowed for. All at once Mieke begins
producing sounds, the words of a talking doll. She tells
the whole battered story in snatches.

Stefaan was in Sri Lanka where he drove the wrong
way onto a highway exit. They drive on the left side of the
road there. Almost immediately he collided head-on
with a large truck. The truck driver was cut out of his tall

cab in a state of shock. As a wrong-way driver you don't stand a chance of surviving something like this. Stefaan was killed on the spot.

It's as if a bag full of water had burst open. The grief wells up. So fresh and new, bubbling up from the darkest core of existence. She drinks from it, slaking her thirst. Ulrike and Evi wrap their arms around Mieke. She allows it for a moment, then stiffens.

'Well, I think the weeds here are really gone.' Mieke frees her shoulders with a shake and apologizes. 'The front door is going to slam shut in the wind. Then I'll be locked out of my own house.' The boxwood pricks her face. One by one, Mieke, Ulrike, and Evi leave the flower bed where the boxwood is located. They're standing in the daylight again at the front door. Mieke steps inside and is about to pull the door closed.

'Mieke, let us help you.'

'You've already helped me,' says Mieke, her eyes lowered. 'Thank you.'

'We don't want to leave you behind like this.'

'I want to be alone.' The door is almost completely shut.

'Mieke, please. Are you sure?' The tears are flowing down their cheeks.

'Please go. Emily is coming home soon. She'll wonder where you are.'

Ulrike and Evi pick up on the signals. She wants to be left in peace. The front door closes.

Lying on their bed in the dark bedroom with a damp washcloth on her forehead, Mieke doesn't think about Stefaan. It still hasn't gotten through to her that he will never lie here again. And yet somewhere there's the realization that she cannot allow this. The insight is there, clear as crystal, and it brings with it a spasm of pain. Her heart tightens like a mop being wrung out. She'll have to fall back on her own resources. She'll have to mobilize everything she's ever learned in life to stand up to this. Her only goal is get her daughter through unscathed.

She goes downstairs to sit in the armchair and wait for her daughter. She's waited for Sarah hundreds of times, but never like this. As soon as Sarah opens the back door Mieke throws her arms around her, to keep her close forever and to protect her from the outside world with her own life.

'Papa,' Mieke sobs. She gasps for air and, with a super-human effort, is just able to utter the words 'killed in an accident.' It's as if Sarah were astonished and resigned at the same time, so softly and intensely does she weep, like a small animal whose leg has been caught in a trap and who doesn't stand a chance of getting free. Animals are strong, but humans are not. Just one tap between two cars and it's all over. What's left is a family that disintegrates. No matter how impossible and abysmally deep the pain is, Mieke finds it reassuring to hurtle down into the blackness with her daughter. It's unclear how long they stand there entwined, but it's a moment that will never return in all this intensity and sorrow.

All at once Sarah pulls herself away and utters one word, endlessly, until it's lost all its meaning and completely erased itself: no.

That 'no' becomes Mieke's new battle cry. This is not going to break her. She will not allow it to break Sarah. No. After a three-hour delay, Mieke succeeds in getting dinner on the table. Elvira has already been on the phone. The news is spreading like wildfire throughout the housing estate. Mieke is grateful that Elvira has dropped in, although she was also here last night, partaking of the hare and discussing a tax shelter system for the companies that are generously sponsoring the foundation.

Everything then was fine and dandy.

Mieke tells Elvira what she knows. The words she uses are totally disconnected from their meaning. She cannot imagine what it's like in Sri Lanka, let alone on the highways there. Stefaan will tell her when he gets back. She stacks one fallacy on top of another. After that half a glass of wine with the steak, of which only Elvira partakes, Mieke completely loses her bearings. In one half of her brain she's telling Stefaan what happened today: that he is gone forever. In the other half she's worried sick about how to go on living without him. It's as if you've spilled paint on a porous floor and then tried to remove it. It doesn't work. It will never work. The thing that connects her two thought furrows is Stefaan himself. She can't excise him or she herself will stop existing. Elvira helps her upstairs. Then she secures the locks on the front door and lets herself out through the utility room.

Wreaths and flowers come pouring in. The flowers have wilted before they arrive, and beautiful floral wreathes are simply non-existent. She returns the white orchid from Ron Hoffman to the flower deliveryman. Tupperware containers stack up in the kitchen. Five different kinds of soup, vol-au-vent with free-range chicken, lemon cookies. Ulrike also gives her a pack of books about bereavement. They're strange books, written by grey-haired sages. Mieke sets them by the front door, ready to give back after a period of two weeks.

There are far more roles to play than she ever thought possible: letter recipient, coffee maker, father, mother, treasurer, landlady, suspect, taxpayer, central figure, starving person, Kleenex consumer, communications director, shopper of black clothing. Something is draining her and tossing her aside like a rag against the ropes of the world's boxing ring. As long as she hasn't been knocked out she keeps on scrambling to her feet. It's more than a full-time job, and that's just what she needs right now. She dreads the day when she'll be sitting alone at the kitchen table and sliding Stefaan's ring onto her finger.

Mieke tenders her resignation as treasurer of the foundation because she is unable to do her job properly under the present circumstances. Elvira declines her resignation. They won't be able to count on her, Mieke protests. Elvira keeps declining. First Mieke has to take whatever time she needs, then they'll see how things are. For Mieke this just means a millstone around her neck. She's being tortured by guilt because she's working indirectly for Ron and is thereby being unfaithful to her dear departed husband.

Her sister Lydia has flown over from the East Coast of the United States. She tried to contact Jempy, but when she called his most recent phone number in Stellenbosch, South Africa, a woman answered who didn't react well to the name Jean-Pierre. Lydia takes a supply of strengthening protein drinks from her suitcase. Lydia is staying in a hotel in the city and comes to see her every day. They don't do a lot of talking. Mieke asks her sister to do her a favour and clear out the hobby shed.

'Don't you want to do that together?' Lydia asks. She doesn't want to encroach on Mieke's memories of Stefaan and get rid of everything without her approval. Mieke agrees to removing most of the clutter together. She wants to leave his tools and the rest of his things undisturbed for the time being.

'Did you know that Stefaan's father committed suicide?' Mieke asks her sister. She doesn't look up from her work, but keeps on stowing open cans of solidified paint in a cardboard box.

'No, I didn't know that.' Lydia has stopped sweeping. She leans heavily on her broom, as if she were in need of support. 'Don't you go getting strange ideas.'

'I want to know.'

'People exaggerate the value of science, Mieke. Science isn't God, Christopher always says. You can analyse all you want to, but the here and now plays a big role that science can never determine. Never. I'm terribly sorry, Mieke.'

Mieke goes to the police morgue to view her husband's mortal remains, which have been flown over from Sri Lanka. She goes through the most horrible moment of her life entirely alone, in the stony chill of the morgue. She will never be able to eradicate that image from her mind. She puts the police report in Stefaan's hobby shed, where her breathing is interrupted by the thought of his scribbles and sketches, which must be lying around there somewhere.

Sarah has turned off her infuriating music for the first time and has come out of her room to address envelopes for the death announcements with her Aunt Lydia. In order to keep her distance and yet to help out, Mieke has baked an apple cake. The ticking oven timer has given her thirty minutes to sit at the kitchen table and watch the grass grow. All sorts of snakes are worming their way through her thoughts.

Completely exposed, she stands in the doorway with an apple cake in her hands. She can't go a step further. She feels an axe in her midriff paralyzing her legs and draining her heart of blood. *You should have seen this coming.* She had a front row seat, watching Stefaan slip further away day after day. She discovered his papers in his hobby shed and did nothing about it. She saw how apathetic he was at the Easter party, but she let it happen because Ron had taken over her thoughts. She knew that Stefaan's father had hung himself. Stefaan committed suicide, too, and if he didn't, then what was he doing on the wrong side of the road? Why did he go gallivanting all over the globe, and why was it impossible to reason with him?

After the funeral and the light snack, which Mieke would prefer to erase from her memory as soon as possible, she returns to number 7 Nightingale Lane. People came up to her with moist eyes to tell her how beautiful the church service was, so dignified. Some of them flew into her arms. It was her job to comfort them, so that the people could go home reassured and she could be alone with her grief. The grief is so great that the whole house is creaking and groaning and coming apart at the seams.

The evening of the funeral Mieke is standing over the kitchen sink, where so many cups have gone through her increasingly wrinkled hands over the years. She rinses the plates off thoroughly before stowing them in the massive dishwasher. He who plucks the towel from her shoulder, where it's been folded into a triangle, and dries a dish with it. She who says it's not necessary, it's really not, she's going to make it easy for herself and use the dishwasher anyway. He who pretends he's a simple-minded little boy who's never heard of a dishwasher before. Were they playing a game all those years, and has he fallen out of his role?

Sarah slips her plate into the cooling dishwater and goes upstairs. They consistently avoid each other. When one is in the bathroom, the other has just enough time to get the water boiling for tea and crawl away unseen. With enormous ingenuity they devise secret routes to keep from having to confront each other. This is how they show their respect. Mieke washes the cups and the plate. Using a scouring sponge, she thoroughly cleans the white inside, the painted outside, and the Wedgwood stamp on the bottom. Outdoors the little yellow heads of the forsythia bushes have come to watch in great numbers. The grass has gotten its second wind after re-emerging from the blanket of leaves and sheet of snow. The sight of their garden hits her like a leaden slap.

You weren't able to stop him.

She opens the drawer with the small tools and takes out a pair of pruning shears. Then she strolls around the garden. Her black heels sink into the earth. She doesn't immediately know which flower to snip off to put in a vase, and finally decides on a thoroughly respectable, thoroughly innocent prunus triloba. Flowers know the great disappearing act of wintering in the dark subterranean soil and reappearing as soon as there's enough sun and warmth. She leaves the flower undisturbed but pulls a petal from one of the roses. She places it on her tongue to see how it tastes. Then she swallows it. Gone. Gone forever.

Stefaan's suitcase has vanished. They have assured her that it will be sent back, but Lydia has gently tried to tell her that there's little chance of them doing so. She wants to have the last thing he touched. She takes the piece of soap he used to wash himself for the last time. As the bathtub fills up, she holds it in her hands. She sits on the edge of the tub and watches it fill to the brim. Then she gets into the tub, in her black suit, with her jewellery still on. She thinks of Jackie O and breaks down completely. She turns on the tap as far as it will go. Under the roaring of the gushing water she can let herself weep. She pulls her head underwater until it occurs to her that she doesn't know whether she wants to come back up.

A persistent pounding on the bathroom door brings

her to her senses. 'Mama, turn off the tap,' she hears Sarah cry out. 'Mama, please.'

SARAH 1998

From now on everything happens retroactively. Banal youth has suddenly come to a horrible end; glorious graduation has taken place in a minor key. During the past few weeks at home Sarah keeps hearing the same noises: the daily, pointless vacuuming, the humming of the dishwasher, the hairdryer that loosens paint, now and then a scant word from her mother. The noise outside the house pours into her empty head with overwhelming force.

Sarah is standing on the lawn of the castle and watching Jules's party, which is getting nicely underway. About a hundred people are scattered among the bushes. The air is quivering from the booming racket, and even the flies are vibrating. She bounces her head up and down to the rhythm of 'Black Steel', Tricky's latest hit. This kind of nodding is really dancing with your head. It's supposed to indicate how relaxed you feel: you can lose yourself in the music.

More and more people are trickling out of the castle through the open patio doors and gathering around the swimming pool. One couple are horsing around at the pool's edge, holding each other in a judo grip; old acquaintances fall into each other's arms. People are enticed by the bright blue water and the mysterious sight of the jagged dark bushes surrounding them in the night. Sarah is standing behind a statueless pedestal, mustering up her courage, when Suri and Emily come walking up to her from the castle as if they had spotted her from behind the tall windows. The nods they exchange in greeting are barely visible. Suri takes a fat Cohiba cigar out of her metal smoking box. The heavy cigar smoke drifts for miles, out to the woods and into the sleeping village, where the last of the roll-down shutters descends at ten o'clock. That's also when the shutters on the mountain are closed and the curtains drawn.

Then around the corner, down the muddy driveway, and right across the carefully trimmed lawn comes a red sports car. The woman behind the steering wheel is roaring with laughter. A young man in a kind of CHiPs police uniform is lying on the roof, holding on to the edges for dear life.

'Come on, Ladies,' says Sarah with exaggerated excitement, 'let's party.' Suri and Emily stare daggers at her. She lights up a Camel.

'Where's the other Lady?' asks Suri.

'I just saw her in the library,' Emily answers.

The library's double door is open. The walls, which are full of crumbling, ancient books, look as if they were leaning more and more toward each other. Sitting in a translucent inflatable chair is Marie-Hélène, murmuring into a telephone receiver with a bare-chested man beside her who is not Barend. He has a body like a snake, white and thin. He places one arm around her and kisses her neck. 'Yes, darling, I understand,' she says into the receiver. She's wearing her standard uniform of heavy combat boots and a minuscule lace dress. When MH sees them, she motions to them to go away.

The guests are converging at the outdoor bar. As Suri worms her way through the crowd to get a bottle of champagne for the Ladies, Emily searches the large, rice cracker-like tiles for something she's not finding, something to talk about. Suddenly she starts conversing at high volume about Lars. Sarah caught a glimpse of Lars ages ago in the smoke-filled cafe across from the school, hanging from his bar stool like a wilted houseplant. Sarah isn't sure whether she should ask about the demo they cut without her, but in fact she doesn't really want to know. The Ladies all felt bad when Jules announced a couple of weeks ago that this time Scott really was going to come over to record the demo. Sarah wasn't able to leave the house the first few weeks after her father's death, but she insisted that the others cut the demo without her. *But then it won't be a Lady Di demo,* Suri objected. Sarah said they shouldn't let the chance slip away.

The Ladies came to the funeral, even though Sarah hadn't sent them invitations (except for Emily). Her mother had sent notices to all the neighbours. The funeral was also the first meeting between her mother and the other Lady Di's. Jules and Xavier weren't there. According to MH neither one of them can deal with funerals, Jules least of all. The sight of the three Ladies sitting in a pew in church had made her wince. It was totally out of place. They didn't have anything to do with her father. They should have stayed away, good intentions or no. Besides, her mother couldn't understand why Suri had come to the funeral in a garbage bag. Did that girl do it to make fun of her husband? Disrespect for the deceased, Mieke decided, that was what it was: a slap in the face. You don't go to someone else's funeral to focus all the attention on yourself.

'I'm going to the bathroom.' Sarah can't come up with a better excuse for escaping from the consequences of Emily's eulogy on her great love. Lanterns are hanging all over the castle. Profusely coloured ribbons are raining down from the high ceilings. In the hallway leading to the regally appointed bathroom there are record sleeves glued to the marble walls. Sarah gasps for breath in the seclusion of the little room. Before going back to mingle with the guests, she smokes a cigarette. *It'll be just fine,* the words her father always said to her when dropping her off at school on the day of a test. It'll be just fine.

Sarah scans all the bodies in the semi-darkness of the ballroom. She sees big burly guys, each with a dangerous edge, brash ladies who butt in on other people's conversations, emaciated goths who stare at the herringbone pattern in the parquet, ordinary girls in flowery dresses, a heavily tattooed black man with a mouthful of gold, recording executives in super sleek suits, Mafiosi with gel in their hair, fanatics who let themselves be coaxed to the pond full of koi fish, only to do an about-face at the halfway point and make for the cocktail bar to hit on a female producer or a businesswoman from Beirut.

No one looks at her, except for a guy squatting next to an amplifier and rooting around in the spaghetti of cables. He asks if she'd mind stepping aside, she's standing on a cable. The guy must have scratched some pimples open when he was younger, seeing from the pinpricks that remain. Sarah takes two serious tokes from the joint the guy offers her.

No one at this party has yet to ask her how she's doing or has given her a spontaneous hug, not like the few times she went outside the house in recent weeks. Four times, to be exact, each time to do some shopping. She went on foot from the mountain to the village with a Big Shopper bag to stock up on a few provisions from the grocer's, all neatly written down in a list by her mother. It was important not to forget anything or her mother would get upset.

At the grocer's in the village a woman spontaneously gave Sarah her place in line. She heard the people thinking, she filled in the text balloons herself. 'There she is, that girl,' 'That must be so awful.' Another woman took her elbow between thumb and forefinger and asked, 'Are you doing all right?' 'I'm all right,' Sarah smiled obediently. When she realized that she was smiling her father's smile, she felt like smashing herself against the counter. He was inside her.

Her mother is making every effort in the world to keep her life at home on track. She's doing this to make a place among the day's worries for the death of her husband, which had descended on number 7 Nightingale Lane so suddenly and without warning. She's working her way through the banalities at top speed: the rugs are being soaked, the living room walls are being stripped, steamed, washed, and re-hung with new wallpaper, and on the side of the fireplace they're being painted over. She loves keeping herself usefully occupied. Sarah knows she shouldn't begrudge her mother this work. The facade is a diversion, a survival strategy. Every generation has its walls, and those of her mother's generation, her small one-person generation, are impenetrable.

'You can keep it,' says the guy with the old pimples. She jumps. Lost in thought, Sarah has let the whole joint burn down between her fingers. She blows on the red tip and takes one last toke on the thick stub. She rubs it against the wall until sparks fly and the butt is extinguished.

An arm reaches around her shoulders. MH has come over and is propelling her in the direction of Jules's entourage. There are about as many people gathered outside as there were at her father's funeral. His body lies buried in the small cemetery at the foot of the mountain. The name of his widow, Mieke Vandersanden-De Kinder, is already carved into the marble gravestone beneath his name. It's a sinister foreshadowing, done not out of stinginess but as a sign of intense grief. To some extent her mother wants to bury herself with him. Sarah feels her heart pounding in her body. It's a virus that is spreading and will not stop until it has possessed her. She stands among Jules's friends and laughs meekly at jokes that get lost in all the racket. She exchanges tepid handshakes with the red-pupilled, gothic zombies and lets herself be hugged by Jules's enthusiastic little friends. They're world famous producers and recording executives who are not much older than the Ladies and whom Sarah has never heard of.

A man in a three-piece suit carrying a dish is wandering from group to group. On the dish are strips of powder. Finally, Sarah says to herself. Months ago, when she took her first hit from a joint, she had thought that the rest would quickly follow, that every possible drug would soon be coming her way. Sarah steps up, takes the long, narrow tube from the waiter, leans forward, and snorts a line from the cool silver. She doesn't even blink her eyes.

'Top quality,' MH says to Jules, who has come to join them. Sarah looks around timidly, at herself, at her feet, and realizes that she is still inhabiting planet earth. She squeezes her nostrils between her thumb and forefinger to make sure her nose isn't bleeding. There are lots of stories going around about ground glass in cocaine.

'Ladies,' says Jules with a thick voice, almost slurring her words, 'don't disappoint me. Don't keep it clean, whatever you do.' She's standing between Emily and Sarah with a hand on each shoulder. She gazes at them intently, first Emily, then Sarah. Then she pinches Sarah's shoulder and says, 'We'll talk.'

A producer who knows Eddie Vedder personally comes

up to Sarah and spontaneously introduces himself. His hands draw figures in the air around her while his eyes are fixed on her face. As he talks she notices that his hands are playing with her. They're warm hands, sturdy but not rough. During his manoeuvres she tries to think of the frontman from Pearl Jam, but this clean-shaven beanpole is absorbing all her attention. An image of two entwined octopuses looms up before her. The image of the octopuses makes her want to extricate herself from his embrace. He's nothing at all like her: too old, too hot-blooded, too untrustworthy. Because the subtle approach doesn't seem to work—explaining to him that she's not charmed by his advances and therefore isn't interested in fucking at this point in time—she pushes him away and shouts, 'Cut it out!' It's the coke that's doing the work for her and making her take an assertive distance. The aggressive producer glides on to a red-headed woman, deathly pale and dressed in a pink catsuit. Someone claims it's Tori Amos.

Maybe it's the cocaine, or maybe it's her aversion to doing any more listening, but Sarah wants to move. Next to the swimming pool is a tall tower of beverage and beer crates. Without even thinking about it, Sarah starts climbing the tower. The construction totters, but she keeps climbing until she's above the heads of the party-goers. The water in the swimming pool ripples below her. She looks down. There's a terrible bitter taste in her throat.

'Hey, Sarah, what're you doing?' MH shouts. The party-goers turn their heads, nudging each other until every-one is looking up at her. For a moment she's the centre of attention. She stretches herself out on top of the shaky tower, takes a deep breath, and pushes off. For half a second she hangs weightless in the air. In that brief opening in time we jump with her into the deep, thoughtless pause in which all movement freezes. The billions of drops of water stand still, the back doors of time open up, and we hurtle through the universe. The next minute Sarah feels the fabric of her clothes fluttering. She feels herself burst apart on the surface of the water like a flower that has opened at lightning speed. After swimming to the side of the pool, she sees MH follow her example and jump in after her. It's a child's game, a chance to let themselves live it up. Sarah and MH scramble out of the pool, grab Suri (who's standing at poolside with a glass in her hand), and pull her into the water. A few more partygoers jump in spontaneously after them.

Sarah looks around in the bracing water, proud of what she has set in motion. Couples blend together in the pool, which is becoming more and more congested. Clothing and cigarette butts are floating in the water, and bottles of liquor are passed from hand to hand. A couple of limber young men climb into the trees. Soon bodies are falling from the treetops like giant raindrops in a fairy-tale cartoon. Someone shouts from the roof of the castle and drops burning strips of toilet paper, which flutter back and forth in the dark yellow light. An owl turns his head a hundred and eighty degrees in order to fall asleep, which he normally doesn't do at this hour, but there will be no hunting for him tonight. Bats dart through the blackness like charred shreds.

Gradually the swimming pool fills up. Sarah pushes herself against the side of the pool and climbs out. The other Ladies are already sitting in the prickly grass. The guests use tablecloths and curtains to dry themselves off. Sarah hears the chattering of her own teeth, like the up-and-down movement of a sewing machine.

She notices that all the little hairs on her arms are standing on end, but it doesn't get through to her, she doesn't experience it.

Male bodies and female bodies, dressed and undressed, at peace or filled with desire, dripping or rubbed dry, are lying every which way on the grass and staring up at the dark puffs of cotton in the sky. The guy from the cable company comes over to talk to her and asks her endless questions about The Lady Di's. The guy strongly advises her to keep the group's name. Their basic principle sounds incredibly good. Music at the crossroads between old punk and trip hop, *that's* the music for these new times, everybody from London to New York agrees with her.

Sarah congratulates herself on her acting talent. She can't even think about rehearsing with the Ladies. She wants to go away, away from her life on the mountain, away from everything bursting with references to her father.

All at once there's a dull thud behind them. A tidal wave bursts up from the swimming pool, a wall of water that rises several feet and smashes against the tiles in billions of fragments. The group of people standing around the pool in a semicircle are suddenly soaking wet, their cigarettes extinguished on the way to their mouths. The red sports car is sinking into the water. After a frozen moment of total silence the world breaks open again. The onlookers laugh themselves silly. A woman worms her supple body through the car window and flaps like a mermaid to the edge of the pool. The woman gives a shout and is fished out by a couple of he-men rushing to her aid.

Many short-lived friendships and many shared glasses and cigarettes later, Sarah is lying next to the cable guy behind a couple of bushes. She thinks he's good-looking, and that's all. Timidly she wraps her arms around him. It's nice to cuddle up and feel his body on hers, but suddenly it feels as if a net had been thrown over her. Even though he's taken the necessary precautions, this is how babies are made; it's how she herself came into the world. Some day she'll be the daughter who makes babies, just like that, so that those babies, too, can die. She pushes this thought from her mind and holds the guy tight.

All right, we whisper in her ear. This is what you want. All that sadness is a waste of time. You have to melt it down into something else. From loss to profit, the most natural progression in the world.

She and the guy fall into a deep, euphoric sleep. When she wakes up, she sees from the corner of her eye a dog's tongue licking the dregs of wine from the glasses. In the swimming pool a ladder is trembling beneath the undulating water. A few articles of clothing and an inflatable shark are floating like silent witnesses on the water's surface. She's frozen to the bone. The coke has worn off. She had expected more from the hard drug, just as she had expected more from the death of her father. Like being out of commission for a specific period of time and then being able to get on with her life. But that's not what happened. It's been a drawn-out, lingering, endless bad trip. It's a torment that she can't explain to anybody. Normally your parents are in the background. But this background keeps pushing itself into the foreground. Will there ever come a time when she can calmly say that her father is dead? No, never, not here. She's suffocating in this country. All she can do here is walk around with that stupid smile on her face, the way her father used to do. She doesn't want to be like that. She refuses to be the daughter of a dead man with a dead brother and a dead father. She will not be a pawn on a battlefield where the slain are periodically brushed from the game board.

Morning light is quickly approaching, as if the lid were being lifted from a big box containing the whole earth. Sarah goes indoors. There are party guests lying in corners all over the castle, like in a Baroque painting in which you keep discovering more and more people. From the depths of the castle she hears momentary laughter, then a long period of silence. She cuts across to the library. The Ladies are sleeping in the armchairs, Suri with her head on the lap of MH, who's lying with her head on the lap of Emily. Sarah won't begrudge them the blissful ignorance that she herself no longer believes in. She blames her father not only for the stupid way his life came to an end, but also for the fact that in his crash her own plans were torn to shreds.

The first beams of morning light come streaming in. Someone has folded a film poster into a crane and placed the bird on top of the piano. Jules is reclining on a chaise longue and paging through a book about animals of the North Pole. Sarah plops down beside her.

Jules asks her how she's doing. She looks sincerely interested. She wants to hear an answer. Sarah shrugs her shoulders. She has no answer, only a handful of facts and the echo of a last phone call. The objective version she tells Jules is a simple sentence, with her father driving the wrong way as the subject and death on a highway exit ramp in Sri Lanka as the predicate.

Jules is one of those people who throws her back on herself, on the Sarah she's stuck with, for better or worse. The Sarah who drags a ton of troubles behind her so it's harder and harder to make any headway. The third person who looks at her and wonders, who are you in my life?

Jules asks Sarah if she knows what her plan is.

'Yes,' she says.

'That's important,' Jules nods. 'Go for it.'

Sarah turns her back to Jules and slips out through the crack of the open door without touching anything. The sunlight pierces the interior through the tall windows and slices the castle into pieces.

'Go for it.' The words resound in Sarah's head. She feels the warmth of the sun penetrate her clothing. At every step she feels herself growing. She goes to the caretaker's lodge and picks up her bag with all her things. Over the months she's been with The Lady Di's she's left more clothes and notebooks here than she realized. Everything has to go; she doesn't want to leave a single trace behind.

At the edge of the swimming pool she sees Xavier, who spent the night with the Polish cleaning woman because parties are more than he can handle. Xavier closes his eyes and absorbs all the sounds around him. His feet are as big as buoys.

'Xavier.' She likes to pronounce his name. The sounds collide with each other. It's a rough name that suits him to a T, the rudimentary, unfinished idea of what a human being is.

As soon as he sees her he gives her a big hug, over-joyed, like a little kid hugging his mother after a ride on the merry-go-round. She puts her hands around his neck, which is too wide to completely encircle. She's sure he hasn't missed her. Now that she's standing right in front of him again, he may vaguely remember or realize that she hasn't been there in weeks. He keeps hugging and stroking her. His raspy voice tries to convey a message. His swollen eyelids tell her he didn't sleep much last night either.

'Bye, castle,' she says as she walks down the driveway with Xavier at her side. The blackberry bushes have already shaken the early dew from their leaves and point to the driveway in large, untamed tufts.

It's her last time here. The mirage has burst apart. A miserable pile of stones, an anachronistic castle in a state of decay, are all that remain. Every step takes her farther away from that crumbling world. She will never be famous with The Lady Di's, she doesn't want to hear a word about the demo, the producer, the release. There's still a small air bubble of music inside her. It's so small and vulnerable that she can't show it to anyone.

Xavier walks beside her, carrying her bag. He follows her without question, like a house pet, trudging along without pausing or turning to look back. Together they make their way through the village. The cousin of the grocer, a man in jeans and a moustache curled at the ends, is sitting on a chair at the door to his shop. A woman like Granny is sitting a couple of houses farther on, washing her wrinkled face in the pure summer light. Xavier waves to them all.

A couple of children are playing in the sunken road at the foot of the mountain. They're steering a remote-controlled truck up the embankment, but it's so steep that the monster truck keeps overturning and tumbling back down. They don't give up. This is part of their game, over and over again. She and Xavier stop and watch until Xavier can no longer control himself. He drops the bag, and without even looking at her he climbs up the embankment of the sunken road like a clumsy ape. He grabs hold of the exposed tree roots and unyielding bushes. She lets him climb, watching as he reaches the top and knocks the dirt from his pants. Then he runs all the way out of her field of vision: Xavier, the boy who feels no pain. She sits down and gazes for a long time at the village below.

Just before noon she rings the bell at number 7 Nightingale Lane. She waits for an eternity, until the thumping at the top of the stairs rolls all the way down.

Mieke, in a pair of white overalls, pulls the front door open. She looks out with screwed-up eyes, as if she barely recognizes her daughter. Then she drags Sarah and her stinking bag of clothes into the house. She zips open the bag in the utility room and stares at the knot of clothes with a face full of disgust. One by one she pushes the garments into the open eye of the washing machine. Only after pouring powdered detergent and fabric softener into the little compartments and setting the machine on boiling does she turn her face to Sarah, who is watching the laundry ritual in a daze.

'I'll go get a piece of beef from the freezer. It'll be thawed out in fifteen minutes, a thin slice of meat like that. But first go take a shower, dear,' she says emphatically. 'Please go take a shower. And then come and eat. It'll be ready in half an hour.'

The house has changed. The smell of paint and white spirits greets her at the top of the stairs. A stepladder is lying full length on the floor to flatten a piece of protective plastic sheeting, brushes wave like seaweed in old canning jars. She goes into the bathroom. She's come back to this house as an outsider. It bears only a vague resemblance to the house of that family with the father who was a deliberate wrong-way driver.

Just when Sarah is about to step out of the shower, just when she's begun to feel that the quicklime has been washed from her bones, her mother comes into the bathroom and pulls the shower curtain back, without any warning. After Sarah was born, mother and daughter never saw each other naked or partially clothed. The liberating message of the sixties fell on barren soil in Mieke's case. It's the record of a generation that got stuck in its groove. Even accidentally walking in on someone in a toilet or bathroom is a crime, and crimes don't take place in this house.

Sarah stands before her mother, stark naked.

'Look at how scrawny that child is!' exclaims Mieke from behind the shower curtain, which Sarah has pulled closed with a jerk. In the past she would have called Stefaan as a witness. He would have stormed up and stood in the doorway, averting his eyes from his naked daughter.

'That can't be healthy!'

'But Mama,' Sarah whines.

'Why are you doing this? Why won't girls eat properly these days?'

'I eat,' says Sarah, and she reaches for a towel from behind the curtain.

'Oh, no you don't,' says her mother, shaking her head in denial. 'Why, for heaven's sake?'

'I don't want to be a fat slob like Shana from Servranx the butcher.'

'You'd have to eat the backside of a cow every day to get that big, and I don't see you doing that anytime soon,' says Mieke. 'You're just being contrary, that's all. But I'm not going to let that happen. Get dressed and we'll talk more downstairs.'

Her mother leaves her standing in the bathroom. It strikes Sarah how banal her rage is. She goes into her old room with the pink wallpaper. It's the room she lived in until she was thirteen, before she got an even bigger room, and it's where her mother does the bookkeeping now. To play for time, Sarah looks at the class photos her mother has hung up here. On the desk are a stack of ironed Dujardin T-shirts and a calendar for the year 1990 with illustrations of birds of prey and regional dishes. Otherwise there are new bookshelves with large loose-leaf binders and books on art and architecture. There's a package of letterhead next to the new printer and envelopes bearing the logo of the foundation and the crown of the royal house.

Finally Sarah goes downstairs. She sees the new rugs rolled up in the entrance hall. She knows her mother is going to keep on decorating this homemade hell forever. She walks into the living room, ready for the confrontation.

'You think you can bring Papa back this way?' She knows the boomerang is going to be thrown back at her.

'I'll have no more of that nonsense!' Mieke shouts. 'I've been waiting here for half an hour. How long have we been standing here?' Mieke is addressing Stefaan, her off-screen husband. 'Half an hour, I'm not exaggerating. I want to know what the plan is.'

'What do you want me to say?' Sarah misses the fight between her parents that this should have been. The fights where she always lit the fuse, and that always ended the same way. Fights so predictable she can dream them.

'Is this how we brought you up?'

'Aaaaaaa.' Sarah lets out a long, drawn-out cry. She herself is startled.

'Oh dear oh dear,' says Mieke, shocked. 'What's wrong with her? She's losing her mind!'

'Yes, I'm losing my mind! I can't stay here anymore, Mama.'

They cannot console each other. The most they can do is avoid each other, as they've been doing all along in such an exemplary fashion. 'I know, dear, I know,' Mieke admits.

'I have to get out of here.'

'We can deal with this.'

'I have to get out of here, Mama. I have to get out of here.'

'Do you want your own apartment? That's no problem. That's fine with me.'

'I have to get out of here, out of this country.'

'Out of this country? And what about your girl-friends?'

'They'll make their own plans.'

'What's wrong with me? Everyone is leaving me.'

'It's not about you, it's about me.'

'No, that's not going to happen.' Mieke shakes her head in total disbelief. 'Your father would never approve.'

Silently, Sarah makes her way through the bowl of hot, unsalted zucchini soup. Somehow she forces the steak with mashed potatoes and steamed spinach down her throat.

'Eat up. It's very lean meat,' says her mother. 'There's not a bit of fat in it. Don't be frightened. Come on, now, just a little.'

After Mieke has washed the plates and the silverware and stacked them in the dishwasher, the widow sends her only daughter upstairs. 'Go up and get some sleep.'

'I'm going to help you,' says Mieke the next morning. She's peeling a banana and slicing it into chunks. 'I called Aunt Lydia. I'll let you go to America for a year, and your Aunt Lydia will help you there. On one condition: that you go back to eating normally. I don't want my daughter doing herself in. No, that's not going to happen. I won't allow it.'

Mieke takes a large container of full-fat quark from the refrigerator. She scoops a white cloud of quark onto the banana and adds pine nuts and a big curl of honey. A breakfast that Mieke herself would never eat.

'Mama, I'm going to eat. I'm going to eat normally.' She's made up her mind.

'That's a good girl.'

The click that Sarah makes in her head is so loud that over the coming weeks she occasionally goes to the opposite extreme and attacks every bit of food like a person who was starved during the war and has finally been released, so that Mieke even has to restrain her. Sarah has chosen life.

Mieke does credit to her obsessive nature and throws herself into this project with an avidity that astonishes everyone. With the help of her sister Lydia, or mostly her brother-in-law Christopher, she makes it possible for Sarah to go to America and arranges for a student visa. She appoints Lydia chaperone so the eighteen-year-old won't be left to fend for herself in the gigantic, life-threatening city of New York. Mieke gives Sarah a run-down of all the different fields of study at the city's top universities, and she keeps having to admit that Sarah is right: it's a brilliant idea to guarantee herself a gold-plated future by studying at an international genius factory like, say, Columbia.

When Sarah asks her mother why she's helping her so much, Mieke says, without batting an eye, that it's going to be hard enough to keep her own head above water in this neighbourhood.

'Maybe it'll work out well for you, too. One of the last things Papa told me was that you wanted to send me away.'

'Well, now you can make him say whatever you like,'

says Mieke. For the first time in months their laughter reverberates through the redecorated house.

MIEKE 2003

Mieke pushes against the wooden gate that symbolically encloses the country manor and its grounds. The rest of the fence—wooden stakes reaching out to each other by means of barbed wire—is lying flat, as if a herd of buffalo had broken out. At the airport in Faro she rented a car at the Avis stand. Their company motto is 'we try harder'.

She's driven here over twisting roads, a bundle of nerves, thinking she was lost at every hairpin turn, her tongue as dry as dust after thirty excruciating miles. Sometime after twelve noon she had stopped at a shabby, improvised snack bar along the side of the narrow asphalt road, where all she could get was a free breadbasket but nothing to eat. The fish still had to be caught. So she ordered a glass of wine, just to be polite. She was given an entire carafe. Continuing on her way, she cursed herself because she was only doing this to prove to herself and her brother Jempy that she was strong and independent.

It's been pretty a wild ride, driving to the heart of the Algarve in that rented car, finally to end up at the remote and dilapidated farm of her brother Jempy.

'You're going to love Portugal,' he had told her over the phone in an attempt to entice her. 'You have to come, because I'm never leaving here and I want to see you. It's already been way too long.'

She shuts the gate behind her and does her exercise. Inhaling and exhaling three times and slapping her chest with every exhale. There's no reason for stress. She's doing this of her own free will. She wants to see how

Jempy is living now. He's always said that the course of every life is written down beforehand in a big book, so he doesn't have to restrain himself. He bounces back from every blow, he prospers everywhere. She's looking forward to being in his company. The first hours will involve sniffing each other out in order to rediscover what they have in common, certainly now that they've grown so far apart. He claims to have found happiness in the great outdoors, and she carries on a daily battle just to enjoy her cut flowers.

It's the first time since Stefaan's death that she's left the country on her own. Elvira has often tried to tempt her to take a trip overseas, but she never felt ready. They've gone on several city trips together, though: Valencia, Vienna, Rome. But she's immediately blocked every one of Ron's invitations to visit Boston.

You can't control everything.

Tomorrow she's going to be fifty-three, and she wants to give herself something: a bit of freedom. It's as if she's let herself out of prison and has stepped up to the gate, timidly peeping. A murder was committed years ago, of her husband, by her husband. That's how she sees it now, after endless self-medication and disciplined therapy, after hundreds of entries in her diary and scrapbook aimed at reining in her despair. Stefaan murdered himself. It's unnatural, it flies in the face of all logic and all instinct, but she's doing all she can to live with this fact. At first she wanted to wring his neck. At half past six in the evening she'd sit down in the armchair with trembling hands, waiting, sliding back into a hole in time, straining her ears for sounds of his return: the click of the garage door sliding open, the car slowly riding in, the removal of shoes. She wanted to hear it so she could storm into the garage and attack him. She hadn't yet confronted him for the insipid message he left on the voicemail, which she didn't listen to until a week after the funeral, a stupid 'I'm sorry, Mieke.' She still can't wrap her head around it. It's a wall of reinforced concrete that she keeps crashing into, over and over again. She's long passed the stage of trying to disguise the suicide as an accident. She'll let the others believe it, though. An automobile accident. They must never know that her husband ended his own life. It's their last shred of dignity as a couple, and she'd do anything to preserve it, at all costs.

Mourning has been an agonizing process. For the first few months the only feelings she could muster for him were negative thoughts and accusations. After a while the whole experience literally brought her to a boil. Then one night, sweating and kicking in her tangled sheets, she made a decision to turn the tide. She went to one of the seven bedrooms, the one that serves as her writing room, and opened a new notebook.

Write down your positive memories of Stefaan, not the bitter eruptions and barbs you fling at him.

The page remained blank. She stared and stared. The whiteness stared back, indifferent, just like the rest of the happy, bouncy world that had nothing for her but a few pats on the shoulder.

Stop with the accusations. Think positively.

She got that from one of those idiotic self-help books Ulrike gave her. With the help of photographs she was able to recall a number of nice memories, but they all seemed tarnished. If she looked at a photo of him holding a spade, back when they were working on the new flower beds, all she could see was a man digging his own grave. A photo of Stefaan with the bashful toddler Sarah on his lap, his gaze fixed on a bowl of fruit porridge, filled her with emotion. What was he thinking about, that he didn't dare look into the lens? Everywhere she looked for foreshadowings of his cruel deed. Gradually something shifted. Stefaan was not a murderer who had felt bad and had taken the easy way out. This was where the real tangle lay: in his past, and in the material from which he was made. At the bookstore she walked past the self-help department, because what she wanted were scientific books with facts. The salesperson had to order them. They had been suggested by Lydia's husband Christopher, recent and older books suitable for laymen. From Darwin she learned that genes persistently soldier on, despite everything. For instance, giraffes developed because deformed deer with overgrown necks could reach the leaves in the trees more easily and were more likely to survive. The first half-deer/half-giraffe probably found it painful to have such a ridiculously long, meandering neck, but thanks to her a new species was created. That's how ingenious nature is. Genes want to survive.

It's hard to detect a useful system in fathers who commit suicide and contaminate the rest of their family. At the very most, serial suicide is a kind of preventive means of self-protection, should life on the planet earth become truly unliveable. She felt herself being dragged into a downward spiral: his whole life had been shaped by a powerless sense of guilt after the death of his father and his brother. Just as her life now has been affected forever and she wonders where she had made a mistake. And Sarah feels guilty, too. And her children will ... It was the cycle that was the cruellest thing of all.

Grandchildren. Something else to think about. Her fear and her hope. As Elvira always says: the world would be so much better off with just women. That's not entirely true, of course, but it is to a certain extent. Definitely in the case of the Vandersandens. She's now inextricably linked to them through Sarah. Her flesh and blood mixed with depressive genes, although Lydia would like to disabuse her of that idea. We do have free will, says Lydia, and it's very strong. Thanks to her free will she sent Sarah away, difficult as it was. They got along so badly that the only thing they could agree on was that one point: living together in one house was out of the question. If they did, neither one of them would find peace of mind. The house was so big that two people living in it produced more echoes than one person living there alone.

Focus.

For their tenth wedding anniversary Stefaan and Mieke had taken a trip to Paris. They were absent-mindedly drinking a thé au lait, totally worn out after having seen about half of Paris in a single morning, when he suddenly disappeared and returned within the minute with a sad, withered rose in a plastic tube. 'I know you hate this, but I'm doing it anyway so everyone can see that you are my conquest,' he had said, and he had kissed her. They had had a good laugh over that silly rose and had thrown it away in the languidly flowing Seine.

Just as she had driven the twisting roads of the Algarve to the exclusion of every other distraction, so she taught herself to focus on one thing at a time. What if an oncoming car were to jump the lane? Whose fault would it be if you collided head-on? These were the kinds of things she shouldn't think about. Stefaan was dead. That was a fact. But her fault or his fault, that was not a constructive way to think.

When his suitcases were sent back, and his office coffee mug along with a few other things were delivered to her door with a card from the office staff, she was relieved.

She made a place in his hobby shed for all such artefacts because they allowed her to focus her attention on him a little longer. Utter foolishness, because he wasn't coming back. What she really should have done was turn away from him and spend as little time on him as possible, but that didn't work.

Everyone tried, in a subtle way, to make it clear to her that he was gone for good. And to ask whether she wanted to keep on living in that barn of a villa. She understood that she had to let him go. Elvira said she ought to create a place of commemoration for him, but that wouldn't bring him back. She listened to it all many times with a great deal of patience while her thoughts wandered. Elvira also said she should be strict with herself, not deny herself everything but take care of herself, eat well, make little forays into the world. Evi brought groceries, everything ready-made and unhealthy. Sweet people who made her feel lonely.

She was strict with herself: absolutely no contact with the outside world that would make her feel guilty. Only a discussion of the weather with the greengrocer from a village twenty-five miles farther on where no one knew her, and a bit of banter about Europe with the shoemaker from the same village. That gave her peace.

Slap your chest three times and exhale.

Then it happened. It was fall, mid-November, a Thursday evening, when families were slowly beginning to get ready for the weekend and she had already begun to look forward to the weekly phone call on Saturday with Sarah. The days were dismally short and the evening TV shows were sleep-inducing. She had been to the greengrocer and had bought a whole supply of autumn vegetables: cauliflower, beets, carrots, and onions. She arranged her purchased wares on the counter and put on her apron.

Outdoors a couple of birds wished each other good night. Mieke looked forward to cleaning the soil off all those vegetables under the tap and to making them completely perfect. When Sarah was little, an inquisitive child who wanted nothing more than to attach herself to her leg and ask questions about the whole world, Mieke involved her daughter in her kitchen activities. She already was in the habit of providing a running commentary of what she was doing, something all housewives do. For her daughter she raised the volume a notch so Sarah wouldn't miss anything.

As she, the widow, was standing in the kitchen and focusing all her attention on pulling the cauliflower into florets, she had what she thought was a déjà vu. For a brief moment, time seemed to be twisted into a knot. She noticed that once again she was announcing what she was doing out loud. She also noticed that he was standing behind her, casting a glimpse over her shoulder. She looked up at the clock in front of her on the windowsill, terrified, and didn't dare turn around. It was twenty minutes to seven, a normal time for him to come home. And a normal thing for him to do, too: look over her shoulder to see what they were having for supper tonight. She thought she was going crazy. She did the exercise. Slap your chest three times and exhale. Just breathe, that's all.

She kept on speaking calmly to herself until she felt able to return to the cauliflower and go on dividing it into florets. She kept on talking quietly. She told him what she was doing, as if she were speaking to a little boy. The gentleness of her own voice surprised her.

She passed through that night in a haze. At ten o'clock, after all the vegetables had been preserved and neatly stacked in the freezer in the basement, she climbed up the stairs. She went to her writing room and turned the heat up. Then she sat down at her table and wrote for a long time before crawling into bed.

Ever since that November evening she has been walking two paths, one as widow and another parallel path, a life she shares with Stefaan and to which she regularly switches over. She tells him what she's going to do that day. She confesses her minor irritations to him. He looks on when she stubs her little toe on the bidet, or when a pot of yogurt slips from her hands. But she can just as easily let him go and walk by himself, like letting a small child go out and play.

Nor did she keep her commentary to herself during the trip to Jempy's farmhouse in Portugal. *It's got to be around this curve. All that turning is making me dizzy. What a dump, but it's just what I expected.* All the way at the back of the property is a small structure filled with rough, grey stones, flanked left and right by non-hurricane-proof lean-tos. She calls her brother and makes up her mind not to spend more than one night here. Sleeping in a car does not appeal to her, but there's no other choice; there's no room for beds in this cave.

Jempy picks her up and squeezes her so hard that she almost faints in his arms. Ten minutes later she's sitting with her exuberant, ever-charming brother at his rusty patio table, her face turned toward the sun. She's less and less surprised by the fact that there are moments when she enjoys being alive, when she's happy. It's an instinctive, ingrained reaction to sunlight and oxygen. She wallows in the nice things he says about her hair and her straight posture, although she doesn't believe a word.

She listens to Jempy's exciting story about a journey through Russia. Switching from a broken-down train to steppe horses, stuck in the middle of nowhere, taking shelter with a circus. The winter was so severe that the elephant had a heart attack. They feasted on its flesh for a long time. Jempy made his way across the entire East Bloc, and when he got back to the civilized world of Prague he sold his whole wine business to a big wine factory with a single phone call and made out surprisingly well on the deal. In the meantime he met the very babe who's now topping up their glasses with watery, refreshing wine. Angelina, the bleach-blond sphinx, smiles amiably. This is their country house. In Lisbon they have an apartment, but her family is living there for the time being. It's all fine with Jempy. He's had his belly full of cities. Soon there will be wild horses walking around here, he says with a broad sweep of his arm, and a whole flock of sheep.

'Ah, little sister, I'm back on my feet. I'm starting all over again. Just you wait.' His enthusiasm would be infectious if it wasn't so ridiculous, pathetic, and implausible. He still has his coal-black eyes and towering plans. She admires the unrestrained, euphoric faith her brother has in himself, but the contrast with Stefaan is too acute. He hasn't even asked about Stefaan yet. To quell her irritation she takes several deep draughts of cooled wine.

A toddler, 'Roberto, Angelina's son', is taunting a mangy peacock with a drooping tail by throwing pebbles at it. When they get to the second bottle of wine and a basket of bread—apparently the national dish—Jempy begins pontificating about how beautiful life is and how glad he is to see her. He takes her hand across the table, which is covered with crumbs and minuscule fish bones: 'stay as long as you want'.

Angelina follows their whole conversation as if she were watching a tennis match, her blonde head turning from side to side, although she doesn't understand a word of Dutch. Her adorable little son calls her back to earth with the universal word for excrement. She vanishes into the house with the mite and doesn't reappear for a long time.

'Jempy, can't you see how rude you are? How can you sit there shooting off your mouth and making speeches about life when you haven't even asked me how I'm doing?'

'How are you doing?'

'Reasonably well. It hasn't been easy for me these last few years.'

'I know. So do I have to ask you about it every time I see you? Does that make you feel better?'

'No, you don't have to ask me all the time, but you just didn't ask at all. I understand it from your point of view. You don't attach yourself to anyone so you don't feel any grief. Like this woman here, the umpteenth frump from a whole line of frumps, she doesn't mean anything to you. You can barely hold a conversation.'

Inhale and exhale three times while slapping yourself on your chest. Let yourself relax, comfort yourself.

'I have a lot of love in me,' Jempy says, 'and I like to give it away. That's true.'

'If sweet-talking a cleaning lady and then giving her the boot is what works for you, then it is true.' Her outburst leaves her speechless, but she's faultlessly navigated herself to her intended destination: a fight. And so begins a futile exchange that runs into the wee hours and is doused in a great deal of wine, most of it consumed by Jempy. Jempy swears he's concerned about her, but concern isn't just a lot of polite talk. And anyway, it's time she crept out of that shell of hers and discovered there's more things in life than grief. And yes, that may sound heartless and crude, but it's the unvarnished truth. And now how about throwing those sardines on the grill?

After the meagre evening meal, Angelina brings out more wine. When Jempy begins blubbering again about Mieke being his favourite, his greatest love in the whole world, she stands up and says she's going to sleep. The alcohol has paralysed her, or she would have poured the wax from the anti-mosquito candles over his head hours ago. Without giving it any thought she crawls into the real bed on four legs that is offered her. Her head is ringing. After tossing and turning for fifteen minutes she gets up and goes outside. All that's there are the moon and the stars. No lighting of any kind for miles around. It's terrifying. She wants to go back to civilization. This is not for her. 'Stefaan,' she says. It's so strange to pronounce his name. As if she were calling a forgotten patient in an empty waiting room.

She hasn't said anything about her birthday the following day. Naturally Jempy, who has also renounced the calendar, knows nothing about it. She's passing Stefaan in age. That's impossible. He was older than she, which is as it should have been. A woman who is older than her husband, that's not right. Now it's happening and she's just standing there without being able to do anything about it: she's going to be older than he.

After a breakfast of milky coffee, rusks, and apricot jam, Jempy comes up with the idea of making cheese. He manages to mention in passing that he borrowed her car while she was still asleep to go to the village and stock up on food and drink. Now she sees how he manages here without any transportation of his own. She congratulates herself for not having brought him a gift; if she had, she'd only curse him again for his endless leeching.

'There's a sheep stuck in the barbed wire. Let's go free it first before we make the cheese,' says Jempy.

'But I don't want to make cheese,' says Mieke, who imagines herself up to her waist in a big mess of sour milk, plodding away with the sphinx Angelina while Jempy 'goes to pick up something' and, six months later in Miami, thinks back on those two twerpettes standing in the Portuguese rennet.

'Whatever you want, but first we have to take the car and free that sheep.' He holds the car door open for her. 'Otherwise it'll die and that would be animal abuse.'

'Who knows, maybe it's a sheep with suicidal tendencies,' says Mieke.

'Ha ha, that's a good one,' Jempy laughs. 'No such thing.'

Suddenly Mieke loses it, completely unexpectedly. She tells him everything, right in the midst of the flock of sheep in the untraceable heart of the desolate Algarve. She tells him how Stefaan had been so coldly calculating, what kind of logic he used. He went on a business trip. Just before committing his deed, he tried to call her. He left a message on their answering machine to say he was sorry, that he loved her. He gave up, just like his father. It's information she hasn't wanted to share with anyone, except for her brother who's dropped off the face of the earth. Jempy nods and wipes his rough hands on his rough flannel shirt before lifting the severed barbed wire higher so the sheep can pass under it, to the freedom of the pasture.

'Are you afraid the same thing will happen to Sarah?' he asks, his red nose up in the air. 'Afraid of the pattern?'

'Yes, I'm afraid. But I can't very well go up to Sarah and say she should be careful, that there's a time bomb ticking in her genes. That she ought to try to defuse it.'

'So you don't say anything, just like you haven't said

anything about Stefaan's suicide all these years?'

'It's not a question of wanting to be silent.' Mieke knows why she's decided to talk here with her brother on a windy pasture among the stinking sheep. Jempy is the only one who has a recipe for life that works: plough straight through it. He's a survivor.

'He couldn't help it,' says Jempy. 'It's more a deficiency of joie de vivre, like a vitamin deficiency.'

She's had a deep need for words since Stefaan's death. Words survive everything and everyone. Jempy is the only one she can talk to without formalities, irritating silences, and barriers. With Jempy she can confess her moments of lunacy, the slips she made after Stefaan's death which only taught her that she's just not strong enough to enter into casual relationships or to satisfy her sexual needs with every guy who comes along. No, she's not going to suddenly become the hedonist she's never been. People seem to think there's a deep longing for hedonism and decadence in everyone. But they're wrong. It fills her with disgust.

She makes Jempy swear never to divulge anything about her outpourings or about the suicide, and not to Sarah, either, with whom he occasionally has long transatlantic phone conversations (she's just heard about this).

They don't make cheese, but they pick peaches for peach jam. Sitting at the rough kitchen table in Portugal, with a bowl full of peaches between them that are bursting from their skins, Mieke thinks back to an innocent afternoon years ago when she was pitting sour cherries with Jempy and Sarah, when she still could get angry at Stefaan over what he had not done.

SARAH 2013

What if she were to buy flowers for Amos, Sarah says to herself as she swipes her MetroCard through the reader at the Union Square station entrance gate. The flow of people suddenly comes to a halt. In front of her is a female tourist whose large Eastpack backpack has become jammed between the metal posts. The tourist waves her arms in the air wildly and wrenches herself loose. Immediately the flow picks up again. In all her thirty-two years of life Sarah has never bought flowers. Where in New York can you find a decent bouquet of freshly cut flowers that won't cost you an arm and a leg? For that matter, why should she buy flowers for Amos with his own money? Isn't that a bit low? One way or another, she wants to do something to introduce the great, unexpected news.

It's nine o'clock on a Saturday morning. The real workaholics of Wall Street who never stop working have been sitting at their computers with cups of Starbucks for more than an hour. The subway cars are filled with befuddled tourists, shoppers, locals. A student is doing pull-ups on a strap while two of his friends cheer him on. Sarah looks straight ahead, gliding through the tunnels under the city. At Washington Square she gets out, along with a young couple lifting a baby carriage. The escalators heave them into the sunny spring day at Washington Square, where the sellers at the organic market glance condescendingly at the passing crowds, rearrange their goat cheeses, and stack up crates of spotted apples. Every time she wanders past the Barnes & Noble bookstore, which is tottering on the brink of ruin,

Sarah is led by means of a whole chain of associations to The Lady Di's. A couple of years ago, when she came here to buy a load of books, Tori Amos happened to be present for a book signing. Sarah links the red-headed singer to the party at the castle, and from there it's just one small jump to The Lady Di's. After all those years the group finally built up a fairly successful career in the European alternative club circuit.

Each month Sarah receives a tidy sum of money: a transfer for the royalties from The Lady Di's' debut CD. A few of the numbers, in other renditions, have become the kinds of hits everyone knows. Sarah wrote practically all the songs on the debut album, but she didn't play any of them. After the death of her father she fled to New York in a state of total shock. The first ray of light in her life was called Amos. Her wild infatuation with him jelled into something totally unique on this planet that only the two of them share: true love that they can't compare to anything else.

Her shoulder bag is too heavy. Or is she already showing symptoms? Shortness of breath and a vague nausea, now that she thinks about it. As usual, all her belongings are hanging from her shoulder. Even the colour rinse and the baking soda for scones. She might bake the scones in the middle of the night, when the ravenous hunger strikes. Would that be a good way of letting Amos know: deep in the night, with a plateful of fresh scones?

Although Amos and Sarah have been married for quite some time, she's still holding onto her former apartment, with a room she had converted into a music studio. That's where she works on her music commissions, or where she just goes to spend a few days by herself when she feels the need. Amos has already given up trying to convince her to move in with him for good.

Every now and then he mentions it. If they're eating an omelette, he'll save the egg box—in order, he claims, to make her a sound proof room in his spacious penthouse. Then she'd be able to make recordings at his place, too, and maybe give up that other apartment. The fact that they don't live together has become a feature of their marriage. At first Amos threatened to end their relationship, but when he realized that Sarah needed it or she'd lose her bearings, he turned it into something they alone understand. Few can afford to live apart like that. In a city like New York, where there are people who live in shoe boxes, having two residences is pure luxury. You have to have plenty of capital to manage it. And Amos does.

Love under one roof is doomed to failure, according to Sarah. Amputating yourself from real life, imitating your parents, who didn't know any better than to live like good, law-abiding citizens—she can't see the point. Nor can she see how people today can keep reconstituting their families, over and over, against their better judgement, until no one can make any sense out of the tangle of offspring or their feelings for the other. Love under one roof condemns perfectly self-reliant people to having a household, a family insurance policy, and garden hoses, and to researching the relative quality of automobile luggage racks. For her, the other variant, in which you're not constantly getting in each other's hair but are still married, is the only viable option, and the only way to stay in the United States following her studies that is acceptable to the American authorities.

'Respectability,' she suddenly hears in her head, a word trademarked by her mother. 'A boy with respectability' was her mother's reaction after that first dinner with Amos. 'You're not going to believe this, but he

makes me think of your father in his younger years.'
After which Sarah walked outside to smoke a cigarette.
Her mother could do that, casually slip her father into
the conversation as if nothing was wrong, as if he had
just gone to the bathroom but would soon be back. In her
eyes, Amos and her father have very little in common.
The two of them might have talked about the steam
mechanism in espresso machines, but she cannot imagine them going any deeper.

There was so much that Sarah didn't understand
during her first years in the cosmopolitan city of New
York, including the complicated American dating culture with its own rules and ways of paying for things.
The more whimsical New York variant was something
she never even tried to grasp. At first she implored Amos
not to have any expectations of her. 'No expectations,'
she kept pounding into him. She was terrified, at times
even furious, that he would get her agitated again and
make her want him so much that she'd wish she had
never met him. She was suspicious whenever he spoke to
her about the connection he felt with her. Who in God's
name had invented the modern, sensitive, needlessly
extroverted man, anyway? At the same time, a sneaky
little voice inside her kept trying to prove that his intentions were far from honourable. What did he want from
her? To use her as a European slut, perhaps? Why did he
ask her so many questions about her guitar? What was
that all about? What did this rich Jewish money-grubber
really have in common with her, a tinkerer who lived
from advances on an inheritance? Wasn't she too far
beneath him, with his hidebound, arrogant Jewish opinions and his pathological friendliness? No other New
Yorker was so considerate. There was something dispar-
aging about it, the voice kept hissing. And when she was

close to exhaustion, and he took both her hands in his own for the hundredth time and, with an intense look in his eyes, declared that he just wanted her in his life for who she was and how she was, and she shook her head in disbelief, put a big kettle of tea on the stove, and began reading yesterday's newspaper, she almost believed he meant it. Yet to be on the safe side she dragged out the names of former girlfriends, photos that happened to fall out of unread books, trips he had taken with other people, so as not to become too attached to him, to create an escape route for when he was finished with her. She was an independent woman.

For the past two days, Sarah has come this close to taking her roommate Stacey into her confidence. She and Stacey have taken a bit of distance from each other recently. There's been no occasion for it, no fight or for-gotten birthday, because they don't celebrate birthdays anyway. You can't tell your friends everything, Stacey said yesterday out of the blue, although they can usually tell with their umpteenth extra sense if you're keeping anything back. It's as if she had been poking around in Sarah's garbage, like any old stalker, and had dug up the positive Predictor sticks. No, Stacey wouldn't be able to keep her mouth shut. Stacey is crazy about children. That's why Sarah hasn't said anything yet. She wouldn't get any support or sympathy, only ear-shattering con-gratulations with her pregnancy. She'd have had to muzzle her in her enthusiasm, to keep her from blasting the news through a megaphone from the Statue of Lib-erty.

Sarah walks further and breathes deeply. She's on her way to the smallest of Amos's coffee shops, the one on Bleecker Street. The smell of something fresh is wafting through the streets of New York. Winter toppling into spring is in the air. The little trees on Washington Square are nonchalantly dropping their blossoms onto the damp asphalt, which was scrubbed hours ago by garbage men. Sarah switches off the music but keeps the earbuds in. She's walking here, the messenger who is carrying the good news within her, and no one knows what it is. No one who happens to look at her.

A child. An American grandchild for her Flemish mother. Unlike the mother, the child will speak perfect American English. From the very beginning of their relationship Amos has refused to give her lessons in pronunciation. It was their first fight. He insisted that her European accent would open many doors in New York. And the doors have opened again and again over the years. She's made her accent permanent, and now most New Yorkers think she's a German.

It's hard to believe she's been living here so long. Months and years pass, like the garbage bags being tossed into a moving garbage truck. She's spent more than a third of her life on the American continent thanks to her father, as unpleasant as that is to think about.

Her relief was immense when she left Belgium and said goodbye to her ashen-faced mother. She walked through the creaking metal jet bridge at Brussels airport, took her seat at the window, and put a Walkman in her ears, ready to re-emerge as another person in another land. The arrangement was that she would be delivered to her Aunt Lydia, her mother's sister, who would take her under her wing. This didn't deter her. Aunt Lydia was too engrossed in her volunteer work as chairwoman of an organization to promote democracy worldwide to get in Sarah's way.

Throughout the flight she had the feeling that she was leaving the contagion of death behind in Belgium.

'They never do anything until somebody dies,' she often heard on the news in reports involving fire prevention or double-parking, but no one ever said anything about how people stand along the sidelines and silently drive each other into the arms of death. She had watched her father walk up to meet his death, step by step, and had done nothing to stop it. She'd have to carry that with her forever. In Europe she'd never dare to dream anymore.

Let's see what America has to offer, she thought, as she emerged hours later at JFK airport with albino-red eyes but wide awake and with all her earthly goods, and dampened her wrists at the sink in the restroom. In the meantime, one American, a balding man with a spherical body in a pair of pocketless jeans, was waiting for her in the arrivals hall, holding a sign in front of his chest with her name on it. It was Uncle Christopher, Aunt Lydia's husband. On the way to their house, which turned out to be in upstate New York, he talked about a cousin by marriage of a great-aunt who had immigrated long ago with his family because the potato harvest in West Flanders had failed miserably. Adventurers who came to try their luck and muscle on the North American continent. There were no inquiries about herself or her mother, much to her relief.

Two and a half hours later they came to a halt in the countryside. All she had seen from the plane was a glimpse of the metropolis. Aunt Lydia and Uncle Christopher lived in a beautiful wooden house of immense proportions, hidden away in the woods. The barbecue alone was as big as a garden hut. The ancient dog waddled back and forth from one end of the deck to the other. Sarah called her mother, as she had promised, to tell her she was still alive. She was assigned a room. It was dismally quiet in the house, but in the evenings Aunt Lydia dispelled the silence with her pleasant chatter. She was the driving force behind this household, a strong woman in whom she saw strong hints of her own mother. Her husband rummaged around like a chicken on barren soil. Aunt Lydia had found a place for Sarah in an apartment with two other young girls in the Village. Even though her school year wouldn't be starting for a couple of weeks, perhaps Sarah would like to go to the city anyway? Sarah nodded her head vigorously, her mouth full of veggie burger and her head heavy with jetlag.

Conversing like adults, they talked about what Sarah might do now. Her aunt gave her the papers for the apartment, the code for the internet, and so forth. They agreed that Sarah could take a taxi to the city when she was ready for it. The other girls wouldn't be arriving at the apartment for a couple of weeks. She could come back any time, day or night. As proof, Aunt Lydia handed her a key to the front door. The next morning her aunt gave her the number of their regular taxi company. They said goodbye, since her aunt, who had to rush off to her volunteers' conference, knew that Sarah would be gone when she got home. Groaning under the weight of a fully-packed hiker's backpack, a guitar case, and a suitcase that would explode spontaneously if you so much as tapped it, Sarah walked to the end of the driveway one hour later toward the yellow cab.

Getting out at Union Square she experienced a hallucinatory moment of pure gold, glittering so obscenely that it dazzled every angel in heaven and made them squint. Standing there on her own two feet in Coca-Cola Land, in no man's land, strolling across a blank page, she thought about her father without a tinge of grief for the first time since his death. He had lived, he had begotten her, she had known him, and she was grateful for it. It was because of all the misery caused by his passing that she had found the strength to take this step in the first place. As if there was meaning in her father's death. Or was it she who just wanted to attach some kind of meaning to the most absurd, the most meaningless thing in the world? Watch me walking here, she thought then, with the power in her body of a fighter jet at take-off. Here she was: Sarah Vandersanden. Eighteen years old. Washed up alone on the East Coast of the States.

She dumped her bags in the apartment and hit the streets again. At the first decent little hotel she came across she went inside and followed the arrows to the breakfast room. She took the elevator (complete with black elevator operator) down to the basement. Three women were standing around a glass dome with tiny little muffins inside, like the three Fates surrounding a globe. Their sole purpose was to lift the dome, hand you ten napkins, and place a muffin on a porcelain plate with a pair of steel tongs. That was their job, their reason for getting up at four o'clock in the morning.

There was little about New York that shocked Sarah during those first days, except the prices. She hadn't counted on things costing so much. Her money disappeared noiselessly, as if she were tanking up day and night with the meter constantly running. Other people had always paid her bills for her silently, unnoticed, but now she had to fork over the money herself. It was so incomprehensible that she released all the brakes.

She was so busy finding her way and falling into bed dead tired that she had no time for reflection. She saw businesswomen walking around the Business District with bidons of water at the ready. Only one person came by on a bicycle, a female courier with a rolled-up pants leg that revealed a tattooed pin-up. Everywhere there were swarms of schoolgirls, splitting up like flocks of loud twittering sparrows.

She couldn't get enough of wandering around and testing the restaurants all over New York. She had promised her mother that she would eat well, and had resolved never again to slip into that false obsession with putting as little in your mouth as possible. She ate exotic dishes at all sorts of strange eating establishments where she always engaged people in conversation. In the music clubs she had her first contact with other musicians, and she made a date to jam with the guitarist of a noise group. She got to know a great many people very superficially, mostly foreigners, because the real New Yorkers kept their distance. In the stream of people on Fifth Avenue she decided to assume the role of big city dweller. At one point she suddenly heard herself cry 'fire', but no one responded. No one had heard her, or everyone acted as if they hadn't heard her. It was wonderful to be no one. In this city she fit right in.

Here she was brave enough to play the guitar on the street, submerged in the anonymity of the passers-by and the sidewalk dwellers. For a little while she even flirted with the illusion that she could earn extra money by busking, but half a day and two dollars later that illusion proved untenable. At night she'd come home alone to an apartment where the only other life forms seemed to come from the walls and the ceilings. Sitting on her rented sofa, totally wiped out, she'd listen to a CD of Jacques Brel's greatest hits, the best thing she'd brought with her from Belgium. She kept all her father's Dylan CDs in a special box. She understood what Dylan meant by 'that wild mercury sound', his description of the ideal music in his head. She wasn't so spineless and transparent that she'd call her mother for money, but one evening, in the depth of her misery, she collapsed on the floor, short of breath, endlessly plodding on the treadmill of failures in her head. She called her mother. As she was keying in the number, she realized that she had never made good on her promise to call every week.

'Ah, you're still alive.'

'Yes.' (Just barely, you should know. I'm tottering on the edge, I'm floating on the Styx.)

'Why are you calling?'

'Oh, you know, no reason.' (How difficult it is to make this call, how happy I am to hear your voice.)

'That's strange, calling me for no reason.'

'I just wanted to hear how you're doing.' (Two minutes to get those sentences out.)

'I'm finally completely finished redecorating your room. It's now my hobby room. I also bought a new desktop. The other one was very out of date, apparently. It's up in the attic. It is a reminder of Papa, after all.'

'I know.'

'Everything is fine, Sarah. It's still difficult, but it's okay.'

'I'm pleased to hear it.'

'You're pleased to hear it?' laughed her mother mischievously. 'That's the first time I've ever heard you use that expression.'

'I don't know.' Suddenly Sarah was fighting back tears.

'Say (Mieke's voice dropped on octave), how's it going there?'

'Fine, fine.' (Chop off her head or ask for money, it's all the same thing. Neither is an option.) She couldn't hold back. The waterfall came crashing down. She began crying.

'Not as easy as you thought, is it, honey?' said her mother softly.

'I'm doing my best, Mama,' Sarah sobbed. 'It's terrific here.'

'And the prices? Everything is expensive, right? Are you getting by with your monthly allowance?'

'Everything costs at least five times as much.'

'I'll transfer some more money,' said her mother. Not a hint of reproach in her voice.

'Aww.' (Brimming with love, the outstretched hand.)

'You're grown-up and sensible now, right? I'm counting on you not to fritter it away. Buy yourself a good piece of meat.'

When Sarah hung up she felt irradiated with affection for her mother. She understood her and agreed with her: money says a lot more than expressions of love.

A card from Suri, travelling by a very circuitous route, found its way to her. There was crocheting on one side and a very compressed text on the other with the title *The Lady Di's have a record contract!!!!* Suri was doing fashion design, Emily was studying psychology at the university, and MH still hadn't decided what she wanted to do with her life. Suri suggested visiting Sarah and asked if Sarah's postal address had changed. The other Ladies all sent their greetings as well. They really missed her and her songs. It seemed like light years away.

Once her new monthly allowance had been deposited, Sarah let herself be persuaded by the neon signs and the buzzing ambience of the clubs. She was foolhardy enough to try an unknown drug—she and a good-looking Jewish architecture student in a horrible T-shirt whom she had met less than an hour before. One minute she was standing at the bar sipping a Cosmopolitan and carelessly accepting an edible postage stamp that Amos handed her, the next minute she felt like a staple had been shot through her spinal cord.

She did remain standing for one full minute, then recklessly collapsed with this Amos into the armchairs in the back room of the club. There he was, panting with excitement, and eager to declare his love for the whole universe, a ten-dimensional universe without borders or vectors, and there she was, panting with nausea, calming herself, and surfing along on that wave of love, but immediately tumbling off her surfboard into the deep, salt sea, after which she came back up, sputtering, her throat raw with bile, staring into a steel wash basin in the women's restroom.

The next day, in the piercing daylight and in an unknown little apartment, she was spat out onto the shore. Looking in the mirror, she saw a girl as grey as driftwood.

'Good evening,' Amos grinned. He plugged a tiny electric kettle into the socket of his wash basin. 'Instant coffee?'

'Yes, great,' she heard herself jabber. She detested instant coffee. The apartment was furnished with multi-functional pieces of furniture he had designed himself, Amos told her proudly. At the head of the bed were a lap-top and a desk lamp.

'What time is it?' It was already four in the afternoon. She could shower if she wanted. Amos came back to bed and resumed his work at his computer. Had she been lying here the whole time while he was working? She sat straight up with her back to him and looked out the window.

She had lost her centre, as if her life were a set of pick-up sticks that a giant had gathered up and dropped again. She couldn't think without everything in her head wobbling. Her disconcerting ability to qualify everything to death dragged her deep into its narrow tunnel. How do you explain something like that to a carefree guy you don't know from Adam?

When she saw her face reflected in the window, she barely recognized herself. Her clothes were clinging to the idea of a girl who was no longer there. The body itself, with arms, legs, breasts, and a nose that was too small, was sitting in front of the window, but it was uninhabited, like an empty room. Her spirit was wandering out there somewhere.

Suddenly Amos was standing next to her with a big, red mug that had MIT printed on it. 'Great,' she said again. Amos watched her try to lurch out of bed, and offered to take her clothes to the basement of the building to wash them, but she flatly turned him down. This guy was much too sweet. She went to take a shower, to escape the coffee and to cry.

When she came back to the living room she was immediately struck by the smell of paint, furniture, and perfume. As if this were a brand-new decor, thrown up in a hurry, she looked for the emergency exit. There was a piece of paper hanging on the door explaining that Amos had gone to pick up a syllabus from a fellow student but that he'd be back soon. He asked her to wait for him. She began snooping around like an intruder. Amos was an orderly guy who had a clean ashtray and kept his important documents in an orange folder. A kippah lay on his personally designed, experimental desk.

Quiet, she said to herself. Go lie down on the bed for a little while. This body is so tired. It's going to stretch itself out and let go of all its thoughts. It'll keep on lying forever. Like a field on the earth's surface. In the summer the heat can dance over it, in the winter it will burst from the cold. Heat and cold will follow each other naturally, whether I want them to or not.

Amos came in with a banana smoothie with ginger. 'This'll help you regenerate,' he said. 'What are you looking at?'

'The window.'

'No, I mean, what are you looking at through the window?'

'The opposite window.'

'You're looking at yourself,' he laughed. 'So would I if I were you.'

It was half past five. Darkness stole into the streets. One by one the lights in the apartments went on. It was the only time you could catch someone at home. Someone could spend the whole evening in a dark room with a bottle of wine and a radio, but when the light was turned on or off you knew for sure that someone was there.

'I've been sitting here watching you for a long time and you haven't blinked once. As if you weren't there.'

'Uh,' said Sarah. She was desperate for fresh air.

'Come on, let's get out of here. How about breakfast?' Amos asked.

Sarah could have known that Amos, every inch the gentleman, wouldn't have dared to just show her the door. She found that both polite and annoying. Without forcing her, but with a reassuring sense of initiative on his part, he took her with him her up the Hudson River. He had borrowed the car from a friend, which hadn't been easy. She didn't even have the energy to mumble that she'd rather go home. Amos drove calmly, bent over the steering wheel, to make sure nothing escaped his attention in the darkness. By the time they had reached the town of Wappingers Falls it was pitch-dark. They went into a diner because Sarah had indicated she'd like to eat there, which Amos said was 'wicked'.

Their stomachs rumbling with hunger, they sat down at the counter on the chrome-plated, firmly anchored stools. On the TV screen was coverage of a shooting that had taken place in Maryland, with lots of police tape, people rushing back and forth, a mother standing with her hand on her pillowy bosom and crying. Amos said he was sometimes afraid a war might break out in America itself. *Maybe that was why Americans were so eager to fight overseas,* he said to her in a whisper, that kind of talk being distinctly unpopular in a Republican joint like this one. When the good-humoured waitress Diane came to take their order, they switched to talking about the weather and about turkeys. Turkeys were so stupid that their mouths fell open with surprise when it started raining. They'd throw back their heads to see where the water was coming from and then drown. After every heavy rainfall there'd be all these swollen turkey bodies scattered in the woods. Diane was a funny woman. When she brought them their chicken wings and Caesar salad she invited them to join her at her dancing school. This evening, after she was finished with her work here, she was going to introduce her students to the tango. Sarah warmed to the companionship of Amos and the waitress. He told all kinds of stories about how wonderful Israel was, and she didn't have it in her to argue. She ate five chicken wings and licked her fingers. Sliding off the bar stool, she heard herself suddenly say, 'I want to go back.'

Amos frowned but didn't object. On the way back she congratulated herself. Another helping hand refused, or more likely chopped off. Amos offered her chewing gum and tried to get the radio going, without success. Neither of them said more than was absolutely necessary. The whole ride back through the darkness felt like crawling into a long sock in order to arrive at the foot, her apartment in the Village. She didn't ask Amos to come up because she didn't dare, and because the last dregs of energy had leaked out of her. She didn't even have the strength to shut the car door when she got out, and he had to lean over to the passenger's side to pull it closed. She saw in his glance that he was glad to be rid of her.

No matter how silly it seemed later on, at that point she couldn't put such experiences behind her. She was terribly disappointed in herself. She had set herself free, taken her life in hand, and now she seemed no more powerful than a bowl of pudding. She hurled reproaches at herself in an endless loop. With her coat still on, she curled up in the armchair and fell into a foggy half-sleep. She dreamed she was married to Amos and that they lived in a small apartment with their five children. When Amos left for work in the morning he locked them all in together. The children were little demons. They attacked their only armchair with a pair of scissors. Where they got the matches from she didn't know, but she had to keep walking from one end of the apartment to the other to stamp out the flames. She threw a sheet over them, tied it up, and left her crying children behind. She stepped into the apartment's garbage chute and slid to the bottom. When she awoke twelve hours later, totally exhausted, she felt as if she were still sliding.

A few more nights of sleep brought no change in her enervated condition. The madness that resonated through the building on Indian summer evenings echoed in her head. All kinds of scenarios played themselves out within her that she couldn't make any sense out of. So it is hereditary, she thought. The sadness. The despair.

Insanity only becomes really deranged and depressing if you can't share it with anyone, and the insanity stole into the apartment with the new guitar and the towers of styrofoam cups, her little hovel that could be completely cleared out in five minutes, that's how few possessions she had with her. After three days of lonely seclusion she went down and ate her first Big Bacon ever from a plastic tray. The Big Bacon failed to provide a solution to her lethargy, so she began wandering through the city that never sleeps.

She walked until the soles of her shoes were as thin as paper. Each of the three times that she smoked backstage with The Lady Di's, waiting to perform, their group ritual was to scrape the soles of their shoes on the ground like bellowing wild steers ready to storm the arena. When she was a little girl and she scraped her shoes behind the shopping cart, her mother would ask: *Are you being paid to mop the floor here?*, at which she would always enthusiastically reply: *Yes.* She could have mopped all of New York, including the subway.

She went back to her apartment. She pulled the stopper out of the bathtub, beat the sofa cushions, and spread the down comforter on the fire escape as the tub let out a deep burp. In no time at all the apartment was straightened up and aired. She crawled under her bed and pulled out her guitar case. Eat well, sleep well, and do what you're good at.

A few days later her roommates arrived. She was going to live with two worldly-wise students who certainly had better things to do than to spy on her. Alicia came from New Orleans and was studying marketing. When the division of the rooms was being negotiated it soon became clear that Alicia had chosen the right course of study. She praised the two rooms she didn't want as if they were suites at the Plaza Hotel. The room she had in mind for herself, which happened to be the biggest and where the sun shone in gloriously every morning, was a room she thought would make a good storage room. But then someone would have to sleep in the living room, so she relented and took that room instead. The other roommate, Stacey, was an Iraq veteran from the Gulf War who was studying on the army's dime. Sarah had almost lost sight of the fact that she was going to be studying, too. The arts, a mishmash of subjects, workshops, and independent projects.

That night Sarah went to buy groceries at the very pricey Whole Foods organic supermarket. The store was packed with watercress still dripping from a shower, mangos blushing with sweet happiness, naked bananas sunning themselves under the store's gracious lights, salmon just back from a swim in Swedish waters and subtly smoked over an oak fire, and blueberries that had been picked in a Canadian pine forest only a few hours before.

The next morning Sarah was standing in the kitchen, rummaging through the drawers and cabinets full of ice cube bags and tumblers. 'God, am I hungry. Anybody know where my muesli is?' she asked.

Sarah almost jumped out of her skin that first time Stacey hiccupped with laughter. Panicking, she wondered whether she had said something with a double meaning, or whether an earbud had gotten lost in her hair, or whether she had managed to make herself look ridiculous. But soon she learned the principles of American laughter. Laughing from embarrassment, laughing to be friendly, laughing to be sociable. It wasn't a form of criticism, nor was it the timid smile of her father. It was just a friendly way of saying, 'Oh, gosh, I'm afraid I've eaten some of your muesli. I'm sorry! Here, have some of mine!'

Stacey's muesli proved to be a super-sweet, sticky, generic brand of Honey Pops, but it was nice of her to offer. If you were to see Stacey sitting at the kitchen table like that with a pink marking pen in her mouth, bent over her three-volume Oxford Dictionary, you'd never believe that not so very long ago she'd been careening through the desert sand in a tank in Kuwait.

Sarah started her courses, which were surprisingly easy and gave her plenty of time to work on her own experimental music. Students spoke to their professors quite bluntly here and saw to it that the amount of theoretical material they needed to know was approximately zero. One evening after a workshop on soundtrack writing and a student meeting about nothing, Sarah came home. She saw that a package the size of a novel had come for her in the mail. It was The Lady Di's debut album. Emily had put a Post-it note on the album with an arrow pointing to the liner notes, where Sarah was the first one to be thanked. Almost all the numbers had been written by her. Suri had wrapped the CD in a piece of fabric that proved to be a T-shirt with three sleeves, a cool consolation prize. It had been Sarah's own decision to leave The Lady Di's for good, but that didn't mean she didn't feel jealous every now and then. As she poured herself a large glass of cider in the light of the stove exhaust fan, Stacey asked if she knew how to spell 'existential'. Sarah scribbled the word on a piece of paper that Stacey had shoved across to her. She saw a whole list of words.

'Hey, nice,' said Sarah, who had adopted the up-beat, enthusiastic tone of her roommates. 'Are you going to write something?'

'Well, not really,' said Stacey. 'Or yes, that's the general idea. But only for myself.'

'Great!' said Sarah. 'Cider?'

'Sure, why not.'

Sarah poured Stacey a glass and pushed it across the table. Stacey pulled a photo album out from under the dictionaries. When she woke up in the middle of the night and all of New York was surrounding her like a jungle, it felt as if an elephant were resting its foot on her chest. She hated those attacks; it was much worse than Iraq itself. She had a photo album, but no words, not enough words.

'Can I see your pictures?' Sarah asked.

They sat down together on the sofa and looked at the pictures of a hefty, muscular Stacey in uniform in front of a military bus on an overcast day, or in a tent with a mess tin and a festively decorated turkey, or pressed in between dozens of soldiers on a boat, most of them with their thumbs in the air. Cheerful photos, dripping with camaraderie, as if they were on a field trip or playing paintball with a group of friends in a desert setting. She pointed to a speck on the photo, an Iraqi citizen. She tore open a bag of sour cream potato chips. 'Did you know I killed someone?'

Sarah was shocked to be given this information so casually.

'It's so easy to kill someone. You're standing there, heavily armed, under the blazing sun. One day you take a picture, the next day you shoot a civilian—or was it a spy, or was it a suicide terrorist with sticks of dynamite stuck all over him on his way to your camp?'

'It was an order. You did it because you had to.'

'No I didn't,' said Stacey, cold as ice, and she shoved a handful of rough-cut chips into her mouth.

Sarah understood Stacey. Stacey felt guilty for the ugliness she had experienced, just like Sarah's father had. There was no word to describe it. No matter how much time Stacey spent gazing at the radar of her dictionary, the word would never appear. It was a defect of the language. Stacey and Sarah discovered that there were many concepts without words. Sarah's English was far from perfect, and Stacey was no intellectual, but they both wanted to know why, after all this time, no one had come up with a word for the fear that everything is going to get worse, the fear of the end times, when it won't be a global conflagration that does you in, but the universal loss of hope. Was there a language that had such a word?

At around midnight they heard a key turn in the lock. Stacey slammed her photo album shut. Alicia came tripping in and stole into the little open kitchen. Deep in thought, she put the tea kettle on the burner and let out an unadulterated American shriek when she saw Sarah and Stacey sitting together in the armchair with a photo album on their laps. The intimacy was broken, and Stacey snorted with irritation.

'Hey, Alicia, what's in the bags?' Sarah asked to break the tension.

'They're body bags,' laughed Stacey huskily, 'she drags all kinds of stuff into our apartment and we don't even know what it is.'

Alicia stifled a giggle, but she didn't understand that Stacey, whose barometer had suddenly registered stormy weather, was expecting a real answer. A wave of anger rippled through Stacey's body. 'This isn't the theatre, you know,' Stacey said. 'It's real. People who've always lived safely in mommy's nest and then get a pile of money to go study in New York, they seem to think you can laugh or scream at everything. But there's a real goddamned world out there. It exists, too.'

The whistle of Alicia's kettle punctured the silence.

Alicia leapt to the kitchen, busied herself with tea cups and cookies in noisy wrappings, and began mumbling to herself under her breath.

'What?' Stacey asked.

'Soldiers are bad people,' Alicia repeated.

Americans were still difficult to size up. The next day Stacey and Alicia were back at the kitchen table, having a good laugh about nothing in particular. It was hysterical, pointless, uncontrollable laughter, and it was infectious. Without knowing why, Sarah burst out laughing, too. They could have been standing in a circle and laughing at each other.

After completing her studies Alicia left the apartment, while Stacey and Sarah grew closer together. Sarah has been sharing the apartment for more than ten years with Stacey, who's slimmed down considerably over the years due to loss of muscle mass. She follows a pathologically healthy diet, smokes on the roof like a Turk, and works hard at irregular hours. She often walks through the apartment in rags, jabbering into the phone and making all kinds of appointments. She and Sarah respect each other's privacy and don't get in each other's way.

Amos and Sarah bumped into each other again in a very roundabout way. Sarah had walked into Barney's in Soho, one of the chain of luxury stores, to buy a new perfume. It took her a very long time to make up her mind, so long that her bladder started jumping up and down. She quickly paid for a vanilla-honeysuckle scent in order to get to the restroom as soon as possible. She held herself in a contorted position over the toilet bowl, carefully avoiding any contact with the seat. In this position, used by the indigenous women of the great American continent when they were about to give birth, surrounded by trees and squatting out there in the wild to ease their contractions, at the glorious moment that Sarah, after a week of serious constipation, was reaching the point of deliverance and felt the universe of her lower body go into a spasm, two hands belonging to some filthy woman slid under the large opening of her stall and stole the bag that contained all of Sarah's belongings, from a student visa and a Visa card to indispensable phone numbers, the fresh dollars she had just earned at Zefirelli's by turning the crank of a pasta machine for ten hours, to the unfortunate purchase of the perfume. Sarah, who had barely had time to pull up her pants, stormed out of the restroom and began delivering an incoherent and indignant tirade about dirty hands in a mixture of Dutch and English to an oak of a security guard. When her indignation turned to rage at the men, who just stood there swaggering instead of running after the thief and getting her bag back, she gave up on any form of help.

After a trip to the Belgian embassy, a three-hour wait, seven transatlantic phone calls with her mother, and a chipped front tooth that came from biting down too hard on a caramel in her anger, her eyes filled with tears when her turn in line finally came up. She was confronted with her first American catch-22 situation: in order to report a robbery, you needed your ID card. When she tried to explain, frantically gesturing, that her card had been stolen, the woman said that wasn't her problem and that those were the rules. Sentences like *it may not be your problem but it sure is mine!* had little impact on the clerk. Sarah had long forgotten that her name was right there in the database. In the constricting tunnel vision of her fury she didn't even hear the clerk calling her back. She went outside and did something that a real New York woman would never do: display her emotions in public.

(With the exception of 9/11, which was well over a year away.)

She stood in the middle of the wide sidewalk and made not the slightest attempt to hide her tears of anger and frustration. The tears did not go unnoticed. They were an irresistible enticement for Amos, who had a good view of the passers-by on Park Avenue from behind the counter of his coffee shop. While doing his best to make a perfect macchiato, as he later repeatedly related, he noticed an attractive woman crying outside his window who was neither homeless nor high and whom he recognized as Sarah the German. A woman of flesh and blood and tears of rage, he said, unlike anything he had ever seen before.

He wanted to know what had happened. She told him how she had been rudely treated—by a security guard, no less. She kept on blubbering, deeply incensed, but she was grateful to Amos that he didn't join her rant about the bully of a security guard. Instead he just handed her his far from perfect macchiato and asked her to wait for him for just a minute. He said he wanted to take her to the roof garden of the coffee shop during his break. Fine, she said. Her blind exasperation had subsided, and now she was just mildly embarrassed about her broken front tooth.

Cup in hand, she followed him to the roof of the tall building. It was liberating to look out over the Big Apple from an almost helicopter perspective, as if it were a movie. Now she understood what her father had found so enthralling about a roof. And not only her father. Amos said that in the Middle East people spend much of their lives on their roofs, to sleep under the open sky or to be safe. From a roof you're a sniper of reality.

She cast a sidelong glance at the man staring off into

the distance. When she asked if he had been working here long, he responded, 'Five months, but it won't be long before I'm the owner.' He was quite attractive, objectively speaking. She found his boasting both clownish and charming. He looked at his watch. They rushed downstairs so he could wash his hands and start a new shift. Amos was hard-working and dedicated. He had three jobs, one of which was the designing of restaurant interiors. Those kinds of people were a dime a dozen in New York, but Amos had lots of ambition and refused to waste his energy on a dead-end job.

Two years later he was already the owner of three successful cafes. He discovered that there was more money to be made in New York with coffee shops than with drinking establishments. He served only coffee and tea. Today he has seven coffee shops, spread out across all the trendy or soon-to-be-trendy neighbourhoods of New York City. Step by step he's realizing his own cunning plan to climb higher up the ladder until he's almost ready to drop. According to Amos, an exemplary Jew is one who skims off the surface of the globe, dreams of his homeland, and earns enough money in the meantime to buy up everything the world has to offer.

During those first years they couldn't see each other before two in the morning. That worked out very well for Sarah, the same Sarah who laughed at the very idea of fear of commitment. She spent all those evenings tinkering with demos that were meant for no one's ears. MH had asked her for new numbers, but she wrote back that she wasn't doing that kind of music anymore. Through friends of Amos she came in contact with a maker of art films, for whom she composed her first soundtrack. It's been a long time since she was able to accept all the requests she received; today she selects only the projects that interest her. She writes and plays music while Amos delegates and supervises.

During their first walks across the roofs Amos taught her the coded language of the New York street gangs. He sometimes cautioned her to look away when they passed corners where crack was being smoked, or not to pay any attention to all the forbidden things that had moved uptown from downtown. Amos knew New York so much better than she did. When she strolled across the roofs with Amos, she felt as if she'd been walking around during daylight hours with her eyes glued shut. He showed her the hanging gardens, the ingenious sleeping shelters for the homeless, beehives dozens of feet above the ground on the flat fields of the roofs. And later, with his friends on the roofs of the Lower East Side, the menageries: rabbits, chickens, and even a couple of goats. It was a whole different world up there, of which the ordinary pedestrians were totally unaware.

Their roof journeys have now become a hobby. You might think the roofs had been inhabited by some nomadic tribe, living high above the heads of the commuters who, until just a few years ago, would only travel through this neighbourhood by AirTrain on their way downtown, never getting out in Queens because of all the problems there. At the present time, however, hordes of hipsters are streaming in, many to visit MOMA PS1.

Today the plan is for Sarah to pick up Amos at about noon. They're going to Governor's Island. Governor's Island was once the private playground of Lord Cornbury, the English governor of New York and New Jersey more than three hundred years ago. He partied there to his heart's content and was able to indulge his proclivity for cross-dressing. At every party he got glammed up as a different woman. It's the kind of place that requires a certain fantasy.

It's about time Amos was informed. How long before it's actually a child? And how long can you keep a child hidden? Recently she read a story in *The New York Times* about a woman who was a professional kick-boxer. She said she felt something after a match and proceeded to give birth in the dressing room. She never even realized she was pregnant. Sarah, of course, is not such a marginal character. How is Amos going to respond to the news of her totally unexpected pregnancy? She's seen how he buys large gifts for the children of friends, quite unashamedly, and how he keeps dropping obscure hints, but at the same time he's so fiercely outspoken about the baby boomers and overpopulation that it's become one of his favourite rants.

Now that she's known since the day before yesterday that there's life growing within her, she feels incredibly strong and vulnerable at the same time. She's the mother of all tissue paper. It's a secret she wants to protect. One minute she has no idea how to handle it all, the next minute she's deep in conversation with her little monster, her explorer, who's about to see Governor's Island.

In Washington Square Park an old black man roars something at her from behind his chessboard, a curse or a blessing, it's hard to tell which. And yet. A child? In these times? In New York? She can't even begin to think about it rationally. In her fantasy she locates her child in playgrounds the size of Central Park, but without the dirty old men behind the trees. But in the world of today and in a metropolis like New York, it's madness just to let your child walk from one end of the street to the other by himself. Or is that her mother talking? Is she going to overprotect her child, too, and is she no better than her mother was?

So here she is, a resident of New York and partner of a

rich Jewish businessman, a musician who is doing what she likes far more than when she was an adolescent grimly trying to prove herself with The Lady Di's, a daughter whose relationship with her mother is steadily improving, much to the surprise of both. The last time they were together was in Boston. Sarah had flown up to spend a day with her mother, who was there for some sort of appointment. They walked the Freedom Trail together, which went past sixteen historical locations. Although Sarah has been a grown woman for quite some time now, her mother flatly refuses to let her pay one cent of the lunch or to let her treat herself to one postcard in the museum shop. It makes Sarah laugh. After all these years she no longer lets her mother get under her skin with her rock-hard principles and her occasional rants about the decline of good manners and traditions.

If she tells Amos she's pregnant, there's no turning back. If she doesn't tell him and decides to terminate instead, will she ever be able to look him in the eye again? Wouldn't she be tearing down the happiness they've been building up all these years? Can a child destroy such happiness? She catches herself thinking in Dutch. When in doubt, the washing machine in her head always switches to a Dutch cycle.

She has to decide before Amos starts suspecting. Should she tell Amos, or is it better not to?

If only she had her mother's consistency. Her mother never doubts. She suffers in silence, but then she picks up a knife and cuts. The price she pays for this are her neuroses, but lately she's grown much calmer. Fortunately I'm not like my mother, Sarah often says to Amos, although she misses her mother's decisiveness when she's back at the deli and is faced with a choice between vitello tonato and maki sushi with tuna, or if she doesn't know whether she wants the red boots or the super-cool hand-braided calfskin shoes. When she suddenly remembers that it's all bad for the environment anyway, she leaves the shop red-faced, promising to come back. Unlike her mother, she can't even decide whether she should decide at all. 'Your mother *is* indecisive,' said Amos after having met her mother for the first time. 'Even there you're a lot alike.' For that he got a *Rolling Stone* hurled at his head.

At a newspaper stand in Washington Square Garden is the most pathetic bouquet of flowers she's ever seen, waiting for a buyer who will never appear. It's plastic, she realizes: a miserable old-fashioned nosegay stuck on a green skewer. She and Amos like to buy ugly presents for each other, for no particular reason. It's their private form of humour. She wonders whether this will make Amos laugh. Maybe it would be better to buy him a tie-dyed T-shirt from the hippie on MacDougal Street. He already has two, both of them hideous. He was wearing a yellow tie-dyed T-shirt when they first met in that club. She couldn't take her eyes off him, so mesmerized was she by that horrible T-shirt.

Two people who fall for each other can later recount those first memories down to the smallest detail. He couldn't believe that she had three kinds of painkillers in her bag (two painkillers and her birth control pill), and that she had drawn a pirate on her foot (it was a koala), and that for their first dinner together she had ordered eggplant millefeuille (chicken wings). As their feelings for each other became intenser and deeper, their memories grew into something that had actually happened, something they repeated so many times that it began to glow and glisten, and all they could do was decide that their first meeting contained within it the fullness of a promise. For twenty dollars she buys the fake bouquet.

Her mobile rings. It's Amos. The Black Keys whistle her ringtone twice. She doesn't answer. It's her right to be out of reach, as it will become an ever greater right for everyone. Her mobile rings again. Santigold rings out; this time it's Stacey. Her mobile is at the bottom of her bag, and both Amos and Stacey know the thing is hopelessly lost, drowned in the confusion of nail polish, lip balm, half a piece of cake, the occasionally misplaced corkscrew, notebooks, squashed popcorn, a recording device for environmental sounds that she never uses, newspaper clippings, etc. She sticks the fake flowers in her bag and keeps on walking.

There's snow in the air. There have been more and more springtime snows in recent years. The city will fall asleep as soon as the snow starts falling. Not that there won't be any people on the street, but the buildings withdraw into themselves, the heating units whine, and no one goes out to face the elements unarmed. Walking through the snow with a newborn baby. She can already imagine Amos calling her back. He's going to be perfect in the role of overanxious father. And she's already conjuring up scenes of horror, something she's very good at.

She keeps repeating the images in her head until there's a whole tree hut growing from one withered branch, an immense structure that has no contact with the ground anywhere but is based on a single insignificant detail and a whole stack of considerations and objections. At any rate, she reasons with herself, the child is an accident. They hadn't planned on conceiving a child, not at all. And although they don't have to tell the child later on, *they* will know it, and that makes for bad vibes. It isn't even three months yet, so it isn't a child.

And while Amos will make a dream father in theory, in practice he's never home, which is why no one really notices that they don't live together. She'll confront him with his ecological objections, too. And she smokes, another argument against keeping it. Sometimes she languishes from self-doubt. She always wants her way. There are thousands of reasons for not keeping the child. She'll strangle the foetus in the womb to protect it from its own fate.

Sarah catches herself hurtling down the street stamping her feet, as if she were trying to literally stamp out the images of doom and gloom. She lets the shame blow through her. No one here knows anything about her life in the shabby Old World. She's so much happier in New York. New York is a beautiful body. Europe is like the innards, a quivering mass of organs with which she would rather not identify, even though they're inside her.

She walks past an advertisement featuring enormous melons swollen to Freudian proportions that sings the praises of a new shower gel. She bursts out laughing. Pregnant women view the world through the lens of pregnancy. She interprets melons as oversexed machismo. Turning the corner she sees the chairs at the windows. Amos has decided against placing bar stools in the front window, which makes the coffee drinkers look like mounted animals on display. He's decorated this coffee bar with antique Chinese seating and the usual kitsch, which also fits in with the Village's hippie legacy.

His headful of raven black curls is immediately visible. Amos is behind the counter, scurrying back and forth. He's got his hands full with aluminium milk foamers, shakers full of ground cinnamon, and ginger syrup. It's very busy in the coffee bar at this hour of the day. The line of people waiting for counter service runs almost as far as the door, and a couple of them are making their coffee themselves. Amos is taking advantage of the recent recession. He charges only half price for coffee made at the DIY counter. The idea is so successful that he's winning on all fronts: less work and ultimately more income.

A Hispanic woman with extravagant earrings and too much glittery eyeshadow to ever appeal to Amos is hanging over the counter and telling him a complicated story. He nods every now and then by way of response and keeps on working. He fills the milk foamer, picks up the dirty cups that a waitress puts on the counter, and knocks out the coffee grounds.

Sarah pushes against the door, and a couple of people in line are forced to step aside. As soon as Amos catches sight of her he waves and purses his lips. His dark brown eyes are laughing.

To give herself a little more time Sarah checks her Facebook page. Suri has put a hilarious image of a fortune cookie on her timeline that says, 'I can't tell you anything cause I'm only a fortune cookie.' Suri, someone else who is indecision personified. They often laugh about it the few times they still see each other: when she goes to visit her mother for the holidays or when Suri comes to visit her. Suri's fashion designs are making a big splash. Her eclecticism has never been so all-embracing: five sleeves and three legs on one garment that qualifies as neither pants nor pullover, one size fits all. Suri can design maternity clothing for her: a dress with not one but five openings to accommodate the bump.

The woman at the counter takes a tiny sip of coffee to indicate that her story is finished. Sarah goes behind the bar and hands Amos the flimsy fake bouquet. He throws his arms in the air and covers his mouth with his hands in sham rapture over the ugliest bouquet in the world.

'I cannot accept this,' he says. 'It's too much, too beautiful. What did I do to deserve this?'

'Not a thing,' Sarah replies blandly.

His iPhone buzzes a new calendar message: Governor's Island! Amos pulls off his apron, steps out of his role as sociable barista, and turns into an urban explorer with faded jeans.

'Subway or taxi?' he asks.

'I'm not going,' says Sarah.

'Hey,' says Amos, who's surprised by the sudden distance.

'No, I'm not going.'

'Don't you feel well? What's wrong? Should I stay in town, too?'

'Don't be silly. Just go,' she says testily. 'I have to write out the orchestral score for Gus Van Sant's soundtrack. He wants to see a proposal by next week.'

Amos is familiar with her moods of sullen silence, and he knows how pointless it is to insist. 'Okay, I'll go with Todd then,' Amos says. He takes a few seconds to walk down the bar and say goodbye to the personnel. On his way back he goes behind her chair and kisses the top of her head. 'Call me if you decide to come anyway, or if there's something else. I'll pick you up later and we can go get a bite to eat.' He lays his hands on her shoulders and kisses her cheek. His stubble scratches.

Lost in daydreams, she imagines a gigantic baby hanging over New York, a little boy with the face of Amos, a kippah on his soft baby skull. He hangs over the city like a zeppelin, his shadow cast over her. She's the only one who can see him and pluck him out of the air. He glances over her shoulder, and the two of them are looking at the open newspaper on the table. There's a photo of a veiled woman staring at her with indifference. It must be nice sometimes to walk around so anonymously, Sarah says to herself. Then a sudden cramp in her lower belly keeps her from reading any further.

We are alarmed. Without asking the permission of the Hispanic behind the counter who has taken Amos's place, Sarah takes the key hanging from the shoehorn and dashes to the bathroom. She shuts the door and locks it as the pain rips through her. Good riddance, she thinks. So be it. No, we admonish her, it's not good, it must not happen. I wasn't ready for it anyway, she sighs in her own defence. You're thirty-two years old, we cry. Of course you're ready. We have to keep imposing ourselves on the world. She's gasping for air. 'No, this is not what I want,' she wails. She takes a wad of toilet paper and checks to see if any blood is coming out of her. Nothing. Not a drop.

A war could break out while she's sitting there on the toilet, hesitating, Sarah says to herself. A war with China. Not a relatively small, local flare-up, but an explosion of violence across the entire Western and Asiatic world. A deadly game of power and prestige. A global coup that will make everyone bleed. He'll sit at the kitchen table and tell his secrets to his little friends in Chinese so that she and Amos won't be able to understand him.

Her stomach cramps subside and Sarah is back in the coffee bar, but nothing has changed. None of the coffee snobs, the chronic fatigue sufferers, or the student coffee bar habitués notice her. Only the woman behind the counter. The woman opens and shuts her mouth like a fish, making every effort to ask her politely how she's doing and what Sarah would like to drink.

'A medium latte, please,' says Sarah with a dull voice. She wants to say something else to the woman, something meaningful. She tries to worm her way into the woman's thought processes and to respond to what's going on around them. Interaction is the greatest challenge of the twenty-first century, she believes—or at least my greatest challenge. She can start with the blueberry cake, China, babies, babies, babies. If an online therapist were to ask her how she's feeling, she would say: 'As if I had swallowed the whole world and I'm going to give birth in seven months.'

Meekly she pays four dollars and ninety cents, exact change, with Amos's money, in Amos's bar.

She finds a place to sit next to a table occupied by an old woman and a boy with a bright red cap on his head, relatively atypical customers in this bar. She listens in on their conversation while pretending to study the fake plants. She takes a first sip and thinks about the baby. The baby is drinking the coffee with her, coffee made with a generous amount of milk. The milk provides calcium for the fingernails.

The boy with the red cap is talking to the old woman. Sarah takes him to be about sixteen years old. His body is growing faster than his gestures can keep up with. He still has to get used to his dangling limbs and burgeoning trunk. He's holding a Mars bar in his hand, peels back the paper, and takes a bite. The boy and the older woman are talking about this and that. Suddenly he tells the grey-haired woman, in a quiet, confidential tone that it may be weird for him because he's not very old-fashioned, but he'd really like to get married.

At another table she sees a pair of lovers. He takes her hands in his and kisses her fingertips. The woman feels uncomfortable with this and giggles it away. A student frowns at her laptop. She types a short message, ostentatiously pushes 'send', and leans back, waiting, sipping from her cup of coffee. As soon as the answer comes rolling in with a bleep, she bangs away at the keyboard. The door opens and two men come in. One takes the coat of the other, who thanks him by kissing him on the lips. The other man sticks out the tip of his tongue and tastes the kiss.

All these little plays being acted out around me, Sarah says to herself, as if I were an extra in some clever ensemble film. The walls are barely visible, but you as the viewer feel them. Each scene sets another scene in motion, and together they form a powerful portrait of the fictional struggle we are all engaged in, the struggle called life. At the end we all lip-sync the same song. This may have been what Jules meant years ago, although in retrospect Sarah suspects that Jules was dealing in anti-establishment clichés.

'How long have you two been together?' the old woman kindly asks the boy with the red cap. She is a confidante with whom he can talk much more easily than with his own blood relations.

'Two months.' (The details fit together nicely). A baby in her belly: is it a two-month-old work of fiction that keeps knocking against her inner walls? If only she could feel him, the argument in support of life would be more convincing.

The wrinkled woman nods slowly. Sarah can almost hear her thinking how trivial two months really are, but she understands that for a beanpole with a cap, two months is a long time because he doesn't yet know how much life is ahead of him and how many tragedies, babies, and deaths will follow so naturally and be forgotten so naturally as time goes by.

'I married young,' the old woman tells him. 'My husband is long dead. I've been a widow for years. If I hadn't shut myself in so much, if I had tried to build a new life for myself, I'd have company now.' The woman falls silent and thinks: it's important that I listen, that I don't start talking about people he's never known, like my husband Fred, who was a road worker and only had three fingers. Stories like that will chase the boy away.

The eyes glimmer in a face full of crow's feet. Her forehead has deep, wavy furrows. The old woman quickly switches to a different topic. Languid beats waft through the bar. She thinks new music is very interesting, she says, but she doesn't know that much about it.

'If I were to buy an album of pop music, what would you recommend? I'd like to do more things with my time.' The woman is overweight, but it's not the obesity of the hamburger generations. She has a body that a whole life has passed through like a patchwork quilt wrapped around her. A woman who chatters to keep from thinking about her loneliness. 'Do you think anyone could still find me attractive?' She says this timidly, more to herself than to the boy. The boy doesn't answer but looks instead at the grey drizzle outside.

Sarah's throat is suddenly as dry as sandpaper. They shouldn't let coffee be called a drink. The more of this beverage she imbibes, the more intensely she feels a raging thirst. She'll go to her own apartment through the drizzling rain and stay nice and dry indoors.

As she wanders past the shops she experiences a kind of invisibility. All her life she's been searching for a margin to manoeuvre in, an air bubble in which she could float happily through the world like a manga figure in a cartoon. She loves looking at an abandoned garbage bag and seeing a little robot, or transforming a street light into a mannequin on stilts, or just walking down the street and hallucinating and fantasizing, with nothing but a medium latte to assist her. Sober, euphoric, and filled with fantasy. It's normal for your brains to supply what your senses only partly observe. But an unborn creature is no fantasy.

Instinctively she places her hand protectively on her belly. It's not having a baby as such that's the problem. She's fine with having a baby. If she could only insulate the child and carry the little block around with her, beyond the past and beyond the present, to a timeless planet where everything just starts with zero and where each little block stands on its own two feet and they don't all get stacked up together to form one big shaky house, she'd sign up for that journey in an instant. But on this planet she has one panic attack after another and she's still too cowardly to let Amos in on her secret. Wrong, wrong, wrong, that's the rhythm of the subway cars as they zoom past her nose.

She comes up out of the subway, and just before she gets home she notices a missed call from Amos. Has that much time really passed? Sensitive, thoughtful, a tiny bit anxious: that's him. Anxious for his own little circle, unashamedly egocentric. She can wake up at night with a start, bathed in sweat and thinking about the injustice in the world, misunderstood Muslims, irritating Republicans, outrageously stupid Democrats, criminal oil companies, the contrast between us and them, all that bad music that no one can even tolerate but that's constantly being nominated, rednecks who exploit their children on reality TV shows and fish out pig's trotters from a tank of slime, European obtuseness, and the complete deplorable lack of solidarity. All that quickly provides enough fodder for a sleepless night. Sometimes she wonders whether her concern for the world isn't simply a projection of her own problems; sometimes she knows for sure it is. Amos always says he understands her when she expresses her anxieties in words. His understanding is like a blanket that you throw over a fire. It suffocates her and totally extinguishes her, while she just wants to keep on raging.

Whenever she tries to explain this to him he nods, full of understanding once again. He takes the toast out of the toaster and puts it on her plate while kissing her and moving on to the order of the day: designing a liquor cabinet for a new cafe, or trying to figure out whether spelt bread is really more nutritious than cornbread.

Sarah keeps on walking. She decides not to call Amos back. What she could really use right now is a whole lot of oxygen and a little bit of alcohol. And stretching out on the wall-to-wall in her music studio with Jacques Brel on repeat.

She enters the apartment building and turns her attention to climbing the stairs, all the way up to the sixteenth floor. It's a ridiculous effort that she'd never otherwise make. Physical exertion is indispensable for pregnant women. She read that last night on one of the pregnancy blogs she skimmed, only to erase the search history afterwards as if she had been lurking around some porn site.

At the front door she bends over from the waist, panting heavily. She lets herself into the apartment, where she occupies two bedrooms: one is perfectly equipped as a music studio, and in the other are her desk and a bed. Stacey pulls a towel over the big mirror in the narrow front hallway. She's walking around in her customary baggy sweatpants and a Hello Kitty T-shirt with whiskers that she got from Alicia.

'What's up?' Sarah murmurs.

Not much, according to Stacey, who slips into the bathroom with some anti-limescale product. Sarah takes a wine glass from the cabinet and senses that Stacey is lingering behind her. She taps her finger against a bottle in the cherrywood wine rack, changes her mind, and pulls out a Montepulciano d'Abruzzo. Would the child have been conceived in her bedroom or Amos's? How could a baby ever walk around here in this artsy chaos, still way too redolent of the student life? What kinds of walls and gates are necessary to provide a baby with safe accommodations? What life-threatening, sharp little corners and objects will have to be done away with for a baby to have free rein here, and what incriminating material?

She struggles at opening the bottle, aware of an uneasy tension hanging over the room.

'Say-Stacey-hey-Sarah-what-should-I ...' Both Stacey and Sarah decide to break the silence at the same time. Their words overlap and interconnect, then simultaneously they revert to silence once again.

'Say,' says Stacey, the first to toss something out, 'I saw you walking around this morning near the Toys R Us on Union Square. You looked a little worried.' She takes the tea kettle and the espresso pot off the stove and puts them on the counter.

'I seem to have a face with only two settings: anxiously awake and anxiously asleep,' Sarah says.

'At least let me know if you want to trade your cute little snoot for my mug.' Stacey goes over the burners with a scouring sponge. Her whole body moves along with her. She pauses for a moment and looks up, strands of hair falling over her eyes. 'But are you okay?'

'Yes,' says Sarah curtly. She's going to do what every

doctor advises against to minimize the chance of a miscarriage: drink. It's wrong and it's reckless, but it's also a useful way of conducting a showdown with herself. She'll leave it up to natural selection. If the little one can survive this, then surely it will be able to cope with everything else. She puts her iPhone in the docking station and plays The XX. A somewhat disappointing second album, a boiled down version of their strong debut. Sarah installs herself at the kitchen table with her glass and the bottle of wine. The table is littered with bottled water, samples of various creams that Stacey has apparently torn out of fashion glossies, Sarah's music magazines, expired discount coupons, and five substantial dictionaries. She thumbs through the Q-Z volume indifferently. Stacey must know those dictionaries by heart by now. They're filled with Post-its and notations made with marking pen. They're Stacey's personal talmud. Stacey herself has withdrawn to her room.

It may be the powerful herbal fragrance from the red wine or the creaking in the speakers, a pale imitation of her earlier cassette tapes, but suddenly she's seized by the idea of calling Uncle Jempy. He's the one man who's willing to listen to her endlessly (at least if she's calling him) and who gives her his totally useless advice only if she explicitly asks for it. But she can't bring herself to get the words out of her mouth. As soon as they come in contact with oxygen, they undergo some weird chemical process that changes them into Problems That Must Be Dealt With.

At the selfsame moment there's someone inside her who is desperate to stay alive. She is now reproducing the species. She is a fertilized flower, a kangaroo with a little one in her belly bag. The conga drums from The XX startle her and call her attention to the fact that there are only two inches of wine left in the bottle. For a seasoned alcoholic that may be a lunch of meagre rations, but not for Sarah. She's giddy and drunk. There's no choice but to keep on drinking and head through the narrow tunnel of her own thoughts.

Sarah thumbs through the dictionaries. One word after another passes through her fingers. The letters drop away and leave her body filled to the brim. It's as if they were pushing against the walls of her insides and shouting: let us out of this miserable, indecipherable body. Stacey sticks her head back in the room and dives into the refrigerator.

'Don't you want anything to eat?' she asks. 'It's three o'clock already.' Sarah's iPhone is humming on top of the microwave. Stacey slices cheese, washes arugula, and toasts a piece of spelt bread. The house phone rings. Stacey answers it.

'Yes, she's right next to me. I'll get her. Bye, Mickey.' Stacey hands her the phone and whispers: 'Your mother.'

Her mother, naturally. Saturday, at the stroke of three: that's her mother's fixed routine, to call at nine o'clock from one of the many rooms in her villa. When Sarah gets on the line her voice is trembling so badly that her mother immediately knows something is wrong. Why are mothers like that? Sarah knows she's making an immense, unforgivably big mistake, but she can't help it. Nor does she care at this point. She breaks down. Throwing all caution to the winds, she tells her mother, startling herself by her own words. 'Mama,' she says. 'I'm pregnant.'

Yes, she's done it. She has just committed a terrible sin against the universal rule that says: never dump an intimate secret on your mother just like that, and especially not if you're pregnant and your whole world is tottering on the brink and the hormones are tearing through you like Ferrari owners on speed on a highway at night—and especially, especially not if you're less than three months gone, and never, ever, under any circumstances, if you haven't told the father yet.

She realizes her mistake, but it's too late. Seized by the same panic that seizes an attacker when he shoots the struggling night watchman, she goes on to take an even bigger misstep and turns off her phone. She doesn't want to know how her mother is going to react. She stands there, her legs shaking, holding the phone in her hand like a contaminated object. The phone is connected to the entire world of phones. Signals travel through wires from the sixteenth floor in NYC to the cables on the sunken road, up the mountain, to number 7 Nightingale Lane. She locks the telephone away in her soundproof studio.

'Another glass of wine?' Sarah asks Stacey.

'Please,' Stacey says. Sarah opens a new bottle and fills both their glasses. They clink without saying a word. Stacey has understood nothing from the brief conversation in Dutch, and she lets her uninformed head bob along to the beat of the music.

Glass in hand, Sarah goes out into the corridor. In the stairwell she takes the narrow stairway going up to the roof. It's quite cold, but she doesn't feel like going back for a scarf or coat. She gently pushes the door, a worthless fibreboard affair that flaps and slams shut behind her.

She kicks a sun-bleached Budweiser can and goes closer to the edge. She's often stood here with Amos. One of the first times she stood with him on the roof of his coffee bar in Queens she threw a can in a graceful arch down to the street out of wanton nervousness. Amos was furious. A hurtling can is a knife, he taught her. A childhood friend of his was hit by such a can thrown from an apartment building and lost an eye.

Sarah stands there for a long time, sobering up in the fresh wind. She's holding the glass so hard that her fingers are clenched around it. She notices this when the door on the roof swings open, revealing Amos in the doorway. Has an intercontinental alarm system kicked in? Has her mother called Amos? No, impossible. She doesn't have Amos's mobile number. Amos comes over to her and takes a sip of wine.

'Hi, statue,' he says. 'I used to practise doing that when I was a kid, being a statue. I haven't done it in a long time.' Amos takes off his anorak and lets it fall to the roof. He stands on one leg, balancing his body and remaining immobile, a flamingo in a concrete river full of lichen, cans, and wrappers. He looks in the direction of Ground Zero, to the most tangible phantom buildings in the world. Sarah is tempted to give him a push just for the joke, but then she sees the seriousness and dedication on Amos's face, and there's something that holds her back. For minutes all his attention is concentrated on standing on one leg. Why is he doing this? To prove he excels in everything? The sceptic Sarah might make that claim, but she'd much rather see it in a different way: he's doing it out of pure dedication to her.

He's been so quiet for so long now that she can no longer say anything, nor does she feel the need to. There are enough sounds in the streets below. From the roof you can still see people walking in the streets, but their faces are erased. Sarah lowers herself to the surface of the roof. She realizes how frozen she is when she sits down on Amos's anorak and feels the warmth it's giving off.

Then Amos breaks off his exercise. Sarah is shaken

from the spell. They look down and fantasize about what they should do with the street below. Bring a mammoth back to life and let him thunder through the streets. They imagine it so vividly that Sarah stretches out her hand to touch the trunk of the mammoth, which has come squeaking over the building, and to feel his rough hide before he goes to die out on the prairies of the Great Plains.

Together they watch a small group of runners. There are five of them. Sarah and Amos can easily follow their movements from the roof. They disappear and reappear between the buildings and the park. There's something very reassuring about just looking at them.

'They're training for the New York Marathon six months from now,' says Amos. 'I saw guys like that years ago in Egypt. Marathon runners with wiry bodies. They run their legs off. Day after day, in the sand, just to do it. Or maybe they had too much energy, or they were running away from something. We saw them pass by every day, but we couldn't talk to them because they were so fast. They didn't seem to do anything but run.'

An hour later she's soaking in the bathtub, dead beat and wiped out, when the bathroom door opens. Amos comes in and kisses her. Without saying a word he takes off his clothes. It's a small tub, yet he succeeds in lying down next to her, so they can soak in the water like a pair of shrimp. Instead of chasing him out of a bathtub on the brink of exploding, eating a couple of pounds of Galler chocolate, and grumbling for a night and a day to make him think she has a problem, she responds to his kiss. Sarah would sooner bite her tongue off than to even consider revealing anything about the pregnancy. She'd rather make love to her unwitting husband.

Their lovemaking follows a familiar routine. Sarah

and Amos know how it usually goes: how he grabs her by the hips, how she wraps her legs around him so they can touch each other with the maximum number of body parts. It's genuine, familiar, sweet sex, not the bungling sort associated with first times and well-buffed, preened, anonymous bodies, but real sex with the rumblings of too much wine and the relaxation of a hot bath. She sinks her teeth into his shoulders: that thick, hard collarbone that she'd so like to bite through. She presses him hard against her, as if she were a moulded form into which he was meant to disappear. He has to pass through her in order to end up in another place. A place where they can lose their way together.

Mothers are too close to reality. They invite reality to their table and wheedle all kinds of secrets out of it. Sarah is sitting at her laptop, reading the date on the airplane ticket in her mailbox for the third time. The message contains the details of a Brussels-New York flight under the name of Mieke Vandersanden. In two days her mother is coming to visit. In a following e-mail her mother explains that she's dropping in because she has to be at a conference in Boston anyway. She's making a stopover in New York so she can visit Sarah in the city as well as her sister Lydia in upstate New York. If it's not an imposition, that is. Her mother has e-mailed her two or three times a day over the last few days, usually on the most trifling pretexts. Should I book a hotel room (because I don't want to be a burden to you two)? There aren't too many steps, are there (because I can't manage that with my hip)?

Mothers don't change, they evolve. Her mother actually seems to have flourished in recent years. She comes to America quite frequently to visit Sarah and her sister.

She travels all over the world for the foundation. Elvira and she are still the driving forces, but there are also many newcomers who are taking the foundation even further. Sarah takes genuine pleasure in watching her mother cautiously get to know new people.

When Sarah goes to JFK to wait for her mother, an odd character approaches her and offers to carry her luggage, although Sarah has only a handbag. She gives the character two dollar bills and sends him away. The stooped little man vanishes into the restroom. Beggars aren't allowed at JFK, but they're infiltrating the airport unnoticed with greater frequency. If things go on like this the whole country will soon be begging at the airports—another way to welcome foreigners to their American dream. Sarah's high heels are not such a good idea from a practical point of view, but they do wonders for her self-confidence.

Like a whale, her mother comes swimming over from the threadbare continent of Europe, covered with seaweed and lichen but more vital than ever. At the first sight of her mother the nerves start racing through her body. Mother and daughter exchange kisses. They have never hugged each other; no need for it. Her mother's appearance hardly ever changes anymore. She probably has her grandfather to thank for that, a man who looked the same on his deathbed as he did in his wedding photo. For years, Mieke, too, has maintained her wedding weight, until she dropped below it after the death of her husband. Not a single word is said about the pregnancy. On the way to the taxi stand, Sarah senses that her mother's nerves are also tightly wound. They haven't mentioned it again, either in their e-mails or on the phone. Sarah has decided to let everything run its course, but she knows without being told that her mother knows that Amos is still in the dark.

Sarah listens to her mother with amazement. It's brilliant how even during an innocent ride from the airport to Amos's apartment she manages to bring up the very subjects that Sarah doesn't want to hear anything about. She tells her that the foundation is restoring the castle at the foot of the mountain, which has been a huge project because the place had been utterly destroyed by the previous owners. She's full of praise for Emily's improbably darling baby, and for Ulrike's oldest daughter's twins, two eight-year-old girls who walk up and shake hands completely unprompted and then let the big people talk in peace. They're not getting an iPad; Ulrike thinks they should just play with wooden blocks. She does exaggerate a bit, however. Moderation is the way to go. You just wait until you have grandchildren, Ulrike says. Then you'll see how much you want to spoil them rotten. It's your first reflex, but Ulrike has armed herself against it.

They walk into Amos's apartment. It's reasonably in keeping with what her mother regards as a decent place to live. What's more, they can talk in peace here. There's no Stacey lugging dictionaries around, and Amos won't be home until this evening. Her mother looks around. They can't get the heating under control. The whole building has been panting from the heat since last night.

'Where's Amos?' she asks.

'He's working.'

'Always working,' her mother sighs. 'By the way, I'll have to get Amos to explain to me what the story is behind that menorah again. Why does a simple candle-holder have so much significance? I know so little about Jewish culture. I know that Jews are fanatics, but they're clever. Muslims are even more fanatical, but unfortunately they're less clever. We've been given another fine example of that.'

'Would you like something to eat?' Sarah asks, interrupting her mother before another of their endless discussions unfolds. She rummages through the closet, between the baking powder, Brazil nuts, and instant pudding mix. She wonders why she's hasn't even baked anything, or taken the trouble to pick up some cakes from Dean & DeLuca.

Fortunately her mother declines any food or drink. She does want a glass of water. Mieke paces back and forth, turning on her heels. There's a crumb hanging on her trousers, a sign that all is not well with her.

'They look good on you, Mama, those trousers. It's the first time I've ever seen you wear them.'

'Oh, I've been wearing trousers for a couple of years now. Much handier than a skirt, and there are such elegant styles. At my age I'm not going to start wearing jeans, of course.'

'How's life in Belgium?'

'Which Belgium?' Mieke asks. 'There's not much left of it.'

'I mean: how is it at home?'

'Fine, fine. They're building a villa on that wooded lot next to us, with a green roof and an indoor swimming pool, and with hand-selected red stones from a special reopened quarry. Guess how much that nonsense costs?'

'Not much, I bet, with this recession,' Sarah laughs, temporarily relieved that they haven't yet broached the Big Subject.

'Four million euros. That's right. And of course they're cutting down all the remaining trees. What's the point of living in the woods?'

'Has the recession had much impact in Belgium?'

'I can't complain, but you see it in the details. Strange things can happen in life. You remember how we used to laugh when we went to the post office and we saw those old matrons with their big fat pocketbooks filled with government bonds? Last year I bought government bonds myself, at 4.3 percent if you hold onto them for eight years. There's not a single bank that pays that much interest. Ha. I guess I've become an old matron myself.'

'You're not that old, Mama. You look very good, actually.' She means it. She's sticking to her resolution not to tell lies or twist the truth.

Mieke looks around the apartment. She sees a real Calder mobile hanging from a length of fishing line and an imitation Rietveld chair from the MoMA museum that still must have cost a couple of months' rental income.

'A very attractive apartment, I must say,' she decides. 'Cosy, not too small, and nice and warm.'

Sarah knows her mother. 'You go rest,' she says. 'You must be tired.'

'For a minute then.' So they continue their little drama, because both of them are eager to postpone the conversation, preferably forever, which was the reason her mother rushed off to America in the first place. She brings her mother to the guest room, where the laundry is still hanging that's been dry for a couple of days. How could she have forgotten to take it down? Mieke pulls over her wheeled suitcase, zips it open, and takes out an envelope from the front compartment containing a coupon for four hundred dollars for the children's department of Macy's, purchased online. She'd rather give her a coupon, she explains, because she'd never be able to buy anything without Sarah thinking it was ugly. 'And now I'm going to sleep.'

Ten minutes later Mieke is back in the living room with a laundry basket full of folded clothes.

'Well, that did me a lot of good.'

'You could sleep a little bit longer, Mama. You hardly had enough time to close your eyes.'

'Thank you, dear. I know. But I can't get any real sleep with all that dust. I'll do a little vacuuming in there later on.'

'Sorry, I haven't had the time, and our cleaning guy has run out on us.'

Mieke gives her daughter an uncomfortably long look. 'How about a snack?'

'No, no, Sarah. Don't trouble yourself on my account.'

'I can just pop over to the store.'

'We're not going to die of hunger, surely.'

'Yes, I'm sorry. I've just been so busy ... ' The spring sun is shining in, but not far enough to reach her.

'You're facing this on your own, too. Amos works far too much. When you have a child, he's going to have to cut down.'

'Stop it, Mama,' Sarah says, interrupting her. 'It's not going to happen. I just can't do it.' There's no other way to make this announcement.

'Look, Sarah,' Mieke begins. Her hand is trembling. Her mother squeezes herself into the space between a kitchen chair and the counter. She takes a glass from the drainboard and fills it from the tap. A blood vessel in her neck is doing a subterranean dance.

For a long time now, Sarah has regarded her mother as an elderly woman who needs to be constantly comforted and reassured. This is a job she cannot take on. That's why she fled Belgium years ago: because grief incites grief. Two grieving people just pull each other down until they end up at the bottom, mourning in the inky darkness. Shared grief is double grief. She fervently hopes there's a devoted man in Belgium, or somewhere, who's willing to take on her immeasurable need for consolation. And even if such a stranger never materializes, she does have to get on with her own life.

'I'm sorry, Mama. That's the way it is. There isn't going to be any grandchild.' She doesn't even feel like giving the matter any thought or arguing about it. She's too sad for that. This open recognition of her total and catastrophic ignorance is humiliating. Keep that in mind, she wants to say: it's the catastrophe that's in my blood. Rather than look at the little woman sitting at her kitchen table, she casts a glance outside.

Her mother, who never used to miss an opportunity to squabble with her daughter, remains silent for an alarmingly long time. Not a word comes out of her mouth. Suddenly she's thirty years older, a tiny, shrivelled-up, hundred-year-old woman with the waist of a doll, sitting on a kitchen chair, caved in, with her hands lying helplessly in her lap, shrouded in profound silence. Sarah doesn't know what to do. Go away and close the kitchen door forever, leaving the little woman to sit there alone? Give her mother a good shake in a rare expression of physical contact? Try to carry on something like a dialogue with a member of the Silent and Corked Up generation?

'If you only knew how happy your father was when you were born,' says her mother out of nowhere. 'If he were still alive and knew you were pregnant he'd be beside himself with joy.'

'You just want a grandchild to compensate for Papa.' There it is, the ghastly accusation, smouldering between them. 'But that's not the way it works, is it? I can't just go ahead and have a baby, can I? Our whole family is contaminated by death.'

Mieke snaps upright. In less than a second she's the

lively woman again from number 7 Nightingale Lane. 'Stop the dramatizing. Listen to me. You are not your father. When your father left us it was his own decision. You would never do such a thing.'

She falls back in her chair and pounds her chest three times, panting and expelling little breaths of air.

'Yes, it was Papa's choice,' Sarah says. 'So you know that, too.'

'For all these years we spared each other, but we're smarter than that.'

'And I'm too smart than to get swept up in that endless repetition of the same doomed Vandersanden pattern. I'm the last Vandersanden, the last of a family that can't find its place in life so it rubs itself out. But not me. I've searched long and hard, but now I've found my place. And I don't want to throw it off balance. Certainly not by a child who in all likelihood would have the same cloudy Vandersanden genes as mine. If I were a good mother I'd put an end to it now.'

'You can't do that, love. It's murder. You'd regret it for the rest of your life.'

'If you could start all over again, you'd make a different choice, wouldn't you? I don't believe for a minute those people who come slogging out of their misery, ankle-deep in muck, cheeks collapsed, marked for life, and who turn right around and swear up and down that they'd do it all again—all of it. Stupid! And arrogant to boot.'

Mieke takes a deep breath and locks eyes with her daughter. They're the eyes of a woman who has lived. There's not a trace of venom in them, no matter how intensely Sarah searches for it.

'After years of fighting I've finally found some form of happiness,' says Mieke. 'And you know I've been strict with myself—and yes, strict with you, too. I did what I thought I had to do. I didn't let myself get talked into anything else.'

That partial admission of guilt is not enough. Sarah wants to have her cake and eat it, too. After all those years she thinks she has a right to it.

'Don't be afraid. Can I be honest with you? I still remember it as if it were yesterday, that day you were born ... '

'Mama, I know that story. There were so many people who came to celebrate on the day I was born, and Elvira had a gold brooch made that I later dropped down the drain ... '

'On the day you were born I forgot all the days that had come before.'

'You won't fool me with that. And even if it is true, it says a lot about you.'

'Stop.' Mieke brings her hand down hard on the table, right in a puddle of sweet-and-sour sauce. She walks coolly to the tap, rinses off her hand, and goes on. 'What I wanted to tell you—if I may proceed, that is, if you will let me have my say just this once.' Like a great orator, her mother lets fall a moment of defiant silence. 'I didn't know what to do when I discovered I was pregnant with you. We had tried for so long. We had had a big house built for lots of children, so it shouldn't have been such a surprise. But it was. Look, I'll be honest with you. Even Papa never knew this. But I'm telling you, those first moments were pure panic. But now I cannot imagine my life without you.'

She picks up the dishcloth from the tap, holds it under running water, wrings it out, and brings it back to the table.

'It's all about the change in your body, pure and simple. Suddenly everything starts rumbling. All the interior furnishings get moved around to make room for something new. And not a little something, either. It comes in and takes over. I can understand that you've been knocked for a loop, but you just have to grin and bear it. With us there was no question of other options. My God, no, I don't even want to think about it. And yes, maybe we were from another generation and we'll never get the hang of this one.' Her consistent use of the word 'we' is annoying. It makes a mockery of reality.

'But does that mean it's so much better now? I seriously doubt it,' Mieke continues.

'So?'

'No, it's something I can't explain, Sarah, but you'll see what I mean once the child is born.'

'A little miracle worker, this baby, curing you of depression and life's insecurities?'

'Who knows.'

'But who itself is utterly miserable.'

'These are confusing times.' Mieke bows her head.

Confusing times? Since when does her mother lie awake at night worrying about the melting ice caps and the suvs that are driving the world to shreds? About the banks that are gobbling up capital and the citizens who are shitting it out? That's never been her concern. As an affluent baby boomer her interests have never been infringed upon.

Sarah says nothing. She looks at the little figure on the collar of her mother's turtleneck. The horseman is lobbing a puck to some unknown place beyond the shirt.

'You look pale, love. It wouldn't hurt for you to rest a few hours, if that's possible in this madhouse of a city.'

'You think it's noisy here?' Sarah asks.

'I think you should get more sleep,' Mieke continues. 'When you're pregnant you need a good night's sleep.

When I was pregnant with you I slept for about nine months.'

'Mama, what are you talking about?' Mieke just ignores Sarah's whole line of reasoning, her doubt and despair. Mieke knows all of propriety's secret pathways, but she can be just as hard and ruthless with her own daughter.

'Oh my dear, we're never going to get along. For the life of me I cannot understand how you can't even find the time to give your kitchen table a good cleaning with a dishcloth, and that's just one detail. But ... '

'Mama, just shut up.'

What if her mother had been allowed to wear trousers when she was young, to wander freely through her parents' vast garden, for example, and pick strawberries? And what if she had been granted permission to consume a glass of beer when she was young, just once, by the society around her and by herself? What if her mother had been a plain old ordinary mother? Would they have been able to get along then?

'Did you come all this way,' Sarah asks, 'to trash my life, which I've worked so hard to build up, and to talk me into exposing myself to a very real possibility of total destruction?'

'Oh, Sarah, you're going to be so glad to see that baby,' she says, as if to reassure her. 'And you'll develop some excellent fighting skills, just like we have.'

'Ha, ha,' Sarah says slowly.

The sound of fumbling can be heard at the front door. Stacey lets herself in. She politely shakes Sarah's mother's hand and tries to engage her in a little small talk, but her mother clamps her lips together and gestures as if she were a deaf mute. Stacey quickly folds up her forgotten tripod. Yesterday she and Amos had a photo session for a new menu for bottled water. You don't have to be a clairvoyant to sense that the atmosphere isn't particularly relaxed. Stacey gives Sarah a wink and disappears once more.

'That's just what I mean,' says Mieke, as soon as Stacey has pulled the front door shut.

'What do you mean, Mama?' Sarah asks calmly. She crosses her arms high on her chest.

'It's always open house here. You can't have that if you want to raise a child, believe me. A child needs structure, order. Fixed times for eating and sleeping and the potty.'

'Mama, you're not listening to me.'

'How can I help you, Sarah? I just want to make my little contribution. I can come to New York more often. Maybe I can rent a room, or stay with Aunt Lydia and Uncle Christopher. Or the little one can come spend a month with me during the summer. I'm not saying you can't do it alone, mind you. To be honest, you're living very nicely here. Yes, I'm glad you're doing so well, although I'd rather you didn't live on the other side of the world.'

Time is standing still, as still as the cactus on the windowsill, which could stay there for all eternity.

Sarah is standing in front of her bulletin board, where a photo has been tacked up along with a number of bills and the folder from the best Chinese takeout in all of New York. She picks a bit at the thumbtacks. 'Why don't you look for a new partner, or just someone to go to concerts and exhibitions with? There are specialized sites for that sort of thing. There's nothing wrong with it at all,' says Sarah. 'I'd be happy for you.'

And then her mother, without a hint of condescension or slavishness, says, 'You can't control everything,

Sarah. If you just consider all the things that can go wrong in life, it's a miracle we live longer than fruit flies. Do you know what would have been easiest for me to do? To have done the right thing and kept you with me when I needed you most, instead of letting you go to New York. But I could see that you needed it. You needed to live your own life and to make your own mistakes, far away from me—mistakes I don't even want to hear about. We all make mistakes, myself included, and I'm happy to let you make your own. But not this one crucial mistake. I won't let you make this one.'

'Now I've got to go to Aunt Lydia's,' she says, 'but tomorrow morning I'll be back here at eleven o'clock, as agreed. Amos is a good man. Tell him, and I'm convinced that together you'll make the right decision.'

Without saying a decent goodbye, her mother continues on her way, tottering with her bad hip and dragging her suitcase, which she hardly opened, to the elevator. Sarah is furious with the intensity that she reserves for her mother alone. It's rude for her to let her elderly mother struggle like that with her suitcase, while with every rasping breath she takes, and by folding her houndstooth jacket over her arm instead of wearing it, she acts out the plea: help me.

Sarah goes to the kitchen and waits at the window until her mother leaves the building and does something that any true-blue New Yorker could only manage with difficulty: she hails a cab. For her mother it seems effortless. She's probably emanating vast quantities of radioactive arrogance, scandalized by the distressing lack of attentiveness on the part of the little men who think they're somebody, with their taxis that go much too fast and are cleaned much too infrequently, especially the upholstery. You have to keep your eyes open.

There isn't a single cab driver who doesn't dare stop for her.

After her mother's visit Sarah crawls into bed, emotionally spent, physically exhausted. Suddenly, without any warning Sarah's body reacts violently. So much has happened and so much is happening.

She lies there between the clammy sheets, steaming on a bed of lava. The fever creeps up to her jaws and sinks its teeth in.

We dab the sweat from her body and whisper encouraging words into her ear. We wrap her up completely so she feels safe with us. We take her along to the side of life she's always avoided. It's very busy there. Words that are never spoken now fly into the air. Sounds she can't otherwise hear are distinctly audible. We ask her to push all the incomplete images together. Some of them disintegrate before she can touch them, others click into place and step out from the darkness into the foreground.

Sarah wakes up in the hole of sheets she has dug for herself. She can breathe again.

We stroll through the city when suddenly we hear a starting signal resounding through the broad streets. Tens of thousands of runners are taking part in the New York Marathon. Tens of thousands of feet beat out the cadence of the city. People stream in in droves to support the runners. Children with blue slushie tongues. Runners' wives with sacks of peanut butter sandwiches that are never going to be delivered because it's impossible to find anybody amid the thousands of runners. A couple of reporters who've stationed themselves at a strategic corner of the Verrazano Narrows Bridge. While the reporter from CNN continues with his excited spiel, we manoeuvre ourselves through the masses. A first group of ten runners catches up with us. Ten athletes with legs like giraffes that barely touch the asphalt.

We walk farther. We're always en route. It began countless years ago, and we're doing all we can to keep on going.

The names that made the difference:

The whole enthusiastic Prometheus crew, with Mai Spijkers at the head and editors Job Lisman and Marscha Holman in his wake;

Matchless first readers, with their brilliant & irritating comments;

Maarten De Rijk, Karolien Debecker, Els Jooris, Isabelle Poppe, and Loes Van Cleemput, sympathetic towers of strength;

11je, the pug whose every word was accompanied by a snore;

Right hand, listening ear, and peerless sister Tanja de Coster;

Editor de luxe, ping-pong partner & light of my life, Inge Jooris.

◆

On the Design

As book design is an integral part of the reading experience, we would like to acknowledge the work of those who shaped the form in which the story is housed.

Tessa van der Waals (Netherlands) is responsible for the cover design, cover typography and art direction of all World Editions books. She works in the internationally renowned tradition of Dutch Design. Her bright and powerful visual aesthetic maintains a harmony between image and typography and captures the unique atmosphere of each book. She works closely with internationally celebrated photographers, artists, and letter designers. Her work has frequently been awarded prizes for Best Dutch Book Design.

The Bauhaus font used on the cover is called Futura, one of the few typefaces that can mirror the letters W and M, held together here by the ampersand in Bella Stencil.

The cover has been edited by lithographer Bert van der Horst of BFC Graphics (Netherlands).

Suzan Beijer (Netherlands) is responsible for the typography and careful interior book design of all World Editions titles.

The text on the inside covers and the press quotes are set in Circular, designed by Laurenz Brunner (Switzerland) and published by Swiss type foundry Lineto.

All World Editions books are set in the typeface Dolly, specifically designed for book typography. Dolly creates a warm page image perfect for an enjoyable reading experience. This typeface is designed by Underware, a European collective formed by Bas Jacobs (Netherlands), Akiem Helmling (Germany), and Sami Kortemäki (Finland). Underware are also the creators of the World Editions logo, which meets the design requirement that 'a strong shape can always be drawn with a toe in the sand.'